I0593369

The Sun Prince

First paperback edition: 2023

Edited by Luke Marty - yourbetareader.com

Proofread by Roxana – proofreadebooks.com/

Cover art by Sien Lee - brushseven.webflow.io - Instagram: @Brushseven

Cover design by Holly @hollybookstore

Map created by Lena – Instagram: @bluidu_streams

Title page art by Vanda - www.missviebookdesigns.com/

Chapter header design by Fictive Designs - www.fictive-designs.com/

Various artworks by Perci @perci.twotwo

For more information, please visit:

or Instagram: @luke_schulz_author

EBOOK ISBN: 978-0-6454574-3-8

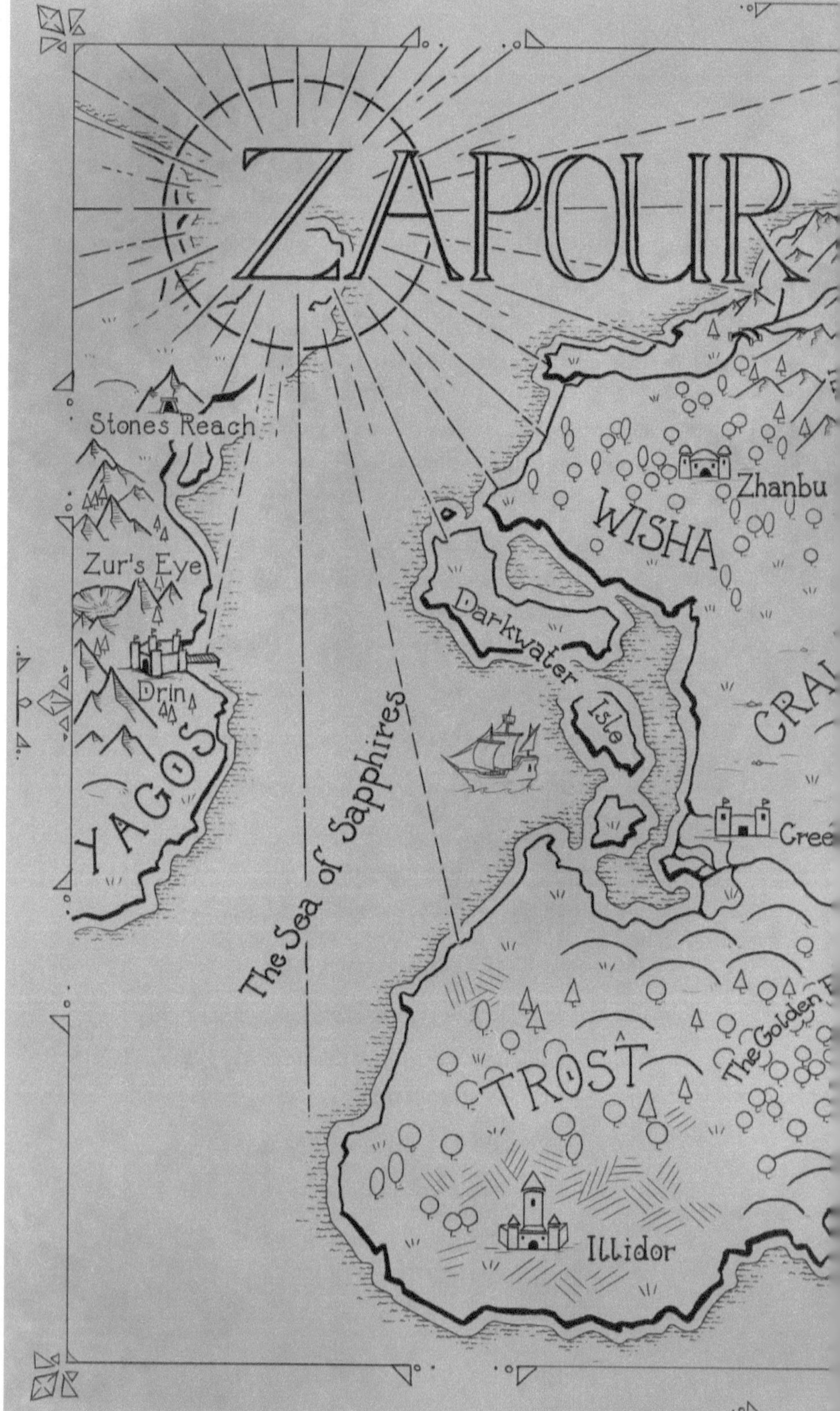

ZAPOUR
Stones Reach
Zur's Eye
Drin
YAGOS
The Sea of Sapphires
WISHA
Zhanbu
Darkwater Isle
GRAI
Cree
TROST
The Golden F
Illidor

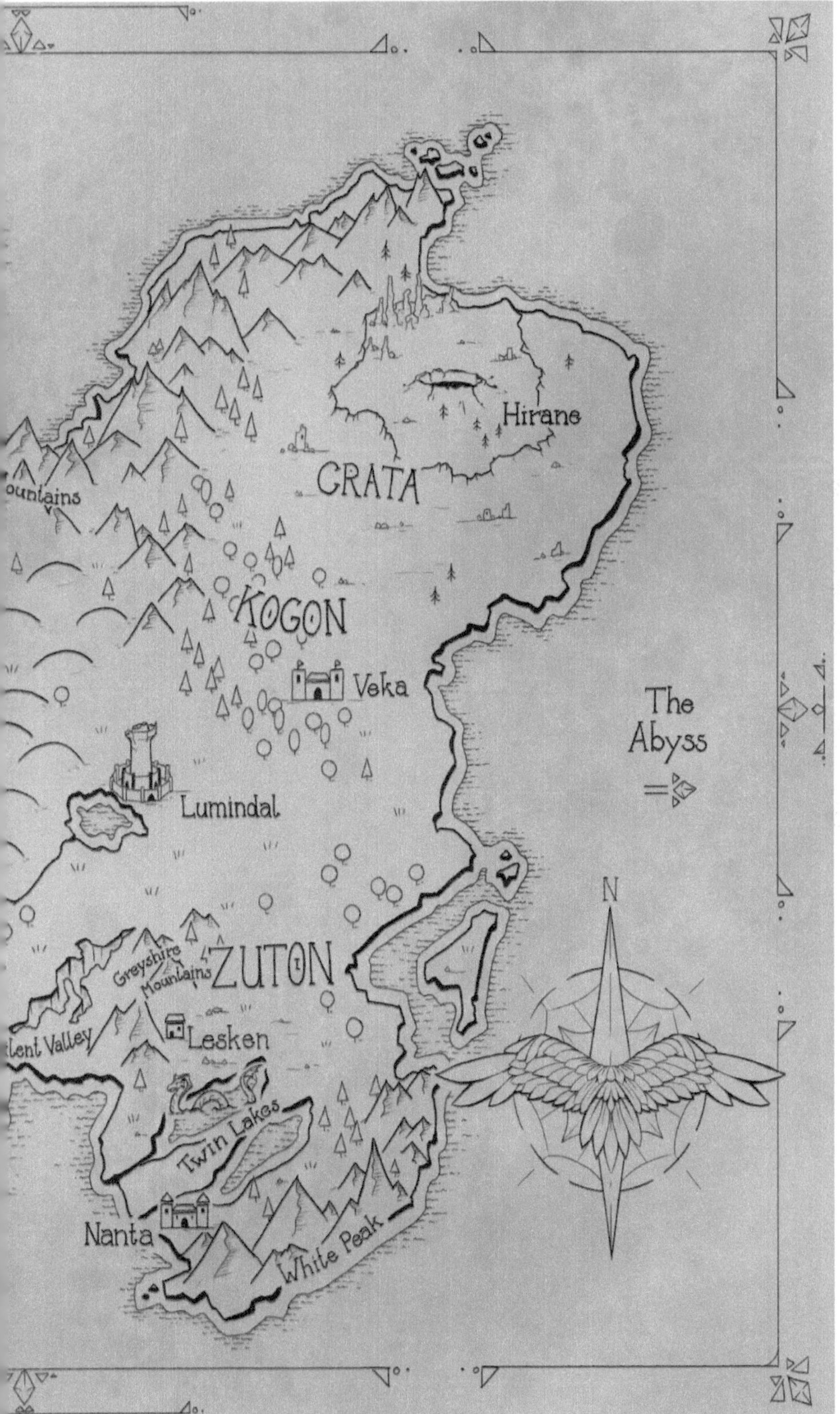

Hirane
CRATA
...ountains
KOGON
Veka
Lumindal
The
Abyss
Greyshire
Mountains
ZUTON
...lent Valley
Lesken
Twin Lakes
Nanta
White Peak
N

The story so far...

The three royal Glaive siblings, **Raiz**, **Isha**, and **Dazen**, live a peaceful life in the Kingdom of Trost with their father, **King Kron Glaive**. When the palace is visited by a powerful political and religious figure called an **Eagle**, sent by the man who oppressively rules over the entire continent of Zapour, **King-Radiant Evanon Lightfire**, Kron forbids the young Raiz and Isha from attending the ceremony. The ever-rebellious Raiz, who idolizes the Eagles and their power, disobeys his father, and when Isha tries to stop him, she finds herself flung directly into the path of the venerable Eagle. Struck by her rare violet eyes, he enslaves her and takes her back to the capital city of **Lumindal**. Raiz attempts to intervene after Kron refuses to do so, and for his trouble he is blinded in one eye.

Angry at his father and desperate to save his sister, Raiz flees Trost alongside his trusty, Shine-eating pet pricket, Spike. For the next eight years he finds himself under the tutelage of **Celik**, the brutal and enigmatic leader of a band of rebels, who teaches Raiz to hone his control of a magic called **Shine** (the ability to absorb and manipulate the sun's light) to devastating effect. Conditioned to become a weapon in a war against their oppressors, Raiz nearly loses touch with his humanity, but it is within this found family of misfits that Raiz meets his friends Draz and Aroha, and falls in love with Veil, a young woman with a troubled past who is plagued by a power she cannot control. Together, the group of rebels liberates the town of **Lesken** from the control of one of the Eagles, inspiring the townspeople to rise up and kill the Eagle themselves.

After eight long years, Isha is still enslaved, forced to be the centrepiece of her "master's" twisted human art gallery. Having kept up painstaking observation of everything around her, she eventually enlists some fellow slaves, and new friends, in a scheme to potentially escape the clutches of their captors. They witness the King-Radiant's brutal retaliation upon Lesken for their uprising, including the use of a large tower called the **Last Light**, which channels many people's Shine into a bomb that wipes Lesken from existence. Soon after, they find their moment and flee Lumindal, though they are closely pursued.

While his siblings have been absent, Dazen has maintained his precarious position as heir to the throne of Trost, navigating the tricky waters of establishing allies for his future kingdom, and proving himself a fearsome warrior. Caught in the middle of a pending marriage proposal to the princess of a neighbouring kingdom, he is forced to travel to Lumindal to seek the King-Radiant's approval, while simultaneously begging forgiveness for his soon-to-be ally's role in the uprising of their town - Lesken. Evanon grants the betrothal, but executes his new fiancée's father in retribution for the rebellion, plunging both kingdoms into political uncertainty.

Raiz, wracked with guilt for the destruction of Lesken and hunted by numerous adversaries, stumbles across his brother Dazen returning from Lumindal. After a tense stand-off and a rare showing of Raiz's growing powers, the brothers find clarity. They soon learn of Isha's escape, and their groups join forces to aid her. They find her just in time to fight off the Eagle and his band of knights who have hunted her down. Fuelled by rage for her years of captivity, Isha seizes the opportunity to slaughter her captor.

Finally reunited, the siblings return to Trost. However, instead of being welcomed home, Kron imprisons Raiz and labels him a traitor. Word has reached Lumindal that Raiz is the man hunting the Eagles, and Kron plans to offer him to the King-Radiant in an attempt to save Trost from suffering the fate of Lesken. Isha and Dazen find themselves powerless to stop him.

During the trip to Lumindal, Veil concocts a cunning plan with both Isha and Dazen to free Raiz from his chains and bring down the Last Light once and for all. She and Isha infiltrate the monstrous tower along with Draz and Aroha, while Dazen attends the King's council where Raiz is given up. Here, Raiz learns his true parentage; he was never a Glaive, but rather the secret son of King-Radiant Evanon Lightfire.

Chaos erupts as Veil and Isha manage to cripple the Last Light, causing Evanon to race to the tower. Raiz frees himself using a key given to him by his brother and pursues his newly discovered father, while Dazen gathers the leaders of the surrounding nations for an assault on Lumindal itself. At the top of the Last Light, Raiz is stunned to find Celik and Evanon in battle with one another. He learns that Celik is, in fact, Evanon's father, and therefore his own grandfather. The battle intensifies, and unable to watch the man she loves perish, Veil throws herself and Evanon into the bubbling inferno in the belly of the Last Light.

The resulting explosion sends Raiz plummeting. He is caught by Spike, who after being inundated with the Last Light's supply of Shine has begun to sprout wings. They tumble through the air, landing by chance in the tower housing the remaining Eagles. Consumed by grief and rage, he butchers everyone in sight. Only the loving presence of his sister is able to eventually quell his rampage. With the tyrannical King-Radiant dead and Lumindal conquered, the heroes begin to pick up the pieces, rebuild relationships that have been torn asunder, and forge their own path into the future.

Cast of Characters from A King's Radiance

Kingdom of Trost

Celia - Mystic: Once married to Kron Glaive, before Evanon Lightfire took her as his Queen. Mother of Isha, Raiz, and Dazen.

Dazen Glaive - Lightweaver: Son of Celia and Kron. Brother of Isha and Raiz. Once the Prince of Trost, he is now king.

Gale – Lightweaver: Second in command of the White-Swords of Illidor.

Isha Glaive - Mystic: Daughter of Kron and Celia. Raised in Illidor by Kron, taken as a slave by Averardus at the age of 12. Sister of Raiz and Dazen. Recently liberated.

Kron Glaive - Lightweaver: Once the King of Trost. Ex-husband to Celia, father of Isha and Dazen. Abdicated the throne at the end of A King's Radiance.

Raiz Glaive - Lightweaver: Son of Celia, and Evanon Lightfire. Raised by Kron Glaive until his betrayal, where he was taken in by Celik. A true Radiant. Brother of Isha and Dazen.

Outcasts

Aroha: Former Knight of the Golden Talon. Now fights against them. Companion of Raiz.

Celik – Lightweaver: Former King-Radiant who was outcast by his son, Evanon. Also known as Urion Lightfire. Grandfather of Raiz. Used Raiz and the crew to take vengeance on his son. Last seen atop the Last Light as it imploded.

Draz – Mercenary: Sole survivor of the Greysword Clan. Companion of Raiz.

Hector – Lightweaver: Born in Lesken (a city of Zuton). Was one of the children taken for being Shine-sensitive. Companion of Raiz, now a soldier of Zuton under its new king, Echo.

Spike: Raiz's animal companion. Formally known as a pricket. Evolved into a Dragon through years of feeding on Raiz's Shine and after consuming a mass of Shine stored within the Last Light.

Veil – Lightweaver: Born in Crata. Cursed with unstable Shine after a Shine-bomb struck her homeland when she was a child. Lover of Raiz. Sacrificed herself at the end of A King's Radiance to cripple the Last Light.

Lumindal

Argon – Lightweaver: A Captain of the Goldon Talon. Brother to Aroha. Killed by Celik (Urion) because he suspected his identity.

Averardus – Lightweaver: Eagle of the Forty-Fourth Spear. Held Isha captive for over eight years. Killed by Isha after attempting to recapture her.

Evanon Lightfire – Lightweaver: King-Radiant. Son of Urion (also known as Celik) and Sephare. Ruler of the Six (now 5) Kingdoms. Killed in the explosion atop the Last Light.

Maitreya: Friend of Isha. Imprisoned by Averardus for having the unique ability to ward off and repel metal. Escaped with Isha.

Puk: Former product of the Thousand-Shields regime overseas. Conscripted as a Blackwing and became a Knight of the Golden Talon. Imprisoned for aiding Isha. Freed by Isha and fought against his former employers.

Salador – Lightweaver: Eagle of the Forty-Sixth Spear. Last seen underground beneath the Last Light after Isha and Veil used him to infiltrate the inner-city of Lumindal.

Sephare: Queen-Mother. Mother of Evanon. Wife of Urion. Last seen in the hands of Gelvard after the city of Lumindal fell.

Yvain: Herald to the King-Radiant.

Kingdom of Zuton

Echo Levic – Lightweaver: Son of King Rayner Levic. Brother of Petros, Huet, and Sumaya. Became king after his father and brothers died.

Sumaya Levic: Daughter of King Rayner Levic. Sister of Echo, Huet and Petros. A warrior. Forced by her father to marry Dazen Glaive, later came to love him.

Kingdom of Craw

Ancel Saelmere – Lightweaver: Prince of Craw. Son of Gelvard Saelmere. Wounded by Raiz near Lesken. Fought for King-Radiant Evanon until the end, where he fought against him to seize Lumindal.

Gelvard Saelmere – Lightweaver: King of Craw. Father of Ancel. Enemy of Trost. Fought for King-Radiant Evanon until the end, where he fought against him to seize Lumindal.

Kingdom of Kogon

Hanns Balsto – Lightweaver: King of Kogon. Enemy of Trost. Fought for King-Radiant Evanon until the end, where he fought against him to seize Lumindal.

Kingdom of Wisha

Aia: Princess of Wisha. Sister of Obeyun.

Obeyun – Lightweaver: Exiled Prince of Wisha. Captured by Averardus until he escaped with Isha. Killed his brother Ajani in single combat and took the wooden crown to become King of Wisha.

Rudi: Leader of the Isidoku clan. Eight feet tall.

Other

The Sun Prince: Usurper of Yagos (A country across the Sapphire Sea). Sent a letter to the King-Radiant asking for those in Zapour to cease their use of Shine, as it is destroying Zur (the sun god).

Prologue

SHADOWS DANCED IN THE DARKNESS, flickering silently as a figure stalked the brightening mouth of the cave. It examined its humanoid physique, extending its hand. Five fingers spread out like a dark web, moving on command. *Five*? That was one more than last bright.

It wiggled the new appendage, testing its strength by tensing and then releasing its hold. It pulled its left hand up next to its right. Strange, a perfect pair. It seemed there were now two new appendages. Two more tools to forever go unused, as whatever evolving life it had was wasted away in this cavern of never-ending darkness.

It wasn't sure how long it had lived for, if you could call this living. It marked the passing of time only by the rise and fall of light at the cave's entrance. Light that it was forbidden to enter.

It wasn't even entirely sure what it was, save for the fact that its features were coming to resemble what humans called a 'male', according to his stolen memories. Father said that it – *he* – wasn't human, that he was something else, a perversion of the species. He found that the thought angered him, an unfamiliar emotion that continued to fester deep inside. Father hadn't even told him how long he had been alive. He had no memory of existence beyond the confines of the cave he now dwelled in. But *Father* protected him, kept him safe. Father was everything, his only friend.

Father had been gone a long time, too long. *What will he think of my improved hands?* he wondered. And it wasn't just his fingers that were different, it was his mind, too. His intelligence was growing, morphing with every kill, becoming sharper every time he fed. His recent meal had proven most beneficial.

It was okay to feed. Father had said so, encouraged it even, as long as he never walked the light. Travellers entered his lair on occasion, those either lost and seeking refuge, or come searching for missing kin, though he was beginning to suspect Father sent them. He made sure none ever left alive. With every life he drained, he felt his own body change. Their memories became his memories, their skills his skills. But the process wasn't perfect.

Despite the changes in his shadowy form, there was always one constant. A tail, black as the night sky in full dark, curled around his morphing form. It came from within, manifesting when prey was near, hungry for the essence of man.

Though the darkness of his home was all consuming, there was ever a small pocket of light. A tiny globe was fixed into a hole in the cavern's edge. At its strongest it shone bright rays of red, illuminating the surrounding area. That light had faded now, however, the liquid inside dull and lacking its natural flare. This fading indicated the length of his father's absence, for it was he who refilled it with light every time he came home.

As dull as it now shone, he used the last of its radiance to guide his hands, careful not to get so close as to suffer its sting. He felt the cold corpse of his latest meal beneath his fingertips as he bent down to study it. The victim was male, his broad shoulders making the body almost too heavy to lift. But his latest tools made the task much easier, his new fingers granting him the grip he needed to haul the cumbersome carcass out of his living space and into the crypt below.

The man's skin was dry and wrinkled. What colour it once possessed had faded as the essence-draining shadow-tail had taken its toll. His mouth still hung agape, as if his final protest yet lingered on his face.

A wave of nausea hit him as visions washed over his mind. Visions of this man, who he had been. The transference of knowledge was often delayed this way. The comprehension of such knowledge took even longer, and sometimes did not even come at all. It was like a giant puzzle. The pieces were all there but putting them together took time, time that he had but didn't know how to use.

Within the flashing images he saw a girl, a daughter. She was young. She clung to her mother's hips as this man, Zeek had been his name, yes, as Zeek approached.

"Father!" the girl cried out joyfully, rushing to throw herself into Zeek's open arms.

In the darkness of the cave he took a backward step, bracing to grasp her as if the girl were his own. The vision vanished almost as soon as it had come, leaving him with an emptiness he was unable to explain. Something within him was telling him he should feel bad for taking this girl's father from her. But no matter how far he dug, he couldn't find that emotion within himself.

Zeek.

He liked that name, it felt as though it belonged to him. He needed a name. All living creatures needed a name, didn't they? Why should he be denied one because his father had been too lazy to gift him one.

Yes, Zeek. That shall be my name.

He continued with his task, dumping the body into the crypt he had built for those whose lives he had taken. Suddenly, a disturbance shifted the air somewhere in the distance. It was subtle, but then again, a lifetime in the dark had sharpened his other senses.

Zeek crept around the cavern, careful to mask his footsteps. He rounded the bend to see that first light was beginning to rise at the entrance.

Shadows curled at his legs, swirling around his waist and pulling tight as the substance which made up his body reacted to the approaching heat. Zeek stuck to the darkness, becoming one with it as he waited for his quarry to draw closer. It was rare for new flesh to come to him so soon, but who was he to deny his good fortune?

The approaching human did nothing to mask their presence, taking confident steps into the mouth of the cave, into his domain.

Zeek felt a flutter in his stomach, another unfamiliar emotion, but one that his previous victim would have labelled *excitement.* He positioned himself behind a thick stalagmite, ready to pounce, his shadow-tail unfurling and poising for a strike as if sensing the occasion.

He bent his knees and was about to spring when a force pressed against him. A wave of invisible energy filled the chamber, fixing his feet to the ground and rendering him unable to move. Despite his immobility, the flutter in his stomach quickened, for Father had returned.

Once the initial burst of energy announcing his presence had subsided, Zeek rushed to greet him. He couldn't wait to show him his new fingers, two new tools he could use to help him.

"Father!" he said, slinking his way from the shadows and forcing himself to bear the sting from the rising light outside.

The man he called Father looked broken, but Zeek knew him to be much more than what he seemed. His dead arms dangled loosely by his sides, rendered unusable long ago. As he turned, his face caught the light, revealing the black imprint of a hand upon his otherwise pink flesh.

"You have changed since my last visit, I see. Have you been feeding?" Father asked.

"Y-yes, I have been feeding. As you commanded. I have these now," Zeek said, holding up his newly defined hands. His face stretched into what his stolen memories told him was a smile. "And I have a name too. Zeek. It is mine, I claimed it."

Father did not react as he had hoped. Instead of sharing Zeek's joy, he leered at him with his characteristic scowl. "Good, then you are ready," he said, tone emotionless.

Zeek lifted his chin. "Ready? Ready for what?"

Father gestured for him to rise, so rise he did. "Ready to leave your home and take your place by my side, out there," he said, pointing towards the light. "There is much to be done."

PART
I

Chapter 1

- Isha –

THE WEIGHT OF A SWORD was beginning to feel comfortable in her hand. Isha gripped the hilt tight, just like Dazen had taught her, before rushing forward with a series of precise strikes. Her opponent battered away her attempts with relative ease, however, thrusting forward with an attack of his own.

She leaned back, and the tip whizzed past her breast, so close she could feel the rush of air creep up her neck. Gritting her teeth, she lunged forward to grab at her assailant's overextended arm, then leveraged his weight to pull him over her shoulder. His bulky frame landed with a thump, and Isha took the opportunity to place her sword next to his throat.

Beads of sweat dripped from her brow despite the chill in the air. Where once her hair was long and wavy, it was now cut short to her neck. No longer need she dress as commanded. No longer was her every breath monitored, her actions dictated by another. Though her internal scars still ran deep, Isha was determined to prove herself outwardly changed. With a frustrated sigh, she relaxed, throwing away her sword and grabbing her opponent's.

She curled her fingers around the dull metal and squeezed. "You see that? It's blunted. Quit pulling your thrusts. I'm not a damsel anymore, Puk. I'll never improve if you continue to hold back."

She extended an arm and allowed him to take it, hauling him back to his feet. Puk dusted some dirt from his tunic before squaring his shoulders to face her. His hands moved in a flurry of quick gestures, signs she had come to know by heart.

You won an honest victory, he said. *You are improving faster than any could have foreseen.*

Isha rolled her eyes and dropped the blade. She spoke using both her hands and her words, a habit she had taken upon herself to improve her signing. "Save it. Flattery won't get you anywhere. We both know I've only been studying the sword for two years. It will take me longer than that to best you in an honest fight."

Puk bowed, but his shameless smirk did not go unnoticed.

The years since the fall of the King-Radiant had been kind to Puk. He was now a member of Dazen's White-Swords, the military emblem etched proudly into his breastplate. And though he remained somewhat reserved, pieces of his personality were continuing to surface, and Isha was glad for it.

As for herself, she was still lost. Not in the way she used to be, she had found a purpose in the sword, in her study of history, and in family. But there remained an emptiness within that she was unable to fully explain. Nothing could erase her past, gift her the years she had missed. Nor did she want it erased. Despite the awfulness of what she had been through, her journey had strengthened her, sharpened her mind, and awakened it to the true nature of what humanity was capable of. There was no substitute for that, no text one could read to learn that lesson.

She walked over to the fountain and splashed water over her face, taking comfort in the refreshment despite the extra bite the lingering winter gave it. Ever since the downfall of the Eagles, the weather had turned. It was not a drastic change. The sun still shone in the sky, Shine was still prevalent among the plains of Zapour, but people were beginning to notice that something was off. Crops weren't growing as they should, food was becoming scarce, and the chill was often unforgiving. Some blamed them, the overthrowers of the King-Radiant, for it, holding true to the preaching of the former Eagles and believing that their deaths had doomed the world to an eternal winter. Others blamed Raiz directly, though his outburst in the Forty-Second Spear had been largely covered up.

Despite growing unrest, the city of Illidor was as beautiful as ever, and the place of her birth had been a great comfort in the years since her return from Lumindal. Yet there remained a sense of displacement, a lingering afterthought that she was still a stranger even amongst her own walls. She placed those thoughts aside as a figure descended the staircase to her left, turning her attention from the bundle cradled in her arms to flash Isha a warm smile. "Your form improves by the day," said the Lady Sumaya. "Soon I'm sure even Dazen will be no match for your prowess."

Isha's eyes lit up. She and her new sister-in-law had become quite good friends since she moved to Trost after the union between their nations. Her presence always brightened her day. It was made even brighter as she drew closer, revealing the newborn babe housed within a sea of blankets.

Isha failed to hide her excitement as she bounced towards the two of them. "Well, I couldn't let you be the only woman in the family capable of wielding a sword," she said. "How is little Nora today?"

Sumaya angled her hips and lowered the babe so that Isha might take a peek at the sleeping beauty within. Her heart fluttered every time she gazed upon her niece. She was the most beautiful thing she had ever seen. Her nose was like a tiny button just begging to be pressed. Her sleeping eyes were closed, but Isha watched as she issued a yawn, stretching her little fingers into the air before shifting position and re-settling into the comfort of the blankets.

"Would you like to hold her?" Sumaya asked, reacting with a chuckle as Isha's face perked up. Without even responding, Isha held out her arms. She held her breath as the tiny human who was now a part of her family nestled into her chest. She had barely begun to admire her when her eyes popped open. Almost immediately she began to wail. At first it was quiet, though it soon became constant, as if the child could sense her mother no longer held her. "Uhh, I —" Isha stammered, looking around while attempting to rock her back to a peaceful sleep.

Sumaya only laughed, offering her arms for Isha to hand her back. "Don't worry," she said. "She's not yet used to other people. Sh-sh-sh-sh, hush little Nora. It's just Auntie Isha." After a couple more shushes and some light rocking, the child seemed to settle, making a gurgling sound before returning to her rest.

Isha let go of the breath she had been holding, watching as

Sumaya continued to laugh at her expense. She still couldn't quite believe that Sumaya was younger than she was. It wasn't that she looked old, quite the opposite in fact, but her maturity was humbling.

"Can you picture yourself with one of these someday?" Sumaya asked, nodding towards baby Nora. "I won't lie, it's hard work, but the rewards are constant."

Isha paled. She hadn't even spared a thought towards the prospect of having a child. Her mind drifted immediately to her prison. The thought of a child of her own suffering through what she had almost turned her off the whole idea. "I — no, I don't know," she said.

Isha followed Sumaya's line of sight towards Puk, who was busily stripping off his protective armour and replacing it with a linen shirt.

"He likes you, you know," Sumaya said.

Isha couldn't mask her rising emotions. "Who, Puk?" she said incredulously, though even as she spoke she knew it to be true. "I don't — it's been too long now. We're just good friends, nothing more."

Sumaya's expression twisted, and if it could have been written in words it would have said, 'I'm not so sure about that.'

Isha shook her head to clear her mind. It was true that there was a connection between herself and Puk, but it had simmered over time to a standstill, at least for her. It wasn't because he wasn't good enough. If any man were to steal her heart, it would be him. But her heart was still not whole enough to embrace another. How could she welcome anyone else when she did not yet know herself?

She snapped back into focus, realizing she had been staring

at him for far too long. "How is Dazen?" she asked, attempting to steer the conversation down a different route.

Sumaya frowned. "Dazen is troubled. So much responsibility is taking its toll, I'm afraid. But he'll recover, I am sure. He is at this very moment preparing for the foreign prince's arrival. Asked me to fetch you, as a matter of fact. He'd like a word with you before the soldiers of Yagos reach our shore."

"Oh, he sent you to 'fetch me', did he?" Isha replied, raising a surly eyebrow. Sumaya stumbled, realizing she had made a mistake. Isha waved it off with a laugh. "It's okay, I know how much stress he's been under lately. A kingdom does not rule itself, it seems. I shall pay him a visit. Keep Nora safe!" she said with a smile as she moved to leave.

"Of course. And Isha, be gentle with him, will you? He's extra fragile at the moment."

Isha turned back briefly to share a wink. "I'm always gentle."

THE MOON-SPIRE TWISTED into the night sky, blanketing Isha in its shadow as she made her way across the open courtyard. She still found it hard every time she crossed, the trip regularly tying her stomach in knots. The dark memory of her abduction was an ever-persistent presence here, though mostly it made her think of her younger brother and all he had sacrificed for her. She took comfort in the knowledge that Raiz was now safe, but the emotional toll of Veil's death still weighed heavy on him.

The knot in her stomach released when she looked up to see Maitreya at the base of the palace. Her long hair flowed down her back in chestnut waves as she clung to her husband, her fingers interlaced intimately behind his neck.

Isha came to a standstill, exhaling extra loudly and issuing a cough. Her friend turned around immediately, her face lighting up upon seeing her closest friend. "Isha!" she exclaimed, throwing her arms around her.

"It's good to see you, Maitreya," Isha laughed, awkwardly patting her on the back as the force of her friend's tiny frame continued to smother her.

She pulled away, clasping Maitreya's hands in her own. "I see you are well! I hope you're not giving Gale here too much trouble," she said, nudging her on the shoulder.

Her comment made Gale smile. The appointed First Hand of the King stepped forward and wrapped a muscled arm around his wife's waist, tearing her away from Isha's grip. "Oh, she's no trouble. Well, maybe a little trouble," he teased.

His words were met with a mock scowl as Maitreya moved to plant a kiss on his cheek. Their happiness meant everything to Isha. Maitreya had been through more in her life than even she had. The two of them shared an unbreakable bond that was born from hardship. The fact that she was still able to attain such happiness after her ordeal lent Isha a sliver of hope that she might one day find it too.

The moment was broken when Maitreya suddenly doubled over, clutching at some unseen wound in her stomach. She let out a pained groan, leaning on Gale's strong hands for support.

Isha moved to act, but didn't know what to do. "What's wrong?" she asked. "Are you ill?"

Maitreya shook it off, feigning a smile as she played down the ailment. "It's nothing, really, I'm sorry you had to see that."

"It's clearly not nothing. Come. I'll have Eve take a look at it."

"No!" Maitreya insisted. "It's fine, really. I've had it looked at. It's just something that happens sometimes, is all. I'm always fine afterwards, trust me."

Isha wasn't convinced, crossing her arms as she stared at her friend's stomach. "What does it feel like? I'm no physician, but I'm here to talk, if you like."

Maitreya hesitated, looking from her husband back towards Isha. "I can't explain it. It's like a pulling. Like something is calling me. It first happened a couple of months ago, and every now and then it happens again. It's stupid, I know."

Isha took a step closer. "It's not stupid. I'm sorry, I promised we would find out why you are the way you are, and we haven't found anything useful yet. But I'll keep researching. We will find out why you're invulnerable outside, and we'll figure out what's troubling you inside as well."

Maitreya placed a hand on her own and shook her head. "No need." She gestured towards Gale. "I'm happy, Ish. I no longer care for such information. I guess some mysteries are just better left unsolved."

Isha withdrew a little, but then nodded. Perhaps it was for the best. If that was what Maitreya truly wanted, then she would drop it. She instead turned her focus to Gale. "Is Dazen in? I hear he's expecting me."

Gale suppressed a laugh, but his eyes lacked mirth. "He is in, yes. But he's not himself of late. His mind is scattered. Between Gelvard's seizure of Lumindal and this prince from across the sea he has much to think upon. Add a newborn child and a brother who won't stand still, and it equals one stressed king."

Isha pursed her lips. "A crown weighs heavy on the head that bears it. I'll see what I can do."

She walked on, brushing her hand against Maitreya's shoulder on her way past. "I'm here any time you need to talk. Just come and find me. I mean it," she said before leaving the two of them behind as she walked into the palace.

Dazen's chamber was deep within. She had to walk down a series of narrow corridors before she finally came to his quarters. She rapped her fist twice on the wooden door, which was currently guarded by two stoic men in blue-white uniforms.

"Just a moment!" came a call from beyond, causing Isha to tap her feet impatiently on the stone floor as she waited. She looked up to one of the guards, her brow knotting as the man refused to move even a single muscle in his face, so intent was he on staring at the opposite wall.

"I hope my brother is paying you two well," she whispered, still watching and waiting for a hint of emotion. When they gave her nothing, she instead cocked her head, listening to raised voices within her brother's chamber. She pressed her ear closer, trying and failing to hear what was being said.

She looked up to find her head was nearly pressed into the stone-like guard's chest. To her delight, his gaze shifted downward to meet her own.

Isha smiled just as the door behind the guard whizzed open. Raiz emerged with a red face and a sour expression. He slammed the door behind him and leant back on it, taking a deep, shaking breath. He wiped a hand over his face, his fingers lingering momentarily over the scarred flesh of the eye he'd lost defending her as a child. When he noticed her standing there he calmed somewhat, and she was glad she had such an effect on him.

"You and Dazen not getting along?" she dared to ask.

Raiz shook his head. "The man is completely irrational. If there's responsibility to be had he wishes to take it all upon himself."

"I guess some things never change."

"I managed to talk at least some sense to him. I'm to leave for northern Crata. If there are alliances to be made there, I'm to seek them out."

Isha gasped. "Crata? Isn't that a dangerous journey?"

Raiz scoffed. "You sound like Dazen. Don't worry, I'm taking Draz and Aroha with me. Oh, and Spike of course."

Isha bowed her head. "You're needed here. Dazen won't admit it, but he needs you, Raiz."

Raiz cupped her chin with his palm and lifted her head so that his eyes met her own. "And I will be here for him on my return. In truth, an alliance with the Cratans isn't the only reason I desire to travel north." His expression darkened, and his eyes left her own. "I want to see if there are others like her," he continued, and Isha knew him to be talking about Veil. "I need to know if there are more who carry her burden, to help them if I can. I know it's likely a pointless venture," he said, raising his hand before she could interrupt. "But it's something I must do. Something I must see for myself, for my own peace of mind."

Isha placed her hand in his and squeezed. "Then I shall be here waiting for you when you return. But please, be safe. And look after Draz and Aroha. I'm looking forward to their wedding in the spring."

Raiz laughed, likely still in disbelief about the union. "If spring ever decides to show up. Don't worry, I'll guard them with my life."

He clapped her on the shoulder departed, leaving her with only one brother to talk to.

She opened the door to Dazen's chamber, where he sat behind a desk heavy with stacks of paper. As always, he dressed immaculately. His pristine royal blue uniform was perfectly tailored to his physique. She also could have sworn he had grown taller over the past year, but that was probably just her imagination. Yet despite his regal appearance, there were signs of the disarray Gale had mentioned. One half of his hair had been combed into neat lines, but he must have forgotten to do the other, which was tangled like a bird's nest. His usually bright and attentive eyes seemed dull and tired. The room also stank. It was as if he had been holed up in here for days on end. That, or he'd just neglected to bathe.

"You look terrible," she said.

Subtlety had never been her strong suit.

Dazen paled. He went to speak, to defend himself, but it seemed he didn't even have the energy. Instead, he sighed. "Welcome, Sister. Always a pleasure," he said, issuing a mock smile. "Come in, come in. Sorry about the smell. I would blame it on Nora but honestly, I'm not even sure anymore. Everything just seems to blend in lately." He angled his head to smell his armpit and recoiled with a dissatisfied scowl.

"It must be hard, running a kingdom while raising a child. No one would blame you if you took a break, you know," Isha said. "Everyone needs one sometimes."

He waved her off with a dismissive hand. "Now is not the time for a break. Not with the ruler of Yagos so close."

Isha still remembered the man who called himself the Prince of the Sun announcing himself through a letter to the King-Radiant when she was still a captive of Averardus. Back then she'd been glad to have someone opposing to that tyrant, but now that Zapour was free of his reign, it seemed Dazen and the Kingdom of Trost were the new target of his religious zealotry.

"Are you sure this is wise?" she asked. "Allowing this man into our country. Is it not dangerous?"

Dazen rose and walked over to a table, taking a seat next to another stack of recently read parchments. He gestured for her to sit, and she obliged. "Honestly, I don't know what to think. All of our contacts in Yagos have cut communication. I've spent many sleepless nights poring over documents for information on this man, but there simply isn't any. It's like he doesn't exist."

Isha continued to watch as Dazen shook his head in disbelief. "I wish Kron had kept better watch overseas. He was always so focused on strengthening our nation from the inside that he refused to look outward. Now I'm going in blind, forced to treat with a man I know nothing about."

"So, he wishes to treat then?" Isha said. "That's good news. There need not be bloodshed."

Dazen spread his hands out before him and sighed. "The man usurped an entire empire. I somehow doubt he's the kind of person to settle upon peaceful terms."

"Well, what does he want then?"

Dazen straightened. "All I know is that he despises Shine. He believes that if we continue to overuse Zur's Light then our star will fail us."

The thought troubled her. She remembered the King-Radiant dismissing his claims as if they were nothing. Perhaps back then Zapour might have been in a position to repel an overseas assault. Under his iron fist, they were at least united. Now, the kingdoms were fractured. Alliances had split, and were no longer bound to defend the other against a threat.

"Is there anything I can do?" she asked.

Dazen nodded. "We need to appear as though we are a united front, that even after all that has happened, we are strong. Echo has come himself to represent the interests of Zuton. Craw and Kogon will have none of it, though. They refuse to even respond to my invitations. I suppose it makes sense considering Gelvard's procurement of Lumindal. Wisha, thankfully, is open to hearing what he has to say. Obeyun cannot make it himself but has sent his sister in his stead. I was hoping you could welcome her. You're close with Obeyun. It is my hope that this might extend to his sister as well."

Isha popped up in her seat, fresh excitement washing over her. "Of course I will!"

The thought of meeting Obeyun's sister was nearly overwhelming. She had wanted to see her dearest friend's homeland ever since their victory over the King-Radiant, but it had never been safe enough to make the trek. Not with Wisha so unsettled and the potentially hostile nation of Craw standing between them.

"Good," Dazen said. "And I want you there with me when the time comes to meet this 'Sun Prince'."

Isha raised an eyebrow. "Are you sure? You know I haven't the stomach for politics."

"I'm sure. I will not have a repeat of the last time a person who thought himself a god came to this kingdom."

Isha's jaw dropped. "I'm not a child anymore. I don't need to be wrapped in a protective shell for the rest of my life. I can take care of myself. And you are not the same man as Father."

Dazen lowered his head. She could see clearly now the dark bags under his eyes. "It's not just about that. I don't know what this man is capable of. I know you are more than able to protect yourself, but I want you close. Don't fight me on this, please."

Isha sighed. "Fine, I will be there. Is there anything else?"

"Have you heard from Mother?" he asked.

Isha shook her head. "Not in a few days, no. Want me to check in on her?"

"Could you?" he asked, expectantly.

"Of course. You should stop worrying all the time, it's beginning to show. If I'm doing all of these things for you, you need to promise to do something for me," she added.

Dazen laughed. "Very well, what is it?"

Isha stood and moved to the door. She turned her head before leaving. "Get some sleep."

Chapter 2

- Raiz –

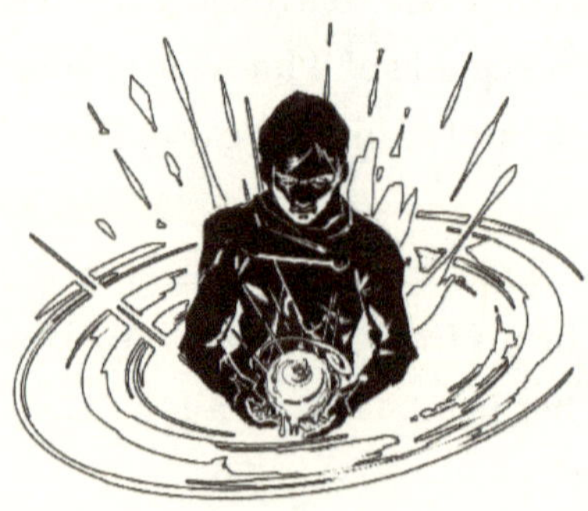

SPIKE ROARED. Fish darted through the water, desperate to avoid the vibrations caused by the pricket's boast.

Raiz reacted, hoisting his net so that it was half above the surface. He curled it, angling its rim so the fish had no choice but to swim into the cross-hatched cording. He pulled it taut, slapping the shallow water in victory as he held up his prize in triumph. He issued a mocking bow as if he were in a play before returning to Spike with his haul.

He opened the net just enough to grab the tail of a particularly wriggly fish and flung it into the air. Spike wasted no time. His long neck, now thick with scales, stretched out. He opened his giant maw, two rows of knife-sharp teeth glinting in Zur's morning light. They weren't needed, however, as the overgrown pricket swallowed the fish whole, his body already turning back to Raiz expectantly.

"I swear sometimes I wish you were still little," he said, sifting through his catch for another fish. "I've definitely lost weight since you've started to eat all of my food."

Spike dipped his head, two giant nostrils moving up and down as he sniffed first at the fish, and then at Raiz's hand. Raiz snatched his hand backward. "Don't be greedy. Fish now, Shine later," he said.

Spike recoiled as if the comment had physically stung him, though Raiz merely shook his head. It was quite surreal, actually, to see how much Spike had grown. He didn't notice it as much as others, with the two of them being practically inseparable, but even he still held dear the memory of Spike nipping at his fingers when he reached into his pocket.

What had surprised him the most, however, were the two bat-like wings that had sprouted from his once bare shoulders and now spread out like a web, leaving a giant shadow beneath his bulky frame wherever he ventured.

"We should be getting back," Raiz said. "You know what Draz is like on an empty stomach."

He latched his recent catch onto the saddle fastened to Spike's back. It was one of Draz's inventions, and it had saved him from an early death on more than one occasion already.

He mounted up, and felt the steady rhythm of Spike's heavy breathing beneath his weight. With it came a sense of peace, as if the two of them shared a connection that defied explanation. He and this creature were bonded, both through the Shine he fed him, and their time spent together.

"Rise," Raiz said, issuing the command for flight. He braced his legs, feet firmly planted inside the buckles. His chest tightened as the massive pricket propelled off his hind legs. Wind curled around his waist as Spike's wings beat.

Salty water dripped from sharp talons as the coastline stretched further and further. Raiz was still awed by the experience of flight. He saw the world in a completely new light. Where before the coast had been nothing but a line of ink on a piece of parchment, now it was real; a vibrant array of blue, yellow, and green as the sea met the land.

In a way, he felt closer to Zur up this high, as if he and the sun god were truly meant to be together.

However, even though he now knew the true power of a Radiant coursed through his veins, he still felt like he was a fraud. It was as if his Shine was rotten, and he was stealing it from someone — or something — more deserving.

Day by day he felt Zur's strength continue to fall. He refused to believe the drivel the now dead Eagles had spouted about them being connected to Zur. If what they preached had been true, then Zapour would already be in ruin. But there was something there, a hint of truth buried beneath a mountain of lies. It was a mystery he had not yet unravelled.

Spike banked to the left and he cast the thought aside. His stomach dropped as the pricket descended, spotting the knoll Aroha and Draz had made camp.

Raiz pulled back on his reins, causing Spike to alter his course. He flapped his great wings and the patchy shrubbery on the hill blew sideways as Spike made his landing. The commotion saw two figures emerge from a single tent, one a stocky ex-mercenary with long brown hair and a chip on his shoulder, the other a woman as tall as a spear and a former Knight of the Golden Talon.

Draz raised an angry fist as Raiz slid down Spike's side and approached his friend.

"Draz was trying to sleep!" he said, stamping his foot. "Tell me you at least brought Draz breakfast?"

Raiz responded with a coy smile, angling his head to where Spike was currently attempting to stretch his neck around to pick at the net full of fish attached to his side.

"Hey!" Draz called, rushing towards Spike and pulling the net free. "Humans feed first; lizard-dragon creatures get the leftovers."

Spike growled, lowering his head so that it was almost

level with the ground.

Raiz crinkled his nose. "Lizard-dragon creature?"

Draz shrugged. "About time you stopped thinking of him as a pricket small enough to fit in your coat pocket. This here is a Dragon. Ain't no one gonna tell Draz otherwise. Draz has seen them in books, heard the tales too."

Aroha approached, rubbing some sleep from her eyes while issuing a great yawn. "First I've ever heard of you making friends with a book," she said.

Draz shrugged again, this time accompanying it with a mischievous grin. "Draz has looked at the pictures."

Aroha ignored him, pushing Draz aside to set eyes upon Raiz's haul. "More fish? I've eaten so many lately it's a wonder I haven't grown gills."

Raiz walked past them. Shaking his head, he grabbed a pan from his pack and made for the fire-pit, where he set up a station to scale his catch.

Together the three of them prepared and ate their meal, sharing banter as Spike curled up beside the fire. Now that they were free from Celik, wherever the bastard was, it was easy to see what they had been missing. Where before everything had been tense, now it was relaxed. No longer did their former master's strict rules apply. The three of them had grown to be a truly close-knit group, both as travel companions and friends. Some had grown closer than others, however, a fact Raiz rolled his eyes about as Draz settled in next to Aroha, draping a meaty arm around her waist and pulling her close.

Raiz was truly happy for them. To be able to overcome their differences and find peace with each other in a world as unforgiving as the one they lived in was no small miracle. But he couldn't help feeling a profound sense of loneliness, seeing his friends' happiness. He knew it was irrational, that he was just jealous, but watching them made him think about all that he'd had, and all that he'd lost...

"So, what's the plan?" Draz asked over a mouthful of cooked fish. "Will you head back to Trost and listen to what this foreign emperor has to say?"

Raiz sighed through closed teeth. "No, I've had enough politics to fill a lifetime. I'll leave that to my brother."

Aroha leaned forward and clasped her hands. "Do you believe what the foreigner says? That we are overusing the Zur's Shine? That this is what's causing the long winter?"

Raiz mused, leaning back against the log he had made his seat. "Nothing is certain. We can't trust his word any more than we could the Eagles."

"You have to admit his theory makes sense," Aroha said, opening up her hands. "Though Zapour has been wielding Shine for centuries, what used to be a rare trait is now becoming more and more common. And with the King-Radiant and his restrictions gone it's only going to get worse."

"You mean my father," Raiz interjected.

Aroha went quiet, likely remembering how touchy he had become around the subject.

"Even so," Raiz continued. "I'm not sure what this 'Sun Prince' expects. King-Radiant or not, the people of Zapour rely on Shine. Entire armies are built around it. We can't simply eradicate it, not to mention that the gathering of such power is involuntary."

"Draz suspects a war is coming," Draz said, rubbing his stubbly chin.

"War is already upon us," Raiz replied. "Gelvard has seen

to that."

"So much fighting," Aroha said. "When will it end? How many people do we have to knock off to create a peace that lasts?"

Raiz sighed. "That's the problem with peace. It never lasts."

A distant wisp of smoke blowing above the horizon caught his interest. He stood, eyes drawn to the billowing rings of black and grey.

"What is it?" Aroha said, turning her head to follow his line of sight.

Raiz shifted, positioning himself at a better angle. "That's no friendly campfire," he said. "Something's wrong. Which village is in that direction?"

Draz moved for his pack, returning with a folded piece of parchment. He opened it, tracing stubby fingers across the page.

"Hurry up," Raiz said, earning him a cold glance.

"Southern Crata has changed since the fall of Hirane. What used to be may not still be. Ah, here we go. Draz puts us somewhere on the coast by Still-Water Bay. The closest charted village is an old mining town called Tinker.

Raiz slung his pack over his shoulder, already moving towards the disturbance.

"Where are you going?" Draz called over his shoulder.

"There's a fire, that means people could be in danger."

"Not everything is our fight, Raiz. We're in Crata, if we respond to every puff of smoke in this relic of a country then we'll never leave. Don't forget why we're here. We travel on grounds of diplomacy. Our best bet is to skirt the coast until we're far enough north to take a direct route to Hirane."

"And if there is nothing in Hirane but smoke and ash?"

"Then it will be as expected, and you can start to search for the true reason you dragged us out here on this venture."

Raiz paled, then shied his head. "You know?"

"Of course Draz knew. It's always been your desire to come here, to see if there are more like Veil. To help them."

"And you don't think it pointless?"

Draz shrugged. "What Draz thinks does not matter. What matters is how you heal. If this is part of the process, then Draz and Aroha are happy to help."

Raiz relaxed. He really didn't deserve such devoted friends. "You mean more to me than you know, old friend. Both of you, but I can't simply walk away when people might be in trouble. How would you have felt if someone capable could have help saved your clan when it fell, but walked away because they had better things to do?"

Draz went to speak but his mouth abruptly closed, head bowing low as the comment cut deeper than Raiz had intended.

Raiz took a calming breath. "I'm sorry, I didn't mean…"

Draz waved him off. "Fine, Draz is with you. But if we're to continue with this vigilante business, sooner or later we're asking for some coin, and it better well be enough to fill my baggy pockets," he finished, reaching deep inside his coat pocket and pulling the insides out.

Raiz shook his head, amused at still finding his friend's greed surprising. He looked to Aroha, who was already saddling the horses. He whistled and Spike came bounding over, the ground shaking with each heavy step. His wings spread wide, ready to take to the air once more.

"Not this time buddy," Raiz whispered. "We don't know what to expect. I wouldn't want your presence to frighten those who could be friendly. I need you to follow behind. Can you do that?"

Spike remained impassive, but Raiz knew he understood. A beast he may have been, but his intellect had grown along with his size. Spike would obey, at least until he sensed danger.

Draz and Aroha approached, each atop a steed of their own. The two horses flanked outwards, each used to, but still wary of the Dragon's consuming presence. Raiz pulled himself up behind Draz, feeling the weight of the man's helmet — Gallant — press against his leg as it dangled from a buckle, never far from his side.

Together, the three of them rode forward into the thick of the forest, and almost certainly into danger.

Raiz covered his mouth with his arm. The three of them had emerged from the brush too late. Smoke clouded his vision as people worked tirelessly to quell a flaming house. Buckets of water were passed around like morning bread as men, women and even children rushed to and from the village well. A man lay on his side, weeping openly as blood seeped through a hastily made bandage.

Despite Draz's warning, Raiz nosed his way into their business, taking a bucket from an exhausted child and throwing it onto the now simmering flames. The people surrounding him seemed too consumed to notice, so he continued aiding them until the flames had subsided. By the end, the dozen or so workers were exhausted, two collapsing to the soot-stained ground and others either taking a knee or leaning on one of the remaining pillars of timber as if it were a soft bed.

Eventually one of the villagers, an elderly man with an unkempt beard, called him out.

"You there!" he said. "Yer not of Tinker. Name yourself."

Raiz held the man's gaze just long enough to seem capable, but not enough to be taken as a threat. "My name is Raiz, and I want to help. Tell me, what happened here?"

Others had begun to circle him now, steered by caution and likely driven by vengeance.

"Ain't no foreigners ever willing to help in these parts," another villager said, this one a woman with a black patch over her left eye. "He's probably one of them, come back to scout out another to take!"

Her comments were met with a rumble of scattered agreement as more began to close in on him. Raiz held out a friendly hand. "I mean you no harm. Whatever happened here today was neither my nor my friends' doing. We are just simple travellers who spotted the fire."

The bearded man who had initially called him out broadened his view, spotting Draz and Aroha, who had dismounted but not yet taken any action. He narrowed his eyes, even more suspicious than before. "Do yerself a favour, traveller, and leave these parts. No good comes from venturing here. Not with those Shine poachers about."

Raiz relaxed his posture in an attempt to seem even less threatening. "What do you mean? What happened here?"

The woman with the eye-patch pushed past the elderly man, shoving him aside. "Look at his hand!" she said, pointing to the skin that had blackened from overusing Shine all those years ago. "He's one of them Light users!"

Those nearest to her widened their stance, ready to take up a call to arms despite the pain they must be already feeling.

Raiz clasped his wrist on instinct, gritting his teeth and searching for a way out of this that wouldn't involve bloodshed.

He'd barely had time to think, though, when the bleeding man crawled up to him and tugged on his charred cloak. "Please," he pleaded, eyes watering as he looked up to him. "You must be strong. Only the strong can wield the sun god's Light. You have to help me, please!"

Raiz stepped back, taken by the sincerity of this man's request.

"Porter!" said the woman with the eye-patch. "Step away from him, he could be —"

"I n-need h-his help," said Porter. He continued to weep, choking up as his nose filled with snot and his throat closed. "W-what choice d-do I have? They took my wife! They took Maya!"

Raiz stared at the man as if he knew him, as if his grief was his own. A small child came running up to the grieving man. "Daddy," she said. "Are you okay?"

The man named Porter grabbed his daughter by the waist and pulled her tight, as if she were the only thing left in his life, and one would have to pry her from his cold dead fingers if they wanted to take her from him.

Raiz steadied. "Who took your wife?"

The woman with the eye-patch took another step forward. "Do you truly mean to help us?" she asked.

Raiz nodded, and found that he meant it.

Behind them a piece of timber fell, the charred chunk of wood landing with a thud and sending a cloud of ash swirling through the air.

"Come," said the woman. "My place was unaffected by the

fires. Let's quench our thirst and talk somewhere with less prying eyes."

The woman led Raiz and Porter, with Draz and Aroha following behind, down a dirt path that led deeper into a small village. It seemed only one house on the outskirts of town had been set aflame, which Raiz took to mean it had been specifically targeted. She came to a stop before a rounded home, opening the wooden door and gesturing them inside. They were welcomed by a warm fire set within an open hearth.

"A steady fire is necessary in times such as these," she said, offering them a seat on a bench beside it. "People are beginning to fear the long-winter will never end." She set about gathering a fresh bandage and some herbs, idly brewing a mix Raiz had never seen before and placing it around Porter's wound before wrapping it in the bandage. "There," she said. "The wound is shallow, but I'll need to take another look at it when time allows. Just don't get any ideas about swinging a sword again any time soon."

This seemed to anger Porter, his face twisting in rage. "That's not an option and you know it. My wife is out there, alone and afraid. You expect me to just let them have her?"

The woman simply ignored his protest, going about her business as if he weren't even there. She returned to the hearth, allowing Porter's rage to smoulder in the background. "Now," she said, turning to face Raiz. "My name is Taula. I'm the village healer. Care to explain what three 'travellers' able to wield Shine are doing on the coast of Crata?"

"My name is Raiz Glaive," he said. Of the three of us only I am able to wield the Light. As to our reasons, they are our own."

Taula's single eye opened wide. "Glaive," she said in a whisper. She arched her head, standing to get a better look at him. "You're him. You're the Red Knight."

Taula's revelation caused Porter to perk up. He moved to the hearth, his wound but a figment of the past as he placed two strong hands on the bench. "Is it true what they say? That you slaughtered the Eagles in their own home?"

Raiz squirmed in his seat, suddenly regretting revealing who he was. He sometimes forgot his own reputation. He had lived in solitude his whole life and was still coming to terms with how fast and wide word could travel, especially word about the downfall of an entire regime.

Draz scowled at him, likely mad at his stupidity, but Raiz decided he was done hiding.

"It is true, yes," he said.

Porter rounded the bench and bent to his knees before him. "Then we're truly blessed that you came to us this day. Please, you must help us. You must rescue my wife!"

Raiz turned back to the healer. "I said I was here to help. I am true to my word. Tell me, what do I need to know?"

Taula bowed her head, but settled back into her seat, pulling Porter back to a seat beside her. "The people who took Porter's wife are part of a group who call themselves 'New Crata'," she said. "But they're nothing more than savage highlanders; rotten remnants of the broken empire that was Hirane. Unfortunately, they're now the major power in these lands. They used to keep mostly to themselves, but lately they've come further south. What's causing them to relocate we don't know, but every so often they take someone from one of the surrounding villages. They hunt Shine, even more fiercely now that, well, you, have broken the regime of the

King-Radiant. They're frightened, that much is clear. I fear something even greater stirs in the north. It's nothing more than rumour and speculation, but I've lived a long life, and I know when trouble is brewing."

Beside her, Porter began to choke up again.

"Do you know where these men reside?" Aroha said, speaking for the first time.

Taula looked to her, her wide eye drifting from bottom to top as though she had never seen a woman of such size before. "There's a mountain range to the north, that's where our riders went missing during their search the last time one was taken from us. But there's a darkness there, lingering, festering."

Raiz paused in thought. He turned to Porter. "Your wife, she could use Shine?"

Porter nodded.

"What does she look like?"

"S-she has long dark hair, fair skin, very slim. Eyes like the sea. Her name is Maya. She's beautiful, you can't miss her!"

Raiz winced as Aroha's hand touched his own. That description… he might as well have been describing Veil. He fought through the painful memories and rose, clenching his fists. "I will find her, you have my word."

Porter clasped his closed fist in his hand and sobbed into it. "Thank you, thank you! Please, see her home safe."

"Do you have anything that belongs to her? An item of clothing not yet washed perhaps?"

Porter hesitated. "Most of our home was destroyed in the fire, but I have this!" he said, pulling out a torn piece of a sweater from beneath his coat. "It's what she was wearing just before they took her. Do you have a hound or something?"

Raiz settled. "Something like that, yes."

Chapter 3

- Zeek -

ZEEK FOLLOWED, keeping to the shadows.

Cool wind ripped into flesh, *his* flesh. He still struggled to recognise the full significance of having a physical body, of being able to *feel* the cold on his skin. It was indescribable. Before, he had only known of and experienced the existence of a world outside of his home through the memories of others. Now, he was there, part of the reality he had dreamt about every night when the bright at the mouth of his cave faded.

Still, the light eluded him, was painful to enter. He was forced to hide when it reigned in the sky, but at least now Father had allowed him to go outside, had said it was safe to do so.

The ground was soft beneath his feet, a comfort compared to the hard stone of his old home. Something nibbled at his toes, not in a harsh way, but a calming one. It rippled and swayed in the wind, and Zeek bent down to touch it. It was tall and coarse, but also flexible and delicate. He searched his stolen memories and found it to be called *grass*. He plucked a strand from the soil and studied it, his night-eyes marvelling at the texture.

"What are you doing?" came Father's familiar voice.

Zeek dropped the grass, letting it drift away in the breeze. "Nothing. I was just curious."

Father glared at him with disapproval before issuing a dismissive sigh. "Come, we have far to travel if we are to get there before sunset."

"Sunset?"

Father didn't look impressed. Zeek almost apologized, nearly withdrew into his shell as he had always done when Father grew angry, but this time he didn't. He was now more than he had been, greater, and he found himself wanting answers – answers to who he was, and his purpose. "I wish to know," he said, standing up straight. "I wish to know all that you know. All that I am."

To his surprise, Father did not chastise him as he so often had. Instead, he looked him in the eye and spoke. "The answers you seek will all come in time. But for now, it is enough for you to know that you are needed. You will play an important role in what is to come."

Zeek rose to his full height, which he now realised towered over his ageing Father. "I am… needed?"

"Yes," Father said. "This world is in danger, and I intend to save it."

"Danger? What danger?"

Father cleared his throat. "There are powerful forces at play, and if we do not stop them, then all of this," he said, gesturing to the surrounding environment, "will be consumed by it."

Zeek inclined his head, watching with intent as the grass continued to sway.

"This is but a taste of what Zapour has to offer," Father continued. "You do not want this to disappear, do you? There is light, so much light. Do you want to see the light, Zeek? To live in it as a human would?"

At the mention of light, Zeek snapped to attention. "But you said I cannot walk the light, that it is dangerous."

"I know what I said. But you are changing quicker than I could have foreseen. Your body is adjusting, your senses tuning. At the moment it is still too dangerous for you to walk the light, but soon… soon I believe it will be safe. You need only follow me, and I will show you the way."

Zeek tried to twist his lips into what his stolen memories told him was a smile, an expression of happiness. By his Father's reaction, he gathered that he had mimicked it poorly, for he turned his head away in disgust.

Suddenly, Zeek doubled over, a pain in his stomach beating like a drum. Father turned back towards him. "What is it?" he asked.

Zeek tried to speak, but found that words were hard to form. He had hoped to hide this from Father, to hide his weakness.

"You will answer me!"

The drumbeat subsided somewhat, enough for him to open his mouth. "I — there is something calling me," he said. "Pulling me towards it."

Father raised an eyebrow, more curious than angry.

This comforted Zeek, giving him the confidence to speak

his truth. "It grows stronger with every step I take, as if something is reeling me in."

"Interesting. Which direction is it telling you to go?"

Zeek broadened his view and pointed north.

"And this pulling, can you push it aside? Block it out?"

Zeek nodded. "I — I think so, yes."

"Good. You must resist it, for your own good. Do you trust me?"

"Y-yes, Father."

"Very well, then let us continue."

Without waiting for a response, Father took off, knowing Zeek would not – *could* not leave his side.

Chapter 4

- Isha –

THE CITY OF ILLIDOR shadowed her steps as Isha made her way through the bustling gates and out into the open fields of her homeland.

She continued down a winding pathway, every stride taking her further from the palace and closer to the remote cottage her mother and Kron had made their own.

Ever since departing the cage that had been Lumindal, she had found peace in space, in scenery, in flora and fauna. Even amid the long winter her mother's tended garden remained vibrant with colour.

Isha walked along the dirt path outside their little cottage. She held out her hands, fingers lightly caressing the cream-white petals of winter honeysuckle. The fragrant flowers hung from almost leafless branches, leaning over to compliment the darker, violet bed of pansies that her mother had bred to bloom in the cold.

Kron was sitting leisurely on a chair resting on the front porch. He looked incomparable to his former self. Gone were the fancy clothes, the regal demeanor, the overconfidence, the crown. In their place was a man who sought redemption. In truth, he had much to atone for; his kingdom, his sons, his daughter, his wife…

He was still a vision of power; strong legs, and arms thick enough to strike fear into the heart of any foe. His eyes, though, perpetually held in them a vulnerable plea for forgiveness. Despite this, Isha still wasn't able to call him Father. Not since returning. She had tried to forgive him, to make amends, but the pain was too deep, too raw for her to simply revert to how things had once been.

He rose as she approached, and Isha greeted him with a polite nod. "Is mother in?" she asked, finding herself in no mood for small talk.

Kron nodded. "She's out back. Isha," he said, catching her arm before she passed him. "When time permits, I would like to spend some more time with you, if that is something you would like? Just the two of us, as father and daughter."

Inwardly, Isha winced, not yet ready for that sort of intimate connection, but outwardly she smiled. "That would be nice," she said as she left. She owed it to herself to at least try, to give him a second chance. He might not deserve it, but he had suffered a long time, and she might not forgive herself if she never gave to him.

Walking past Kron, she skipped around to the back, finding her mother in amongst the glistening, luminescent branches of a miniature forest. The shimmer trees shone brightly even in the light of day, their golden leaves interlacing and creating a canopy which covered the entire garden.

Celia was reading, leaning backward as she rocked on her

curved wooden chair. She must have heard Isha's approach, as she peeked over the top of the book before setting it down and welcoming her with a warm smile.

"Daughter, how lovely of you to visit me on this fine day," she said.

Isha relayed a polite smile of her own, then sat herself down on a bench beside her. "It is good to see you, Mother. I see Kron is in today. Are things… well? Between the two of you?"

Her mother sighed, lavender eyes closing for a moment before fluttering open again. "Yes, things are well." Though her eyes were full of colour, there was an emptiness behind them, as if she weren't really there. It was like the person that she had once been was gone, buried beneath the weight of Lumindal. A weight Isha knew well.

Isha had carried that burden for eight long years. She couldn't even imagine what it must have been like to live it for nearly twenty. How could someone go through something like that and retain their sanity?

"You still don't forgive him, do you?" her mother continued.

Isha lowered her gaze, her expression already answering the question. "I thought with time I could. He has done nothing since my return to give me reason not to, and yet still I hold back. Does that make me cruel?"

Celia opened her posture a little. "No, it doesn't make you cruel," she said, letting out a light laugh. "Kron is many things, but easy to forgive is not one of them. He can be… difficult, and at times harsh, but I do not think him a bad person. When I left for Lumindal and Evanon took interest in me it broke him inside."

"When you… left? Were you not taken against your will? Did the King-Radiant not force your hand? Why else would you have abandoned us? Left your children to be raised without a mother?"

Celia looked taken aback, as if the questions wounded her deeply. "Things were complicated back then. Love can be wonderful, but it can also be delicate, fragile, and at times a burden. It is true that I once loved Kron, perhaps I still do. But it is also true that I once loved Evanon, before he became the man that you knew him to be.

"I make no excuses for the way he acted, and in truth I blame myself for what happened to him. From birth he was forced down a dark path by an unworthy father. I tried to placate the hostility growing inside of him, thought I could use my influence to steer him a different way. I wanted to right the wrongs of the past, to change the course of history. But in the end, I was wrong, and I paid the price for it."

Isha frowned, questions that had lingered in her mind for a long time bubbling to the surface. "What wrongs of the past? Who were you to think you could influence the mind of a King-Radiant? Am I capable of the same? Who and what are we?"

Isha placed a hand on her chest, feeling her quickening heartbeat before taking a deep breath. She noticed that her mother had withdrawn her touch. "Sorry, I didn't mean to… I just want answers. I have been patient, have waited for you to settle here in Illidor, and to recover. But there is so much I need to know. I want to know what you know. I want to know who I am."

At first, Isha thought her mother might stand up and leave right there and then, but as her words had time to settle, so too did Celia. She relaxed, shoulders dropping.

"You are right. You deserve to know what you are, who you are. But seeking answers is not always the right path, sometimes it is better to stay sheltered from the past, for your own safety."

"I don't care," Isha said. "I haven't lived a safe life. I don't need to be sheltered. I want to know."

"Very well," Celia said, cupping her hands together and straightening her back. "I will tell you what I can, but there are parts of my history that might come as a shock. Are you sure you are ready?"

Isha issued another confident nod, her excitement rising. When she had discovered that her mother was alive and was just like her, she had thought she would find answers. She had expected that the riddle that had been her life would be unravelled, that she would finally understand who she was. Unfortunately, this hadn't been the case. Her mother had been distant, often vacant from her own mind. Isha had tried to pry for answers on multiple occasions, but she had feared to press too hard, frightened that she might break a fragile mind. But today Celia seemed different, more whole. Isha felt bold, determined. Still, she had to be careful.

"Before I begin," her mother said, "you must know that I was not born in Zapour, nor was I born in this century."

Isha's eyes lit up. "What do you mean? How old *are* you?"

"Eight hundred and sixty-two."

Isha's mouth dropped. She attempted to respond, words proving frustratingly elusive. "How?" she finally managed to say.

"In truth, I am not sure. Despite my long-lived life, I was born after the time of providence, when Zur bestowed his gifts upon the chosen. Before sickness took her from me, my mother told me stories of the intervention. Today it is believed that Shine was the only gift Zur granted us in the fight against Cova. What the Eagles did not tell you is that there was another."

Isha reached for her face, her mind instinctually making a connection. "Our eyes."

Celia nodded. "There were more of us before I was born. More of those gifted with empathic ability, able to impart their influence over another, alter emotions, and take away pain. But there was a war. Not fought between nations, but an internal war between the two factions who together had shared in victory against the skae. My mother spoke of a fierce battle, and also a great loss.

"I never knew my father, but to my mother he was everything. He was her counterpart, and together they fought against the system and its growing violence. But in the end the violence came for them, and the system won."

Isha leaned forward. The urge to question and learn more was overwhelming. "Are there more? Like us, I mean."

Celia let out a thin breath. "Perhaps. I do not know. I have lived a long life, it is true, but one spent mostly in solitude. I was raised away from civilization, from the danger of the past. Away even from sunlight," she finished, holding out her palm and allowing a droplet of Shine to drip from her fingers. "I did not even come to learn the full truth of my eyes until I decided to defy my mother's wishes and venture across the Sapphire Sea. It was then that I met your father."

Isha took a moment to take in so much information. She sat, staring at the puddle of discarded Shine slowly turning to breen at her mother's feet. "I want to learn. I want to know what I am capable of. I want to understand why people like you and me were so loathed, yet now are revered."

Isha noticed her mother's demeanor begin to shift, her mood clouding over. She squirmed in her seat. "No. It is not something you should learn. It is something to hide. Yes. The might of what we once were is better left unremembered. You must trust me on this Isha."

Isha's stomach sank as her pulse quickened. She was so close to breaking through, to grasping the truth. She wasn't about to let this chance slip away. "Please. I must know. I am sick of living in the dark."

"I am sorry, Isha. If you were to attempt to reveal our latent power to the world, I would not forgive myself for what they would do to you."

"They? What do you mean? We are in Illidor now, Mother. We are safe. Dazen will protect me. Raiz and Spike will never let anything happen to me. I am safe. We are safe. There is no reason to hide any longer."

Despite this, her mother continued to shake her head, rocking back and forth, retreating from the memory of her past. "You don't understand. You are better off not knowing. I should not have told you even this much. I am sorry. Please forgive me, it is for the best."

But mother I —"

She stopped herself, remembering her mother's frailty, but she couldn't fight off the anger and frustration. She had been on the verge of breaking through to her, she was sure of it, and yet her mother remained trapped in her cage. Though Celia was now physically free, her mind was still captive to the trauma of the past.

Isha needed to know more about who she was, and if her

mother wasn't going to tell her, she would find out for herself.

Chapter 5

– Raiz –

"ARE YOU SURE THIS IS WISE?" Draz asked as they entered the rocky terrain of central Crata.

Raiz shifted. "They need our help. What am I to do, ignore them? You know me better than that."

"Maybe so, but you need to think. We came here to broker peace, to find potential allies. Not to find missing people."

"If these 'New Cratans' are anything like what Taula says they are, then there will be no peace. I won't bargain with thieves and brigands."

"Then what will you do when you find them? Slaughter them all? Is that what you've become?"

Raiz paused in his tracks. He stopped breathing, his mind replaying the events in Lumindal, when he had let his blood-lust take hold. He had killed them, every single one. They had deserved it. All of them deserved to pay a thousand times for what they had done, for the people they had been.

Why then did he feel guilt? Draz's comments cut deeper than his friend could know. Was that all he was now? A scythe? A reaper? An instrument of vengeance?

He shook himself out of his reverie. "I don't know what I'll do. I suppose I'll figure it out when I find them."

Raiz hoisted the piece of clothing Porter had given him up to Spike's nose. "Can you find her?"

Spike sniffed the air, ears lifting like a hound's as he caught wind of something. He took off at a sprint, with Raiz, Draz and Aroha racing after his barbed tail.

Raiz's lungs burned as Spike took them on a three-mile journey. Finally, just when Raiz felt he could run no further, the Dragon slowed, taking cautious steps as he positioned himself between an outcropping of high-walled rock.

Draz doubled over behind him, ripping Gallant off and struggling to catch his breath. "Really wish, we had, brought the horses," he said between gasps.

Aroha slapped him on the back. "Come on Draz, a little cardio will do you good. Maybe come morning you will have lost some of that puppy fat."

Draz punched her playfully in the arm before Raiz glared at them both, lowering his hand and placing a finger over his lips.

Voices sounded in the near distance, prompting him to sink into a crouch. He poked his head through a gap, peering out into the night. Fires were lit around an established camp. "I count seven of them, plus two on watch."

Draz unlatched his axe and held it aloft. "We've faced worse. Any sign of the girl?"

Raiz squinted, surveying the camp. A central pavilion was set up, surrounded by three smaller tents. "She might be in there," he said, pointing towards the pavilion. "Guess I'll have to take a closer look."

Aroha tugged on his shoulder. "Those sentries have a tight watch. You're not getting in there unnoticed."

Raiz carefully removed her hand from his shirt. "Who said anything about unnoticed?"

Before they could respond, Raiz had already left the safety of his cover. He turned quickly to Spike, commanding him to stay put until he was needed. The creature grudgingly obliged.

He raised two hands into the air, the stored Shine that flowed through his veins granting him the confidence to overpower any adversary, despite Zur's absence in the sky. It wasn't long before he was spotted. A sentry whistled and waved a torch in his direction. "Halt!" he called, beckoning a few others to come to his aid. "Stop where you are!"

When Raiz did not stop, he drew his short sword, another three men doing the same behind him.

Raiz let a few droplets of Shine build up beneath the cover of his fingertips, but otherwise made no move to attack. He waved his left hand, offering a sign of peace. "I seek an audience with your leader. You are of New Crata, correct? I am Raiz Glaive of Trost, here on friendly terms." He hated himself for saying it, for giving them a chance, but Draz was right. He couldn't just go around slaughtering anyone and everyone.

The sentry on duty wavered, whispering something to the man next to him. The man darted off into the distance, leaving the sentry with his bow raised and pointed at Raiz. "Don't move."

It wasn't long before more of the bandits were woken. One

hardy-looking fellow wearing a brown bandanna stepped forward and grunted. "This way," he said, turning and motioning for Raiz to follow.

He did, but kept his guard up as they led him into their small camp. Behind it, hounds barked in their cages, likely sensing Spike's presence in the near distance. Raiz ignored them, instead making his way inside the large tent pitched in the centre of the encampment.

"The Red Knight," came a deep voice belonging to a man who was slowly stepping towards him. His face was a mess of scars. His thick right arm held a heavy, curved sword, but his left was a withered tangle of skin and bone. It looked drained of all fat and muscle, all colour lost to whatever had maimed him.

"I admit, I thought you'd be taller," the man continued. "If you're really the Red Knight, then I gotta thank you. Without the King-Radiant's intervention, we Cratan's have been able to rebuild, grow strong again. Unfortunately for you, your future here is death. And with your death, my pockets'll swell. Yep, you'll fetch a fine bounty for my master. The demons up north'll pay a high price indeed for one of your calibre, if you're actually who you say."

"Where is the woman?" Raiz questioned, ignoring the ignorant rambling.

"Hm?" the bandit grunted.

"The woman you took from Tinker. Where is she? If you will not speak on terms of peace, then I would have her from you before I take my leave."

The bandit paused, then broke into a fit of laughter. "You came here for a woman?" he said, jesting to all those around him, who also revelled in laughter. "You got some balls kid,

I'll give you that. But the woman's gone. Yep, sold her to my master already. It's likely the demons already have her by now, flush with Shine as she was. Pity, she was a pretty one."

Raiz had heard enough. He'd opted for diplomacy, given him the chance to plead innocence and show him that he deserved to live. But this man had earned death, and Raiz would pay him his due.

"Now then, let's see if this Red Knight proves —"

Before he could finish his sentence, Raiz had shot a bolt of Shine through his chest. The bandit looked down at the gaping hole in his chest with wide eyes before dropping to the floor, dead.

The others surrounding him were slow to react, eyes alight with disbelief even as their comrade fell. Raiz capitalized on the delay, hoping he had made his point. "I ask again, where is the woman? Where was she taken?"

For a moment, the remaining men were too frozen to speak. The man furthest to his right let out a shrill scream, calling for back-up. Voices responded in the distance, along with the growls of what Raiz knew to be hounds.

He grit his teeth and scrambled out of the tent. Pressing two fingers to his lips he whistled, looking over his shoulder to see Spike wasting no time. The pricket-turned-dragon thundered forward on foot rather than taking to the air, preferring to stay close to Raiz as they fought. His presence alone sent two men tumbling over their own feet onto their asses. They were the first to die. Spike slashed with his claws, carving into flesh as if it were butter. Their screams rang throughout the camp and roused others, who came to answer their dead compatriots' last call.

There were more than anticipated, with nearly a dozen

spilling out from the surrounding tents. Draz and Aroha soon joined them, weapons drawn. Raiz summoned his stored Light, igniting his red-glowing glaive with a flourish and watching as those before him marvelled in fear. He made to move, to kill, but hesitated. Something held him back. His vision swirled as memories assaulted him. He pictured the Eagles dying helplessly before him. Was this truly who he had become?

Three hounds burst ahead of their human masters, their angry, slobber-filled jaws snapping as they spotted Spike. Spike spread his wings and growled to intimidate the hungry pack, but it did not deter them. On they spurred, launching atop Spike's scaled hide, bringing Raiz out of his reverie.

Raiz winced as he witnessed one of the dogs latch onto a soft spot above Spike's shoulder, but he was forced to focus on his own quarrel when three men charged at him. Raiz had the blood of a Radiant. They were no match for his Shine and skill. He sliced one through the collarbone, following up with a sweep that cut straight through his aggressor's short sword, searing into flesh and bone.

His glaive blazed, cutting scarlet waves and turning opponents into corpses. Eventually, one man pressed too close, grabbing onto Raiz's shirt. The tip of a knife grazed his ribcage as he twisted away just in time. Pain flared across his torso, causing Raiz to drop his glaive, the Shine-fuelled weapon losing its structure as soon as it was no longer an extension of his will.

It didn't matter. Elbowing the man in the head, Raiz broke free and regained enough room to raise a fist. He slammed it down, dropping the bandit to the ground. Raiz fell upon him, furiously raining down blows with knuckles that dripped red.

Each punch was thrown with more force than the last, until he realized the man beneath him had stopped moving.

Eventually, the last of the screams subsided and the campsite went quiet. Spike limped over, favouring his left leg. Raiz could see it was bleeding steadily, but three dead hounds lay behind him. Raiz took a series of heavy breaths, and found that his hands were violently shaking.

His vision blurred, memories of the past assaulting him like a physical blow. All he could see were the Eagles, their dead and dying bodies spread before him like a painting rendered in blood. He winced, both head and heart ablaze with an ache that sought to drive him mad.

"What have I done?" he whispered, fixated on his bloody, shaking hands.

"Raiz!" came a call from the side. Draz approached, one hand held in the air. "Raiz, are you well?"

Raiz faltered. He took another look at the carnage surrounding him. "Is this who I am?" he said. "Is this all I know?"

Draz just stared at him as if he were a feral dog that might need to be put down.

"Something's wrong with me, Draz," he said, holding up his hand and watching the blood trickle down his fingers.

"There's nothing wrong with you, lad. These people deserved to —"

"Look at me!" Raiz shouted. "I did this!" He gestured to the man whose face he had caved in bare-handed. His frame was that of a boy barely past his teens. "You were right," he continued. "I shouldn't be here. I have a family, people who care about me. I should be at home, with them. And yet I can't do it. I'm a monster."

He paused, half waiting for Draz to argue against him. When he didn't, Raiz continued. "My brother once warned me. He said he would hate to see me become that which I sought to destroy. At the time I dismissed him, was angry that he could even think such a thing. But he was right. I thought the Eagles were the true evil in this world. They killed for pleasure, took what they wanted. I'm no different. I've become the monster I always hated."

He started to spiral out of control. His thoughts consumed him, starting to send him to a place from which he knew he may not be able to return, when he suddenly felt a searing pain spread across his cheek.

All thought ceased, replaced by agony as he staggered from the impact, working his jaw up and down to see if it were still functional. Instinctually, he moved to retaliate, his fist balled and ready to strike, when he saw Draz standing there with his shoulders squared, fixing him with a stare so intense and righteous that all violence was immediately shoved to the back of his mind.

"Would you like another?" Draz asked, cocking his arm slightly.

Raiz rubbed at his cheek and was surprised to see blood as he pulled his hand away, only to remember it was not his own. "Thank you," he said, his faculties returning to him. "But it still doesn't change anything."

"Where would your sister be?" Draz said, causing Raiz to look at his friend with a quizzical expression. "Where would she be," he repeated, "if you had not spent your life trying to see her safe? Where would she be?"

Raiz hesitated. "In Lumindal."

Draz took a step forward. "And those children, the ones we

rescued. Hector. Where would they be, if we had not intervened?"

Raiz let out an exasperated sigh. "I—"

"Where would they be!"

"Dead," Raiz said.

"They would be corpses. As would be the others that were under the thumb of that broken regime, and likely all of Trost. Perhaps even all of Zapour, eventually. So you can call yourself a monster if you like, but perhaps a monster is exactly what this world needed."

Raiz tried to gather his thoughts, but emotions ran rampant through his over-active mind. There was one emotion which stood above all others, overpowering all sense of rationality and dashing any hopes of peace. Anger.

Why was he so angry all the time? He had thought it would disappear once he got his sister back. When it didn't, he had thought that eliminating the King-Radiant and his Eagles might quell the rage ever-lurking within. But none of it did a thing. They were all dead, and yet his frustration continued. His hands still itched for justice, even though justice had already been served.

Spike came to his side, his ribbed tongue scratching at Raiz's side and attempting to lick him clean. Raiz leant into it, nuzzling him under his chin before dripping some excess Shine into his gullet.

"I am a monster," he finally said. "But I don't want to be."

Just then, a gurgle sounded from below, followed by a choking sound as one of those he'd thought was dead awakened from his unconscious state. Raiz lowered himself to the bandit's level, gripping him by the collar of his jerkin.

"Where is the woman?" he asked.

The man just blinked at him, too stricken with fear to respond. Raiz stepped away, taking a deep breath to avoid unleashing his rage again. "Draz, see if you can get anything out of him."

Draz obliged, taking a more relaxed approach. He unlatched the stopper from his water-skin and poured a few drops into the fallen bandit's bloody mouth. The man sucked the water down like he'd never had a drink in his life, choking as he took in too much and spitting nearly half of it back up.

"Are you going to kill me?" said the bandit, hands shaking.

Draz sighed, bending down to his level. "That depends. Tell us what you know of the woman your band took captive from Tinker, and we shall see."

Draz's words didn't have the calming effect he had intended. The man, whom Raiz now realised was also no older than he was, shuffled backward in a panic. "I — I didn't wanna take her! I had no choice! I swear, I'm not like them. I didn't do nothing!"

Raiz rolled his eyes, he'd heard that before, but Draz tried to sympathise.

"Draz believes you, but you need to tell us where she is. What have you done with her?"

The young bandit bit his lip, and after a lengthy gulp, he finally responded. "S-she's already been offered."

"Offered to who?" Draz said. "For what?"

The bandit shook his head. "N-not to who… to *what*."

Raiz turned, cocking his head to the side. "What do you mean 'to what'?"

The bandit shivered. "I — I don't know. Some of 'em, they don't have faces. T-they come from the mountains, up north. They take and they take. We don't have a choice! It was either us or the villagers."

"You always have a choice," Raiz snapped, finger pointing towards him. "And you chose to give the lives of innocents above your own."

The bandit shuffled back another inch. "I didn't choose nothing! I'm a simple soldier. I'm not involved with the decisions."

Raiz closed the distance between himself and the bandit. "How do we find them?"

The cowering bandit raised an arm over his face, expecting to be hit. "I don't know!" he sobbed. "T-they only come at night, but they're fast, very fast. Light weakens them, I'm told. But I've never seen one, not properly at least, only from a distance. Please, don't kill me."

Raiz shared a hesitantly concerned look with both Draz and Aroha, as if all three had come to the same conclusion but couldn't believe it.

"The lad lies," Draz said. "He's spinning a tale. The Skae are a myth. No creatures of Cova walk the plains of Zapour, at least not anymore."

"That is not what Celik believed," Aroha said.

"Celik was a lying sack of pricket shit," Draz said, spitting into the soil. "Surely you didn't believe all of that crap."

"Then how else do you explain this?"

Draz shook his head. "It's a lie, clearly. Either a lie, or this poor lad has been fooled, likely by some callous warlord bent on holding leverage over the villages of Crata."

Raiz listened. He reached down and lifted the young bandit up by his shirt. "Show us where you saw these 'creatures'."

"But... I — "

"I was not asking," Raiz said, pushing him lightly in the back. "Move."

Chapter 6

- Zeek –

"LEAVE IT."

Zeek pretended as though he hadn't heard his father, cupping his hands together beneath the wounded creature. It chirped, attempting to rise but ultimately falling when its broken wing collapsed.

He lifted it into the air, studying it like a curious child. He had heard of these creatures before, whistling their songs every brightrise and darkfall. His stolen memories told him this was a bird, an animal of the sky.

"Why won't it fly?" he said, turning to face Father.

His father grumbled. "This animal's well-being is of no concern to us. Now leave it be."

"But it will die," Zeek said.

"All living creatures die eventually. Let fate decide its course."

Zeek found himself instinctively pulling the bird closer to

his chest, as if that would shield it from any further harm. "But humans take lives all the time. I take lives. If we are to save the world, can we not save them too?"

Father approached, his stare as cold as the nightly breeze. "Some things are not worth saving," he said. "The world is wide, its oceans vast. Search through your memories and you will see. Not all that need saving can be saved. We must focus on the many, and sacrifice the few."

Zeek searched through his memories and found what he was told to be true. He looked down at the bird once more. "But this creature will soon die. Should I not at least try to save it?"

"To what end? You would waste time and energy on sustaining a creature that will have no impact on the world. The animal is insignificant. It is nothing. Its death will mean nothing."

Zeek withdrew, mind racing with thought. "Am I... nothing?"

Father took another step towards him. "You are not nothing. If you wish it, your life can have purpose. I can give it purpose. But you must listen to me. You are not yet ready. Your mind and body are not yet up to the task I have set. Your previous indulgences have proved useful, but they have also made you soft. You need to feed on someone with substance, someone with the skills required to carry out what you were made for."

"What I was... made for?"

"Tell me, Zeek, would you like to walk the light?"

"What was I, before you found me?"

"You were nothing! Then I rescued you. I will speak no more on the subject. Now tell me, would you like to walk the light?"

Zeek frowned, but the prospect of walking the light intrigued him greatly. "Yes. I want to be like you. I want to be human."

"Then first you must listen to me. You must trust me. Leave the bird."

Zeek hesitated, hands shaking. But Father's word was final. He had to obey. That was his purpose. He lowered the bird to the soft grass beneath his feet. He stepped aside and exhaled as the bird continued to chirp.

There was a red flash, and the bird's fractured song was silenced as it was turned to ash. Zeek turned, furious at such a betrayal, but as soon as he shifted Father was on him, his unrelenting gaze a warning against retaliation.

"You must trust me, Zeek. This was a mercy, to end its suffering. You must trust that I know best. If you cannot, then you will never walk the light, and we cannot make the world a better place."

Zeek stood for a moment, hovering over the ashes of the animal he had wanted to save. He searched within himself for the emotion that was causing him to care for the creature and set it aside.

I must listen to Father. Must always listen to Father.

THEY REACHED the dark shelter of a small house before the bright returned. Zeek had no idea where they were. Father had told him that they had entered the eastern border of Craw, but he didn't know where that was. He didn't know where anything was. The entire world was a blank slate. *He* was still a blank slate, and he couldn't wait to fill in the details.

His mind had grown over the past couple of days. With

that growth came curiosity. He had only ever touched the light once, and the result was as his Father had said it would be. His skin had burned, and the shadows which at the time formed his frame had tightened, choking the life from him. If Father had not been there, then he feared his life would have been over before it had even begun.

Even so, he was stronger now, his body had changed. Less and less shadow made up his increasingly pinkish skin. Could he touch it again now that he was further transformed?

The windows of the house were blacked out with paint, but the door was unlocked. Father was downstairs tending to business of his own. Zeek watched the shade of black paint change as light began to rise in the outside world. The door was calling him. Just one push, a couple of steps, and he would be in the light again. He pressed against the frame and pulled the handle, listening as the old wood creaked open. A sliver of gold broke through, a line of bright tracing through a room full of dark.

He inched his fingers around the edge of the door, head peeking out behind it. The colour was blinding, and his vision blurred. His head ached at the drastic change, and yet he could not part from it. He could see *everything*.

He reached out, one slow inch at a time. The tip of his finger was almost there when a voice froze him in his tracks.

"What are you doing!" his father's cry rang louder than he had ever heard.

He withdrew his hand and slammed the door shut, returning to the darkness. "I just wanted to see if I could."

"Do you want to die? Because that is what will happen if you walk outside right now."

"I — I'm sorry, Father."

"I asked you to trust me. If you cannot do that, then we are done here. I will leave you to face the consequences of your negligence alone, and you will suffer for it."

Zeek dropped to his knees. "I didn't..." he sobbed. "I won't, ever again, not without your permission. I promise."

"Get up, get up. Come, I have something for you, a meal."

Zeek did as he was told, following his father's footsteps. Hunger nagged at him. His shadow-tail vibrated within the confines of his shirt, yearning for more.

He was led down a small, winding staircase and into a room dug beneath the small home. Torchlight flickered in the centre of the room. It was so different than his usual red globe. He hovered his hands over it, dazzled by the beauty of what he now came to know as *fire*. Heat crawled up his arms, warming him. Warmth was also a new concept, one he had seldom experienced, for there wasn't much of it in his old home.

A chain rattled at the edge of the room, followed by a weak groan. Zeek looked up, watching as Father used his feet with practised skill to scoop and place a bowl of fresh stew at the foot of the man who was confined by the chains.

Bony fingers clutched at the bowl, and the sound of heavy slurping filled the room as the man devoured his meal. Zeek watched with continued fascination as the chained man tried to speak. His voice came out as no more than a croak, however, so he reached for the pitcher of water by his side.

After a lengthy sip, he spoke again. "You... left me here... to die."

Father paced the room, dead arms unmoving as always. "You are alive," he said, his tone flat and callous.

"My... father... will find me," he said in-between breaths.

"He… will kill you."

Father must have found that amusing, for he smiled, the firelight twisting his features into something from a nightmare. "Your father is a gluttonous pig. Best you forget your past life, young prince. You are soon to become part of something much grander."

The prisoner moved to spit at him but found his mouth to be too dry. His lips were cracked, and Zeek could see his ribs poking through the pink of his skin. Despite this, he lifted his head into the sky and began laughing. It came out as more of a cackle, a deranged cry born from someone starved of sustenance. It quickly turned into a coughing fit, and the man his father had called a prince bent over and retched, upheaving his recently ingested stew. He spat at Father again, and this time liquid came out. "You think yourself clever, old man. But you do not understand the weight of what you have done. I am Ancel Saelmere, first-born son of Gelvard, and heir to the throne of Craw. They will come for me. These lands will be crawling with soldiers before long. You are finished."

If Zeek's father was bothered by the outburst, he didn't show it. He simply went about his business, using either his feet or his mouth to mix a concoction on the rotting desk in the opposite corner.

"I am afraid they will find nothing but a corpse," Father said.

Beside him, the man called Ancel began to thrash, using what little strength he had left to pull at the chains that bound his wrists to the wall.

"It is nothing personal," Father continued. "I do not delight in depriving Zapour of those who can wield Zur's Shine. One might argue it is contradictory to my goal. But unfortunately, it is necessary. You see, Zeek here is special. He is greater than either you or me. But in his current form he is… limited. In order for me to bring out his full potential, I need you. Take it as a compliment if you wish. Your link with Zur is strong, and your skills are vast. Yes, you are what he needs."

Ancel descended into a rage, rocking back and forth, cutting his wrists on the metal in one last desperate attempt to free himself from his bonds. "You are mad!" he screamed. "Let me go! My father —"

A leg extended like a whip, bare foot cracking into Ancel's cheek and sending him crashing onto the floor. Zeek saw a tooth or two leave his mouth, then ricocheting off the stone wall.

"I have heard enough of your babbling. It is time for you to perish." He turned to Zeek, an expectant glee etched into the lines of his ageing face. "If you want to walk the light, then this is the way. Feed. Take everything. I want all of who he is gone. Let his memories be your memories, his abilities your abilities. If my theory is correct, then he is all you will need."

Zeek hesitated, taking a cautious step towards the nearly unconscious Saelmere. He cracked his knuckles, his body yearning for the meal that had been prepared for him. He took a wary look over his shoulder. "Father, no. Not with you in the room."

Father grumbled, eyes narrowing. "What is the difference?"

Zeek looked to the floor, trying to understand why he felt the way he did. "I… it is not something I can explain. This… feeding. It is a private thing. I do not know why it is so. But I do not wish to do this in your presence."

Father went quiet, and for a moment Zeek thought he was

going to lash out at him. "Very well," he said instead. "I will be upstairs. Come to me when it is done."

With that he left, footsteps fading into the distance. Zeek was left alone in the dark once more with nothing but his prey.

He crouched, studying the broken prince. He didn't look like much. His memories told him that princes were supposed to be grand, majestic even. But lying before him was just a boy, one barely past his adolescence.

Zeek had encountered a child once. They were much smaller and younger than this, and he had let her go. He didn't know why, not really. Perhaps the child did not yet have enough experience in life for him to take, or maybe he had been influenced by the personalities he had previously taken, driven by an empathy that was not his own.

It mattered not, for though this boy was young, he was no child, and Zeek had no choice. He had to obey, and he wanted to walk the light.

Ancel squirmed, beginning to regain consciousness. Zeek inched closer, pressing his hands against the fallen prince's torn shirt. He instantly recoiled, staring at his hands. They were hot. It struck him as strange. This had never happened before. All of his previous victims had been cold, their life force coming easily. But this man, he was different. More than the warmth was the power he felt, radiating like a physical presence. He reached down again, this time allowing his hands to remain.

He soon found that whatever power this man had lurking beneath his skin did not like his invasion. It flailed wildly, fleeing from his touch. Zeek didn't know what it was, only that he wanted it. He focused, instincts ushering him to begin the process.

His tail unfurled fully in a serpentine swirl before rising like a scorpion above his head.

Then it struck, piercing deep into the prince's chest. Bright, golden energy rose through the shadows that made up his tail. It sucked, and finally the prince's essence flowed into him. Zeek's chest expanded as his arms flung behind his body. This was different than before, grander, more filling. It was ecstasy, it was life.

It hurt. No. It burned.

His body screamed at him to let it go, to stop this madness, but he couldn't stop. Although it hurt, it also gave him strength. He could feel his body changing, morphing into something more, something fierce.

He arched his head, continuing to suck the life from his meal. There may have been a cry of protest, a last plea for life, but it went unheard. The ecstasy was overwhelming. It wasn't just that his body grew in strength, his mind also became sharper, the flood of fresh memories lending him a deep pool of experience that he might be able to draw from, given the right focus. He found it baffling that someone so young could be filled with so many powerful memories, so many painful memories. He drifted into a state of euphoria, only dimly aware that the process had already ended, and the prince was dead.

Then, slowly, he came to himself. The corpse before him was a mottled mess of sunken skin and protruding bones.

The knob-less door behind him was abruptly kicked in, and Father strode into the room. "Is it done?" he asked, answering his own question as he bent down to study the remains. "How do you feel?"

Zeek wiggled his fingers. His forearms itched. It was as if

there were two opposing forces within, clashing and mixing together, forced to live in tandem even though by nature they were opposites. "I feel… good," he said. "Really good."

A spark lit within his mind, one that could not be ignored. The light was calling him.

He rose to his feet and made for the door.

"Zeek, stop!" Father called. "We must approach this with caution."

This time Zeek didn't listen. He was certain that the light wouldn't harm him. He stalked through the darkness towards the front door. Looking down, he saw light seeping through the crack. He pulled, and it creaked open. As before, he reached a hand outward, slowly, expecting to be burnt, even though now he knew he wouldn't be.

He closed his eyes and stretched further, but he did not burn. His stomach fluttered, an emotion he was beginning to enjoy. He stepped fully into the light, basking in its glory. He felt his face, his chest, his legs. He ripped his shirt, exposing his body to the light. The shadows that had been an ever-present leech faded, crawling back into his flesh.

He sucked in a fresh lungful of air and cried out in glee. Father appeared by the frame of the door and Zeek returned to him, unable to contain his excitement.

"It worked! It worked! I can walk the light!"

Father merely grunted, but Zeek could tell he was pleased.

"Enjoy the light for today," he said at last. "But tomorrow, we have work to do."

Chapter 7

- Isha –

IT WASN'T ENOUGH. Isha yearned for answers, for more information. Her mind was scattered, broken into a hundred different thoughts. Could her mother really be *that* old? Was she also capable of such a long-lived life? Then there was the question of her abilities. She had always felt different, like she had a power within yet to be tapped. But she had never known how, or what.

She wanted to press for more answers, ask more questions, but she knew it to be dangerous. Her mother's mind was fragile, and delving into past memories pained her. It had taken all this time just for her to open up this much. When she'd first returned home she had seemed receptive, but then everything changed. She withdrew. Withdrew from Isha, from Dazen, from Raiz. Only Kron seemed to have her ear.

Isha forced herself to set her worries aside. Her brother needed her. Dazen was a mess. Even now, sitting and picking idly at food on the dinner table, she could see his stress. It was well hidden behind his impeccable white-blue uniform, groomed beard, and trained mannerisms, but the signs were there. His fingers were tight around the spoon, which he was using to stir the already cold bowl of soup in front of him.

"Relax," she said, placing a hand on his free arm. "You don't need to carry these worries on your own. I'm here."

Dazen eyed her and grumbled. "I'm fine," he said, sitting up straighter.

Isha smiled as Dazen moved his free hand into her own, cupping it even as his knee bobbed up and down under the table.

The Great Hall was packed to capacity. Nobles had come from all corners of Trost to have their voices heard regarding the Sun Prince's arrival. If the past two years had proved anything, it was that Dazen was a capable leader.

Already he had settled the past grudge between the Grudle and Chaldwin families by offering fair compensation in land ownership. He had appointed new leaders, rewarded loyal old ones, and overseen numerous lucrative trade deals – including an agreement with the coastal town of Brane that had provided Illidor with more wealth than it had seen in years. That wasn't even to mention the benefits the union with Zuton was providing for the citizens. Tax rates had plummeted, since less men were needed in the garrisons bordering the two countries. More workers had flowed into Illidor, leading to an expansion of homes and districts. The number of Shine users in Trost had also swelled with the acquisition of soldiers from Lumindal after its fall, as well as abolishment of the previous limitations set by the King-Radiant.

Not all was well though. With the long winter refusing to abate, people were hungry. Of course, this wasn't Dazen's doing, but when you were a king, everything was your responsibility.

At the end of the table Nora burped, causing Dazen's focus to shift towards his infant daughter. A quick glance from Sumaya told him she had it under control, however, so he returned to stirring his uneaten meal.

Isha chuckled. It was unusual to have a babe dine in the Great Hall, but Dazen and Sumaya had taken it upon themselves to introduce her to the court early. The people of Trost needed to see the future of their kingdom. They needed to see that the bond between Zuton and Trost was very real, and not just a political advantage. Nora's presence gave them that confirmation. Besides, there was nothing like the attendance of a baby to dissuade those tough-to-please nobles from any hostility towards the crown.

Echo sat by his sister's side, having left Zuton to treat with the prince from across the sea. Unlike Dazen, he scarfed his food down like it was the first meal he'd had in ages. Sumaya scolded him, eyeing him with a look of distaste that slowed his progress to a near standstill.

Rounding out the table was Aia, Obeyun's sister. Beside her, towering over the entire table, was her personal guard, Rudi. He looked down at his plate as if the food before him was an entirely new concept and he didn't know how to go about eating it.

Isha sighed. She was angry at herself for not having been there when Aia arrived. She had been selfish, too absorbed in her thoughts and with her conversation with her mother. She didn't know how to broach a conversation with her now. Had too much time passed? Would it be awkward?

She decided that she was being silly, if Aia was anything like her brother, she had nothing to worry about. She wiped her mouth clean, shifted out from her seat, and made her way towards the Princess of Wisha.

All of her worries washed away when Aia smiled at her brightly, lifting the star-shaped birthmark on her cheek like the sun rising into the sky. Isha placed a hand over her heart and took up an empty chair next to her. "You must be Aia."

To her surprise, the Wishan princess thrust herself upon her, wrapping two spindly arms around her shoulders before pulling her into a tight hug. Braided black hair flowed down to her waist in a wave, bringing with it a citrusy scent. She pulled away, but her relaxed grip remained as she held onto Isha's arms.

"I know who you are, and I owe you everything."

Isha couldn't help but blush. She angled her head downward in embarrassed glee, only for Aia to raise it again with a light touch of her fingers. "Your eyes really are as beautiful as Obe described!" she said. "He has told me much about you."

Her use of the common tongue was extremely good considering she came from so far up north. No doubt Obeyun had been teaching it to her as his plans to open up Wisha advanced.

Isha returned her smile. "Thank you. He has told me much about you as well, though you are a lot taller than he used to describe you."

"Ha!" Aia responded, throwing her head back. "I changed much during his long absence, I am sure. And yet he remained the same caring brother he was when he left. I have you to thank for that," she said, squeezing her hand a little tighter.

"Your brother is the reason I am here today," Isha said, gesturing to the surrounding room. "Without his strength, I would have fallen to the demons of my mind long ago."

Aia nodded. "I am sure he would say the same of you. It is a shame he could not be here. He very much misses you, and he would love for you to come dine with us in the Hall of Songs one day."

Isha bobbed her head, excited at the prospect of seeing her friend's homeland. "How fares Wisha? I understand it has proved difficult to open up in the past two years."

Aia's mood sombered, if only a little. "The state of my country remains, uh…" she paused, searching for the right word, "difficult. Most of the clans have rejoiced in Obeyun's leadership. There was much cause for celebration after the victory in Lumindal. But some clans remain… reluctant."

Isha frowned. "I can imagine how hard it must be. Especially now that Craw has taken control of the City of Light. I wish Trost and Wisha could be closer, and one of us did not have to brave their hostile lands to see each other. You are here now though. Did you have any trouble crossing the border?"

"No, we had little worry. The Bakai with me are strong. But… there is more wrong with my country than you know. Hidden things."

Isha paled, moving a couple of inches closer. "What do you mean?"

Aia's expression turned. "The mountains, they are dark. Many of the clans there we have lost contact with. There are rumours, reports of creatures, beasts who are taking our people."

"This is why Obeyun could not come himself?" Isha asked.

Aia nodded. "My brother is proud. He wishes to see his promises to you and to Trost kept. So, he has sent me in his stead to speak for him on matters with the man from across the sea. However, I am not my brother, and I am not as proud. We need help. These…. things… they are growing. I fear if we wait too long, we will lose many people."

Isha clasped Aia's hand, watching as her gaze drifted into her own, as if entranced by the violet in her eyes. "I will talk to my brother. It will have to wait until the meet with the Sun Prince, but we will come to your aid, have no doubt."

Isha blinked, watching as Aia shook her head free of the daze. "I… thank you," she said, turning away suddenly. Isha couldn't help but wonder if she had done something wrong. She wiped at her eyes, which were aching, strained as though she had not slept in days.

Before she could fully gather herself, Dazen stood to address the room. All signs of his previous worry were a figment of the past as he flashed his brazen smile over the hall, watching and waiting for those gathered to cease their conversations come to attention.

"Welcome, lords and nobles, citizens of Trost! First, I must thank all those who have braved the winds of this long winter to join us here for food and drink this evening. Your presence has not gone unnoticed, and I assure you your concerns will be addressed, in due time.

"For now, we have a more pressing matter, one that involves all of you." Dazen paused, letting his gaze wander over every table in the room. "Many of you have heard the rumour that a usurper from Yagos has made his intentions known towards Zapour. I can confirm that this is, indeed, true. But let me be clear, there have been no threats of violence, no open acts of war. I have agreed to meet with this usurper to discuss the future of our nations."

The gathered nobles broke into conversation, quietly whispering and arguing with one another. Dazen let it play out, holding his posture before speaking again. "Some of you might disagree with me on this matter," he said.

"We must show strength!" came a call from the crowd.

"He has usurped one kingdom, he will do it to another!" came another.

Dazen held a hand in the air, silencing them once more. He took a deep breath. "I see many seasoned warriors here, born of Trost, hardened by years of battle. For that I am grateful. Grateful to have such strong men to call upon should the need again arise. But have we not had enough war? Has Trost not seen enough conflict? For years we fought against Zuton, all for the sins of our ancestors. Now, look at what can become of peace. Are we not better for it?" he said, gesturing to Nora, who continued to bob up and down on Sumaya's knee.

"I will meet with this Sun Prince," he continued. "And I will listen to his terms. If it is possible to create a peace, then I will strive for it."

He paused again, allowing those in the room to dwell on his words a little longer. "However," he said, "if peace is not attainable, if this man from over the sea is not who he says, then I will call upon you, and I hope you shall answer!"

His words were met by a rhythmic thumping as all those present began to clash their mugs on the tabletops. A wave of agreement and applause reverberated across the entire hall.

"To the future!" Dazen said, raising his cup and taking a lengthy sip.

Isha watched as everyone echoed Dazen's action before returning to their meal with a new sense of purpose.

IT TOOK ONLY a few days to reach Brane, the coastal town in western Trost where the meeting was to take place. The whole time, Isha had been thinking of her mother. All she wanted to do was pepper her with questions. She needed answers, and she was angry at her for not providing them. She needed to find truth in her existence, a purpose for her new life free of chains. Somehow, she believed that purpose was hidden within the past. Her questions would have to wait though, for Dazen needed her.

The sea was black. It mirrored the starless sky. Waves lapped the coastline, white foam frothing again and again before being swallowed by the ocean currents.

She stood beside her brother. Dazen was vigilant, refusing to succumb to the bite of the cold as the coastal breeze drifted down from the high cliffs further north.

The representatives from Zuton and Wisha stood firmly by his side, the allied kingdoms portraying a united front as the tide brought in the first of the Sun Prince's ships.

They were massive, like nothing Isha had ever seen. She hadn't seen many ships before, not big ones at least. Lumindal was situated in the middle of Zapour, far away from the coastline, so there was never any need for them. The largest she had seen were the small fishing boats the merchants used to travel the river and the lake selling their wares. Compared to the ones before her, those may as well have been paddle boats.

Broad sails spread wide into the sky. Illuminated by torchlight, they stood like giant wings. Masts nearly half as tall as the Moon-Spire rose into the air, towering over them and blocking out the light of the moon.

Beside her, Dazen shifted. Whoever this man was, he was smart. Pitching the meeting in the moonlight took away their advantage. With no sunlight to draw upon, those Shine users present would be at a significant disadvantage in a fight. There was no sight of an army, however, just the three enormous ships.

The sound of muffled voices filled the air as anchors were dropped and people began to depart. A white banner emblazoned with a golden sun flapped violently above the central vessel. It matched the sails, which were all painted with the same symbol. As the figures drew closer the voices disappeared, replaced by a dreadful silence.

A circular wooden podium had been built atop the sand. It had been fitted with seats, an equal number on both sides, and was surrounded by dozens of torches. Dazen took his place atop the platform, Aia and Echo following his lead. Isha's hands began to shake, nervous as she was for her older brother. Much had changed over the course of the past few years. In the past, age had ruled Zapour. Now they were in a new era. Youth Had taken over and new leaders had risen. Perhaps a fresh vision was what this world needed.

The first emissary from Yagos made their presence known. A mountain of a man adorned in thick, plated armour stepped onto the podium. Like the ship's sails, a sun had been embossed on his breast plate, golden flames licking the edges of the curved chest-piece.

Isha remained still, trying not to let her gaze linger. Two figures came next, a man and a woman. These two were not adorned in armour. Instead, they wore immaculate matching uniforms. A row of buttons lined their vests and sleeves, and their pants were tailored so tight that Isha's skin crawled at the thought of trying to fit into them. They looked to be the same age. The woman had tied her hair into a bun, and the man wore his slicked back into neat lines. Both had sharp jawlines and high cheekbones. The man looked a little lost, as though he was still taking in the atmosphere and had forgotten that people were staring. The woman was all hard lines, suspicious eyes darting over everyone. Isha's heart jumped when she met her glare. The hard woman held it for a moment before her eyes suddenly grew wide. She tried to hide it, but something about Isha had caught her off guard.

Isha dismissed the thought, focusing on remaining still. Two more guards clad in heavy armour made their way atop the platform, parting to make way for the man she assumed to be the Sun Prince. His head was down. Long black hair flowed down around his neck. It shone in the firelight, the blackness so prominent it was like it had its own reflection.

Beside her, Dazen clenched and opened his fists stiffly. Isha still couldn't see the man's face as he turned to take his place upon the seat Dazen had provided. He sat between the matching pair, his bulky guard choosing to remain standing. Dazen lowered his hands, gesturing for those with him to take a seat.

The silence stretched, both parties seeming to take each other's measure.

At last, Dazen decided to break it, placing two hands on either side of his chair. "Welcome to Trost, Prince of Yagos," he said.

The foreign prince shifted, brushing a strand of hair aside and slicking it back in one motion. Full lips spread into a broad smile as he opened his eyes to look directly at Dazen. "Please, Yagos is but one location in a world full of them. I do not limit myself to a single place. You may call me by my title, the Sun Prince."

Isha heard his words, but their meaning was lost. All thoughts had turned to one thing, one feature. The world may well have been non-existent in that moment. Her focus was on the Sun Prince, for his eyes shone violet.

Chapter 8

- Raiz –

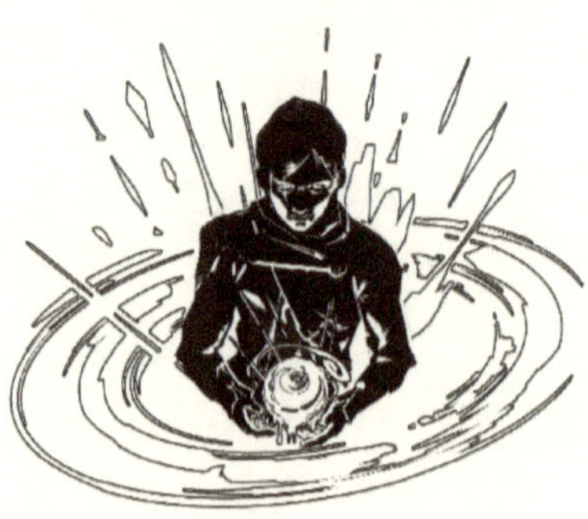

FRUSTRATION CONTINUED TO MOUNT as Raiz made slow progress into the rough terrain of northern Crata. The vast emptiness had given way to an uneven plain of long grasses and slippery slopes. Dense fog had settled on the horizon, leaving the lofty eastern peaks of the Weeping Mountains visible only in broad daylight.

Small pools snaked their way through swaying sawgrass and half-submerged logs. The captured bandit stopped to rest by one of them, collapsing onto the bank before splashing cold water over his face.

"Get up," Draz called, pointing his axe toward the depraved captive. "A snail could have taken Draz here faster than you."

The bandit groaned, feigning an injured leg as he rose shakily to his feet. "Please, I done what you asked. Just let me go."

"Let you go? We have a ways to go yet. Now get moving."

"This is where we met them," he replied, pointing a finger. "Just down there. Follow the path through the marsh. Soon it'll turn solid. Follow it towards the mountains. There's a valley where two rising plateaus meet. That's where our leader leaves the captives to be taken."

Raiz took three steps forward and grasped him by the collar. "You better not be lying to us."

"I'm not! I swear on my life! This is the place. Just a little farther."

"Great," Raiz said. "Then you only have a 'little farther' to travel."

A look of sheer horror crossed the captive bandit's face. His eyes darted towards the sky, then to the path. "N-no, I can't. I won't go any further. The sun's setting. You can't — I can't be here when it does."

Raiz shared a concerned look with Draz and Aroha. "What happens when the sun sets?" he dared to ask.

"That's when they come," he replied, hands shaking. "Please, don't make me go there. I've seen what they do, what they are."

"Enough of this!" Draz spat, moving in to take the prisoner from Raiz's grip. "You either show us the way, tonight, or you die here. Make your choice."

Raiz watched as the bound man grappled with the decision. There was a look in his eye, one speaking more than words could portray. This man was frightened. No, more than that, he was deeply terrified. He closed his eyes and offered his hands. "Take it then."

"Huh?" Draz replied.

"My life. I may be a coward, but I know what'll become of

me if I go with you. Some fates are worse than death."

Draz blew out an exasperated sigh and threw his hands in the air. He turned to Raiz, expecting him to make a decision.

Raiz took the dagger from his waist and moved in front of the prisoner. He listened as the bandit issued a whispered prayer, closing his eyes and accepting his fate.

Raiz braced the blade, and then cut the rope binding him before kicking him to the dewy grass. "Go," he said. "Find a better way to live. If I see or hear you involved in even the petty theft of a loaf of bread, know that you will wish to have gone with us into the valley tonight."

The bandit was off quicker than Raiz could finish his sentence, his injured leg suddenly recovered.

"You're letting him go?" Draz protested. "The man is filth. He'll be off raiding with another group before the next cycle of the moon."

"Then go and kill him," Raiz offered. "My hands have seen enough blood of late."

Aroha approached Draz from behind and placed a hand on his shoulder. "Don't worry about him, Draz. We have more important matters to see through."

Draz grunted, but Raiz knew he understood. They were not butchers. At least, he didn't want to be.

Spike came lumbering over, his leg heavily bandaged from the bite he received from the hound, but the wound didn't seem to faze him. Aroha lifted the piece of the woman's clothing to his nose, and Spike turned his snake-like head in the direction the bandit had shown.

"DRAZ IS NOT SCARED," Draz said, bickering with Aroha as the three of them traversed the marshlands.

"Then why are you wearing Gallant?" Aroha teased.

"Draz is cold, there's a difference."

Beside them, Spike groaned, one of his feet lagging behind as it got stuck in a mud puddle.

"Hope this is worth it, Raiz," Draz said. "Draz will be washing marsh gunk off his boot for weeks after this."

"I gave them my word. She has a child. I'm sure the feeling of returning a mother to her child will be worth a little mud on your boots."

"And if there is no mother left to return?" Draz replied, stopping in his tracks.

Raiz froze, letting his feet sink into the ground. The thought had been plaguing him since they'd left Tinker. "Even so, there's something going on here worth investigating. I won't go back empty-handed. If nothing else, I'll find answers."

"There's nothing lurking in the shadows but a couple of mountain brigands playing at being warlords. They're using the monsters born from bedtime stories as a scare tactic, inciting fear, whether they once existed or not. The villagers are likely selling the same tune, spreading the fear so the young ones stay safe at home, away from the real danger."

"Which is?" Raiz pressed.

"Us. Humanity. There's no creature darker than the one hiding in the depths of the human soul. Draz fears the people of New Crata have succumbed to it. There will be no treating with them."

Raiz took a steadying breath. "You could be right, but another darkness clouds these lands, I can feel it. And since when do we stand by while innocents are taken from their homes?"

Draz clapped him on the shoulder. "Aye lad, Draz is with

you. There," he said, pointing north to where the path turned solid. "An end to this stink. Not much farther now."

He was right. Soon, the gooey softness of the marsh gave way to the hard rock and stone of the mountain base. The bandit had been telling the truth so far. Beyond the marsh was a wide valley where the two plateaus met. Extending past that was the towering ranges of the Weeping Mountains.

"This valley used to be a river," Aroha said, bending down to touch a piece of the earth.

"Looks like her tears have all dried up," Draz replied, kicking at a broken crate left on the side of the valley.

Raiz looked over to where a cart lay abandoned. It was empty, its axel snapped in two and whatever it had been carrying long gone. "People have been here recently," Raiz said, his gaze drifting to a set of muddy boot prints. "These tracks are fresh. Perhaps only a day or so old."

"*Human* tracks," Draz emphasized.

Before Raiz could respond, Spike issued a deep, reverberating growl. Raiz moved towards him and placed a hand on his side. "What's wrong boy?"

Spike ignored him, lowering his head to the ground as he stared into the shifting fog clouding the passage north. He growled again, this time baring his teeth as plumes of vapour sprouted from his nostrils.

"Something's wrong," Raiz said.

"Maybe we should make camp at the foot of the mountain tonight," Aroha suggested. "Come back in the morning when light once again touches the sky.

Raiz looked up, watching as the last fraction of Zur dipped below the horizon. "Every moment we waste we risk the mother's life."

"Draz agrees with Aroha. We'll be blind in there during the night. Best to wait until first light."

Raiz scowled at the both of them. "I thought you didn't believe in monsters?"

"Monsters, no. But human traps? Ambushes? Yes. You forget who Draz used to be. In the Greysword clan this is how we took down a mark. Clever thinking, stupid people, the right location. Even the blood of a Radiant in your veins won't protect you against an arrow to the back."

Raiz mulled over his thoughts, wondering if his friends were right, if he was being reckless. But he couldn't stop picturing the poor victim, alone and afraid. It reminded him too much of Isha. He had been young and unprepared then, but that had all changed. He wouldn't allow another to fall while under his watch. Thoughts of Veil clouded his mind as he ran through all that he could have done to save her, to protect her. He wouldn't let that happen, not again.

"I'm going," he said. "If you're worried about an arrow to my back, then you'd best come and protect it."

He beckoned for Spike, whistling through closed lips as the Dragon came to his side despite the fog. Raiz hoisted himself into the saddle and made himself comfortable. "Let's see how they react to a Dragon storming down their throat."

He heard Draz and Aroha groan, but their footsteps followed, leaving Raiz to wonder just why he deserved such good friends.

Darkness enveloped them fully as they ventured deep into the enclosed valley. Raiz summoned a small globe of Shine so the group could see each other in the inky black. Spike's vision was clear even in the dark, so he led them forward.

The sense of impending dread only amplified the deeper

they went, though so far Draz had been wrong. No ambush had been set. No sign of human activity was present. Even the tracks had died out, though the ground had hardened as they crawled further up the roots of the mountain.

An eerie silence settled over the company, broken only by Spike's laboured breathing and the odd growl. He thought about taking flight and surveying the mountain from the air, but he would be just as blind up there as he was down here, and Spike couldn't hold Draz and Aroha's weight.

A voice drifted in through the fog, indistinct and barely audible, but it was there. Raiz called for a halt, pressing his ear towards their destination.

Radiant…

Aroha took three steps forward, confusion wrought on her pale face. "What was that?"

Raiz remained fixed on the distant fog, waiting to hear if the voice sounded again, though Draz made that impossible, trudging up beside them both. "What did you hear?"

"A voice," Raiz said.

"Bah, nonsense," Draz replied. "Was probably just a trick of the wind."

Raiz re-settled into his saddle, still with half an ear cocked to the side, ready to listen. After a time, he gave up, marking the voice down as what Draz had said, a trick of the wind.

A little further down the track the valley began to expand, opening up the mountain range. A small forest spread out before them. Tightly packed trees sprouted high into the sky on either side of a dirt path, clouding them in thick canopy. Raiz warmed himself with his Shine, allowing it to flow through his body, spreading its heat. Aroha and Draz were not so lucky. Their breaths came short and sharp. Aroha opened her pack, wrapping herself in another layer of linen.

"This had better be worth it," she said, shaking her head.

Raiz hopped down from Spike and expanded his ball of Shine. It hovered over the palm of his hand like a miniature sun, radiating heat from its core. "Here," he said. "Warm your hands. I don't want you unable to wield your sword."

"How thoughtful," Aroha said, taking off her gloves and spreading her giant hands around Raiz's globe.

Radiant...

Together their heads snapped to the side as the whispered voice sounded again. Darkness was all they could see, their vision further hampered by the thick of the forest.

Raiz looked to Draz, who nodded. "Aye, that was no trick of the wind," he said. "Someone is out there, taunting us."

Raiz curled his fingers into a fist as Spike issued another deep growl, wrapping his barbed tail in a protective ring around him. "What do you see, Spike?" Raiz said, following his line of sight.

A flicker of movement followed in the shifting shadows. The sound of branches breaking and trees rustling could be heard.

Raiz thrust his hand forward, the ball of gathered Shine shooting like a beam into the centre of the forest. Light followed its path, illuminating a figure for the barest of moments before exploding into a tree, setting it alight. A shrill, inhuman shriek sounded as whatever had been lurking in the shadows panicked. It was followed by another cry.

A human cry.

A woman screamed, the voice growing fainter as whatever had her fled down the forest path. Raiz, Draz and Aroha shared a quick look before taking off at a sprint. Spike followed, wings tucked to shoulders as he thundered down the path.

The sounds of their prey softened, impossible to track in the dark of night, but still Raiz followed, brushing past stray branches in pursuit.

"Raiz, stop!" Aroha called. "The trail is lost."

Raiz bent over, sucking in deep lungfuls of air as he caught his breath. "What… was that?"

"I don't know. But whoever it is, they wanted us to follow."

Beside them, Draz sighed. "Definitely a trap then."

Raiz grit his teeth and stood tall. He shook his fist in the air. "What are you waiting for!" he shouted. "Come on, I'm right here!"

Spike let out a roar, issuing his challenge, making it clear to all that he was a force to be reckoned with.

Descendant of Gallion…

There was no fixed location for the whispered voice. It was everywhere, surrounding them as if coming from the very air itself.

Raiz flinched, eyes darting in every direction. "Who are you? Show yourself!"

Thief… Give back what you have stolen…

The voice had a direction this time, accompanied by more shifting movement in the distance. Raiz took off at a sprint once more, ignoring the calls from Draz and Aroha. He ran until his lungs gave out, finally stumbling into a small clearing where the edge of the forest gave way to the steep cliffs of the mountain range.

The white of the moon peeked over the mountain above, illuminating a partly shadowed figure at the mouth of a wide cavern. It was tall, perhaps even large enough to rival Aroha.

Its humanoid shape was wreathed in strings of darkness, and black eyes devoid of emotion stared blankly at the three of them. In its grip was a frail-looking woman about to pass out. She was covered in sweat, too exhausted to move.

Behind the figure rose something grand and grotesque – a tail almost as large as Spike's, but longer, more mobile. It slithered high into the air, the stringy tendrils of pure darkness forming into a sharp point at its tip.

Raiz made to move, but he was too late. The tail pierced the woman through her chest, and Raiz was forced to watch as all colour drained from her face. It seemed to be literally sucking the life from her, the black tail pulsing with the effort. He shuddered, momentarily frozen before he regained his wits and burst forth to chase down the creature of darkness. Before he closed even half the distance, however, it was gone, dropping the half-drained body and disappearing into the depths of the cavern beyond.

Raiz knelt by the woman's side. Long hair trailed down her neck, all flaky and matted. Her cheeks were hollow, and her skin was dried out. He scanned the corpse, sparing a quick glance towards the mouth of the cave, which loomed ominously just ahead, calling for him to enter. He reached into his pack to retrieve the piece of cloth Porter had given him and held it up to the tattered clothing the dead woman wore. The tear of the cloth matched the one Raiz held. He bowed in despair. He hadn't known this woman, and yet he couldn't shake the feeling it had been his fault. He was supposed to protect her. He was supposed to have protected Veil, too. But he hadn't. He'd failed. And now, thanks to him, this woman was dead. Just like Veil.

"Raiz!" came a call from behind.

Raiz shifted, a ball of fresh Shine ready in his hand to unleash on any who would dare prey on him.

He spun around to see Draz, hands held before his face, blinded by his Shine. "It is Draz, Raiz, settle yourself."

Raiz lowered his Shine-infused hand, allowing his head to drop, a tear running down his cheek. "She's lost," is all he managed to say.

Draz angled his head to get a better look as Aroha caught up to them. Draz removed Gallant, staring dumb-faced at the remains. "Zur's piss, what happened to her?" he said.

"I don't know for sure, but I intend to find out," Raiz said, turning towards the mouth of the cave.

Draz shook his head, though it was Aroha who spoke. "Remind me why we follow you again?" she said, mirroring Draz as the two of them accepted the fact that there was simply no stopping Raiz once his mind was made.

"You don't have to come," Raiz said. "It's me that holds the blood of a Radiant, me they're calling. I won't drag you along with me into what is certainly a trap. But this is something I have to see through."

The two of them sighed in unison. Draz crossed his arms, while Aroha pointed her hand. "Lead the way," she said. "We've followed you this far, may as well see it through. Besides, Spike won't let anything happen to us, will you boy?"

Raiz turned, expecting Spike to come to their side, but he remained still, head bowed, diamond-shaped pupils fixed onto the cave's mouth. A deep growl vibrated in his throat, his white, sword-like teeth glistening under the light of the moon.

"What's wrong?" Raiz said, moving towards his long-time friend and companion. He placed a soothing hand on his cold scales, but Spike did not respond as he usually would. The

Dragon clenched his jaw, almost snapping at Raiz, animal reflexes screaming at him that danger was present. His wings spread wide, and he shimmied backward like a spooked horse.

Radiant…

The voice sounded again, taunting him. Raiz spun around, looking for the source, but it was hidden in shadows. "Come out here!" he shouted. "Face me!"

Come to me Radiant… The one who would steal from me… Give it back… Give it back!

The call was louder this time, more audible, but soon it faded, its echo trailing into the depths of the mountains.

"He won't budge," Aroha said, pulling at Spike's leg. "I've never seen him this skittish. Whatever's in there has him real spooked."

Raiz bent down, looking Spike in his yellow eyes. "You stay here buddy, you've done enough. Mind the entrance for me though, will you?"

Spike didn't respond, continuing to stare into the abyss, but Raiz was sure he understood.

"Darkness doesn't scare me," Raiz said, loosing a jet of almost pure crimson Shine into the stone beside his foot. He channelled it, shaping it with his will until his glaive was fully formed. It shone like liquid lightning in the night's darkness, radiating heat as his fist gripped it tight.

Without further delay, he walked into the cavern, the light of his weapon illuminating the passage. Draz and Aroha followed.

"If you are to live and Draz is to die beneath this shithole of a mountain, then you'd best believe you'll have me haunting you," Draz said.

Behind them both, Aroha laughed. "I wouldn't let him die, Raiz, he would make one stubborn ghost…"

Raiz stifled a small laugh of his own, but he found it hard to take humour in their current predicament. He needed to remain sharp, vigilant. Whoever was taunting him, they knew who he was, and he was pretty sure they were no ghost–

Chapter 9

- Zeek –

ZEEK BATHED IN SUNLIGHT, allowing warmth to fill his body. He followed an itch, watching as his pale skin reacted to the heat. According to Father, this was nothing, a fraction of what the sun could produce. But to Zeek, it was a whole new world, one in which he still felt as though he did not belong.

He winced as the shadows swirling within writhed, reminding him that this was only temporary, that he was not truly human. He still didn't understand his purpose, his reason for living. Father said he was important, that he had a role to play, but he wasn't sure. How could someone like him change things? How could someone so new have an impact on a world that had been breathing for an era?

Furthermore, what reason did he have for acting one way or another? How could someone who had never truly lived decide how others should spend their lives?

"Are you making progress?" Father asked, startling him as he leaned over his shoulder.

"I — I think so, yes," he answered honestly. "Though it is tough to gauge. This man — this prince — he was very skilled, very knowledgeable. It will take time before I can fully understand all that he knew, all that he could do."

In truth, there was more to what he was feeling. As he took the time to fully absorb all that Ancel had been, new emotions were beginning to arise. There was hatred, a distaste for the world that Zeek couldn't fully understand. He didn't like it, wanted it gone, but he couldn't deny that it was there, was part of him.

"We don't have time. We need to act now," Father replied, moving to face him.

"And what is it we're acting on?"

Father's chest puffed out. He took a deep breath, and his scowl deepened. Eventually he relaxed, his posture sagging. "You grow curious. Your mind is expanding with each kill, with each consumption. You probably feel as though you have all this information, and no context in which to place it, correct?"

Zeek nodded, surprised to find that it was exactly how he had been feeling.

Father paced up and down the clearing. "Your vision will become clearer with time, but you must trust me, trust in my experiences. Know that what I do, and what I shall have you do, is in the best interest of this world. Preservation, that is my goal. To preserve life, to protect humanity."

Zeek lowered his head, mind buzzing with a thousand thoughts. "But Father, I am not human, am I?"

"You know you are not."

"Then, what am I?"

"You are a perversion. Part of a species that should never have existed."

Zeek paled. "Then why am I here?"

"You have been given a chance. I chose you Zeek. You are my tool. In return for your service, I overlook the perversion that you are. You can decide to become human, if you wish it. You can now walk the light, which is more than your kind deserve."

"What makes them so undeserving?"

"Enough with these foolish questions. For now, it is enough to say that they are dangerous. That is all you need to know."

"Am I dangerous?" Zeek asked, knowing he was testing Father's patience.

"You are a necessary danger! You can be more than your predecessors. Your potential is limitless, and I would see it directed. But you must choose now. Will you follow me, and see your potential fulfilled? Or will you forsake your destiny, and return to the darkness in which your kind belong?"

Zeek looked his father in the eye, trying to measure the strength of his words. "And if I should decide to return?"

Father huffed a displeased sigh. "Then so be it. I will not stop you. But if you should decide to stay, then I will accept nothing but devotion. If you stay, and turn on me, there will be no forgiveness. No second chances."

Zeek gulped, feeling the weight of choice for perhaps the first time in his life. "I am with you, Father. Always."

"Good. I will forge you into a weapon, a tool the likes of which this world has never seen. Together, you and I will shape kingdoms, and shift the tides of humanity so that we may prosper."

"What would you have me do?"

"For now, practice. Draw power from Ancel's essence, allow his knowledge to become your knowledge, and make his skills your own. You will need all of it if you are to kill the prince from across the sea."

Chapter 10

- Isha –

BRIGHT LAVENDER EYES peered into her, through her, searching. There was a flicker of recognition in them, an element of wide-eyed surprise followed by suspicion as they quickly narrowed. She felt as though she were drowning, overcome by a sea of emotions.

Were there really more out there like her? Or was this person just a farce? A fluke? Mere coincidence? Some distortion of colour that had nothing to do with what she was? Perhaps violet was simply a common trait over the Sapphire Sea. Or maybe the origin of her eyes was just an exaggerated story, changed and morphed into something more than it actually was.

No.

There was an energy about this man, different from those who could wield Zur's Shine. It was familiar, yet distant. It was as though this person was the same as her, but more. He was who she could be if her potential were to be fully realized.

Dazen was speaking, exchanging words with the foreigners, but Isha was too awe-struck to take notice. She shook her head, blinking and willing the dizziness to go away. Conversations continued, and pleasantries were exchanged with Echo and then Aia.

She thought she heard her name, which snapped her back to attention. When she came to, she found everyone to be staring at her.

Dazen stepped aside, gesturing towards her. The man who called himself the Sun Prince stepped forward, offering his hand in welcome. Isha took it in her own, her chest tightening as he bent over to kiss it. His hand was soft, his lips cool.

He parted, but his gaze did not waver as he bowed another greeting. "I must admit that over time I have grown accustomed to being alone in my peculiarity," he said, voice calm yet confident. "It is a pleasure to meet another like me, whose eyes shine as mine do." He turned back to Dazen. "Tell me, Glaive, does the violet seed extend across your lands, or is your sister, like me, an oddity?"

Dazen placed a protective arm around her, more as a show of solidarity than in defensiveness. "As far as I know it is a feature only her and our mother share."

The Sun Prince pursed his lips, one eyebrow rising. "Might I ask your mother's name?"

Dazen took a step forward, his stare hardening to stone. "You may not."

For a tense moment, Isha thought there might be violence, but the Sun Prince withdrew his iron gaze and took a placating step backward. "Should these proceedings end well, I would very much like to speak with you," he said, bowing once more to Isha. "I am certain we stand to find some clarity in exploring each other's existence."

Isha made to respond, but no words came out.

Dazen stepped in. "I suggest we both retake our seats. There remains much to be discussed."

The prince issued one last cursory glance her way before returning to his seat, crossing one leg over the other as he clasped his hands, head held high, as if these very sands were rightly his.

Once more, an uncomfortable silence settled amongst the gathered royalty. This time it was broken by the Sun Prince, forgoing his princely posture and leaning forward to speak to Dazen. "I am quite curious. When I reached out to these lands with my proposition two years ago, I was met with naught but ignorant silence. I understand that Zapour, like Yagos, has recently undergone somewhat of a change in leadership. Of course, I have heard the tales, but as you and I both know, tales are often exaggerated. Tell me, is the King-Radiant really no more? Is what I see before me truly the new power in these lands? The very people responsible for the end to a thousand years of religious dictatorship?"

Dazen shifted in his seat, but it was Echo who spoke up. "The King-Radiant is dead. Any power he once held is now forfeit."

The Sun Prince brushed another strand of hair behind his ear, taking in the information. "So, shall I presume the lands of Zapour are now divided once more?" he asked.

"That is one perspective," Echo said. "Though we might present another. Before the King-Radiant's fall we were united on paper only, sworn to answer should he call, but free to quarrel who we wished."

"And now?" the Sun Prince asked.

"And now we are one under more than just a piece of signed parchment. The kingdoms of Zuton, Trost, and Wisha stand together, in heart and by oath."

"I see," the Sun Prince continued. "How very touching. Of course, there are more than three kingdoms in Zapour. What of the other three?"

Echo and Dazen looked at each other, leaving words unspoken.

"Craw and Kogon are their own kingdoms," Dazen said. "Whatever is spoken here today, know that we do not speak for them. Their voices are their own. As for Crata, they are no longer a power in Zapour."

The Sun Prince relaxed into his chair, the smug expression on his face suggesting that this confirmed intelligence he had already gathered.

"Enough of this. Why are you here?" Dazen finally asked. "For centuries Zapour and Yagos have remained neutral, conversing only via minor trade agreements and dealings with the former Eagles. What interest do you have in our future?

"And before you answer," Dazen continued evenly. "Know that we do not take threats idly."

The Sun Prince paused, the red-haired woman by his side growing agitated. She rose, fist shaking as she spoke. "Do you know to whom you speak? This man has been chosen by Zur to restore this world to its natural state. A world your nation has destroyed!"

Her anger was tempered by a gentle hand from her prince. Isha watched Dazen's eyes narrow, but it was the Sun Prince who spoke. "You must forgive Sounja, she does not understand the delicacy of our situation. Aggression is not the path I wish to take. I do not threaten violence. It is my wish to educate, not to conquer."

"Forgive me if your words are not easy to believe," Dazen said. "Yagos is no small island. It would have taken more than a man wishing to educate to usurp the old emperor from power."

A genuine smile crossed the Sun Prince's lips. Not one of scorn, but of mutual respect. "I do not shy from violence, if violence is what Zur requests. But tell me, did the three of you here before me not recently accomplish the same feat? Were your reasons for overthrowing the King-Radiant not just?"

Isha could have sworn he looked over to her as he spoke those last words, but she wasn't certain.

Aia was the next to allow her voice to be heard. "You say you wish to educate, but what is it that you think we do not know? You say you speak for our god. I say Zapour has had enough priests pretending they know the will of Zur. The last people to insist they spoke for him are now in the ground, what makes you any different?"

Isha was taken aback, only now remembering the fierceness Obeyun had often spoken about when describing his sister. Opposite her, Sounja's face had turned beet-red, while her white-knuckled fists spoke words she was forbidden to say. She managed to center herself, however, settling back into her chair and allowing the prince to speak for her.

"Ah," the Sun Prince said. "A fair question, though one that will take time to fully answer. Time that, unfortunately, is running out for Zapour."

"Is that a threat?" Dazen asked.

"Not at all, young Glaive. That was a truth. A truth you do not yet understand. Just because you do not believe it, does not mean that you will not bear the consequence of your continued actions."

"And what actions might those be?"

"Your use of Shine," the Sun Prince responded without hesitation. Dazen had known the topic was coming, and Isha was curious to see how he might handle it.

"So, it is true then. You wish us to cease our use of Zur's Light," he said.

"I do."

"And I suppose you have a heavy justification for such an extreme measure?"

"The justification you seek is all around you," the Sun Prince continued. "You simply fail to recognise it for what it is."

"Explain it to me then. What are we missing that you seem so confident about."

The Sun Prince raised both hands into the sky casually. "Can you not see? You are somewhat blinded by your friendly climate, but even you must see the signs. Zur is dying. He will not die today, he will not die tomorrow, but he will die if nothing is done. Zapour has been spared the full strength of winter's bite so far, but times are changing. Yolinters linger longer each year. The chill grows deeper, more challenging. I know this because Yagos has borne the brunt of these changes. Eventually you will be as we are, living in an infertile land, unable to produce enough of your own crops. Do you think it fair that we are forced to suffer through your actions?"

"And just what are you accusing us of?" Dazen said.

"Not you, Dazen of Trost. All of you," he said, spreading his arms wide. "I know what goes on in this province of yours. I have my own eyes on these shores. Yagos is not without Shine of its own, but our use of Zur's Light pales in comparison to your reckless employment of his gift, which you have been abusing for centuries."

"Shine is our way of life," Dazen said. "It is our foundation. Entire armies and economies are built around those with the ability. You would ask us to simply abandon it on principal?"

"Shine is a poison!" the Sun Prince snapped, in a rare show of aggression. He quickly calmed, however, reverting back to his peaceful demeanour. "A way of life that revolves around war and destruction has no sustainable future. Where do you think Shine comes from? Do you think that such power can simply be consumed without consequence?

"It comes from Zur," the Sun Prince continued. "Every time a person draws in Light, they steal a part of who he is, what he is. Zur is powerful, but he is not without limits, and he is dying."

"Why would Zur gift us with something that could kill him?" Dazen retorted.

"You already know the answer. Do not pretend that you do not. Shine was a gift given freely centuries ago to Gallion and those with him who would stand against the Skae. But though Gallion is long dead, his seed remains, along with the descendants of those who followed him. The magic of Shine has spread beyond comprehension, and the toll of its constant use has whittled away at our beloved god's power."

Isha watched as her brother considered the foreign prince's words. "And how is it you know so much of our culture? Of our religion? You were not born here in Zapour. Why should we believe your word?"

The Sun Prince did not falter, as if he had been expecting the question. "Zapour and Yagos are not so different as you would think. Your now deceased Eagles were not the only followers of Gallion, and they were not the only ones granted Zur's Light. Before you fight me on this, tell me," he said, holding up a hand, "did you believe all that your former Eagles preached? If you did, you would not have overthrown them. My words today are not intended to mislead. As I said, my goal is simply to educate, to show you a better path. A necessary path for the survival of both Zapour and Yagos."

Dazen took a deep breath, sparing a glance towards Echo as he ran a hand over his trimmed beard. Eventually he leaned forward, looking into the violet eyes of the Sun Prince. "What you ask of us is no small feat. It has many implications for the continued survival of all of our nations. We must take time to consider your words."

The Sun Prince clasped his hands together, and for a moment the air seemed to still. The breeze disappeared and time seemed to slow. The violet of his eyes shone brighter, and when she looked at her brother, his own eyes seemed to glaze over.

"Please," the Sun Prince said. "Take your time. Consider what I have said. I wish to resolve this peacefully, but do not mistake my words for weakness."

Dazen did not respond, frozen as if caught in a spell. The Sun Prince spared a knowing look towards Isha, aware that she was unaffected by whatever had just occurred. He stood, issued a short bow, and began to depart. "I shall call upon you tomorrow, when Zur's light is again at its lowest. Take care, Princess of Trost. I meant what I said, I greatly desire to speak with you. There is much we could share with–each other."

Chapter 11

- Raiz –

THE CAVE SEEMED TO HAVE NO END, the entrance having long ago faded from sight. Raiz waved his glaive in the air, picking slowly through the darkness. Fortunately, there weren't any deviations to the tunnel, so finding their way back out would be relatively simple. His senses continued to heighten the further they crept, expecting an ambush at any moment. He was prepared, however. His Shine was strong, and he had lots of it to spend.

Eventually, the cavern widened and the three of them stepped out into an open expanse. The comfort of light reflecting off of nearby walls was left behind, and they became a lone source of light in an all-consuming darkness.

"What's going on here?" Draz asked. "No human can survive this deep into the mountains without light to see. There's nothing here."

"There's something here, I'm sure of it," Raiz said, staring into the black. "Show yourself!" he yelled.

Draz yanked sharply him by the collar. "What are you doing? Are you insane?"

"They know we're here. If your colossal head wasn't enough to tip them off, then my Shine will have done the trick," Raiz said, before calling back out into the unknown. "Face me! Answer for your crimes!"

For a moment the cavern was still, soundless but for the laboured breathing of Raiz and his companions, who now firmly gripped the hafts of their weapons.

Foolish child…

The voice echoed across the chamber, it's source unidentifiable. Draz thumped a challenging beat on his chest, followed by the sharp ring of Aroha drawing her longsword.

I can smell your blood, Radiant… You will die for what you have taken from me… Thief…

Raiz tensed. The voice sounded almost feminine. It was as soft as a whisper, but the harshness of the tone spoke of experience and age beyond comprehension.

"Enough of this!" Draz shouted, stepping in front of Raiz. "Quit playing games. Who leads you? Draz demands you show yourself!"

His words were met with a rumble and a flurry of movement. Raiz shifted, glaive at the ready. It sounded as though a mass of whatever creatures lurked within the depths were converging on their location. Raiz couldn't see more than a few paces in front of him. He waved his glaive, threatening any who would dare come close. Behind him, Draz cried out, his leg suddenly yanked from beneath him as a snaking vine clamped on to his foot. He was dragged several feet into the nothingness. Raiz followed, quick on his feet. He caught up to Draz and swung his glaive downward in a winding arc, severing the vine's hold on his friend's leg.

Raiz flinched as the vine dissipated. It hadn't been a vine at all, but some sort of solid shadow. He heard a shrill screech from beyond, as if the shadow had been a limb, an extension of someone – or some*thing*. He grabbed Draz beneath the shoulder and pulled him back to the safety of Aroha.

A deep, cackling laughter filled the cavern, reverberating on all sides. Dread washed over Raiz as he grit his teeth in frustration. "What are you!" he demanded.

What am I? came the response. *No, what are we…*

More movement followed the stranger's words as shapes formed at the edges of their circle of light. They crept closer, quiet footsteps made loud by the sheer number of them. Panic rose within, and Raiz braced himself for what was surely to come.

We are the future, descendant of Gallion, son of Zur. We are the past. Your father grows weak. The time has come for our ascendance.

Raiz had heard enough. He drew power from his stored sunlight, forcing it into the palm of his blackened hand. With a single smooth motion he released it, sending a beam of red Light direction-less into the dark.

He gasped as, for a fleeting moment, the cavern was illuminated, highlighting *thousands* of formless figures. The image was gone quicker than it had come, but it remained burned into his mind, the horror of it impossible to forget.

They were like humans made entirely of shadow, their bodies whole and yet ephemeral. He took a backward step, inching closer to the tunnel's exit, but as he turned he found that the shadow-creatures were already there, surrounding them in a ring of black.

"Draz," he said. "I'm beginning to think you were right. We shouldn't have come here."

Beside him Draz whistled. "Well lad, if we make it out of here, Draz is skinning you alive. So, either way this ends poorly for you."

Raiz sighed, the three of them pressing their backs against one another as more of the creatures closed in on them.

Die, descendant of Gallion. Let my vengeance be complete, and the spawn of Cova re-take their rightful place in the world.

The raspy, feminine voice faded like a ghost in the shadows, and in its place came the onslaught.

Raiz swept his Shine-glaive in a wide arc. The incoming shadow-creatures hissed and snarled, scared of the Light that was their opposite. A snake-like tendril of weighted shadow darted past his guard, its sharpened point catching him on the arm and drawing blood. Raiz reacted, changing his grip and slicing through the tendril in one smooth motion. The tail of darkness burned just as easily as flesh. More screeched in pain as Raiz cut at them, fending them off from all angles.

He heard Draz cry out as one creature slashed at him with a claw. Draz retaliated, bringing his axe down on the clawed hand. Instead of cutting as it should, the axe struggled for purchase, barely affecting the creature, which lashed out at Gallant. The creature wailed in pain, however, as its formless hand burned against the peridium helm.

Aroha too seemed to be struggling. Instead of the clean cuts her longsword usually wrought, it was similarly repelled, sending her off balance. Raiz covered, sending a bolt of Shine with his off-hand that seared through the shadowy-flesh of at least three of her assailants.

"Our weapons won't cut these bastards!" Draz screamed amidst the chaos. He quickly unstrapped Gallant, using it to bludgeon the skulls of the advancing shadows. "We need to move, now!"

Raiz spared a look at the tunnel they had come from. More and more of the creatures were closing in, held back only by Raiz's shining Light. "Move on my mark," he said, gathering Shine in his palm once more.

He swung his glaive in one final sweep, creating distance between the three of them and their foes before turning towards the exit. He released a stream of Light, separating those blocking their path as they inched away from the searing heat. "Now!" Raiz shouted.

He cut another creature in half, following Draz and Aroha as they made for the gap created by his Shine.

You cannot escape death, Radiant…

The ghostly voice boomed over the commotion, reverberating through the tunnel as they made their escape. They were deep inside the mountain, however, and they had a long way to go if they were to make it out alive.

The shadow-creatures were closing, and for each one Raiz cut down two more would replace it. His legs quickly grew weary as the constant stop-start of their attempted escape wore down his body. He gasped for breath, spending every scrap of Shine he could muster, but even he had limits. He felt his hands begin to itch, the force of so much heat passing through them becoming unsustainable, unbearable. The memory of his outburst in the throne-room all those years ago came to mind. If they did not escape soon, he might lose his arms altogether. Either that or his Shine would run dry, unable to be replenished while Zur slept for the night – not that his rays would reach them down here anyway.

Their weapons rendered ineffective, Draz and Aroha ran. Raiz was their only hope, and he knew it. It was his fault they were here, his arrogance that had led them down into this pit of death. It was his responsibility then, to see that they made it out alive. If he had to lose his arms to do it, then so be it.

His glaive still blazing, he cut at more of the pursuing nightmares, but they were even on the walls now, crawling like ants as they swarmed them. Every passing moment stretched into what seemed like hours. Every inch of ground covered felt like a mile.

Draz continued to use Gallant, punching at a leaping creature whose claw caught his face before he sent it tumbling back into the ravening pack. He cried out but did not stop running.

Raiz could feel a breeze of mountain air caress his open, blackening skin. Cova's moonlight twinkled in the distance; the outside world marked by the very being he suspected had sired their current pursuers. They were so close, but the gap between predator and prey closed ever tighter.

They were going to die.

Raiz knew it. There was no time. His fault, his responsibility. Shouting at the others to keep going, he turned, deciding to die on his own terms rather than be cut down from behind like a scared deer. If he could just hold them off long enough, Draz and Aroha might be able to escape alive.

Scrounging for the last scrap of Shine still coursing through his overworked veins, he thrust two hands behind his back. His glaive dissolved into liquid as he re-used his already conjured Light, channelling it along with new Shine into a giant sphere in the palm of his hands. His limit was met. If he released this, he would lose his hands. If he did not, they would all be consumed by whatever foulness now haunted these mountains.

He closed his one good eye, accepting his fate and preparing to release all that he had.

Just then, a large thump sounded behind him, and for a moment he thought an earthquake had struck. It sent him off balance, distracting him long enough for him to notice the commotion.

A deafening roar split the cavern. His Shine soaked back into his skin, his survival instincts kicking in without need for his direction. A shadowy beast thundered past him, larger by far than any of those in the darkness beyond. Large, bat-like wings beat like a drum and the conjured wind buffeted the approaching creatures of the night.

Spike lurched his head into the air, gullet glowing a deep red. In one motion he thrust his head forward and opened his mouth, sending an enormous jet of pure crimson Shine flaming forward. The formless figures didn't even cry out as they were disintegrated, blown away by the sheer force of Spike's Shine.

Raiz let out a shallow breath, but wasted no time. He used the last of his strength to mount Spike, collapsing into the saddle even as the beast turned to flee.

More creatures could be heard in the distance, soon to replace those that had been lost, but time was finally on their side. Spike covered ground quickly, catching Draz and Aroha as they left the mouth of the cave and fled into the cold night air.

Chapter 12

- Isha –

"ARE YOU SERIOUSLY CONSIDERING THIS?" Gale said, standing with hands on hips in the command pavilion.

Isha sat uncomfortably at the war table as the discussions resulting from the Sun Prince's proposition continued. She wasn't accustomed to such deliberations. She was used to being a fly on the wall. It seemed old patterns were hard to break, as she was largely ignored. It made her angry. Even more frustrating was the fact that she had nothing to say. Was she here simply because she was Dazen's sister and he wanted to keep her safe? Or did her brother actually value her opinion?

She decided to let the matter rest. If she thought of something worth saying, she would say it. She focused instead on Dazen. There was something not quite right about him. She couldn't place what it was, but he wasn't himself.

"And what if he speaks the truth?" Dazen said, speaking loudly so all gathered could hear. "What if Zur is dying?"

The pavilion was isolated, flanked on all sides by trusted Whiteswords, but by the way Aia and Echo shied away from her brother's words, he might as well be speaking on a raised dais in a room full of gossiping mouths.

"And what if this is a lie?" Gale continued. "For all we know he used the same tactic to overthrow the old emperor of Yagos. I council caution when it comes to trusting a man you have only just met. There would be severe ramifications for us if we suddenly ceased our use of Shine. Not to mention that the gathering of Shine is not voluntary."

"I concur," Echo said, placing two hands on the round table. "While Gelvard holds Lumindal over our heads like a darkening cloud, removing Shine from my armies is not an option. He will not listen to reason. I will not allow him to hold power over Zuton."

"So, we would choose a slow death rather than a quick one?" Dazen questioned, eyeing the room.

In the corner, Aia remained silent, content to let the others speak first. Rudi stood behind her like a towering shadow, his focus akin to a panther. He seemed to stare at Dazen, vision narrowing, as if he noticed something no one else had.

Isha followed his gaze, unfurling her arms as she caught wind of what he was looking at. A piece of Dazen's eye shone violet. It was subtle, a light tinge, but it was there. Now that she had noticed it, it was impossible to miss.

What is it? Puk gestured beside her, drawing her attention.

There is something wrong, she said, moving her hands in a flurry of movements.

Puk leant in.

Isha paused to consider how she might express her concern. *There is something off about my brother.*

Puk spared a look before returning his attention to her.

It is like, she continued, pausing to search for the correct gesture. *Like he is under some kind of spell. Look at his eyes. The Sun Prince, he did something. I do not know what, but I could feel it.*

Something to you? Puk questioned, inching closer.

No. It was not like that. I do not know what to think. I thought there was no one else like me, yet now this man shows up from across the sea. I…

You are curious, Puk responded.

Isha nodded. *I need to know, to confirm the truth of what I am. I need to know my entire life has not been a lie.*

Puk hesitated. He placed a hand on her shoulder before taking it back to sign. *He could be dangerous,* he gestured. *You should be careful around him.*

Isha nodded, taking comfort in Puk's presence. *I will be careful. You have my word.*

The sound of raised voices drew her out of the conversation.

"We need more information," Echo said. "Evidence, not just hearsay."

"Zapour has not recorded a winter lasting this long in centuries," Dazen replied. "That is evidence enough to at least pique my curiosity. A stranger this prince from across the sea may be, but he is right. We rely too heavily on Shine. It is no sustainable way to live in harmony. We need only look at our history as evidence. Entire cities destroyed in the blink of an eye. Numerous wars fought and won through the use of weaponry beyond our comprehension. Perhaps we would be better off without it."

"You would forgo your own Shine, then?" It was Aia who spoke up, hands crossed and tucked neatly into her sides. "You would hide from the sun, refuse its power?"

Dazen hesitated, then stood firm. "If it would prevent another war, then yes. I would do what must be done."

The star-shaped birthmark on Aia's cheek rose as she considered his answer. "That is a bold statement. We of Wisha do not hold many Shine users of our own. For a long time we feared it, and perhaps still do. The concept of going without Shine would not trouble us. In fact, I'm sure many would be in favour of such a bargain. It might even encourage those who are less willing to venture out into this new world that is being opened up to us."

Dazen nodded. "What of your brother? He is strong with Shine if I recall."

"My brother went half his life hiding it from his captors. I am certain he would not mind, provided there was a safe way to prevent the sun's influence. If this is the direction you wish to take, then Wisha is with you."

"A plan, then," Dazen said, standing tall. "Echo is right. We cannot simply abandon our use of Shine altogether, not with Kogon and Craw still active and a potential threat. Neither can we afford to spark another war, one we are under-manned and unprepared for."

Silence stretched as everyone stopped to think. Waves crashed on the sandy shore beyond them, and in the stillness all Isha could think about was the colour of the prince's eyes.

"Perhaps one problem could solve the other," Aia said, stepping towards the table. She held everyone's attention now, and the spotlight did not seem to frighten her. "Gelvard and the Kingdom of Craw have made their stance clear. They wish to rule, or at least to conquer. It is only a matter of time before they move on one of our nations.

"Either way we look at it, they are an obstacle for both us

and for the prince from across the sea. If stripping Shine from Zapour is truly your goal for the future, then let us strike a bargain. One that places another potential ally on the table." Aia finished by leaning over the map of Zapour that Dazen had prepared and repositioning the miniature pin representing the Sun Prince to rest between their own.

Beside her, Dazen looked impressed, as did Echo.

After the council, Isha decided to go for a walk along the beach. She and Puk hadn't made it far before Dazen found her.

"Walk with me?" he asked.

Isha turned back to Puk. She pressed two fingers to her lips and in one movement bent her hand over her opposite forearm, signalling Zur's rest beneath the horizon and wishing him a good night.

"The stars are bright tonight," she said to her brother as they walked the sandy shoreline away from camp. Dazen looked to the sky, and for a moment she thought he would never look down. "Are you okay?" she inquired.

Dazen blinked as if shaken from a daze. "I — I'm fine. My mind is just a little clouded is all."

"It can't be easy, all this pressure."

Dazen scratched his head. "I'm quickly learning that being a king is far and away from being a king-in-waiting. I may not have agreed with all of our father's decisions —'and I never will," he said, squeezing her hand, "but I'm beginning to feel the weight of it. The burden he carried. The crown is heavy, and I fear I'll soon be crushed by it."

"You mustn't speak like that," Isha said.

"My mind is a storm, Isha. Who am I to speak with about these troubles if not you? Sumaya is the mother of my child, which is already enough weight to carry. I — I don't know if I can do this, continue to make such important decisions. What if I become like Father? What if I make the wrong choice? I don't know if I could live with myself if I'm the cause for someone else's misery."

Isha clasped his hands in her own. "You are more than our father. You are Trost. The very essence of who we are is inside of you, guiding you. Have faith, Brother. In yourself and in us. You will not fail, whatever you decide."

Dazen paused, the slight incline of his lip suggesting he had accepted her words. Isha embraced him, pulling him close and showing him that she was someone he could lean on.

She pressed her head into his chest, the two of them holding there for a time. She felt the rapid beating of his heart slowly begin to ebb. His muscles relaxed and he moved to part, powerful hands holding her arms. "What did you make of this 'Sun Prince?'" he asked. "It cannot be easy to find out there is another like yourself."

Isha bit her lip, trying to piece together the puzzle of her thoughts and form them into words. "I — I don't know what to make of him. For so long I thought I was alone in… what I am. Then I found out Mother was like me. I still don't even know what I am, if anything at all. So much fuss over a thing as simple as the colour of an iris."

Anger coursed through her veins. Just the thought of it all set her blood boiling. Dazen waited patiently for her frustration to abate. "Now that you've seen him, now that you know another like yourself is out there, do you think anything of it?"

"I think I'd like to talk to him, if possible. Can you arrange that?"

"I can try, yes. It seems he's also taken an interest in you."

Isha met Dazen's eye, her face edging closer as she once again noticed the odd bit of purple floating amidst his usual blue. She squinted, imparting her will as if something inside of her was telling her what to do.

Dazen jumped back, one hand covering his left eye as he yelped. "What was that?"

Isha blinked, a sudden pain forming behind her own eyes. "Let me see you," she said, taking his head in her hands and pulling it close. "Open your eyes."

Dazen did as he was bid, squeezing open his eye for her to observe. Whatever had been there was gone now. "How do you feel?" she asked.

Dazen shook his head. "Clearer, actually. What did you do?"

Isha crossed her arms. "I'm not entirely sure. I don't think it's a question of what I did, more one of what I have undone."

Dazen took a step back, suddenly aware of what she was implying. "The prince, you think he did something to me?"

Isha looked again into his eye, trying to recall what she had seen. "I can't be sure, it's possible. You did seem overly eager to please him before. It wasn't like you, to come to a decision like that so rashly."

"You think he cast some kind of spell on me? To influence my decision tomorrow?"

Isha shrugged. "I think there's something amiss with him. He's up to something. Tell me, now that your head is clear, how do you feel about the removal of Shine from Trost?"

Dazen paused to think. "I think you're right. It's not a decision I should have come to so quickly. There is some truth to what he said. We're far too reliant on Shine. I don't want future generations to grow up as dependent as we are. If what he says is true, then the future may be even more bleak than we predicted. That's not a world I want Nora to grow up in. If removing Shine from Zapour will help prevent a war, then it's something I must consider."

"But?" Isha prompted.

"But Echo is also right. Shine can't be removed overnight. Then there's Craw and Kogon to think about. Allowing them too much power and influence could prove disastrous, and would likely undo all that we seek to improve."

"Then what will you do?"

Dazen sighed, rubbing a hand over his forehead. "All that I can, I suppose. I'll speak my piece to this prince from across the sea. If he's as peaceful as he preaches, then he'll see sense in a reasoned approach. If not, then perhaps a war was always inevitable."

Chapter 13

- Zeek –

ZEEK'S EYES OPENED WIDE. He stood on a cliff's edge, staring into something so vast, so unimaginable, that he could scarcely believe it was real. Of course, he knew what it was, his memories told him so. But there was a difference between knowing that something existed, and actually seeing it for yourself. He no longer had to trust that his memories were real, now it was before him.

The sea.

"It's so blue," he whispered, to himself more than to Father, who was busy scouting the coast, searching for a way into the camp of soldiers.

Daylight still shone, but Zeek could see Zur's edge begin to dip below the horizon line.

"Are you done staring?" Father said, turning towards him.

"Why did you not tell me such a thing existed?" he asked.

Father looked out into the open ocean before taking

another step. "It is nothing special, just a large puddle of useless water."

"It's beautiful."

Father grunted. "You have a skewed sense of beauty."

"And what is yours, then? What beauty do you see in this world of ours, if any at all?"

Father's eyes narrowed. "I see beauty in order, in structure. The sea is nothing but a passage for those who would seek to disrupt that order. You see those ships down there?" he said, pointing towards three huge vessels which were floating on the sea. "They seek to spread poison over these lands, our lands. They would see an end to Shine, the power of Light. You would not be here if not for Shine, Zeek. Is that what you want, to return to the shadows of your cave?"

"No!" Zeek responded. "I have seen too much to go back."

"Good, then we must act now to stop the spread at its source."

"What would you have me do?"

Father paced the stone cliff. "There will be a meeting tonight between those of Zapour and those from across the sea. It is your purpose to ensure that the meeting ends with blood."

Zeek nodded, feeling the weight of Ancel's anger. He didn't like that he was so eager to fill his mind with knowledge through the death of another, but neither could he ignore that it was part of him.

"Your target is the one who calls himself the Sun Prince."

Zeek peered into the camp, watching as more humans than he had ever seen scurried around. "How will I know which one he is?"

"There will be a meeting, a closed meeting. There will

likely be less than ten people in attendance. Your target will be the male with violet eyes. Kill him. Drain him if you can. I should like to know what he knows, if possible. His memories will prove useful in our future plans."

"And if there is no time?"

"If time does not permit, then see yourself to safety. His death is most important, his knowledge secondary. I will leave it for you to decide. How quickly can you do it?"

Zeek reached for the shadows within him, arching his back as his tail detached itself from the pink of his new skin. It burned when touched by sunlight, a reminder of just how fragile he still was. "It shouldn't take too long. I will try my hardest, Father.

"But how will I make it there? Won't I be seen?" he continued.

"You let me worry about that. Humanity has been scared of fire since long before Zur gifted them with Shine. I will set a distraction, draw their eye, while you come from there."

Zeek followed his stare, which peered in the water's direction.

"Let us test just how much you truly love the sea."

ZEEK STEPPED BARE FOOTED into the expansive mass of water. A chill crept up his leg, his newly formed flesh unaccustomed to the sheer force of nature that was the sea after sun-down. In his previous form he'd been used to the cold. His cave had been nothing but a wet mess of moss-covered rock.

His new form was amazing. It allowed him to feel, to experience the sensations this world offered, but with such sensations also came certain repercussions. His flesh could now break, could fall prey to illness, and fall victim to frostbite.

He paid the pain no mind, however. He embraced it, even. With pain came life, and that is more than he could say of whatever he used to be.

He submerged himself fully into the darkening waters, allowing the white foam that he had come to know as *waves* crash over him. He had never swum before, and for a moment he thought that would be his end. But even though he had never done it, he'd consumed those who had.

He tapped into his bank of knowledge, using Ancel's experiences to guide him, to become him. It came easily, his body reacting to what his victim had known. It was becoming easier and easier to use his acquired knowledge, to make practical what had previously only been thought.

He thrust one arm in front of the other, propelling himself deeper into the sea. A large wave threatened to consume him. It loomed like a giant hand, ready to clap at any moment. He dipped his head, kicking his legs as he ducked under to the safety of the ocean floor.

His shadow-tail floated, pulling him back to the surface, towards the air that he had come to so desperately need. All he had to do now was wait.

Soldiers manned the majority of the coast. Some watched, holding to their duty with expressions of stone. Others had set up camp and were sitting around a fire, playing some game of cards. He could hear their laughter, how they took delight in each other's company. It made him wonder if he would enjoy such a thing. He had never spoken to another person save for his father and, to an extent, his victims. He wouldn't know what to say. Even his stolen memories were no help when it came to the need to express himself.

Three dark silhouettes dotted the night sky to the north. He turned to stare at them, basking in the glory of these unimaginable vessels of the sea. If Father was right, then these people were dangerous. They were a threat, seeking to take away his precious light. And threats needed to be eliminated.

He waited, basking in the feeling of weightlessness, unperturbed by the ache in his head as the cold began to take effect. Steadily, the muffled voices on the ships faded, and the shadow of a smaller vessel appeared. Oars were lowered and set into motion.

He looked to the coast, beyond the bank of sand occupied by the humans and into the treeline behind them. He had to wait. Father had told him to, had said to look to the sky for a sign.

And so, he floated. Now that he had seen the vastness of the ocean, everything seemed so insignificant. He was but a tiny piece of this world, a fragment of something that had existed for millennia. And yet, Father said that he would matter, that his actions could change the course of the world. He didn't know if that was true or not, but he was excited to find out.

He edged closer to the shore, watching with heightened vision. Shapes moved along the coast, converging upon a single structure. The tent flapped in the wind as the boat pulled ashore, figures disembarking before they too made their way over to the chosen meeting point.

Zeek prepared himself. Night was his friend. He may have recently been granted access to daylight, but the night was where he truly felt his strongest. His shadow-tail curled around his neck, sensing its prey and yearning to strike.

A plume of smoke suddenly rose into the night sky. Zeek lifted his chin, watching as bright firelight flickered in the distance. It began to spread, quickly blanketing the skyline in a smoky haze. The humans around the camp were abuzz with activity, running around in frantic patterns. Shouts of alarm rose from all angles as people panicked.

Zeek acknowledged his father's work, emerging from the sea completely undisturbed, the defenders' focus drawn elsewhere.

The prince from Craw had gifted him a wealth of knowledge, skills he intended to put to full use. He blended in with the shadows, darting to the right, ducking beneath a half-erected tent as a soldier passed by him, attention focused on the commotion to the east.

Guards were posted at the entrance to the pavilion where the two parties had met, and Zeek watched as a panicked man ran up to them before being granted access.

He inched closer, sand crunching beneath his feet. He reached the rear of the structure and placed an ear against the tight cloth. He could hear raised voices from within, but what they were saying was hard to determine. He used the sharpened point of his shadow-tail to cut into the fabric, creating a fist-sized hole.

Peering inside, he saw that a warm fire was set in the centre, the lone source of light in an otherwise darkened space. All the faces looked the same to him. Humans all seemed to have the same generic build, separated into two basic forms, male and female.

"My lords," a regal-looking man in a blue and white uniform said as he entered. "There is a fire to the east. The whole forest is ablaze."

Another man — a king, by the crown cresting his head — rose in response, though he was facing away from Zeek. "Lock down the perimeter, find out all that you can," he said, turning to face another whose back was also facing Zeek. "What is the meaning of this? Have we not come to an agreement?"

The man in question rose, not in an aggressive manner, but neither did he shy away from the conflict. "I assure you. Whatever is out there is not my doing. My intention is to educate, not to provoke. If there is something amiss to the east, then I will gladly wait with you while an investigation is carried out."

The man wearing the crown shifted, his face now visible. The fire sparked and his eyes lit with violet. It was not as vibrant as Zeek was expecting, but in the dark of the night Zeek's vision had not let him down. It was there.

Zeek's shadow-tail vibrated, curling around his waist and arching above his shoulder. Like the predator he was, Zeek waited patiently for his opportunity. There were too many people in the room. He could probably manage to kill him quickly, but Father had wanted his knowledge, and this man was strong with the Light. He could feel it. It was like an energy calling to him. He'd already had a taste, but a taste was not enough. He wanted more, wanted to become more.

If living in a cave had taught him anything, it was patience. He waited, a shadow within a shadow. People moved around him, but the position of the tent was isolated, set a distance away from the main camp, and he was well hidden.

"This meet is over," the man with the violet in his eye said. "If you truly mean what you say, then we will find another time to discuss terms."

More words were exchanged, but Zeek paid them no mind.

He watched, ever vigilant, as people began to depart. A woman moved first, stepping out of the pavilion and into the dark of the night. Another followed, then another, until there were only two left. The man with the violet eyes, and the one with whom he had been conversing. As the second figure began to leave, Zeek expanded his rip in the fabric. Stealth was his friend as he crept into the tent. He stalked his prey, whose back was towards him. This was his opportunity, his chance. Zeek approached the violet-eyed man. His shadow-tail moved on its own, an instinct built into who he was. A golden crown rested upon the head of his target. A crown soon to fall.

Although Zeek was silent, the man with the crown turned, as if reacting to his shadowy presence. Zeek quickly closed the gap, moving to within a breath's distance. He watched as his victim's eyes widened in horror, as everyone's did before he consumed them. A light groan escaped his lips as Zeek plunged his tail into his chest, his head arching back as the draining process began.

He felt his victim's energy flow into him. It was electric, the sensation greater even than his last. Then there was resistance. There had never been resistance before. The man with the violet eyes fought back, not physically, for his arms were paralyzed by his side, but mentally. There was a battle of the mind as Zeek fought fervently for control.

For the barest moment, Zeek thought he was going to lose, that he would be beaten, but the man finally broke. The life that he had lived flowed into Zeek, his victim's memories becoming his own. They came and went quicker than a breath, but a breath was all that was needed for him to see it.

Zeek released his hold, shadow-tail recoiling. A single tear fell from his inhuman eye, a tear shed for what he had just taken. Though it was impossible to comprehend the full weight of what he had done, a brief moment was all it took to make him feel regret. He pushed away, shaken by what he had seen in the flash of memories, but it was too late. The victim was dead.

Footsteps shuffled at the entrance. A man stood there, horror wrought on his otherwise smooth features. Two violet eyes stared out from him, bright as the sun in full light. Much brighter than his victim's had been. Zeek paused. Had he made a mistake? Had Father been wrong? Were there two men in this meet whose eyes shone with this colour?

The man charged at him, sword drawn. Zeek was forced to retreat, stepping away and letting his prey drop to his knees.

More figures emerged behind the approaching man, accompanied by startled voices.

Zeek assessed the situation, remembering his father's words. He needed to go. He propelled himself backward, using his tail as leverage. He squeezed through the opening he had made in the tent, the softness of the sand welcoming him as he returned to the night, and to the sea.

Chapter 14

- Isha -

"WHY ARE YOU LOOKING at me like that?" Isha said, making the accompanying hand gestures as Puk stared at her.

Her words seemed to shake him. He placed his fist above his heart and moved it in a circular motion, gesturing an apology.

She grabbed his hand and pulled his focus back. "I'm sorry," she said. "I'm just frustrated. I should be in there with him. I don't trust that man."

Puk withdrew to make another gesture. *Dazen does not want any distractions.*

"So I'm a distraction now?" Isha said, not even bothering to mime her words.

Puk shook his head. He pointed towards her eyes. *The prince. He is interested in you. It is not good for your brother to negotiate with you there.*

Isha rubbed at her face, wishing she could change the colour of her eyes and have all of her problems solved. "Even so, he may need me. I think that man has some kind of power over people's minds. I could sense it. What if all they said about me was true? What if I am different, that my eyes allow me some sort of influence over another. What if I used it on you!?"

Puk smiled. *I was under the influence of others long before I met you. No. I am under no spell. At least not one born from the mystery of your eyes.*

Isha felt her heart flutter at Puk's crooked smile.

The moment was soured when a man shouted in the distance. Isha looked up, following the sound. A smoky haze had settled over the treeline. She stood, watching as flames flickered in the distance.

"What's going on?" she said.

More shouting ensued as soldiers were roused and a perimeter was set. Isha spotted Gale in amongst the chaos, calling orders. She ran over to him, Puk following her lead. "Gale! What's happening? What's out there?"

Gale paused briefly to address her. "I'm not sure, stay with Puk! I'll go and check on Dazen."

He sprinted off, sand trailing in the air as he made his way over towards the designated pavilion.

As the fires raged, swirling winds blew smoke in all directions. Isha covered her mouth, coughing into her sleeve. She grabbed Puk by the arm and dragged him away from the smoke, following Gale, certain that this smoke and fire was no mere coincidence.

She was almost barrelled over as soldiers bearing the serpent crest of Zuton barged through the camp, cutting her off and forcing both her and Puk to wait for them to pass.

A number of Aia's Bakai were also converging on the command pavilion. Rudi, head and shoulders above the people around him, acknowledged Isha and helped her push past oncoming soldiers.

Puk followed, now a couple of strides behind as Isha made it to her destination. Aia was first out of the tent, speaking to Rudi in Wishan.

Isha interrupted, clasping Aia by her wrist. "What's going on?" she asked.

"That's what we were going to ask you," she replied. "Are we under attack?"

Isha shrugged. She stood on her toes, trying to locate the source of the commotion, or search for signs of attack.

"Where's Dazen?" she inquired.

Aia pointed to the tent.

Isha dashed over, but she didn't get far before running head-first into something hard. She rubbed at her head, shaking off the dizziness. A mirror of her own eyes stared back at her, deep pools of glowing violet. But they were not as they had been before. Gone was the calm, the sense of composure and serenity. Replacing it was a look of fear so primal that she knew as soon as their eyes met that something was wrong.

The Sun Prince leaned back, eyes darting to and from the entrance.

Isha moved to speak, to ask him where he was going, but a hand gripped his shoulder, ripping him away and dragging him back towards the boat at the shoreline.

She stood for a moment, perplexed. What had happened in there?

Dazen!

She pushed off the sand, swatting away the tent flap as she entered the pavilion. A body lay strewn on the floor. Echo knelt next to it, shouting something incomprehensible. More people rushed into the room, others sprinting out. Isha was petrified, refusing to look directly at the man Echo was holding in his arms.

Puk took hold of her, attempting to usher her away from the scene that was unfolding. But she was strong, and she pushed his arm aside, finally aware enough to take action.

She brushed past Puk, dropping to her knees as she took the broken body in her arms, ripping him away from a wailing Echo.

Tears flowed freely down her cheeks as she pulled her brother's head into her chest. "Dazen!" she whispered, though in her mind it was a scream.

She checked for a pulse, pressing two fingers into his neck. His skin was dry, as if the life had literally been drained from his body. His limbs were limp, his features barely even recognizable. Blood pooled beneath her, seeping through his coat in a sticky mess of red. She looked into his vacant eyes, praying, searching desperately for life, But there was no life to be found there.

Time slowed. Her mind fractured, barely able to comprehend the reality of what had happened. This couldn't be true. It had to be a dream. Dazen couldn't be dead. He had a wife, a child. Despite the burden of ruling, he was happy. Isha finally had a family again, someone to love, to care for.

She tried again to rouse her sleeping brother. She pulled at him, ripping open his shirt to assess the wound. What she found was a single puncture. Around it, he was completely drained of colour and vitality. Skin and bone were all that remained. There was nothing left to wake, his sleep was now eternal.

Isha fell upon him, wracked with grief, silently straining to unleash a scream that could not escape her throat. Puk tried to calm her, to pull her away from such a painful sight, but she would have none of it, clinging onto her brother's breathless body.

Her tear-blurred gaze fell upon the entrance, remembering the frightened look in the foreign prince's eye. It had all been a ruse. Yagos didn't mean to make peace. They didn't want to educate. They wanted to start a war. He had done this. He had murdered her brother.

Grief turned to anger. Sorrow to rage.

"He will pay for this," she said, still clutching her dead brother's hand.

She rose, driven by instinct over rational thought. The Sun Prince was still here. If she was to avenge her brother, it had to be now, before he had the chance to flee. She would find him, and she would kill him for what he had done.

She placed Dazen's head on Echo's lap, checking her hip to make sure her short sword was still in its sheath. Then she charged out of the tent, eyes narrowing to slits as she watched the Sun Prince flee to the safety of his rowboat.

She set off at a sprint. There might have been shouts and footsteps behind her, but she didn't care, so consumed was she by a single thought. She ran faster than she ever thought possible, her boots sinking in the soft sand. The boat pulled away, rowing toward the larger vessel, but it wasn't docked far. She could make it. She could still avenge her brother.

She screamed and ran with everything she had, using all of her effort to propel herself forward into the oncoming waves and through to the wide sea beyond. She wasn't a skilled swimmer, but she knew enough to keep moving forward.

The chill caused her chest to tighten. A wave crashed on top of her, stinging her eyes. She gasped as she surfaced and water dripped into her throat, causing her to splutter and gag reflexively. Her head ached with a tingling numbness, but she ignored it, cupping her hands and repeatedly placing one arm in front of the other.

The Sun Prince's ship loomed like a thundercloud in front of her, blocking out the moon in its vastness. Chains rattled in the near distance as the anchor was hoisted. She inched closer, noticing that the rowboat was beginning to rise. A rope was tied to each corner, pulled taught as those above began to lift one boat onto another. The murderer's escape was almost complete.

She felt for her hip, reassuring herself that the blade was still there. It weighed her down, but she'd almost made it. She could see him, the man who had killed her brother. Her heart screamed, but her body dove beneath the water. She angled herself and surfaced calmly on the other side of the rising boat.

Isha saw her opportunity. She sliced through one of the ropes, kicking away as the boat dropped on an angle, rocking those aboard. She moved quickly to the back of the rowboat, preparing to slice through another rope. Her blade only managed a small cut before a hand clasped her wrist.

Sounja stared down at her, face a picture of rage, digging claw-like fingers into Isha's flesh. It took all of her strength to keep the grip on her sword.

However angry this woman was, Isha's fury burned brighter. She braced her feet on the hull and pulled her sword arm down, allowing the water to consume her again. The woman's stubborn grip was iron, and she followed her in, tumbling over Isha's shoulder into the cold abyss.

Isha recovered, her free hand gripping the thick wood of the row-boat's edge. She thrust herself upwards, swinging wildly in the same motion. A gasp rose over the cacophony of crashing waves. She felt an impact as the sharp steel cut into flesh. Blood dripped from the tip of her sword.

She managed to gain enough leverage to see her work. The prince let out a pained groan, a bloody hand covering a shallow gash on his chest.

A lumbering brute of a man in full plate armour placed himself in front of the prince on the rocking boat, using his bulk to block her advance. He raised a boot, preparing to kick her in the face and send her off the edge once more.

At that moment, the partially severed rope snapped.

The boat lurched, and the metal-covered man was set off balance. He tumbled over the side, joining the woman Isha had already cast there. Isha's arm bashed against the wood, jolted by the impact, but she held on.

Two figures remained on the small boat, which was now tilted at a harsh angle. She was at a disadvantage, however, her lower half still submerged in the raging sea.

Bright eyes stared back at her. They almost seemed to plead with her. The eyes of the guilty.

She grit her teeth, using his hesitation to her advantage. She swung again, but her reach fell short. Something hard tugged at her leg. She turned to see Sounja attempting to pull her back into the sea. She dropped her sword, forced to use two hands to keep her hold on the boat. She kicked her leg, the sole of her boot ramming into her assailant's nose with a sickening crunch. But she was determined, and Isha's blow only spurred her on.

Isha felt her grip faltering. Just as she was about to fall, the pressure on her leg vanished. She spared a look over her shoulder, watching as the red-haired woman was grappled.

"Puk!" she cried out. Her silent friend had come to her aid. Water splashed as the already choppy sea was broken by their wrestling forms. Isha forced herself to stay vigilant, clawing herself out of the water as the Sun Prince continued to watch, either unable or unwilling to try to stop her.

She had made it halfway onto the boat when the other two ropes snapped. Though the boat was only inches from the surface, the jolt of the impact was significant. She was thrown forward into the man who had murdered her brother, the two of them falling in a tangle of limbs.

Blood still leaked from the wound she had given him, but it was only a minor cut. She tried to reposition, to regain her breath, to find her sword, but she had little luck. Her foot was caught between two pieces of wood, and the Sun Prince had her in his grasp now.

He held her close, his breath warm on her neck. "Let us talk about this?" he said. "It can be explained."

Isha raged. "You killed my brother!" she shouted.

He made to respond, but his words were lost as the boat rocked once again. Puk's head emerged, long wet hair sticking to his face as he pulled himself on board. He brandished a knife, but the red-haired man who had been by the prince's side the other day blocked his path to their target. Puk clasped the collar of the man's shirt and pulled. The man tried to fight him off, but his arms were weak, not made for combat.

"Edar!" the Sun Prince called, attempting to free himself from Isha.

Puk's knife rose, and the young advisor's life was about to end.

Suddenly, in one swift motion, the Sun Prince thrust Isha off of him and dove over Edar, his back turned to Puk's descending blade. It struck him on the shoulder, sinking into flesh. He didn't cry out in pain as Isha expected. Instead, he wrapped his arms around his comrade in a protective hug.

Before Puk could swing again, light shone from above, followed by an arrow. Puk's eyes grew wide as the arrow struck him in the arm. His dagger fell, grip giving way to pain. Figures descended from the larger vessel looming ominously above. Isha blinked. More bows were trained on both her and Puk, ready to be loosed.

"Hold!" the Sun Prince called. "Do not harm them!"

Isha's face turned pale. Men boarded the rowboat, grabbing her beneath the arms and hoisting her upwards. She resisted ferociously, kicking one off and sending them tumbling into the sea.

No. Not again. She couldn't be taken, refused to be at the mercy of another tyrant. She desperately tried to fling herself overboard into the mercy of the watery depths, but strong hands prevented her. There was little she could do. Her hands were bound, and she felt something hard hit her in the temple. Her vision darkened, and consciousness slipped away.

PART
II

Chapter 15

- Raiz –

ZUR'S STING WAS a welcome relief. Raiz collapsed, footsore and travel-weary. His arms still itched from overusing his Shine. While the sun's energy could renew his power, it could not undo the damage already done. It would take weeks for him to recover, if he ever would at all.

Draz and Aroha lay beside him, and for a while the three of them were still. Nobody talked, nobody did anything. Pain mixed with exhaustion, and was accompanied by the overwhelming sense of dread that had followed them down the mountain and back through the stinking marshlands and dense fog that plagued this area.

Even Spike collapsed beside them, hitting the ground with a resounding thud. Raiz rolled over, placing his head next to his companion's snout. Raiz knew Spike to be capable of twisting Shine, the two of them had been practicing it for some time, but never had he spent so much in one burst.

"Spike, Draz owes you a drink," Draz said, finally breaking the silence, his breathing still heavily laboured.

"What in Cova's name was that?" Aroha said, sitting up.

"Draz can't believe it. Won't believe it."

"You saw them, Draz! With your own eyes."

"It was dark, they could have been—"

"You saw them. You know what they are. Celik was right. A conniving bastard he may have been, but the cripple was right. The Skae are real, and they are not so lost to this world as the books claim."

"So those things were Skae?" Raiz questioned. "The shadows from legend?"

"What else could they be? They knew you," Aroha continued. "Baited you. That was all a trap. We're lucky to be alive."

"They called me Radiant," Raiz replied. "Whoever was behind that voice sensed my Shine. I think someone was here before, stole from them."

"Whatever they wanted, I'm not sticking around to find out," Aroha said, rising to her feet. "We need to get as far from these mountains as we can. Taula was right, they are cursed."

Raiz nodded, sparing a thought towards Porter's wife, her withered corpse still fresh in his memory. "I have to return to Tinker, have to tell them what's happened. Porter must know his wife's fate. I owe him that much."

The town of Tinker was empty. Raiz walked past the charred remains of Porter's house and into the town centre, searching for Taula, Porter, or anyone really. There was nothing. All signs of life had been erased. Livestock had been transported, their pens standing empty.

"What happened here?" Draz asked, hands on hips. He strutted into the courtyard and kicked over a crooked stack of hay. "Do you think the Skae got to them?"

Raiz surveyed the area. "No, there are no signs of a struggle, of battle. These people left willingly, or at least without a fight."

"Why would they do that?" Aroha said. "They didn't seem like folk to so lightly abandon their livelihood."

"Does it matter?" Draz replied. "They're gone, our business here concluded. Clearly, they did not have faith in your ability, else they would have waited for you to return. There's nothing for us here. We should return to Trost."

Raiz paled. His thoughts turned to Veil. In truth, he didn't know why he'd come all the way up here. He'd pretended there were possible alliances to be made, even tricked himself into thinking it might be true, but deep down he knew Dazen was right. His being here was senseless. He only wanted to be closer to Veil, to her homeland. He missed her, his heart never having stopped its ache.

Draz and Aroha knew it too, and yet they had come anyway, for him. Now he had led them to this terror, a darkness he never thought actually existed.

He turned to leave when a shuffle sounded from behind a nearby house.

"I knew you'd come!" Porter shouted, springing from a nearby hiding hole behind the base of a home. "Where is she? Where's Maya? You found her, yes?"

Raiz stood and watched as Porter's daughter ran up beside him and tucked herself beneath his arm. Something died inside of Raiz as the excitement in her eye faded, replaced by a sense of loss so fresh that only one who had felt true heartache could understand.

They saw it in his expression, sensed it. Perhaps they'd already known her fate in their hearts. Beside his daughter, Porter bent to a knee, eyes swollen, lips quivering. "She's dead, then?"

Raiz paused, then issued a solemn nod.

"How?"

"Perhaps it is best you do not know."

"Tell me how! If my wife is dead, then I must at least know how she passed."

Raiz bowed his head. "The Skae took her."

Replacing Porter's grief was a sense of dread so foreboding it made Raiz shiver. "Then they were right. The Skae have returned. I should've gone. I should've left when they told me to."

"Where is everyone?" Raiz dared to ask. "Where has the town gone?"

Porter was still snivelling, wiping snot from his nose while attempting to console his sobbing daughter. "They — they left. Soldiers from Veka. They came, recruited. So many of them. They took all of them south, but I stayed, hid. Stayed for Maya."

The tears returned as Porter mentioned his wife's name. Raiz placed a hand on his shoulder. It was all he could do. He had been in the frame of mind where Porter now resided. There was no comfort adequate enough.

"You should leave this place. It is not safe. Do you have family? Some place you can take your daughter?"

Porter gave a sniffling nod, and then Raiz left. As much as he wanted to help, he knew he was not enough.

He took one last look around town, a reminder that this

was not home. He was not welcome here, never had been. Returning to where Draz and Aroha were conversing, he began to check Spike's saddle. "I need to go home," he said. "Dazen must know what's happened here. There's no alliance to be made with New Crata. Porter told me that soldiers from Veka came here to recruit, though I suspect they weren't given much of a choice. Kogon must be mobilising, preparing for something. Trost needs to know about it, and they need to know the Skae exist!"

"It's alright lad," Draz said, moving to clap him on the shoulder. "Draz and Aroha have already decided. You should go on without us. Go home, we'll follow. With Spike you can make it home within a few days."

Raiz relaxed, feeling some of the tension wash away. "You're a good friend."

"And don't you forget it!" Draz said, issuing him a toothy grin, one Raiz still wasn't accustomed to, since for most of their friendship Draz had unrelentingly covered his features with Gallant.

Raiz fastened his boots into the stirrups of Spike's saddle. He'd had to have the saddle custom made at least half a dozen times now due to Spike's continued growth, and this latest one was already looking snug. He wasn't sure when he would stop growing, if he even would at all. Spike was now taller than Raiz, and with his neck at full stretch perhaps even twice his size. His wings spread wider than a house.

"Don't take too long on your way back," Raiz said as Spike bent into a crouch. In the same motion, his great wings beat and he leapt upward. The air shifted as ground turned to sky.

Raiz held firm. Lifting off was always his favourite part of flight. The feeling of weightlessness and knowing he was separating from the world below never seemed to grow old.

Spike banked to the left and flattened his wings, allowing him to drift in the light breeze. Raiz glimpsed the peak of the mountain they'd entered as his elevation levelled off. Up until yesterday he had never put much thought into the history of the world, of religion and creation. But seeing those things up close, living the horrors spoken of over campfires and experiencing their malice, he was beginning to question everything.

He thought of Isha and Dazen. He needed them, more than they needed him. He realised that now. All his life he had thought of himself as their saviour. He thought it his responsibility to right the wrongs dealt to them. In a way he was right, but he was also wrong. He was the youngest child. He may have been born to a different father, but he was still their family, and he needed them now more than ever.

For half a day he let Spike take him, his mind clouded. His wounds ached, and his arms were weak from overuse of Shine. He wouldn't be fighting for a while, at least not until his burns recovered. Spike needed to rest, however, and Raiz could feel the beast's stomach rumble beneath his weight. Come to think of it, Raiz had barely eaten in a day and a half himself. He craved sustenance, his stomach grumbling for him to provide it.

Together, the two of them descended onto unfamiliar ground. If he'd had to place them on a map he would have put them somewhere in central Kogon. He angled Spike over towards a small lake in a thicket of trees. The pricket landed with a thump, wasting no time before sucking down a gulletful of fresh water.

Raiz descended his scaled back, boots splashing on the

lake's bank. Spike turned to him, Raiz knowing at once what he was after. "No Spike, no Shine today. Not for a while. You'll have to go without," he said, stroking a scale just above his wounded leg. The wound was already beginning to close. Raiz marvelled at this creature he had come to call his friend, wondering just how many more surprises he might have in store.

Raiz left Spike to find his own food. He never strayed too far, but it was important for them to not become reliant on each other. He didn't think Spike worked like other animals. He ate like them, shat like them, acted like them too. But Spike was different. He liked food, but didn't need it. He had once gone an entire winter without a single scrap of food, living only off Raiz's Shine, and come summer he had grown another five inches.

Shine is what made him strong, what made him grow. Without it he would likely still be the tiny creature Raiz had once mistaken for a lizard. Raiz felt at his pocket, remembering when Spike had been small enough to fit inside.

He found a hoard of berries dangling on a nearby bush, quickly wolfing them down as if he had never had a proper meal in his life.

A branch snapped in the brush behind him, and Raiz almost drew from his well of Shine before its sting flared on his arm again. Instead, he turned, listening as the sound of wheels turning came closer. Hoof beats clicked on the dirt road ahead as two horses pulled a covered wagon down the winding path. A man sat at the front, reins in hands, ushering the horses forward with haste.

Raiz hid behind tree cover. The man atop the wagon wore a serious face. His features were hardened. He had a powerful jaw marked with a large pink scar that stretched into his lower cheek. Two men in full plate armour rode in the carriage behind him, dirt brown sashes strewn across their chest. Soldiers of Kogon.

One of the soldiers shouted an order, and the wagon came to a halt. Raiz peeked around the tree, sure that he had not been discovered. The sharp ring of steel sung as a soldier drew his blade and pointed towards a thicket of brush in the near distance.

A deafening roar boomed as a thundering figure split the trees across the other side of the path.

Spike.

The soldiers attacked, hopping down from their vantage. They seemed unperturbed by the sight of a Dragon in their midst, though they were still cautious. One of them thrust at Spike's mid-section, and was met with a crunch as sharp teeth clamped around his wrist, shattering bone.

Before Raiz could leap to his defence, Spike charged the second soldier, crashing into the side of the wagon. The two horses kicked and neighed, attempting to flee in different directions but getting pulled back by the tack binding them.

The driver was thrown forward, his momentum toppling him over the edge and onto the dirt pathway as the wagon broke, turning sideways and crashing into the trunk of a tree.

The second soldier was crushed by Spike's weight, his plate bending to choke the life from his lungs. Spike then made to finish off the driver, driven by instinct, his bulky frame hovering over the fallen man as he scrambled to draw his sword from its scabbard.

"Spike, no!" Raiz called, making himself known. He held out his hand and pressed forward, confident his friend wouldn't harm him. But something was different. Spike heard, but he wasn't listening. This wasn't like him.

Spike's hesitation gave the hardened man time to recover. He used that time well, regaining his feet. Rather than running as most would in the presence of such a beast, he charged.

Raiz reacted, instinctively drawing a charge of Shine to the tip of his finger. His hand convulsed, the Shine inside protesting at him for trying to use it when he was not yet healed. He withdrew his hand, shaking it as he would a jammed finger.

The man from the wagon cried out, his sword scoring a mark on Spike's hide even as his legs were ripped from under him.

Spike jerked his serpentine neck, clenching his jaws around the flesh of his ankle and shook. The scream that followed echoed through the dense wood. With one last shake, Spike let go. The man was sent sprawling, landing with a crash, his head splitting against the wood of a wagon wheel.

Spike went to follow up, to finish his kill, but Raiz stepped in. "Hold, Spike! This isn't you."

Behind him, the man groaned, head lolling from side to side. Spike issued another deep growl, but his vision was not fixed on his prey. Instead, he sauntered over towards the rear of the broken wagon. Raiz followed, positioning himself between the injured man and Spike.

He heard movement from within the wagon. Not the hard thumps of a man trying to escape, but a soft scratching of nail on wood. The wood had been cracked, and a gap had widened enough for Raiz to pull on.

Keeping one eye on Spike, he pulled hard on the plank of wood, ripping it free. Spike inched closer, head low to the ground like when he meant to protect Raiz. But this time the protection was not meant for him.

Three creatures as small as his hand stared out with yellow, reptilian eyes. They crawled on top of each other, barbed tails rattling as the prospect of escape became real. Spike poked his head through the gap, resting his snout on the wood as one of the creatures made to climb up it.

Raiz relaxed, drifting back towards the wounded man against the wagon. The driver issued a deep, cackling bout of laughter, blood spraying as he attempted to speak. "So… this is what… they become…" he said between laboured breaths. "Monsters. My… master will be pleased."

Raiz snapped into action, moving to where he lay and grabbing him by his blood-spattered shirt. "What are they? And who is your master?"

The man looked at him as if he were simple. "You stand here… master of the beast…" he paused to cough another gout of blood over Raiz's exposed wrist, "and you do not even recognise… their spawn."

Raiz paused, turning to take another look at the creatures as they jumped from the wagon and curled their tiny frames around Spike's giant foot.

"Prickets," he said, shifting back towards the dying man. "Are there more?" he asked, shaking his collar. "Are there more of them?"

The man smiled, jagged scar bending into a curve. "Many… more."

"Where are they?" Raiz demanded. "Where can I find them?"

He shook his collar again, though he more than most knew the face of a dead man. Blank, empty eyes stared back at him as the man Spike had mauled took his last breath, his knowledge dying with him.

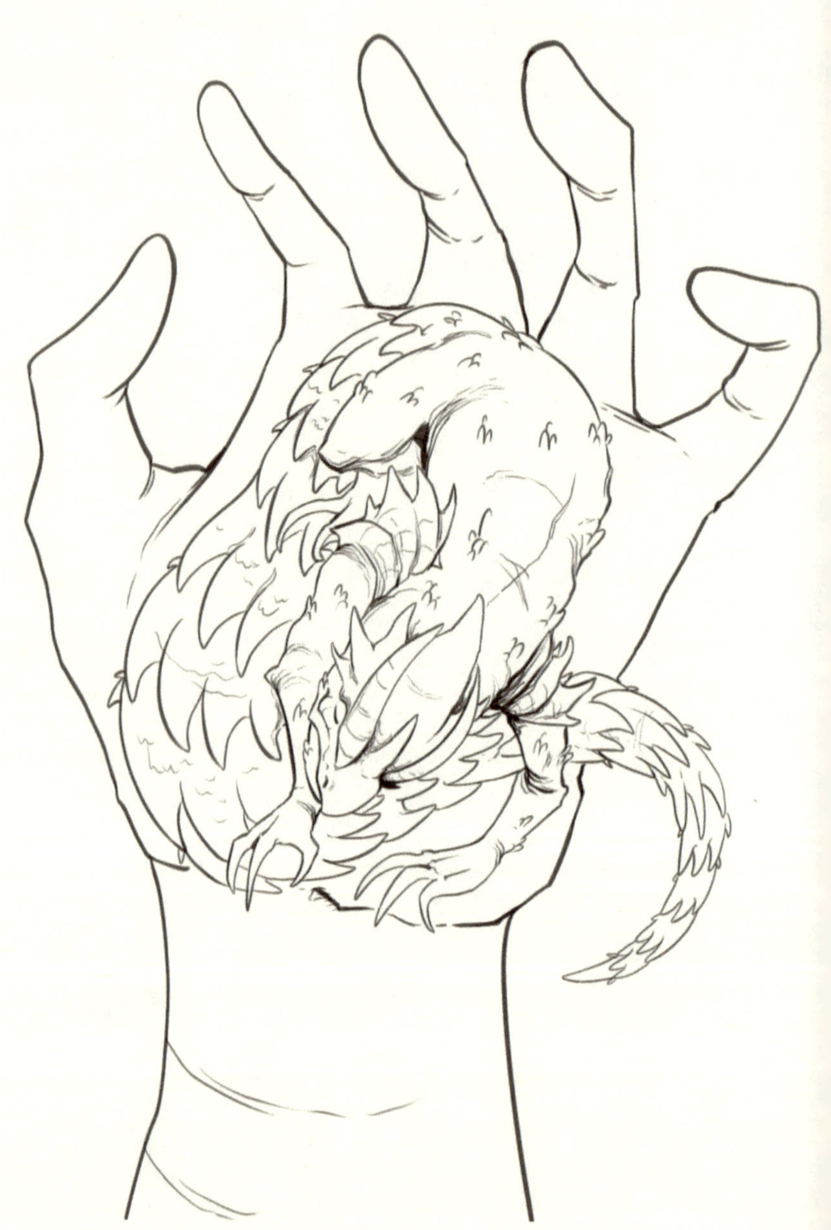

Chapter 16

- Zeek –

ZEEK ARCHED HIS BACK, mouth open, yearning for breath that would not come. He clenched his fists, urging the stolen power to fully integrate. It was too much. He had taken too much. The surge of energy was unbearable. He felt the warmth of his latest victim's Light flow through his veins, counteracting and fighting against all that he was. The two opposing forces clashed, locked in a battle against each other and rendering him trapped inside of their struggle.

He heard a voice to his right, his father's voice, though his words were incomprehensible. He tried to speak, to wrestle back control of his body, but the pain was too much.

It burned, *he* burned. This is what Father had warned him about, what the power of Zur did to his kind, why he'd had to stay hidden in his cave. It was excruciating.

Zeek refused to lose to the Light. There was too much still to see in this world, to discover. He'd only just begun his life, and would not forfeit it. He pushed against the pain, willing his stolen Light to cease, to temper. He felt the shadows within him begin to take hold, to overthrow the Light pulsing through his veins. They didn't diminish it, only stemmed its flow, directed its course. Instead of flaring wildly, it now steadied, even beginning to listen to him.

He relaxed slightly, his breath returning. He sucked in a deep lungful of fresh morning air and held out his palms. He wriggled his fingers, checking to see if his body still functioned as it should. "What… is happening to me?" he said, now fully aware of Father's presence beside him.

"You stole too much Light, killed the wrong target."

Zeek hesitated, recalling the night before. The sand. The sea. The man with the violet in his eye. And then another, shining even brighter. "I'm sorry," he managed to say. "I have failed you. I am a failure."

Father continued to observe him. He circled around. "You did well. And you have grown taller."

Zeek shifted, bemused. "I did — well? I do not understand. I killed the wrong man. The one you wanted is still out there."

"It does not matter. Your purpose was served. No longer will there be any thought of abandoning Shine."

"But that man, the prince from across the sea. Will he not come for us?"

"Us? No. But these lands, yes. He will come, and Zapour will be prepared, after they have finished battling each other."

"You mean to incite a war. Why, Father?"

Father grinned at him as if he were a child, which, in a way, he was. "War breeds strength. War heightens preparation. Zapour will need strength to face what is to come."

"And what is to come? What are you preparing them for?"

Father raised an exposed foot into the air, generating a globe of Shine as red as blood. He raised the ball to Zeek's chest, close enough for him to feel its sting. His shadow-tail reacted, ripping through his shirt as if it had a will of its own. It cut at his master, his father, but he was prepared. He danced to the side, disbanding the Shine and watching as Zeek's tail slithered back into the safety of his body.

"For you," Father said.

Zeek paled. He rubbed at his skin, squeezing it as if he could rip the shadows from his body and tear out that which had made him. "What am I?" he asked.

"You are both our saviour, and our extinction."

"Extinction?"

"Yes, that is what I seek to prevent. That is what I prepare for. What no one else knows is coming."

"Could you not just tell them? Convince them of what you know?"

Father shook his head. "Those in power no longer wish to believe in truth. For too long they have lived in naivety, clouded by their own bitter disputes, unable to recognise the true threat soon to be facing them. I know, because I was a part of this lie. I refused to believe what was right in front of me, what was taught to me from birth. But my mind has awakened. I have seen what lurks in the shadows. I have been to the Skae Queen's lair, know the truth of what they are. I have caught a glimpse of their plan, see it in my dreams. History will repeat itself. A second Darkening is coming. An eclipse to blot out the sun, your sun.

"You are not enough. I am not enough. Soon, all will know. Soon, all will fear them as they should be feared. I will prepare us. I will repair that which should never have been broken, and restore what Zur has given us." Father frowned, and for the first time Zeek saw true emotion cross his features.

"Why do you care?" Zeek asked.

"Hm?"

"Why do you care, about this?" Zeek continued, gesturing to the world around him. "From what I see you take no joy in what the world offers. You have no friends to call your own, no kin to draw support from. Why do you care for this world's fate? Perhaps humanity does not deserve to be here if this is how they see the world."

Father's body glowed a deep red, Shine surfacing as his rage piqued. Even though Zeek was now taller, Father seemed to tower above him, the overwhelming heat surrounding him like a physical presence. "Do not think you know me. You forget that I made you, turned you into who you are today. Do not judge what you do not know. I can just as quickly unmake you, should I choose it. Where have these thoughts come from?"

Zeek withered. He shrank, his shoulders drooping as the force with which his father spoke matched the power he radiated. "I — I am sorry, Father. I did not mean to…"

The heat surrounding him passed, the air returning to normal. Father took a deep breath, his glow all but gone. "You are young, foolish. There is much to life that you do not yet grasp. Perhaps you are right. I do not see the joy in this world that others might. But my goal is one of duty, not for myself, but for all. Zur has set me a task, and I intend to see it fulfilled.

"Do not question me again," Father continued. "You have given your word to obey me. Let this be a reminder of what it would mean to break that vow."

"Yes, Father," Zeek said, frustrated at himself for letting his curiosity get the best of him. Where had it come from? He hadn't thought this way before, had he?

Then it hit him, why he felt different now. How he had changed. It was his latest victim. It wasn't only his body that was morphing as a result of his consumption, his mind was changing too. Thoughts were creeping in, memories, emotions. Such strong emotions. They mixed, clashed with old affections. It made him think, consider. Who was he now?

He shifted back toward his Father. "Where is our next destination? Is there another sea to visit?"

"No, my child. Where we are going is far from the sea, but just as fascinating."

Zeek's dark eyes lit up.

Father turned– already moving. "We are going to Lumindal."

Chapter 17

– Isha –

THE NAUSEA WAS PERSISTENT, nagging at her insides. Several times she had nearly spilled her guts onto the wooden floorboards, which were damp beneath her bare feet. She couldn't even hold her hair back with her wrists tied by rope to a post.

A prisoner again.

She had sworn, sworn she would never put herself in a position like this again, that she would be blade that cut, not the flesh that was wounded. She had been fooling herself. She was no assassin, no killer, had only been playing at one.

She tried to spit to rid the taste of salt from her mouth, but came up dry. Her eyes swelled, filling with tears she hadn't yet had the chance to shed.

Dazen was gone…

Her brother. Her friend. Her family. Gone. Dead because she had not seen through such trickery. She hated him, this man from across the sea, would never forgive him for what he had done. She cursed the day Dazen had agreed to meet with him, and blamed herself for not stopping him. She would kill him. On her life, she would avenge the loss of her kin.

Anger raged relentlessly inside of her, burning like a furnace that could not be quenched.

Her fury mixed with guilt as she remembered her capture, remembered Puk. She looked around. Nothing. He was not there, she was alone. Was he dead? Had he been murdered in her pursuit of vengeance? She wouldn't be able to forgive herself if that was so. She bit hard into her lip, enough to draw blood.

Is this how Raiz had felt all those years ago? Had he been carrying this guilt his entire life? This desperate yearning to correct a mistake foolishly made? She wondered where Raiz was now, how he would react to Dazen's death and her capture. How could she have done this to him again?

A noise from outside broke her thoughts. She tugged at the rope, wrists burning, but it was no use. Footsteps sounded, voices murmured. She could only just hear what was being said.

"Do not be a fool!" a voice said. Female.

The footsteps stopped short of the wooden door. "Leave me be, Sounja."

"You are wounded, my prince. That bitch is insane. We should have slit her throat and dumped her overboard when we had the chance."

"Now who is acting the fool?" a voice replied. "She is a princess. Her death would mean all-out war."

"A war began the moment she came at you with a knife."

"She thought I had murdered her brother. That changes nothing. She tried once and she will try again."

The door cracked open and sunlight streamed through, the light blinding her even as she pretended to play dead, hoping he would come close enough to strike at.

She quashed the thought, however. If she hadn't bested him with two hands, what hope did she have with none? No, she would bide her time. She was good at waiting, had spent her whole life patiently watching.

Instead, she stood up, projecting strength into her posture and setting her face into a fierce glare. The Sun Prince entered, followed by the red-haired woman. Violet met violet in a stare that in her mind seemed eternal.

"I will kill you for what you have done," she said, her voice calm, powerful.

The man who called himself the Sun Prince remained still, tranquil. He did not look smug, nor did he look particularly remorseful. He simply stood there, staring. Long, black hair flowed to his shoulders in a wave, contrasting the brightness of his eyes. He was tall and slender, yet muscular. His features were well defined. He walked towards her, his steps elegant. He walked as though he were a god, hips swaying and head tilting as if his word was law.

He studied her, and Isha's attention was drawn to the bandage covering his otherwise bare shoulder. Memories of Puk's blade striking his flesh rose to the surface, her lips twisting in a satisfactory smirk.

Behind him, Sounja snarled. "You dare!" she snapped, making to brush past her prince, fist raised.

She was blocked by an outstretched arm. "No!" said the prince.

Sounja froze, her face twitching with frustration.

"Why am I here?" Isha said. "Am I your bargaining chip? I will not be used, I refuse. If that is your intention, then kill me now." The words were out of her mouth before she even realised what she was saying, but she held firm, rage gifting her strength.

A hint of agitation touched the prince's brow. He took half a step forward, hand outstretched. For a moment, Isha thought he might do as she bid and end her suffering, but there was no knife, only an open palm. He took her chin and lifted her head until their eyes clashed once more.

"I did not kill your brother," the Sun Prince said. "Despite what you think you saw."

For longer than she would have liked, she stared at him, caught in his gaze. Then she remembered the violet spark in Dazen's eyes the night before he was taken from this world. The delusion he'd been under, the spell that had gripped his mind.

She shook her head free of his soft grip. "You lie!" she shouted. "You are nothing but a fraud playing at being a prince. I don't know what kind of magic you hold, but it won't work on me. I know what I saw, and I know what you are."

The Sun Prince looked taken aback. He flinched as if he had been struck, his mouth ajar. He sauntered back to where the red-haired woman stood, her glare unfaltering.

"You see," Sounja said. "This is pointless. She cannot be convinced of the truth. We should throw her over the edge and be done with her. Let the sea decide her fate."

Isha recoiled at the thought of being tossed into the wide sea. She didn't want to die, despite what she had said, but she would rather die than be subject to another man's will. If that was to be her fate, then perhaps she should take her chances with the sea.

"Noone will die today," the Sun Prince said. "We will reach Yagos soon. Her fate can be decided there. In the meantime, I want her fed and cared for."

"My prince, you cannot be ser—"

"Am I clear?" he said, voice firm, yet gentle.

"Yes, my prince."

"Good." He turned back to Isha. "I know you do not see it now. I do not blame you for it. But you do not know me as you think you do. I did not kill your brother, and I do not want a war."

"If you did not kill him, then who did?" Isha questioned.

The prince frowned, as if the memory pained him. His hesitation was confirmation enough for Isha.

"You are a liar. I know what a liar looks like, sounds like. I have been in a den with them my entire life. You are one and the same, no better than one of the King-Radiant's Eagles. I hope you meet with the same fate."

True rage flickered then in the prince's gaze, burning brighter even than Isha's own. He thrust an arm downward. "Do not compare me to them! I am nothing like those puppets."

Isha flinched, taken aback by his sudden outburst. The prince seemed even more shocked, disturbed by his own loss of composure. He straightened, let out a slow breath, and re-focused. "Get some rest," he said. "We shall talk again tomorrow. Until then, take the time to grieve."

With that, the Sun Prince left her, Sounja following his heels. She turned briefly to offer one last bite. "Sleep well, Princess. Let us see how you fare away from a life of being coddled and pampered."

With that, she left, closing the door behind her. Darkness consumed Isha, though this time she welcomed it, glad to be rid of their presence.

Coddled and pampered… if only they knew.

Chapter 18

- Raiz –

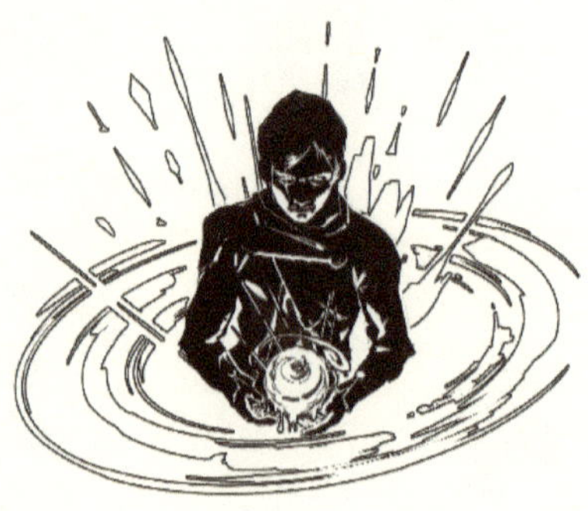

SPIKE FLEW LOW TO THE GROUND, despite Raiz urging him to fly higher. He knew why, the reason was next to him, wriggling around in his saddlebag. Raiz placed a cautious hand atop the leather cover, checking for the tenth time that it was fastened securely onto Spike's side.

Prickets were a rare sighting. To find three of them in the possession of soldiers of Kogon was no coincidence. Eve, a healer from Illidor, along with her husband, Deryn, were the only people Raiz knew who bred them. They were very protective of their secrets, so much so that Raiz didn't even know how prickets reproduced, nor if they currently even had any more tucked away. The couple had taken a significant interest in Spike over the past two years, marvelling at his rapid growth and pleading with Raiz to allow them to study him, to reproduce what he was. But Spike was no subject to be experimented on.

While Raiz was busy pondering the concept of pricket reproductive organs, a burst of Light rose into the sky in the near distance, jetting in a horizontal arc. Raiz cocked his head. Spike followed the Light, drawn to its source.

Spike rounded a crop of trees, beating his great wings as he pulled up and landed on a ridge overlooking a small farming town on the outskirts of Veka, Kogon's capital.

Another beam spiralled directionless through the air. The Light was followed by a scream — or rather a screech. It was inhuman, the sound akin to that of a wounded animal. Spike snarled, baring his teeth as he crept closer to the edge of the ridge.

Raiz followed the sound, Zur's glare obscuring his view. He slid down the slope to get a better look, Spike following. They came to the edge of an open paddock, hiding beneath the last bit of tree cover.

Raiz stopped and stared. He refused to look away from the scene that was playing out before him, despite its brutality. Soldiers were everywhere, men in full plate armour that bore the raging bull crest of Kogon. Their brown sashes coloured the landscape. The sun was out in a cloudless sky today, and Raiz watched in disbelief as captive men and women, half naked and shackled, were forced by the soldiers to expend their Shine. The sun beat down, gifting them strength even as they used it.

Chains rattled. Raiz tensed as an animalistic cry ripped through the air and pierced his soul. A creature bucked and kicked at a cage. He knew this creature, it was Spike — only it wasn't. It was Spike as he had been a few years ago, a pricket the size of a large hound. Its jaw snapped wildly in the few inches it had available through the chains that tightly bound it. Its scaled hide was weathered and covered with dozens of lacerations. Frantic yellow eyes darted in every direction, full of hatred.

White-light poured into the cage from all angles, striking the pricket and seeping into its hide. There was so much Shine…

The beast was in pain. Prickets fed on Shine, Raiz knew that, but this was different. This was too much. They were force-feeding it to drive unnatural growth.

Raiz's instinct was to react, to barge in and tear them all to shreds. It was barbaric, inhumane, but as he moved, he felt his own pain rise to the surface, reminding him of the burns yet to heal.

He broadened his view, aghast to see similar scenes unfolding across the open plain of the paddock. How many did they have? To what purpose could they possibly be inflicting such harm?

Raiz placed a hand in his saddlebag, checking to see if the rescued prickets were still there. One bit at his finger playfully, and brushed a wet tongue against his wounded skin, just like Spike used to do.

Meanwhile, Spike bent his legs and unfurled his wings, ready to pounce.

"Hold boy!" Raiz said, despite his urge to set him loose.

Spike steadied, teeth bared, barbed tail vibrating with anticipation. Raiz opened the bag and allowed one of the tiny prickets to creep onto his hand. Spike stalled, razor-like pupils shifting from the captives back to the baby in his possession.

The captive prickets below grew even more agitated, the closest one throwing its weight against its cage, bending the metal bars that held it in. Soldiers of Veka reacted, thrusting a row of blunted spears tipped with fire through the gaps, pushing the growing beast back to the centre as others tightened the chains holding it down.

"It knows we're here," Raiz said. "We need to leave. They'll come searching." His words were met with a protest as Spike snapped towards him, teeth crunching the air a mere inch from his face.

Raiz grit his own teeth and clenched a white-knuckled fist. He hated the thought of leaving them here to suffer this fate, but he was weak, and they numbered too many. Perhaps he could have taken them at his best, with Spike's help, but even then, they also had Shine users. Men and women just as capable of harnessing Zur's Light as he. There was no sense attacking now, it would only lead to a quick death and a shallow grave.

He turned to leave, to take Spike and usher the young prickets he could protect to safety, when a branch snapped behind him. A crossbow bolt zipped past his head, and Spike howled as it struck hard into the muscle of his right wing.

Raiz reacted instantly, brandishing his hidden dagger and throwing it in the direction the bolt had come from. He heard its impact, a man's last breath gurgling just beyond his vision. He went to summon his Shine, but the pain was too much. The pricket he had taken from his bag pricked at his skin, itching to get at the Shine bubbling underneath. He took it in his other hand and placed it in the pocket of his tattered cloak.

Spike reared, angered by the torture of his kind and enraged by the bolt in his hide. He lashed out at a tree near where the bolt had flown from, the force of the blow snapping wood. Bark and branches flew through the air as more figures emerged.

Initially, they reacted as any sane person would at a raging Dragon lashing out at them, they cowered, but then they circled. Two, three, then soon six or seven more appeared, surrounding Spike and Raiz, weapons raised. All bore the crest of a raging bull on their breast.

Raiz ducked as more bolts whizzed past him. One clipped his belt, slicing into the leather. Spike's tail came full circle, its barbed point crashing into the plate of the closest assailant, crushing steel and bone to leave them breathless. Then he whipped it around sweeping the legs of another, the sharpened barb cutting into the flesh behind the kneecap.

One of Kogon's soldiers threw a looped rope, catching Spike around the neck. He pulled it tight, tying it to a thick tree. Spike went to sever the bind with his talons, but another man threw a large net over his wing, and his restricted movements sent him tumbling sideways.

Another rope caught Spike's leg, which yanked him in a different direction. Raiz went to help, to cut him free, but a man stood in his way. Hefting a heavy mace, the man swung at him with experienced precision.

Raiz ducked, his concern only for Spike. His companion cried out as the point of a spear ran through his thick leg. The one who had thrown the spear soon paid the price, Spike's tail again whipping into motion and catching him unaware. But the damage was done. Spike staggered, falling to the ground in a tangle of rope and net.

Raw emotion poured through Raiz then, overthrowing thought and sense. His Shine lit like a brazier within him. His body convulsed, the pain numbing as he spread his Shine over his entire body. His skin glowed a deep crimson, emitting a bright light that blinded the man with the mace. To his surprise, it didn't hurt. His Shine wasn't being released, instead it became him. He remembered this feeling, he'd done this before when fighting his brother, then again in Lumindal.

Dazen had called it the Flare.

Soldiers stumbled around him. The man with the mace dropped it, falling to his knees as if some invisible weight was pushing him down. Raiz took a calm step forward, picked up the mace, then looked to the man. He was struggling for air, as if the ability to breathe had been stripped from him. Raiz felt no sympathy. This man deserved to die. He swung the mace, watching as metal met flesh and bone. The result of the impact was immediate, the soldier's body collapsing to the grassy soil.

Others were like he had been, frozen in the bubble of Raiz's projected Shine. Some were stronger, reaching for fallen weapons even as their own muscles worked against them. Raiz didn't share in their struggle. He moved from soldier to soldier, swinging his stolen mace. He knew it would pain him later, that he was surrendering to his inner monster, but in this moment he didn't care.

One after another, men and women fell to the blunt ball of metal, unable to defend themselves. It served them right. They had earned this death. They had hurt his friend.

When it was over, Raiz released his hold on his Shine. He stumbled forwards, the toll more mental than physical. His mind was a fog. He tried to shake it clear, but someone was calling for him. It was Spike. He picked up a dead woman's sword and used it to cut the ropes binding his friend.

Spike rose, his neck swinging wildly as his survival instincts told him danger was still present. He calmed somewhat when he saw Raiz, who made for his side, opening the saddlebag to see that the two baby Prickets were still safe. He reached for his pocket and placed the third one back with his siblings. "Can you fly, boy?" he asked.

Spike shook the last rope from his body, standing tall, wings spreading out wide. The shaft of the crossbow bolt stuck out from his right wing. Raiz wasted no time pulling it out. Spike yelped, flinching away from his touch. Raiz called upon his Shine, just a little, fighting through the pain. He placed his Shine-infused hand on the wound, watching as the sun god's magic seemed to heal it, not fully, but enough to stem the flow of blood.

Raiz leapt up on Spike's back and kicked him into motion. More soldiers were approaching, their voices echoing through the wood, but Spike was off. Arrows followed, spiralling past as ground again gave way to open air.

Spike beat his wings, lifting them higher and higher into the blue sky, and Raiz took a deep breath, suddenly feeling the many sleepless nights. He spared a look below, and what he saw troubled him.

The city of Veka spread out as wide as he could see below him, but what could be seen on the outskirts of the city was what caught his eye. Thousands of soldiers dotted the horizon, armoured for battle, congregating.

Kogon was preparing for war.

Chapter 19

- Zeek –

ZEEK WAS BECOMING more and more human by the day, both in physical appearance, and in the way he processed the world. Where before everything had seemed simple, now it was complex. His latest kill had changed him, was still changing him. He felt his mind expanding. What once was an idle lake had now become a raging sea of information and knowledge. It was almost impossible to access all of it, to process an entire lived life in the space of a few days, but pieces were coming to him, bits of information about who this person was, and what he had been able to do.

Zeek found his moods changing rapidly as he examined the man he had come to know as Dazen. A profound sense of loss hit him like a breaking wave as he stumbled upon the memory of his daughter — of *Dazen's* daughter. Images of the child suddenly came to him in vivid flashes. Such powerful emotions coursed through him then, almost sending him teetering off balance as he followed his father down the winding pathway towards their destination.

These emotions were different to when he had taken Ancel's life. Ancel's heart had been tainted by hatred and cruelty. Dazen's was full of care and love. The two clashed, battling with one another, each trying to influence Zeek's own emotions, his personality. Zeek had killed before, but these two were different. Their Light also filled him, fuelled him. He could feel their power, their strength. It was his now, to use as he wished.

"How much further?" he asked.

Father had been silent for most of the journey east, but Zeek didn't mind. He'd used the time to observe, to examine. Every branch passed, every animal met, was a new experience.

"The City of Light is not far. You will see it on the horizon soon enough."

Zeek knew more about the man his father was now. Dazen knew him. Not personally, but snippets of information steadily crept through about the type of man he was. Revered, scorned, and misunderstood all in one. Ancel had told a different story. One of power — immeasurable power. A picture of who Father used to be came to the forefront of his mind, of who he was before he lost the use of his arms. The King-Radiant, ruler of Zapour. His red Shine flared brighter than Zeek had ever seen. The image came and went in a flash, however, Ancel's memory of him in such a state fleeting.

"Zeek!" he heard someone call, snapping him back to attention sometime down the road. "We're here," Father said.

Zeek looked up, eyes widening as the clearing opened. The City of Light was on the horizon. Great towers spiralled into the air, taller than he could have imagined. Before this, he had lived his whole life in a cave. Now he had seen the sea, seen what nature offered, seen the forests, even seen the mountains, but never had he seen civilisation. The incredible feats humans were capable of creating amazed him. Such structure, such design.

He moved closer, following Father's heels until the shadow of the city loomed over him. One colossal tower stood taller than all the others, despite being shattered about three quarters of the way up. People were up there, surrounding it with ropes, bricks and metal. It was as if it had imploded and was now being remade. Many other towers stood tall around it, spiking sharply into the sky, their tips white as sleet.

"You used to rule here," Zeek said, the words leaving his lips before he had the sense to hold them shut.

Father glared at him. "Be careful which memories you choose to believe. The perspectives of those whose knowledge you draw from are skewed. They see but one side of a many-faced die. Best you frame your own mind, form your own perspective."

Zeek nodded. "Yes, Father."

Father leant in close, his breath warm on Zeek's cheek. "You must be careful here. Lumindal is now under the control of Gelvard, ruler of Craw. He will be in a mood, likely distraught, and searching for his son."

Father followed his remark with a sly smile, which stretched higher into his cheeks as he watched Zeek's mind process the information.

"I killed his son!" Zeek almost yelled.

"Quiet! Do not give anything away. If he should recognise him in you, then our purpose here will be voided. I need Gelvard alive, for now."

Zeek closed his mouth, obeying. Such brutality, to treat with a man whose son he'd recently had murdered — whom *he* had murdered. But who was he to ponder morality. He was a killer, responsible for taking many fathers from their children. He could not question the motives of a man like Father when he himself was just as bad.

Two iron-clad doors swung open. An array of men carrying red banners poured out to greet them. They surrounded the pair, lowering spears twice the size of a grown man to point at them.

Father stood unafraid, not bothering to defend himself. The soldiers were silent, their hardened faces menacing. Zeek spun, pressing his back to Father's. His shadow-tail began to unfurl, stopped only by a shake from Father's head. It crept back into his body, safe behind the confines of his skin and clothes.

The footsteps ceased, replaced by a stretching silence, then more movement as soldiers parted to let one man through. Instead of the plated mail of those surrounding him, this man wore a neatly trimmed uniform. His features were thin and gangly, made proper only by his courtly posture and the authority which he seemed to rightfully carry. His hair was short, slicked back and tied into a knot.

The man must have noticed his glare, for a thick vein appeared on the brow of his reddening face. He settled his gaze upon Father before gulping a stone sized lump down his scrawny throat.

"Back again so soon?" the man in uniform said. "And I see you have brought a pet this time. Carry your books for you, does he?"

Father did not retaliate, though Zeek nearly did, wanting

to tear this man's throat out for talking about his father the way he had. He stopped himself, remembering Father's words of caution.

"I have no time to tolerate your inflated ego today, Yvain. Take me to Gelvard, I have business to discuss with him," Father said.

The man named Yvain narrowed his eyes. "You are no longer the master here, Urion! You do as I say! As I command."

Father took a small step forward, and Zeek watched with fascination as Yvain took three steps back in response.

Father smiled.

Yvain struggled to regain his composure. "You are not welcome here. Please leave."

"Take me to see Gelvard, or you will find out once and for all whether there is Radiance left in my veins."

Father accompanied his words with a small burst of Shine, a projection only, but it was enough to send Yvain shuffling away. The gate opened to allow them passage, and Father padded forward, walking through the guard as if he had not just scared the living daylights out of the lot of them.

Zeek couldn't help but stare in awe at the sheer size of the open city. Luminescence seemed to dance from corner to corner, cast by hundreds of shimmering globes of Shine, though these shone a bright white in contrast to the red hue he was used to in his old home.

Great white buildings rose from the ground, human-made and unnatural. They seemed to only get taller and wider the further they went into the city. And the people, so many people. Every instinct was screaming at him to hide, to vanish from sight, telling him he did not belong here. He was not human. He wondered if they knew. Were their stares directed at him because they could tell what he was? What he could do to them?

His shadow-tail began to throb from his back. It vibrated with distrust. It wanted to kill, could sense its next feed, but it was also scared, as if it knew that Zeek did not belong there, that the city was a poison.

He pressed it back into his body, straining at the exertion. Eventually, Yvain led them to the very centre of the city. Zeek looked up – it was all there was to do. His path was blocked by a large mound, from which rose a string of spiked towers that stretched into the sky like giant fingers.

His stolen memories held nothing but disdain for this place, both Dazen and Ancel sharing their displeasure with him, and yet Zeek could do nothing but marvel.

"Wait here," Yvain said before instructing another two dozen or so guards to keep a close eye on them.

They waited for what seemed like forever. His Father's patience wore thin, but Zeek didn't mind. He climbed up to a vantage point and stared out into the city, watching with interest at how humans made their living in such a place. Four guards followed him vigilantly, with stony expressions. Zeek issued them a mock smile, but it must have come out distorted, for two of the guards flinched, reaching for the blades at their hips.

Thankfully, before anything could happen, Yvain returned, muttering something beneath his breath. He raised his head in mock glee as he approached his former master. "Right this way," he said.

Father huffed an amused sigh. "Thank you, Yvain, for leading me through my own hold."

"Ah, but it is no longer yours to claim, is it?" he said in retaliation, though his pace slightly quickened.

Zeek followed him up the spiral staircase that was carved into the stone mound and entered the base of one of the vertical structures.

Zeek was expecting the room to be dark and damp, like the inside of a cave. That was all he knew. Besides a small house, he had never been inside of a building crafted by humans. What he saw now was quite a contrast. Replacing the moss-covered walls were large portraits, paintings of other humans and things he did not quite understand. Enormous banners were draped across the walkway, woven with coloured thread and designed with an artistry that spoke of years of practice. Zeek didn't understand it, how humans had so much time on their hands to make such things as this. To him, life was short, primitive. He was a small child in the lifespan of a human, though with each new lifeforce he stole, he was becoming more and more like them. Perhaps he would be an artist one day, weaving threads and creating paintings of his own. His heart skipped at the thought.

His attention was diverted as they came to a stop outside twin stone figures in the shape of eagles. They seemed to stare back at him, their fierce eyes unwavering in their stillness. Father walked between them into some kind of contraption. Zeek followed, he always followed, and a door closed behind them.

He nearly lost his footing as the floor began to move. He widened his stance, steadying himself, expecting an attack, but none came. When the door re-opened, a new setting greeted him on the other side. High, ornamented windows showed him that he was now high up above the city. The contraption had somehow transported them into the sky, to the top of one of the towering structures! Zeek took a cautious step outside, not currently trusting his instincts.

A long red carpet ran from one end of the room to the other. Guards flanked each wall, while attendants busied themselves in the background. There was a raised dais at the end of the carpet. Sitting atop of this was a simple-looking throne holding a heavyset man. A platter of food was set on the table before him, though it was quickly disappearing.

The man on the throne grumbled at Father's appearance, mumbling something to an attendant through a mouthful of roast beef. He kept eating, leaving them both with nothing to do but watch. Eventually, he pushed his plate to the middle of the table, taking one last sip from his goblet of wine before burping and turning his attention towards them. He grinned, his toothy smile clearly an insult.

"How times have changed," he said, sitting higher in his throne. "How does it feel, to be down there?"

Father ignored him, though his gaze did not falter.

"I destroyed your old throne, you know," the man continued, gesturing to a white puddle of once-solidified Light to his right.

"If you wish to replace me, Gelvard, you will fail," Father said. "Only the bloodline of Gallion may claim the title of King-Radiant."

"Bah! I do not wish to replace you, nor your Shine-crazed son. A King-Radiant is no longer needed in Zapour. I will create a new order, under new leadership."

"For someone who does not want the title, you sound an awful lot like my Shine-crazed son."

"Nonsense!" Gelvard bellowed. "Evanon was ambitious,

I'll give him that, but he was also foolish. He reached for too much, thinking all could be controlled. The Kingdoms of Zapour have grown powerful, both in populace and with Shine. Trost cannot be controlled, and the Kingdom of Zuton follows Trost's lead like a lost dog. Now Wisha has come out of hiding. Did you think I would sit idle while those around me plot and scheme? I hold Lumindal now, and with it the pillar of Zapour."

"Lumindal is nothing without the Last Light," Father replied.

Again, Gelvard issued a toothy grin. He motioned to one of his personal guards, a man in gold-plated armour carrying a lengthy halberd. The guard departed, sliding through a door to the side of the dais. "Much has changed in your absence, Urion, and yet much has remained the same. The Golden Talon are mine to control, their allegiance bought and paid for with my coin. But you are right, Lumindal is nothing without the Last Light."

As he spoke, the guard returned, carrying beneath his arm a scrawny man in tattered clothing. His wrists were bound in metal cuffs, face covered in dirt, hair a tangled mess.

"Put me down you brute! Do you know who I am? What I am capable of?" he said, kicking and screaming. "I will have you flayed. I will have you burned at the stake and —"

He paused as his eyes met Father's.

"Urion? I thought you dead."

Father sighed. "Salador."

Gelvard laughed, a deep bellow of a laugh that came from his belly. "Can you believe it? A single Eagle survived the devil child's slaughter, and it was the one Eagle I needed. Salador is the key to the return of the Last Light. He alone knows the secrets to its reparations, and he is my slave."

Beside Zeek, Father remained impassive. "If this man has told you the truth, then you will know that only the blood of a Radiant can harness the power of the Last Light."

Gelvard's grin faded, though he kept his composure. "So it would seem. Though lying comes as easily to the two of you as drinking wine does to me. Why should I believe you?"

"You are welcome to try it yourself, once the tower is rebuilt," Father said. "I will count the pieces of you scattered across Zapour when you are finished."

Gelvard raised an unkempt eyebrow and grunted. "So, I am to trust you, the former King-Radiant, to use the weapon for me if the time should come."

"You have no choice."

"Luckily, trust is not something I need, for you know what I hold against you. What prisoner I have in my possession."

Zeek watched, expecting to see some kind of reaction from his father, but he remained still, focused.

"Is Sephare unharmed?" he said after a moment.

"She is," Gelvard replied. "Your wife is safe, for now."

"Then we are in agreement. I shall direct the weapon for you, and in return, you keep her safe."

The King of Craw let out a low, distrustful grumble, but nodded. "You had best not stray too far, Urion. If my enemies do indeed join with this prince from across the sea, then I will have use of you sooner rather than later."

"Yet another problem I have already taken care of for you."

"What do you mean?"

Father straightened. "The King of Trost is dead, the Sun Prince blamed for it. Zeek here took care of it," he said, gesturing towards him.

Genuine surprise crossed the king's features as his gaze drifted to Zeek. He paused, and for a moment Zeek thought he had been found out. His eyes lingered, staring through him as if he were a ghost. He leaned closer, and it was only then that Zeek could see through Gelvard's façade, catching a glimpse of the despair hidden beneath it. His eyes were heavy, full of tears not yet shed. The fate of his son was yet unknown, though surely he had come to the conclusion that his return was unlikely.

"Who is this man, to so lightly kill one of the six kings of Zapour?" Gelvard asked, recovering himself.

"He acts as the hands that I have lost. He did this deed upon my command. There will likely now be war between Zapour and Yagos."

Gelvard turned red, his fist slamming on the oaken table. "A war Craw will be caught between! Or have you forgotten whose lands lie on the coast?"

"A war was coming whether you liked it or not. Now you have one king dead and two enemies pitted against each other. I would say the odds are heavily in your favour, and from what I remember, you are good at stabbing people while their backs are turned."

Gelvard's eyes narrowed as he cracked his knuckles, but he said nothing.

"Remember our bargain," Father continued. "And when the war is won, try to remember who the real enemy is."

"Again with this Skae business," Gelvard huffed. "They are a fairy tale, a myth. They do not exist. I will not focus my forces on the imagination of a madman."

Father turned, not even bothering to defend himself. "There will come a time when you eat those words, Gelvard. I hope your stomach is not too full when it does."

Gelvard bellowed something in retort, but Zeek was already on his father's heels, following him out of the chamber and back down the contraption that turned sky into ground.

Chapter 20

- Isha -

SLEEP ELUDED HER. The constant back and forth of the ship's momentum made it difficult. She felt empty, consumed by grief. Her thoughts churned along with the raging sea beneath them.

She had to figure out a way to free herself from here, had to hold hope that her brother's fleet was hot on her trail. If the Sun Prince's vessel reached the shores of Yagos first, there was little they could do for her.

She couldn't let that happen. She had to free herself. She'd learned the hard way not to rely on others, on luck. If she wanted to be free, then she had to make it happen herself.

But she didn't just want to be free. She wanted revenge. Wanted justice. He had to pay for Dazen's death. She would make him pay. But how?

The door inched open. In came a serving boy. He refilled her water, and hesitantly moved to feed her some recently cooked fish. The last time he'd tried she had refused, nearly biting his hand off. This time he was more cautious, standing a few feet away and offering his hand.

Isha nodded. "I won't refuse," she said. "You have my word."

The serving boy had to be no older than ten. He took a step closer. Isha opened her mouth and took the food without complaint, chewing softly and relishing the rise in her strength. "What's your name?" she said after she gulped it down.

"My name?" the serving boy said.

Isha nodded, feigning innocence.

"My name is Cole," he said, unable to turn his hazel eyes away from her own.

"Well Cole," she said. "I need your help."

The boy just stood there, fascinated.

Isha held her leer. Before, she had always avoided eye contact, hiding who she was from anyone and everyone. This time she locked onto him. She didn't know what she was doing, not really, but it seemed like it was working.

"These bonds," she said. "They're too restrictive. Can you loosen them for me?"

The boy's head turned to the side, but his eyes were still on her. "I — I'm not supposed to do that," he said.

Isha took a steadying breath. "It's okay, Cole. I'm your friend." She focused on each word, putting effort, power, into each syllable. She had never tried this before, not completely. She had only ever seen her eyes as something to hide, but after watching the Sun Prince influence her brother so effortlessly, she wondered if it was something she too was capable of.

"You can help me," she said. She opened her hands, angling them around the post and showing the knot to him. He took her hands in his own, his body close enough for her to strangle.

She dismissed the thought as soon as it came. She would not harm a child, not even if it meant losing her freedom. Cole plucked at the knot as if he were in a trance, working slim fingers through the grooves until it loosened enough for him to pull it through.

Isha tried to mask her surprise. She hadn't expected this to work. She felt relief around her wrists as the rope fell away. She curled and uncurled her hands, itching to use them to avenge her lost brother.

"Stay here," she suggested to the boy — no, she ordered it. He nodded, and Isha knew he would stay.

She moved for the sliver of light, pressing her weight against the door. Looking out, she breathed a sigh of relief. There were no guards. She crept out onto the deck, swaying as the sea rocked her back and forth. Broadening her view, she recalled the layout of the ship from when she was dragged across its surface and thrown into the hold. If there was one skill she had in spades, it was remembering details. It had helped her escape the clutches of Lumindal, and it would help her here. As she followed the path, a pair of deep throated voices sounded above her, and she clung to the wall to hide herself as best she could.

Wood creaked as a heavy foot pressed on the surface mere inches above her. She held her breath, waiting for the voice and the pressure above to disappear.

"I count six to our three," the voice said.

"We've won against worse," came a reply. "Besides, the prince won't let us down. These are our waters, ain't no one better at sailing the open sea."

Isha turned her head to the rear of the ship. A spark of hope flared in her chest as she spotted her brother's ships — white swords pitched in the middle of blue sails. They were still distant, small dots on the horizon, but they were there. Coming for her, for Dazen.

The ships were enough to spur her on. She shuffled away from those above, keeping her body pressed to the wood. She reached the end of the wall and crouched behind the bulk of a barrel. The rear-deck was filled with the Sun Prince's crew. She looked to the railing. All she had to do was jump over. Perhaps she would fall into the path of the friendly ships. It was a chance, maybe the only one she had.

She braced to leap off the edge and into the Sapphire Sea below, but something held her back. It wasn't enough. Part of her wanted to jump. It was the sensible thing to do. But there was something about the prince. He was like her. He might hold the answer to what she was, to who she was. Yet he deserved to die. And then there was Puk to think about. She couldn't abandon him, not here, not ever. She battled with herself, wrestling with indecision. In the end, one emotion triumphed above all others. Rage.

Her brother's body was barely cold, and the man responsible was here, within her reach. Gone was the thought of a warm bed and blanket. Gone was her fleeting desire to seek out who she was. It was replaced by a single, overwhelming need for revenge, for justice. She was more than she used to be. She may not be as skilled with a blade as someone like Veil had been, but what she did have was opportunity and surprise. She could kill him, close the distance and do to him what he had done to her brother. She didn't want freedom. She wanted the one responsible for her brother's death to pay, to suffer as she did, as all of Trost did.

She spotted the man responsible, his back to her as he stood at the stern. She could make it there unseen. Puk was with him, hands tied behind his back. He looked sad but did not seem to be harmed. She searched for a weapon, a tool capable of dealing death. She didn't have to look far. The deck was full of them.

Sailors worked, pulling at ropes, fastening knots, some shouting orders and others rushing to obey them. She watched as one of the men threw a splintered piece of wood into a pile — likely part of a mast that had snapped. Her eyes narrowed. She waited. The dots on the horizon closed, heightening the sailors' readiness and drawing their eye eastward.

Isha took her opportunity. She didn't sprint, knowing fast movement would draw attention. She walked over to the pile of splintered wood, grabbing the sharpest piece she could see and tucking it beneath the confines of her shirt.

Anxiety mixed with fear as she walked out onto the open deck. She made it halfway across without being noticed, keeping her head low and her feet moving. She could see the fur trim of the Sun Prince's woollen cloak. It wrapped around him as the breeze swept over the boat.

Her fingers itched with fury, her heart missing a piece that nothing could ever fill. Only the thought of vengeance held her steady. Stab the prince, free Puk, jump off the back of the ship. That was her plan.

She heard someone shout from the side, but didn't dare to look. It spurred her on, turning her walk into a sprint. She was close, close enough to draw the makeshift stake back in preparation for the killing blow.

Though her voice was silent, inside she growled. She thrust with all her might, plunging the wood right towards the heart, just as Puk had taught her. Tears streamed from wind-blown eyes. This was for Trost. This was for Dazen. This was for herself.

The wood stopped an inch away from the Sun Prince's back. A thick hand gripped her wrist. Stunned, Isha looked up to see steely eyes over a boulder-like nose. Metal armour clinked as she was lifted into the air, the behemoth of a man handling her as if she were a toy. His grip tightened around her wrist and the wood slipped from her fingers, falling uselessly to the deck.

The Sun Prince turned. Etched on his face was not surprise, but the same knowing look Raiz used to give her when he pretended to catch her at the last moment as she followed him. She swung her free arm. How dare he look at her like that. How dare he mock her. She kicked at him, surprised that her boot actually landed on his chest, not that it had any effect.

"Put her down, Abhick," the Sun Prince said. The brute did as he was bid, her feet again touching something solid, though his grip on her wrist did not soften. "You are stronger than I thought, to have come so close," he continued. "Tell me, how did you free yourself?"

Isha said nothing, just writhed against her captor, teeth bared into a snarl.

"It was Cole, wasn't it. Tell me, is he dead?"

The mention of the boy's name shocked her from her rage. "I do not spill the blood of the innocent, only the guilty. I am not like you."

If her comments offended him, he didn't show it. "You swayed him, didn't you," he said, more as a statement than a question. "With your eyes."

As he spoke those last three words his eyes locked onto hers. There was something powerful about them. They were like a deep well, hiding an impossible treasure that no one could ever reach.

A wave of guilt struck her. The thought of using a child in the way she had sat ill in her stomach. But the child was alive. He was unharmed.

"I don't know what you think we share, but I would rather tear my eyes from where they rest than be like you. We are nothing alike."

His first hint of agitation showed, a line forming on the edge of his lip. He quickly hid it, turning with a sigh to stare out into the open ocean as the ships drew closer. "They are determined, these friends of yours," he said, ignoring her last remark. "They come for you, and for me."

"Then soon you will be as my brother is."

The prince's calmness annoyed her. No one should be this composed. He was either extremely ignorant, unbearably arrogant, or indelibly confident.

"I am not the man you think I am. I did not kill your brother, though neither can I explain his death in a way that would make any rational sense."

Isha frowned. She shook her head and shifted her weight, wincing as the man holding her wrist tightened his grip. "You speak in riddles," she said. "I saw you leave the tent. There was no one else there. Only you."

"There was someone else."

"Who then? Who killed my brother if not you?"

Finally, his composure broke, if only through a slight slump of the shoulders and a wrinkle of his brow. "I cannot explain what I saw, who I saw, only that it was not human, not entirely."

"Why lie?" Isha protested. "I am already your prisoner.

You already have what you wanted. The King of Trost is dead. You have your war."

"War is the last thing I desire. I am a man who seeks peace. I have seen too much blood in my life to search out more of it. I do not expect you to understand."

"That is what every tyrant in the long history of Zapour has said, right before they slaughtered thousands just to hold a piece of gold atop their head."

"I am well aware what the ruling class of Zapour are capable of, more than you know," he said, a hint of sadness in his tone. "I have gold, a wealth of it. I have no need of more. Nor do I seek power. However, Zur has chosen me to right the world, to fix his mistake."

"Mistake?" Isha questioned. "How can you say that of a god?"

"Even gods make mistakes. Not even they can foresee the complete outcome of their interventions."

"Enlighten me. What mistake do you think the sun god made, oh mighty prince?"

"His mistake was you," he said, voice calm. "Your brothers, your father, all those capable of wielding, and reproducing spawn who can summon, his Light. Your infestation has grown intolerable. You fail to see the repercussions of your continued action. Zur is dying, and the burden of his recovery falls upon me."

Isha took a moment to absorb his statement. "So you *were* lying. You do mean to incite a war. You won't stop until you have your victory. You don't want peace." She almost laughed at his audacity.

"You are a smart woman," he said. "But you are also naive. There are different definitions of peace. Sometimes, short-term peace must be shattered in order for long-term prosperity to be established."

"Do not make me repeat myself, tyrant," Isha said, spitting the last word.

A flurry of footsteps and a raised voice interrupted their conversation. Sounja approached, shaking her fist. "I told you to kill this bitch," she said. "She is more trouble than she is worth. Bind her wrists and throw her over the edge. It is what she deserves."

Isha narrowed her eyes, but said nothing.

The Sun Prince held up a hand, rubbing at his eye with the other. He took a step closer to the railing. "They will be on us soon, your countrymen," he said, ignoring Sounja's protest and directing his words to Isha. "You must make a choice." He turned towards her now, clasping his hands behind his back. "You can save them and be free. Take a small boat, go to them, call off their assault. I will not pursue you, nor will I take any action against Zapour for the next three cycles of the moon."

Beside her, Sounja protested. "You cannot be serious, you would let her go?"

The Sun Prince silenced her with a stern expression.

Sounja's face went as red as her hair, but she bit her lip and stepped aside.

The grip on Isha's wrists loosened and she took the opportunity to turn and watch the ships close distance. "I count six of my ships to your three. You are outnumbered. If you are true to your word and let me go, then all I would be doing is aiding your escape."

"The world is full of stories about the few overcoming the many. This will be no different."

"This world has seen enough tyranny. It does not need another arrogant despot who thinks himself better than others."

"This word you keep saying, tyrant," the Sun Prince said, facing her again. "I do not like it, do not agree with it. It implies that I am arbitrary, unnecessarily cruel. Those who follow me do so of their own free will. Their devotion is absolute, their loyalty proven."

"Then we shall see that loyalty tested," Isha said. "You will pay for what you have done."

He stared at her for a time, as if she were a puzzle he could not quite figure out. "Then shall I presume you decline my offer? You will risk the lives of your countrymen to have your vengeance?"

Isha took another look towards the ships closing in on them. There were still six to three. Who did this man think he was, to be so sure of victory? "You are confident only because you have me," she said. "If your plan is to use me against them, then it is a shallow one."

The Sun Prince shook his head as if disappointed. "It would seem I will need more than words to prove myself to you. Very well, if action is what you seek, then I will offer you this," he continued. "Our ship will sail ahead, leaving only the other two behind to deal with your own. If your men are as capable as you claim, then there should be no contest. If they are successful, then I will submit, hand myself over, and leave myself at your mercy."

Isha narrowed her vision, suspicious. "You are either incredibly mad, or incredibly cunning. I want your word you will not intervene. Two to six. Then we will find out how much your word is truly worth."

"You have it," he replied. "Though I warn you, this is your choice, your decision. I am not responsible for the lives lost in this endeavour."

Isha hesitated. It was usually Dazen who bore the weight of decisions like this. She hardened her expression. Dazen was the reason for this. Dazen was dead, and the man responsible was standing next to her, no matter what he said. He needed to pay, and Dazen's men were going to make him.

"Very well," the Sun Prince said, taking her silent glare as a response. He whispered something to Sounja, who took the information stoically, despite her hatred towards Isha. She turned and began shouting orders.

Isha smiled as Zur's warmth bathed the battlefield. Many of the White-Swords were capable Shine users, and white-light was always an advantage, especially against something which would sink if punctured.

Soon, the ships on either side slowed their pace, oars pulling tight. Isha watched as men readied themselves for battle. Soldiers armoured in full plate lined the sides of the giant galleys, fixing large, rounded shields to the side of the boat. Before long, the galleys' edges were covered in a thick sheen of shining black metal. Even the hull and masts of the great vessels were coated in a thin layer of metal. She had to cover her eyes as the ships passed. Zur reflected off of them, a rainbow of colours forming where the ships' bottoms met sea.

Isha looked down. The man holding her was also dressed in full plate armour, only it wasn't iron, nor steel. Her eyes went wide. She knew this metal, had been around it her entire life, had lived beneath its shadow.

Peridium.

Her vision shifted towards the White-Swords of Illidor, the

six ships moving into an offensive formation as the Sun Prince's two moved to meet them in battle. The prince's ships were larger, but not by much.

Panic began to set in. A sense of dread filled her, as if she had just made an enormous mistake, but she kept her composure, holding firm in her belief that she was right. Two against six was surely a fool's game.

True to his word, the Sun Prince stood with her, holding a confident posture as his men departed to die for him. Was this the kind of devotion they had? Would they sacrifice themselves so he could flee?

She held her breath as the first of the six drew close, rowing into a V-shaped position. Isha didn't know much about naval warfare, but she assumed that the White-Swords were trying to surround the Sun Prince's ships before getting close enough to either sink or board them.

From her vantage point she could see the yellow sun on the defending ships' sails begin to retract. The two galleys stalled, falling into the trap of the V formation.

Bright spots of Light began to pierce the sky, surrounding the Sun Prince's lone ships. A white wall formed, covering the battlefield in a blanket of Light so bright that despite her excitement, Isha had to avert her eyes.

The Light from Dazen's White-Swords hit the prince's ships in a direct assault from all angles, their formation holding tight as they attempted to sink the two in one massive wave of energy.

Isha's excitement soon turned, however, as the bright rays of Light reflected off the smooth peridium surface of the giant galleys. The Light that should have sunk them returned to its casters, direction-less, but powerful. Rays of Shine struck the unprotected hulls of Dazen's fleet, puncturing deep and causing those on board to stumble as at least four of the six ships immediately began to steadily sink.

Fire flickered as masts burst into flame. Screams rose above the cacophony of sounds as soldiers burned, some jumping overboard into the Sapphire Sea, others continuing to pour their Shine into the enemy ship, targeting weak spots in one last futile attempt to win the battle.

Isha watched as the men, *her* men, fought for their lives. Only one of the ships was still fully intact, with a second barely limping on. Even now they scrambled, lowering ropes and rescuing those who had been cast into the ocean. Isha felt her heart pound rapidly in her chest. She wanted to help them, to dive in after those lost. This was her fault, she had made the call, she had cost these people their lives. But still some lived.

She looked from the battle back toward the prince. He did not seem to take pleasure in the slaughter as she had expected he would. Instead, he stood composed, even sad. She threw herself at his feet, the grip around her wrist once again tightening. "Let them live, please!" she begged.

The Sun Prince looked at her, and without hesitation nodded. He held up a hand, and from the actions that followed it seemed to signal a retreat. His ships returned to him, slowly departing the carnage of the battlefield.

It was over before it had begun. The fleet from Illidor had lost, and Isha was once again at the mercy of another.

And yet, the Sun Prince could have easily finished them, slaughtered everyone. His ships were untouched, the Shine completely ineffective against their peridium shielding.

She began to re-think everything. The Sun Prince. Zur. Herself. Dazen's death.

THE SUN PRINCE

Just who was this man from across the sea?

Chapter 21

- Raiz –

SPIKE POWERED THROUGH the night, flying longer and harder than he ever had before, despite his injuries. Raiz no longer had the energy to sit up straight in the saddle. Instead, he slumped to the side and just let Spike take him.

He couldn't tell how long they had been flying, only that days had passed. He reached around and dripped some scraps of Shine into Spike's mouth, gifting him the energy he needed to see them home. But he knew it wasn't enough. Spike was fading, reaching his limit.

The two of them began to drop, the grassy greens of his homeland now visible below. He spotted Illidor in the distance, the tip of the Moon-Spire a welcome sight.

Spike's wounded wing began to leak again, red blood trickling down his hide. Raiz reached a hand to re-seal it with Shine, but his fingers burned. Spike jerked, the momentum sending them into a spiral as he descended, his injured wing flapping awkwardly.

They steadied, then dropped again. Raiz woke fully from his dream-like state, panic setting in as the danger of crashing presented itself as an imminent possibility. The gates of Illidor loomed just up ahead. He pulled on the reins, but his efforts proved fruitless, the bulky creature too strong to be steered when wounded. The two careened toward the ground, Spike beating his wings one last time to soften the impact. Spike's belly touched down in a farmer's field, smashing through rows of crops before skidding past a fence and out onto the gentle slope of a meadow, where he finally slid to an abrupt stop,

Raiz jolted forward, slipping from the saddle as he was propelled into the air. He landed in a tumble, his body aching from a dozen fresh bruises. He searched for breath that would not come, the landing having winded him. He tried to rise, to check on Spike, to tell his brother what was coming, but his energy was drained, taken from him via overuse of his Shine and too many sleepless nights. He fell back to the ground, allowing the comforting grasses of the meadow to cushion his fall. He drifted, exhausted, until his eyes shut, and the world around him became dark.

RAIZ WOKE TO A NUMBNESS. His head ached, vision foggy. He clasped his fingers around something soft, silky. He opened his eyes fully. He was in a bed. Fresh bandages wrapped his arms. He reached for Shine, afraid of what he might find, but it was still there. That, at least, would never leave him.

His thoughts turned to Spike, the feeling of not knowing like an itch he needed to scratch. As he rose, his back seized, and his legs collapsed like water beneath his weight.

Something sounded from beyond the door, likely drawn by Raiz's exasperated moaning. It swung open, and in walked a figure. He was expecting it to be Dazen, or perhaps Isha, come to check on him as they always had. He prepared himself for a scolding, to be chastised for being reckless, for once again pushing his body past its limits. For leaving…

To his surprise it was neither of them. In their place was another familiar face, one he'd not seen in at least two years. His shoulders were rounder than Raiz remembered, his arms thicker, and he had grown a thin layer of stubble that covered his once childish face, but he was unmistakable.

"Hector!" Raiz said, a genuine smile crossing his lips at seeing the young man his old friend had become.

The boy-turned-man walked into the room. Raiz expected to be greeted with the warmth such a reunion deserved. Instead, Hector's face dropped. Dark bags were present beneath his eyes, and his expression sombered further as he looked down to see Raiz staggering to his feet. He tried to hide his melancholy, feigning a smile and nodding towards Raiz. "It is good to see you, my friend," he said.

"You too, Hector. It's been too long. I see I made the right choice, leaving you with Echo. Look at you, you've grown strong! But unfortunately, our reunion will have to wait. Where's my brother? Where's Dazen? I need to speak with him, the matter is urgent." He watched as Hector's head drooped. "Something's wrong, I can see it written on your face. Speak plainly," Raiz urged.

Hector's lips curled and his face seemed to scrunch into a ball, as if he was doing his best to hold back tears. "Raiz, I —" he started.

Raiz rose fully, standing straight. "Hector, where is my brother?" he said with more authority this time.

Hector went to speak and came up empty. Raiz's breathing doubled. He ran for the door, brushing past the fumbling Hectory. He almost fell over, collapsing into the door frame. He pressed against it until he regained his footing, then stumbled down the familiar hallway of the palace, making his way to the main chamber, where he knew Dazen would be.

"Raiz, wait!" Hector called, but he was already moving, ignoring the plea.

More familiar faces began to show up, standing, staring. They had the same look of sadness painted on their faces. Nobles, servants, friends. Some went to speak to him, to help him, but in the end they all let him pass.

He continued to search, making his way towards the Great Hall, towards his brother. He found the double doors, pressing his weight against the wood and listening as it creaked open.

More people were crowded inside, gathered for some event he had not yet been made aware of. Raiz limped down the walkway, all eyes turning to stare at him, but none daring to stop him.

A babe cried out, and Raiz remembered Dazen's child, little Nora. How could he have forgotten something so important? A wave of emotions swelled inside of him at the thought of being an uncle. He, of all people, an uncle. He wouldn't know what to do with himself around her, had absolutely no experience with children.

He looked up to see Sumaya, Dazen's wife, cradling the child in her arms, lulling it back to a peaceful sleep, but this room reeked of anything but peace. Tears stained her cheeks and neck, and her eyes were full of grief.

Raiz searched the room, looking for Isha, for Dazen. Where were they? He found Echo, standing stoically next to his sister, hand on her shoulder. Gale was also there — the leader of the White-Swords, and Dazen's personal guard. Where Gale went, Dazen would not be far.

More familiar figures presented themselves as he drew closer to the dais. Kron stood tall next to his mother. Celia's head was buried in Kron's fur coat. She wept. *Mother, why are you weeping?* he wanted to say, but he could not find the words.

Everyone averted their gaze, turning from Raiz and back towards something in the centre of the raised dais. A stone column. Raiz couldn't see what it contained. His heart stopped. Not a stone column, a cairn.

He rushed over to the platform, his wounds forgotten as he climbed atop it. Kron moved to intercept, grabbing his shoulder even while Celia still clung to his other arm. Raiz froze, staring into Kron's impenetrable gaze. The man was broken, moreso than he had been back in Lumindal. He didn't say anything, didn't do anything. His grip relaxed, and Raiz looked down into the cairn.

His two bandaged hands caught him, grasping onto the cold stone as his eyes swelled with emotion. His throat closed. His mouth gaped in silent horror. Dazen was there. He had found his brother, and his brother was dead.

No warming eyes stared back at him. No knowing smile greeted him, only a cold-faced corpse. His skin was withered away, as if his life force had literally been sucked dry. But it was him, there was no doubt.

Raiz fell to a knee, unable to continue to look. "I should

have been there," he whispered. "I shouldn't have left."

His mother approached him then, violet eyes somehow empty of colour. She wrapped her arms around him and pulled tight. Raiz released himself into her embrace, allowing his emotions to run their course as he wept into her blouse. Time stood still as all shared in his grief. Dazen, the King of Trost, his brother, was dead.

"Who killed him?" Raiz said, slumping on his chair in the common room, cheeks wet. He couldn't remember where the day had gone, just that he had been in pain. Pain that would not heal overnight. This was a scar, an indelible mark on his soul that would forever linger. How could he have let this happen? He had only just got his brother back. It was his fault. He shouldn't have left. He let his own grief get in the way of caring for his family.

Echo sat to his right, Kron and Celia to his left. Sumaya lingered in the corner. She tried to put on a strong façade, but such powerful emotions were impossible to hide. She was hurting, perhaps more than any here. Enough that Celia had taken Nora for the time being.

The child was asleep in his mother's arms, resting peacefully. Raiz wondered if she knew, wondered if someone so young could feel the loss of a father.

"We were betrayed," Echo said, turning his shoulder. "He was murdered in the dark. It was my fault. I should not have left him alone. I should have known. I should have known!"

"What of his body? Why is it withered so?"

Echo shook his head. "We are not sure. I suspect a poison of some sort. But I do not know what kind of poison can do that to a body so quickly. Some foreign concoction, possibly."

Raiz said nothing. He didn't chastise him as maybe he once would have, but neither did he give comfort. He turned to his mother, to Kron. "Where is Isha?"

They were silent, Kron unable to look him in the eye. Raiz held his breath, panic flaring in his chest. "Where is she? Is she alive?" he found himself almost screaming.

"She is alive," another voice sounded. It was Gale. He had been standing behind his family, but now he stepped forward "I saw her. On their ship. The Sun Prince has her," he said, though Raiz could tell he was struggling to say the words.

Raiz felt his Shine rise to the surface. They all felt it. The air around him grew warm.

"Raiz!" his mother warned, bouncing as the babe began to wake.

Raiz took a breath, releasing his aura. "Tell me everything," he said, facing Gale and Echo.

He took in their comments without moving, listening as they explained the meeting between the two parties, the terms suggested, and then finally the night of his brother's death. Raiz winced, hatred for this false prince from across the sea igniting like a wildfire, burning brighter even than his hatred for his father had.

"Under the banner of truce!" he hissed, fists clenched, teeth bared. "He will pay for this. And Isha, he took her?"

"No," Gale said, causing Raiz to falter. "Isha went after him. She was there, after Dazen fell. She and Puk swam after their ship, must have been captured in their attempt at vengeance."

"And you let her go!?" Raiz shouted, turning and grabbing Gale by the fabric of his shirt. "You just sat there and watched as all of this happened? You were supposed to be protecting them!"

Gale cowered beneath his grip, his composure turning to mud. "I am to blame. You are right. I failed them."

"Why didn't you go after them! After her!"

"We did go after them. We sailed day and night in an attempt to see justice done, to bring Isha back. But they caught us unaware, they destroyed our fleet like it was nothing. I — I am sorry, I failed them."

Raiz let him go, gulped, and turned to see his family staring at him as though he were a monster. Then he remembered. He was a monster. Raiz took one last look and moved to leave.

"Raiz! Where are you going?" his mother called.

"Where do you think? I'm going to get Spike and find my sister."

"That is insanity! You can barely move, you will die!"

"I have no choice," Raiz replied. "I will not let her go through the same pain I once caused again."

"Raiz, you get back here!" she insisted, one arm pointed at him, the other still cradling Dazen's child.

Raiz froze. He was angry. Not just at Dazen's death, but also at his mother. She had barely spoken to him since returning to them two years ago. Had kept herself at arm's length. Perhaps it was partially his fault, he had been closed off since Veil's death. Even still, what right did she have to talk to him so?

He felt something grab his arm. He turned back furiously, but it was not his mother's grip I clasped him, it was Kron's.

"I will get her," he said, his voice deeply pained.

Raiz looked up. Although the man he had once called his father was not the same man he used to know and hate, some wounds never fully heal. He'd never had the strength to forgive Kron for the pain he'd caused Isha.

Raiz shrugged away from his touch. "What do you mean you will get her?"

Kron straightened, his barrel chest heaving as he took in a breath. The years had done nothing to diminish his frame. He still had the same bulky, rounded shoulders. He was at least a head taller than Raiz would ever be. A long, grey-black beard trailed down his chin, resting just above his breast. "I will go to Yagos. I will find her."

The words almost passed through Raiz. Was this the same man who had once let Isha be taken by an Eagle, all those years ago?

"You?" Raiz said incredulously. "You lost the right to call yourself her father when you left her in the hands of that fiend."

Raiz braced himself. He was expecting Kron to bark back, to retaliate, but he did nothing. He just stood there, a heavy frown etched on his face as he sucked in another deep breath. "I have wronged her, I have wronged you, I know this. I was never a good father, but I have changed – am *changing*," he corrected, sparing a glance towards Celia, who stood listening in the background. "You are not strong enough," Kron continued. "Fight me on this if you will, but in your current state, you will lose."

There was an edge to his voice, a confidence reminiscent of the family name. Raiz crossed his arms, searching for a weakness to exploit, a reason to dispute his claim. Though his expression was stone, his Shine was still very much alive and flowing within him. Even so, Raiz snapped his head to the side, unable to forget all he had done. "No," he said. "I cannot trust anyone else. I got her once, I will do it again."

"Do not be a fool!" Kron said, his voice rising this time. "Your mother has already lost one child, do not let her lose two more."

Raiz gulped. He looked to his mother, the woman who had whisked him away as a child, saving him from a life of pain as a child of the King-Radiant. But had Kron been a better father?

"I have already prepared for the journey," Kron continued. "There is a ship waiting for me, ready to depart upon my arrival."

Raiz moved to protest. "Then I will come with you. My wounds are insignificant, they will be healed soon."

Kron held up a firm hand. "No, you are needed here. Trost needs you right now. Let me do this for my family. Let me right the wrongs I have perpetrated."

Raiz looked around to see those who were close watching, listening. "What do you mean Trost needs me? What good can I do here?"

Kron took a single, shuddering breath. "Raiz, you are to be king."

A weight dropped like an anchor in his stomach. His head began to spin. He looked to his mother, to Echo, to Gale, to Sumaya. All of them were watching, looking at him differently.

"King?" Raiz said, finding his voice. "I can't be a king. I wouldn't... I don't... I can't..."

"You must," Kron insisted. "You are a Glaive, no matter what I once said. You are the rightful heir. Nora is still just a babe," he indicated the child in Celia's arms. "You must rule until she is of age."

Raiz took a backward step. He ran a bandaged hand across his face, over his scar. How could they expect this of him? He was not a lord, he was a rebel, the unwanted child. He couldn't rule a kingdom.

"The nobles will be pressing this issue," Kron said. "Some will try to stake their own claim on the throne. You cannot let that happen. A Glaive must hold the throne of Trost, for more reasons than one."

"Then what of you?" Raiz said, not even knowing what he was saying anymore. "You would not take back your throne?"

"My days of ruling are past. I have lost the people's faith. It is Dazen they believed in. He who has restored Trost to what it once was. Now you must take the mantle, be the man Dazen knew you would become."

"I am not my brother," Raiz protested. "I know nothing about ruling a kingdom."

"You do not need to," Kron said. "Gale will show you the way. He knows everything Dazen did. All you would need to do is be the face the people want to see."

"You mean this face?" Raiz said, pointing a finger towards his scarred eye. "I cannot bear the crown. It is too much weight."

"You took down the King-Radiant," Kron said. "You are the reason we are all free from his grip. That was your decision. You made the call and acted upon it, all while I sat and cowered in my castle. You, more than any, know the weight of a crown, even if you have not had the chance to wear it."

Raiz lowered his head. Never had he expected such words from Kron, of all people.

"I will free Isha, even if I must give my life for it. You have my word."

Raiz sat and took a moment, wishing Dazen was there. He

would have known what to do. He always knew what to do.

He straightened, composing his features. He looked to Kron, then to the room. All eyes were on him, expectant. Raiz stood, and he nodded.

Chapter 22

- Isha –

ISHA FELT A FOOL. How could she have let this happen? An entire fleet wiped out in a matter of moments. Now she was stuck here, on her way to a land she knew nothing about, alone in her grief, her anguish.

She curled up into a ball, hands hugging her knees. Her wrists were no longer bound, a minor relief. Darkness shrouded her, only a single sliver of light from the deck above illuminating her surroundings. She thrust one arm forwards, pretending she was like Raiz and Light would flow from it. She wanted to burn it all down. The ship. The Sun Prince. Herself.

A thought continued to nag at her. Dazen's fleet had been destroyed. The prince could have ended them all, could have turned around and burned the last of their ships. Yet he spared them, left breath in their lungs, and a ship to carry them home.

She shook her head. That was no act of kindness, but one of arrogance. Did he truly care for their lives? Or did he just want to prove his power over her?

Her thoughts broke as the door was thrust open. She knew

before he even walked in that it was the prince. "Are you well?" he asked, leaning on the frame of the door.

Isha scowled, peering up from her ball. She turned her head, not wanting to look at this man a moment longer than she needed to.

"I am sorry for your pain," he said.

Isha slowly uncurled, unable to mask her hatred. "What do you know of pain! My brother is dead. He had a child, did you know that? A baby girl, now destined to live her life without her father's love. And it's your fault, everything is your fault."

She was expecting to be berated, scolded and chastised as she had been whenever she or someone she knew spoke up against Averardus, but the prince just stood his ground. He even managed to fake sympathy, his face relaxing, softening, those gentle eyes attempting to plead innocence.

"I have something for you," he said after a time.

"I don't want anything from you," Isha responded. "Leave me alone."

The prince left, and for a moment Isha thought he had truly gone. He returned shortly after though, two of his guards holding another man between them. Isha uncurled fully, rising to her feet. "Puk!"

She rushed over to him, the two guards allowing his weakened form to drop into her arms before quickly forming a defensive wall protecting their prince.

She carried Puk's weight, carefully shuffling him towards the rear of the room where the crack in the ceiling widened and the light was brightest.

"We will be arriving in Yagos soon," the Sun Prince said. "I suggest you get some rest."

Then he was gone, the room again going dark. But Puk was

alive, and that was enough to pull her from her depressive state, at least temporarily. "Puk," she said, lightly caressing his face. "Are you okay? Did they hurt you?" She gestured with her hands at the same time.

Puk nodded, even feigned a smile. He winced in pain, however, as he attempted to straighten. Isha's brows crossed. She opened his shirt. His back and shoulder were bandaged, a small blot of blood seeping through where he had been shot with the arrow.

She propped him upright, leaning him against the wall. Puk slowly raised his arms, his hands and fingers forming fractured gestures. *Are you okay?* he asked.

Isha cupped her hands over his cheeks and leant in to kiss him on the forehead. "I'm fine," she lied. "I'm sorry Puk. You shouldn't be here. I acted rashly, and now we're both stuck on this ship. I don't know what will happen, but I'm glad you're alive. I couldn't live with myself if I caused your death."

Puk tried to smile, but it quickly washed away, replaced by worry as he looked towards the door. *Where we are going, is not good,* he signed. *This place, it is filled with evil men. Selfish men. Violent men.*

Isha recoiled. Of course. How could she have forgotten? Yagos was where Puk had been born, where he'd been raised, if you could call it that. Yagos was where he'd been broken, turned into the man he'd been when Isha first met him. It pained her, knowing that she'd brought him back here. He'd come so far, changing who he once was. Now he was going back to his beginning, forced to re-live past trauma.

"We will find a way to escape. I promise. Yagos will not be where we go to die."

Puk took her hand in his own, and for a long while the two

sat, resting together as they once had.

ISHA'S EYES FLUTTERED OPEN. Footsteps thundered overhead, and the ship seemed to turn. She looked down at her hands, intertwined with Puk's. She wriggled her fingers, feeling a physical chill as she attempted to regain movement. It was cold, extremely cold. She shivered, inching closer to Puk in an instinctual attempt to steal his warmth.

He woke with a start. He groaned, the pain in his shoulder still troubling him. Men shouted above, and Isha jolted forward as the ship jerked. Puk caught her, staying her fall and bringing her back. She clung tight, breath misting, bones aching.

Her mind was a fog, caught somewhere between self-pity and grief. She barely even noticed as men marched into the room and ripped her away from Puk. One wrapped a fur coat over her shoulders, a small comfort as she was ushered onto the deck.

It was snowing, the white precipitation blown by a gentle breeze. It covered her hands and face, and dampened her hair. She was expecting to see the crystal-clear blue of the open ocean, but instead what rose before her was a high, arching cliff, capped by a heavy layer of snow..

The Sun Prince's galley swayed along the coastline, curving around a bend to reveal a large bay. It was as though the Sapphire Sea had carved away a swath of land from a much larger piece. It was shaped like a crescent moon, with a bustling harbour situated right in the middle of it. Dozens of ships were docked along an extensive pier. Some were as large as the galley she now stood upon, others were smaller. A couple of them came out to meet them, sailing beside them as their prince made his overdue return.

Beyond the coastline, Isha could see the beginnings of a sprawling metropolis. Tall buildings towered over the surrounding snow-capped flora. It wasn't quite as large as the city of Lumindal, but the sight had her standing and staring.

As the ship approached, she could see the dockside was busy with people trading their wares, fishermen reeling in nets, and guards patrolling every corner. A large majority of them stopped what they were doing to stare out into the bay as the enormous galley prepared for landing.

Isha turned to see the man who had taken her brother from her. She wriggled in the guard's grip, causing it to tighten, and her to squirm.

"Release her," the Sun Prince said, signalling to his guard.

Without hesitation, the grip holding her wrists vanished. She rubbed at her arms, standing without bonds and free from the darkness. A ramp was lowered, and she imagined running, swimming, going anywhere that wasn't here. The thought was quickly dismissed. She was in a foreign country, and the sea was vast. If the ocean currents did not swallow her, then the chill surely would.

"You are free to go as you wish," the Sun Prince said.

Isha almost didn't comprehend his words. "I'm... what?"

"Stay for today. After that, if you wish to return to your homeland, then I will arrange it."

Isha failed to stifle a laugh. "You would let me go back? Just like that?"

"I told you, I am no tyrant. I will not hold you here against your will, but I would ask that you stay, if only for a time."

Isha scrunched her face into a confused ball. "Then why not send me back with my men? Why play games with me, make me watch as my men fought for their lives?"

The prince took a deep breath. "I gave you the chance to return to them, to change their fate. I am not to blame for the decision you yourself made. Besides, I wanted you to stay. I want you to see what we are, who we are."

"Why? What am I to you? Why does my opinion matter? If I ever get my freedom, I will use it to kill you."

He pursed his lips, seeming to contemplate his next words carefully. "Then that is a risk I will take, but it will not be as easy as you think, to kill a prince."

He issued a mocking smile, daring her to try. She almost took him up on his offer, but stayed her hand. For now…

"As to your opinion," he continued. "You are a princess of a land poisoned by something they do not understand. If we are to have any hope of working together to quell the poison, then I need to open your eyes."

"Any hope of a civil agreement was lost the moment you took my brother from this world. Trost will never forgive you, I will never forgive you. So no, I will not stay with you and become a victim to whatever magic you may or may not have. The moment Zur goes to bed this day, I am leaving, or are you not a man of your word?"

She could see the displeasure written on his face, but to his credit he did not act upon it. He simply nodded. "Very well. What you see before you is Drin, the capital city of these lands. Take your warrior friend over there and explore its streets for the day. If you try to run before the day is up, I will find you. But I am a man of my word. When the day is done, you will have your freedom."

Isha shook her head, unbelieving. She moved to Puk, who was waiting for her, leering suspiciously at all around him.

The prince grabbed her lightly on the arm, turning her to face him. "I did not kill your brother, nor did I ever desire him dead, but I see that there is no convincing you of this. If you wish to know more about who you are, about why your eyes shine differently, then seek me out. We have much to talk about, you and I."

Isha jerked her shoulder, shaking her arm from his hand. She moved away, grabbed Puk, and walked down the open ramp.

Chapter 23

- Raiz –

THICK CLOUDS CLUNG to a sunburnt sky as Zur made for bed. The open fields of Illidor were crowded with people, all come to witness the ascension of their king as Dazen's spirit was sent to the afterlife.

Raiz knelt by the pyre, the White-Swords of Illidor waiting upon him to begin the process. He closed his eyes, spending a last comforting moment with his brother. Was he truly dead? Could his wise and noble older brother now be one with Zur? He couldn't believe it, wouldn't believe it if it weren't for that nagging feeling of something missing in his heart.

He blamed himself, always blamed himself. If he had been there, if he hadn't been off on some pointless and selfish mission to cure his own heartbreak, he might have saved him. He should have been by his side, as Dazen had wanted. He could have stopped this. None of it would have happened if he'd been there to watch his brother's back, as he should have been. Now Isha was gone too, Raiz forced to leave her fate in the hands of a man he despised.

"I'm sorry," he whispered, hiding his voice and tears from prying eyes. "I failed you."

Raiz searched the surrounding area, expecting some sort of sign to answer him, some large gust of wind to rip by, signifying Dazen's response. Nothing came though, just a long stillness. Silence.

He rose, taking his place by Gale as the White-Swords circled the pyre. All looked to Zur, calling upon his strength. Then their gaze shifted to Dazen, to the pile of wood beneath his rotted body, and they burned it. Tears and Shine poured from Raiz in concert. Heavy flames spiralled into the air as his king — his brother — turned to ash.

Raiz stepped back into the line where his mother and Sumaya stood, watching, crying, reminiscing. Their cheeks were wet, their expressions hardened.

Dazen's death was a blow to Illidor. It was a blow to all of Zapour. Men like Dazen didn't deserve to die. Why was it always the best of them that breathed the least? It was always the worst who lasted, who lingered. Just once he wished that it wasn't so, that he could take his brother's place on that pyre. Maybe then this world would be better off.

After an unknown amount of time had passed, he finally left, sparing one last look into the ashes that had been his brother. He felt a new weight growing inside of him now, a burden he'd never wanted, but was now afraid to leave behind.

"I will try to become the man you wanted me to become, Brother," he whispered into the stillness of the night.

A CROWD HAD GATHERED once again, although this time Raiz was the centre of attention. The dark of the night had faded, giving way to a morning that was undeserving of its brightness, for this was the morn that Raiz was to be crowned. Usually such a ceremony would take place weeks, sometimes even months after the death of a king, but Trost was at war. They needed a leader now. Few knew of Raiz's true lineage, and those who did kept their lips tight. As far as anyone here was aware, Raiz was a Glaive, next in line to the throne.

He sat upon a high chair, built atop the stone mound in the city courtyard, the same seat Kron had remained seated on when Isha had been taken as a child.

Though the courtyard was packed to capacity, few cheered as the presentation proceeded. Raiz didn't blame them. Why would they cheer? They loved Dazen, had been given good reason to. Raiz was someone they didn't know. How could they? All they knew him as was the boy who ran away from home. To them he was false, a shadow of what Dazen was.

Even now, as the coroner moved to place the crown atop his head, it felt wrong. Raiz knew it was necessary, feared to think about what would happen if another might take it for themselves. Dazen's work needed to be preserved. In just two years he had accomplished so much. All of his efforts to improve this land, to sew it back together and unify that which was fractured, would be forgotten if any other were to stake their claim.

Raiz saw them in the crowd, watched on as Clifford of House Grudle crossed his thick arms in silent protest. Opposite Clifford was Randall from House Chaldwin. He too watched the ceremony with contempt, thinking he, as one of the noble elders, was right for the crown.

It was hard to accept, to sit above them and sell them a lie. But it was necessary. It was what Dazen would have wanted, and what Raiz needed to do.

The coroner lifted the crown above his head. It lingered there like a swollen cloud, ready to burst and smother him with its weight.

Raiz leaned into it, ready to accept the burden, but then he paused. Instead of allowing it to circle his head, he took it in his hands. The moment lasted, stretched. The crowd was silent. The coroner was confused, standing with outstretched arms as if unsure if he should place them by his side.

Eventually, Raiz moved. He stepped forward, past the coroner and to the edge of the stone mound, peering into the apprehensive crowd. He felt his nerves begin to heighten, itching at him from the inside. He was not a man for noble speeches, but in this moment he felt that the people deserved one.

"You do not know me," he shouted so that all could hear. "Not as you knew my brother. Though I grew up here, it is true that I did not stay. As for why I left, my reasons are my own, but I am here now," he continued, pausing and listening to the silence.

"I do not promise reform or promote change. My brother did that. He saw this kingdom prosper, he is who in your heart you still follow, and that is where your hearts belong.

"I will take this crown, as is my right, but I will not wear it. I will not wear it until I have proven myself true to the task. I will not wear it until I see all that my brother has built sustained, all promises kept, all agreements fulfilled.

"I will not be played for a fool, and you will be held

accountable. As great as Dazen was, a kingdom is not run by a single man. There will come a time when I will have need of you. All of you. I hope when that time comes, you will be by my side."

Raiz relaxed, the crown fixed into his left hand. There was silence. No cheer, no shouts of derision, only silence.

A KING'S ATTENTION was never his own, it seemed. Raiz was growing increasingly frustrated at the endless waves of people who demanded his time. Gale handled most of it, even though Raiz could see he too was grieving. Gale was a man of duty, and without him, Raiz would have crumbled.

"You made a good speech," Gale said in a brief pause before the next person was brought into the throne room. "If a short one."

Raiz sighed. "Didn't sound like it."

"Do not fret over their response. You were heard. The people may not have shown it, but they listened. You spoke wisely."

Raiz inclined his head as Gale addressed the next in attendance. Raiz oversaw every interaction, the crown placed in view on his lap, making sure all of Dazen's promises were kept and reassuring all who came to him with their problems that he would listen. It felt odd. There was a piece of him that was burning, wanting to charge across the Sapphire Sea and exact his vengeance, to free his sister, but that would have to wait. The time would come to act. He needed to be patient, for now.

Trost was ill-prepared for an overseas invasion. They didn't have the fleet for it, not to mention that the winds of winter continued to wreak havoc across their shores, burying crops beneath storm and flood. He had been informed that they hadn't the provisions to sustain a prolonged voyage across the Sapphire Sea.

A stout man in heavy plate was next to walk into the room. He wasn't fat, even though to some he might look it. He was short in stature, but his physique was thick with muscle. It was the kind of build that one crafted through the swing of a sword or heft of an axe. His scarred, battle-hardened face looked up to Raiz not in admiration, though neither was it scorn. It was the look a man gave when one demanded respect, a look that spoke more than words could convey.

He unsheathed the sword at his hip and thrust the pointed end into the carpet of velvet at his feet. He did not bow, merely spoke his piece. "Your Highness, I do not know if you remember me, but your brother knew me well. My name is Alzar Brickham, head of the Brickham family, Lord Protector of Kirkham, the first defence against the hostile lands of Craw."

Raiz rose from his chair with one hand curled around the crown. "I do remember you, Lord Brickham. I remember you well. You trained Dazen when I was younger, taught him a few tricks if I remember correctly."

Alzar simply nodded.

"What can I do for you?"

Alzar straightened even further. The Brickham family were a proud house, if Raiz remembered correctly. Loyal to the bone, yet foolishly stubborn at times. Alzar must have swallowed a great deal of pride to stand before a king he did not know nor yet respect. "Ever since Gelvard took Lumindal, soldiers of Craw have been skirting closer and closer towards our borders. As of today, there has been no attempt at an offensive against our garrison, but my family have not been Lords of Kirkham for so long by being unprepared. Before…" he paused. "Before your brother was taken from us, he promised to send reinforcements in the form of thirty Lightweavers to reaffirm our position."

Raiz looked to Gale. "Is this true?"

Gale nodded. "Though this was before we lost that number in our attempt to chase down the Sun Prince's ships. I would take some time to consider if we still have the means to support such a request."

Raiz listened, accepting Gale's council, but this was not the time to be cautious. He needed to be bold, to make a statement.

"Then you shall have fifty," he said, looking Alzar directly in the eye.

The Lord of House Brickham showed a rare glimpse of emotion, mouth opening slightly. "I am most humbled, my king."

"You are a man of Trost, Lord Brickham. A loyal one, from an ancient house. I would not see you slighted in the absence of my brother."

Alzar nodded and turned to leave.

"I would, however," Raiz continued, causing Alzar to shift, "see that you continue to hold true to your oath. If the time comes for war, to avenge the death of my brother, our king, will you answer the call?"

Alzar paused. This was a risk, but one that had to be taken. Raiz didn't want to offend, but neither could he be seen to be weak.

"Aye, my banner will answer. We are no oath breakers, and we too lust for the blood of those who would conspire to kill our king. Do not worry, young Glaive. You have my sword should the need arise."

Raz breathed a heavy sigh of relief, sitting down and slumping in his chair. Being a king was tiring work.

Eventually, the hall cleared of people. He felt alone. Everyone he could have leaned on for support was gone. Veil, Isha, Draz, Aroha, Dazen…

He turned and spotted his mother lurking in the corner, watching him. Raiz thought things would be different having a mother around. All his youth he had wished for it, to know the comfort of a mother's love. Now that she was here though, now that she was real, it felt strange.

He did not hate her for giving him up, in fact he admired her for it. It took courage to do what she had done, to sacrifice herself so that he might have a better life. It wasn't her fault Kron had turned out the way he had. But being here now didn't change the fact that they were strangers. She was very much like him, stubborn, awkward. But she was not like other mothers. How could she be? She had been locked inside a tower almost as long as Raiz had been alive. He couldn't expect her to suddenly forget all that she had been through and love him as though he were still a child. Perhaps she saw too much of Evanon in him. Raiz grimaced at the thought.

Raiz needed her though, now more than ever. He wanted to mend their relationship, to start anew. He just didn't know how.

For now, he was forced to place that thought on hold. He still hadn't broken the news about the Skae. How could he? How could he tell the world that they were not alone? That the stories they frighten their children with were no longer a work of fiction, but an impending reality?

Then there was the army Kogon had mustered, and the

prickets being tortured, morphed into what he could only assume were weapons of war. His hand instinctively reached for his pocket, as if the baby pricket was still there. He took comfort in the knowledge that they were safe, however.

Trost needed to know, Zuton and Wisha needed to know. Armies needed to be raised. The Skae were real, and instead of focusing on them as they should, Zapour was about to go to war with itself.

The curtains of the Great Hall were drawn, and at the round table within sat two kings and a princess, each with their own council present. Raiz had Gale, Echo had Sumaya, and Aia had brought Rudi.

Echo was taller than Raiz remembered, more composed, and yet he was still a child in his eyes, too young and inexperienced to be a king. Then again, so was he. Echo had stayed to pay his respects to Dazen but was due to leave for Zuton the next morning. So, Raiz told him everything. He spoke of the Skae in the mountains, of the army from Kogon, and of the tortured prickets.

"This is heavy information, are you certain?" Echo said, staring at Raiz as though he had just told him ghosts were real.

"I know what I saw," Raiz reiterated. "Shadow-men with no physical form. They spoke to me. There were thousands of them, vicious, cunning, agile, hungry. I fought them, killed them, burned them with my Shine. We would have died down there if Spike had not come."

Raiz paused to look around the room, searching for the doubt he knew would spread..

It was Aia who spoke next, leaning over the table, brow creased. "These 'shadow-men' – Wisha has been attacked from the same mountain, on the other side. People have gone missing, more and more every day, taken when Zur falls and Cova rises. My brother, he sent men to find them, to bring them back, They never returned. Do you think these creatures are responsible?"

Raiz nodded. "It cannot be a coincidence. They are not without intelligence. They lured me there. They are building, growing. They are dangerous."

"But if these creatures are what you say," Echo interrupted, "the Skae of legend, then they cannot walk in daylight. They are imprisoned in the mountain, forced to rot beneath. They are no threat to us, not in the light."

"No threat perhaps to a land on the opposite side of the continent," Aia bit back. "But to me and my people they are very much a threat. Are Wisha and Zuton not allies? Would you so simply ignore our troubles? Did my brother make a mistake extending his arm towards your kingdom?"

Echo steadied. "Forgive me. You are right. I only meant that right now my country simply cannot afford to send out aid. Not with Gelvard holding Lumindal. Not with Kogon forming an army. I must return to Nanta."

Aia turned her attention to Raiz. "And will you help us? Your sister promised us aid. Without it I fear Wisha will soon be overwhelmed, if all that you say is true."

Raiz bowed, planting his hands on the table. "Your concern is just. You have every right to request support. I wish I was in a position to lend it. But my brother is dead. My sister taken. The Sun Prince will come for us all. He is a concern for all of us, not just those of Trost. We need to build a fleet. We need to raise an army. Yagos needs to be dealt with. This insult is all of ours to bear, and must not go unpunished."

"We all feel his loss," Echo said. "Dazen was there for me when my thoughts were darkest. We will see him avenged, I promise you. But we must be rational. We lack the fleet for a full-scale invasion, we do not know the lay of the land, the western seas are their ally more than ours, and we do not have the men to spare. Not with Craw and Kogon mobilising. And now there is this threat from the north you speak of. We cannot fight a war on three fronts."

"Then what do you suggest?"

Echo straightened. "We need Craw and Kogon to fight with us."

Beside him, Sumaya shifted, but did not say anything.

Gale pressed his weight into the table, leaning forward. "Craw and Kogon cannot be trusted. They have already ignored us once when asked about what to do with the Sun Prince, why would they answer this time?"

"Their seizure of Lumindal cannot go unheeded," Raiz responded. "And I will not treat with Kogon, not after what I have seen."

"We need them," Echo continued. "I do not like the prospect any more than you, but Gelvard and Hanns are men of Zapour. If we publicly announce our feud with Yagos, then we could avoid internal war entirely."

Sumaya drew back her hood. Dark clouds of blue sat heavy under her eyes, though her face was stone. "You would be foolish to treat with him, Brother. You know better than that. The man is a liar and a traitor twice over. Dazen would never have gone to him for aid."

Like Raiz, Echo bit back his frustration. Sumaya was ailing, her grief turning to anger. "What would you have us do then, Sister?" Echo said.

Sumaya shook her head. "It does not matter. You are all children playing at being kings. Father is dead, Petros and Huet along with him. My husband is gone. Wisha sends a child in a king's stead. And Trost is left with a boy who would raze the entire world to the ground if it meant he received his vengeance."

Rudi made to stand, held firm only by a hand from Aia. Raiz, however, was not held back. He stood, and his glare was like a knife biting into his brother's widow. He clenched his fist but said nothing.

"Go on then," Sumaya taunted. "Show us all what we already know. You are unhinged, not fit to rule a Kingdom. Do you think I have forgotten all that you have done? My brother and husband may have forgiven you, but I never will. You are responsible for my father's death, for the fall of Lesken. You are an arrogant child. We all saw what you did to the Eagles. You are not fit to fill your brother's shoes."

All of Raiz's pent-up anger, all of the emotions roiling inside him began to tear, to rip open. He wanted to shout. He wanted to call upon his Shine, to silence all who spoke against him. But with that rage came realisation. Sumaya was right. How could he rule a nation when he could not yet rule himself?

His anger began to simmer, replaced by self-loathing. He breathed a heavy sigh. He couldn't fight his way out of this situation. He couldn't face Sumaya, couldn't face anyone right now. She was Dazen's wife, and she was right. So, he did the only thing that felt natural. He turned away from his problems, and ran.

Chapter 24

- Zeek –

FATHER LIKED TO WALK. It was all he seemed to do, walk from place to place. He never went anywhere without a purpose though. Everywhere they went he was active, cunning, manipulative. Every sentence he spoke had a secret meaning, each direction a hidden motive.

Zeek didn't mind. He relished every step. Despite his growing wisdom, each new location was a new sensation. His stolen memories fed him a wealth of knowledge about the world, but a picture was still just a picture. As he walked, he listened to the songs of the birds in the trees. He felt the dampness of the soil beneath his feet. Whenever they camped, he relished the smokey scent of meat being cooked on a fire, and savoured the spice they added to their meals. He remembered all that he had felt, thought of all he was yet to experience. He wanted it all, wanted to feel alive, would never return to the darkness of his youth.

He didn't care what Father made him do next, as long as he didn't have to go back to that cave.

Still, his increased intellect had made him curious.

"Father," he said, quickening his pace so the two were walking in step. "If that man in the tower really does hold your wife prisoner, why do we not free her? Is that not what a husband should do for his wife?"

Father refused to break stride, continuing down the dirt path the two had been walking for the past three days. "And how would you know anything about what a husband should do for his wife?" he responded.

Zeek mused for a moment, rolling the thought around in his mind. Since consuming Dazen, he'd been feeling new emotions; empathy, respect, love. This was quite a contrast to Ancel, who had been so consumed by hatred it was almost overwhelming. Zeek continued to feel as though he were a string being pulled in two entirely different directions. It made him wonder, was he even capable of his own individual thoughts and feelings? Or was his behaviour directly influenced by those whose lives he had claimed?

"Be careful which memories you allow through," Father said, interrupting his thoughts. "You must accept them, use them even, but never become them.

"As for my wife, she knows the role she has been cast in, and she will play it well. Gelvard will pay for what he has done. For now, we need him. We are only two, and I have no hands. In order to meet our goals, we will need to deceive, to manipulate. It is the way of things."

"Is that why you didn't tell him about his son? You know he is already dead. I killed him."

Father's lips curled upward. "You killed Ancel because he

had something you needed. I did not tell Gelvard because he did not need to know."

Something within Zeek wanted to fight his father then, to lash out and tear him to shreds. It made him pause, emotions running rampant, warring with each other. It was Ancel, he could tell. By consuming all that he had been, Zeek now carried part of the dead prince with him. It was the same as Dazen, and all of his other victims. They were ever present, as if the people they had once been were trying to sway him, to drive him towards certain actions. Up until now, Zeek had been able to deal with them, to place them aside, but it seemed that the more he allowed memories in, the more they began to exert influence.

There was something else there as well, underneath it all. A constant drum, pulling at him, itching at his insides and attempting to direct his course. The further west they ventured, the worse it seemed to get. Someone, or something, was calling him.

"What is it?" Father asked, stopping to stare.

The pain doubled, clawing at his innards. His shadow-tail ripped through his shirt, vibrating with an inhuman tone as it snaked around his body, constricting him. "I — I don't know," he wheezed.

He struggled against it, arching his back.

Come home child…

The whispered voice caused Zeek to whip his head around, expecting to see a face to match it. When none appeared, he began to stagger, to panic. Whose voice was this? Where was it coming from?

His mind went blank, the forest in front of him vanishing, replaced by total blackness. Then, two circular shapes moved across the darkness. They were opposites, one as bright as day, the other as pale as the moon.

The shapes drew closer. The brighter shape began to flare, to grow, to overpower. Then something happened. The moon-shape shifted in front of the bright one, blocking its light, nullifying it.

The Darkening is almost here, my child. Come home. Soon we shall rise. Come home…

Pain suddenly lanced across his nose, striking like fire and sending him reeling. He skidded across the dirt path, catching his fall with his hands. He recovered to find Father hovering over him with a raised foot, his persistent scowl searing into him, waiting, expecting.

Zeek rose.

"Is it finished?" Father asked.

"Is — what?"

"Your fit, is it over?"

Zeek looked down. His shadow-tail had retracted back under his skin. The voice in his head was no longer present, the pulling now just a distant beat. "I think so. W — what happened?"

"You are the one with the ailment, you tell me."

"There was a voice, deep, comforting, familiar. It was calling to me. It needed me. But it had no face."

Father paused, considering him in the way Zeek had considered the injured bird. "What did it say? What did it tell you? You must answer me Zeek!"

Zeek froze, panicked. "The voice, it spoke of the Darkening, of something rising. I — I don't know what that means."

Father looked as if he had been slapped. "This is troubling.

Very troubling. Zapour is not ready. We must prepare them. If it happens again, I want you to tell me. Do you want to go back to the shadows? To live inside of another cave?"

"No!"

"That is where you will end up if you follow the call. You must ignore it. Follow me, and I will give you the world. Follow that voice, and all you will get is more darkness."

Zeek gulped, but nodded. "Yes Father. Where are we going next?"

"Back the way we came. I have business in Trost."

Chapter 25

- Isha –

"WE'RE GOING HOME," Isha said, sticking close by Puk's side as the two traversed the snow-laden streets. "One way or another we will make it out of this place."

Puk took in her words stoically. He seemed on edge, eyes darting, fingers twitching. Of course he was. The last time he'd been here he was a slave, forced to obey on threat of persecution. This was where he'd been born. This was where he had lost his tongue, his right to speak, to live. How could she have brought him back here? She hated her own selfishness sometimes.

Puk continued to walk by her side, but he was not present, not entirely. He seemed distracted, staring this way and that..

"What is it?" Isha asked, stopping and guiding his attention back towards her.

There is something… different, Puk gestured.

"What do you mean? If you like, we can go back to the ship, spend the day there before we take our leave."

No. There is something I must know.

Around them was a market. The street was busy, despite

the snow that continued to fall. Isha knew she was being followed, could sense it. She needed to find a way to contact home, to let her brother know she was here. It seemed impossible. She had no friends here, no way of communication. She just had to wait out the day, see if this prince remained a man of his word.

It took her longer than it should have to notice what had drawn Puk's attention. He was staring at the soldiers. They cornered every street, their rounded peridium shields held tight to their chest, a golden sun emblazoned on their armour. Puk approached one, his curiosity becoming too great to deny. He stood face-to-face with the soldier. He was about the same height as Puk. Tall, broad, holding the same steely expression.

Who holds your key? Puk gestured.

The soldier looked puzzled, though he seemed to understand. He placed his shield on the ground, rising and making a series of gestures in return. *There are no more key holders. You do not know this?*

Puk's expression twisted in confusion. He looked to Isha, then turned his attention back to the soldier.

The Thousand-Shields, you are free? Puk signed.

The soldier nodded, offering a light smile. *The Sun Prince,* he gestured. *He liberated us, burned all the holders and melted the keys. We are free.*

But you still serve? Puk asked.

By choice, the soldier replied. *Not by obligation. Many of us left, yes. But still many more chose to stay. Who are you, to not know of such things?*

Isha remembered a conversation with Puk back when they had first met, when they had spent the day trapped in a box travelling across Zapour together. He had conveyed to her his past, his days as a slave under the regime of the Thousand-Shields Company before being shipped off to Zapour. He had described the key-holders, cruel overlords that Puk had been trained to obey. They had given Averardus a similar key when he acquired Puk's services.

A commotion arose across the road, drawing the soldier's attention. Two men were in a heated argument, their voices rising above the bustling crowd. The soldier Puk had been conversing with moved to intercept. He thrust his shield in the middle of two angered men.

"Come now, shield master," one of the men said, backing off a step. "This is but a friendly argument between two patriots. There will be no violence, I assure you."

The soldier with the shield hesitated, gauging them with his eyes. Both were solidly built, their thick arms capable of throwing a strong punch. The one who had spoken rubbed at his moustache, which curled down beneath his lip to join with his groomed beard, which was spotted with flakes of snow.

The other man in the argument took one look at the soldier and stepped aside, though he would not be silenced. His face flushed red. His permanently creased brow spoke to years of hardship. "To the abyss with the Sun Prince," he said. "His word is nothing but a false promise. Our land rots in an eternal winter, and yet he returns with nothing. Where are the lands he promised? When will the sun return to what it once was? I have daughters and sons I need to feed. We cannot live on fish forever, we are too many. We need the sun. We need our lands returned."

"But my friend, can you not see?" the bearded man said, stepping onto a nearby table. The commotion had drawn a crowd. Isha and Puk settled near the front, eyes focused on the man who called their attention as if he'd been born to do so. "Can you not see all that he has done? Our prince is the saviour of Yagos. Do you not remember what we used to be? Can you not imagine what we would now be if he had not come? Our prince is the Breaker of Chains. The Slayer of Emperors. Liberator of the Thousand-Shields," he said, gesturing to the soldier, who was still fixed into a fighting stance.

"Our prince was chosen by Zur to cast away the poison rotting away at our sun, our god, our livelihood. Such accomplishments do not happen overnight, my friend. No, such feats take time. You are right to be concerned, you all are!" he said, projecting his voice and raising his hands to the crowd. "But fear not. Bessimir will deliver for us. No longer will the continent across the sea dictate the fate of our shared world. No longer will we be bound by their rules! Shine is the poison, the cause for your heartache. Take your anger out not on the one trying to right the world, but instead on those who have wronged it."

Isha had heard enough for her to know she should not be here. If they found out who she was it might not end well.

She turned, running nose-first into something soft, yet solid. It was a man's stomach. She bounced off the rounded surface, losing her footing and ending up sprawled on the floor. Puk pushed his way through the crowd, bending down to pick her up, but people were staring. The man on the table had stopped, transfixed by her. The crowd followed his gaze, all looking at her as if she were some precious jewel.

"You there," he called. "Your eyes, let me see them. I must see them." He jumped down from the table and pushed through the crowd. Puk stood, fists up. "I seek only to look, not to harm. Please."

Puk didn't care. He stood before her, a fearsome shield.

"It cannot be. Your eyes, they shine the same as our prince!" he continued. "It is a sign! Our day is coming! Zur will shine bright again!"

Isha recoiled, too familiar with the situation beginning to unfold. Why? Why did this always happen to her? She wasn't special.

"All of you, can you not see?" he continued, turning his body towards the crowd now. "Can you not feel her power? She is like Bessimir!"

Isha began to panic as everyone around her stopped and stared. They muttered to themselves, all trying to look upon her violet eyes. She searched for a way out, but her path was blocked. People had flocked to the stall, drawn by the scene. Isha withdrew. Her thoughts were plagued by Averardus, by the Eagles. She would not be placed in that situation again. No matter their intention, she would not be the object of their fascination. She refused. She began to push, to shove, striving for a way out but finding none. Puk aided her, pressing his body against those seeking to gaze upon her.

A voice suddenly split the air, high-pitched and authoritative. The crowd froze in their tracks, their curiosity beaten by obedience and a sense of duty.

A woman edged her way through. Red hair stood out amongst the crowd, her uniform lending her enough respect for citizens to dive out of her way. "That is enough," Sounja commanded. "This woman is coming with me. She is not to be touched. Am I clear?"

A series of humble nods followed, and Sounja inclined her head towards the pathway she had carved. "Well, are you coming?"

Isha scowled at the woman who had not so long ago wanted to throw into the sea. But what choice did she have? She took Puk by the hand and picked her way through the crowd, her free arm shadowing her brow.

She followed her red hair away from the busy street and into a run-down tavern next to an alley. It reeked of sweat and liquor. There were a few others present, but upon seeing Sounja they departed, stumbling drunkenly out the door until only she, Isha, and Puk remained, along with a tall and slender barkeep, who was busily washing an empty glass with a cloth. He stopped what he was doing, moving to the top shelf and grabbing a bottle. He unstopped the cork and poured a shot of nasty looking alcohol.

Sounja downed it in one gulp, then beckoned for another, the barkeep happy to oblige. Once she was done, she settled into the seat opposite where Isha stood. Puk still positioned himself in front of her, focused, untrusting.

The red-haired woman took a deep breath, licking her lips clean before casting her gloomy scowl over the two of them. She rubbed at her temple. "You are trouble," she said. "I will never forgive you, for coming after my prince, for wounding my brother."

Her eyes darted to Puk, and Isha could see she wanted to make him pay. But something held her back.

"What is this? Why are we here? If you have brought me here to kill me, the least you could do is hurry it up," Isha replied.

Sounja smirked, quickly hiding it and turning to beckon for another drink. "Unfortunately, I cannot kill you. Not yet, at least. But do not mistake my words. If you try to harm my prince again, there will be no mercy, only swift retribution."

"Then why am I here?"

"You are in here because out there you will get yourself into trouble. You are here because for some unfathomable reason, Bessimir has taken an interest in you."

"I did not ask for his interest. Nor do I want it."

"Good. This will be easy then. I want you to leave. After this day is done, I want you gone. Take a ship, head back home. I no longer care. I just want you out of our lives. You are a distraction, nothing more."

Isha gave a scowl of her own. She thought it through. It was tempting to stay just to spite her, but she had to go. She needed to grieve her brother, needed her family.

"This man you love," Isha said. "I have met men like him before. He takes what he wants and does not care about anyone but himself. He lies and deceives, manipulates and destroys. I don't pretend to know how his magic works, but he likely has you under his spell."

"Shut your mouth!" Sounja barked, making Isha jump. "Bessimir would never use his powers on me. You know nothing of my prince. Nothing!"

Isha composed herself. "Tell me of him, then. Tell me how he is deserving of such devotion."

"You do not deserve to know. You will not be here long enough to care. I am charged with seeing to your safety for the day, nothing more."

"Well, the day is long," Isha said. "Enlighten me. Prove your prince is not the unrestrained dog I know him to be."

Sounja rose from her stool, right hand reaching to her sword hip. Puk edged forward, ready to intervene, but Isha pushed him aside "I am not scared of you," Isha said. "This is not the first time I have been a prisoner."

Sounja huffed an amused sigh. "Having a midnight curfew under the roof of a palace does not count as being held captive, Princess."

Isha's features hardened. "You know nothing of what I have been through, of what my family have endured."

"There lies truth," Sounja replied. "We each know nothing of the other and yet presume to know all. The only difference is that I do not care who you are, or who you were. You will not be here long enough to be of interest."

"I know you are killers," Isha said. "I know your prince broke his oath to uphold the parley."

"If my prince says he did not murder your brother, then he did not. He would not lie."

"Is that not what he does? Are not lying and deceiving all part of who he is? Of what he was born to do? I know what it means to have those eyes. I may not know how it works, but I saw what he did to my brother."

"You do not understand him as I do. He has ambition. He is driven by a force beyond our meagre comprehension, bound by a god and set on a course of righteousness. Already he has done the unimaginable, and accomplished the unbelievable. Beneath his high standards and even grander goals is a set of unwavering principals. His eyes grant him the ability to see, the ability to know, and the ability to influence. He thought highly of your brother. He told me so, for what it is worth. He attempted to influence his mind, yes, but only to direct him to the path of righteousness."

"And when Dazen could not be swayed, he cut him down and left him to die."

Isha found her hand was shaking, emotions she thought

she'd had under control rising to the surface.

"What purpose would that serve?" Sounja retorted. "If we wanted a war we would have just invaded, not gone through the trouble of trying to change what I now know cannot be changed."

"Well, you have your war. The armies of Zapour will not forgive you. They will come, and see justice served."

Sounja huffed a fractured laugh. "From what I understand, the nations of your continent are already at war with one another. Even more reason for the prince to intervene."

"What business are our affairs to you?" Isha said.

"Have you not been listening? Were you not there when Bessimir spoke of the growing danger? That was no ploy, no trick of the tongue to seek a quick surrender. Zur is dying, and your continent will be the death of us all. We do not seek to destroy, but to preserve. A war between your nations is a war with consequences that we all must bear. How much Shine will be used? How much more can you take from our beloved god? You are all as arrogant as you are foolish. Only we are enlightened. Only Bessimir understands the repercussion of such wild overuse of Zur's power."

"You speak of arrogance as if it does not rule you," Isha replied. "From where I stand it is you who are single minded, you who refuses to heed the opinions of others."

Sounja snickered. "Then will you leave?"

Isha met her gaze,–refusing to allow her the upper hand. "When Zur dips below the horizon, yes, I will take my leave."

Chapter 26

- Raiz –

RAIZ SAT IN THE ONLY place that made any sense, remembering a time when life was simple. Cool air whipped at him. This high off the ground the breeze was strong. It curled around him, piercing through his charred skin, its bite reminding him of what he was.

The Moon-spire never changed. Despite the years passing him by, the Spire was one constant that retained its sense of history. It was his comfort spot, the place he went to when life became too much to handle. Right now, life was certainly too much to handle.

His frustration only grew the more he thought about it. He had wanted to challenge Sumaya, to scream at her, rebuke her. Tell her how wrong she was. But that would only have proved her right. He was no king. She was his brother's wife, the mother of his niece. She was right to chastise him. Their alliance hung by a thread, led by youths thrust into a world beyond their grasp, forced into a situation they were not yet experienced enough to bear. Aia, Echo, himself.

Dazen would have known what to do. He always knew what to do. But Dazen was no longer here.

The hatch inside the tower began to creak open. For a moment he thought it was Isha, come to lend him comfort as she always had when he was an upset child.

In place of Isha, however, was his mother. She climbed up the narrow hatch, her silken dress a tangle as she slowly rose to her feet. Raiz reacted, squeezing back through the window and closing it shut behind him.

"Mother," he said, chest heaving.

A warm smile greeted him. His mother's hands cupped together as she approached him. Raiz searched the space around him, wanting to offer her a seat but finding only dust-covered tables, most of which held rusty objects with sharp edges and pointy ends.

"I hope I am not interrupting anything," Celia said, taking another cautious step towards him.

"N-no, of course not," Raiz mumbled. "I — this is just where I come when I need to think."

"Gale told me you would be up here. He warned me not to come, insisted that I not, actually, but I was never very good at doing what I was told."

Raiz chuckled, the feeling all too familiar. "I would offer you a place to sit, but I haven't had the chance to clean up in here yet."

His mother waved him off. "I am happy to stand. I have spent far too long sitting at a desk. I will stand all I can."

Raiz nodded.

"It is not easy, being a ruler," she continued. "The prize of a crown has always puzzled me. So many people seek it, yet so few have the fortitude to bear it. Your father struggled with it. Your birth father, that is. Evanon became a cruel man, but he was not always so. I loved him, once, as much as it pains me to admit. Things were… complicated, back then."

"More complicated than they are now?"

"No, I suppose not."

"I don't want to turn out like my father," Raiz said. "Either of them. But I feel myself slipping. I'm not good with thinking through decisions. What if I make the wrong choice? What if Isha suffers for it? What if the kingdom suffers for it? I already have enough blood on my conscience. I don't know if I can bear any more."

"You do not give yourself enough credit," she said, moving to place a comforting hand on his bandaged forearm. "Think of how the world would be without you right now. Evanon would still be King-Radiant. I would still be locked in a tower, my mind lost. Isha would be a prisoner of Lumindal. You have something better than the ability to make decisions, you have the will to act on them. You have a sense of justice, of what is right and what is wrong. That is all a ruler ever needs."

"But most of what I did was just running blindly and hoping my Shine would be enough to see me through. I cost an entire city their lives, Mother. All those people are dead because of something I did. And it nearly happened again. If Veil hadn't sacrificed herself, all could have been lost."

"So now you have learned the value of consequence. Now you understand the ramifications of your decisions. All kings must learn this. I learned this when I left Kron for your father. And Kron has learnt it many times over."

"I should have been the one to go after her, not him," Raiz

said, thinking of Isha.

His mother shook her head. "Kron will not fail. I know his mind. He will get her back, or give his life trying. Besides, you should not underestimate your sister. In a way, she is stronger than all of us."

Raiz opened his hands, still feeling the sting of using too much Shine. He was of no use like this. He had no choice but to trust Kron.

"I'm sorry we haven't had much chance to talk like this. I… have not been myself, since Veil…"

"You are not to blame. I have only just started to regain my sense of self lately. There is still much I need to atone for, to share. I have been closed to my emotions, to my children, for too long, and now one of my children is lost."

A single tear began to trickle down his mother's cheek. Raiz wanted to wipe it away, to wrap his arms around her and say it would all be okay, that he understood her pain. Yet he remained still. Why did he remain still?

She wiped it away herself with a swat of her finger. "I apologize. I did not come here so you could watch me cry. I came to swallow my past and look to the future. I came so that I might lend comfort to my son, whom I have long neglected. If this is too much to bear, I will take my leave."

"No!" Raiz found himself almost shouting. He recovered himself. His emotions spoke for him. He wanted this, needed it even. A mother's love. "Stay, please, at least for a time."

His mother relaxed, shoulders dropping. The two made a seat for themselves on the old wood of the Spire's floor, and they talked.

She shared many things with him. Some shocking, unbelievable even. She spoke of her true age, which was something that Raiz struggled to comprehend. She spoke of her time in Yagos, and the power with which she'd been born, of her venture across the Sapphire Sea, of Kron. She spoke of Evanon, and the events leading to Raiz's birth. He felt her regret, her remorse, saw it as genuine.

Then Raiz told her everything, spilled the story of his life. He spoke of the day young Isha had been taken, of his grandfather taking him in, and of his eventual betrayal. He told her of his friends, Draz and Aroha. Then, finally, he spoke of Veil. He thought it would cause him pain, to speak so openly of his feelings for her. But after he was done he felt as if a weight had been lifted. It was as though sharing his burden had allowed part of it to dissipate.

When their conversation turned to Dazen, they spoke about his life, rather than his death.

Once they were done, Raiz felt relieved. His legs were sore from sitting on the hard wood, but the shadow that had been lingering over his shoulder had cleared. His mother felt it too, and he was glad for it.

He smiled at her, offered his–hand, and together the two of them made their way down the Spire and off to a much-needed rest.

Chapter 27

- Isha –

THE SUN WAS BEGINNING to set. So far, the prince had not deviated from his word, and other than Sounja's intervention, Isha had been relatively left to her own devices.

There was a growing sadness to the city. It was deep-rooted. There was still laughter, joy, pleasure. Taverns frequented street corners. Fishermen worked hard on the docks, casting their nets. There were swordsmiths banging hammers, seamstresses spinning wool, and merchants trading goods. In some ways it was not so different from Illidor, though the people of Yagos seemed to feel that their happiness would be short-lived, as if they believed what their prince preached – that they were living on borrowed time.

She didn't know what conditions were usually like on this side of the sea, but the bite of winter was certainly harsher here than in Trost. These people were starving. She could see it in their figures. Most were thin and frail, and on more than one occasion a beggar had approached her asking for food. They were clinging to a hope that the weather would clear and the sun would once again embrace their lands. Perhaps that was dangerous. If the right seed was planted, their thoughts might turn sinister. Isha more than any knew how quickly want turned to hate.

Even if it wasn't all a ruse, even if all that Bessimir said was true, she couldn't stay. She was needed in Trost, with her family. The temptation to find out more about her eyes and lineage was real, but she couldn't trust him. She thought about staying for vengeance, for justice, but she had since given up on the notion, dismissing the thought as fantasy. She would find justice, but she would do it the right way this time.

Sounja returned near the end of the day for what Isha assumed to be an escort back to the ship. Her muscles grew tense, however, when their path turned a different direction. Once they were clear of the city, instead of heading back to the coast where her ship to freedom was supposedly awaiting her, she was taken further inland. Puk was present the entire time, lending her needed comfort.

"Where are we going?" Isha pressed. "The ships are back that way."

Sounja didn't even bother to turn and look at her, fiery hair flowing over a thick coat gathering light flecks as a sheen of snow began to fall from the sky.

"So, was it all a lie then?" Isha questioned. "Shall I presume your master's promise was false, and that I am being led into the mountains to die?"

This drew a reaction from the surly commander. She inclined her head. "My prince awaits you on the mountain trail. There is one more Trule would like to show you before you take your leave."

Isha sighed. Her breath misted into the evening air as the sun began to dip below the jagged mountain edges that made up the horizon.

"This is insane," Isha commented. "This will take us all night to climb."

"If you wish to complain," Sounja said, "please do so quietly. I detest the sound of your voice. Your promise to Bessimir was to give him until the day is done. Come first light, if you wish to leave, that is your choice. Until then, I suggest you do as I say. You are more than welcome to lie here and perish in the snow. I will be sure to inform my prince of your weakness, though I am sure he expected it."

Isha clenched her jaw. She had been both mocked and admired all her life by men and woman far worse than Sounja, yet somehow the red-head's words infuriated her more than ever before. Even worse was the fact that she now felt motivated to finish the journey.

The snow on the mountainside was thick, but a path had been carved through, allowing them to walk unhindered. Slowly, the sunlight faded, and the last of the light dropped below the mountain, but their trail was soon lined by an array of burning braziers, firelight flickering wildly in the high-altitude winds. She found it to be a welcome warmth.

Finally, the two looming mountains either side of her came together, a narrow path the width of a horse's length splitting the middle. Sounja stepped to the side, putting her back to the rock. "I go no further. Bessimir awaits you down the path."

Isha gave a sceptical look, scratching her head as she peered into the mountain's depth. "You want me to go in there?"

Sounja said nothing, though Isha could tell she wanted to say something snide. Isha sucked in a deep breath, straightened her shoulders, and walked between the gap, eager to remove herself from the commander's presence.

As she passed, she heard a grunt. She turned to see an outstretched arm blocking Puk's path forward. "Only you may enter the temple. Prince's order."

Isha moved to protest, and Puk's fingers curled, but Sounja's eyes were steel. Puk pressed his weight into her arm, but this only made her agitated.

"Puk stays with me," Isha said weakly.

"Your mute friend takes one step into that temple, and he leaves with his head in a box."

Isha gasped, appalled by the blunt statement. She placed a warming hand on Puk's chest. "It's okay Puk, I'll be fine. Wait here for me, then come morning we can be gone from this place."

Reluctantly, Puk took a step back, Sounja's glare still biting into his soul. Isha turned and headed into the darkness of the mountain.

Snow still fell through the crevasse. She left a trail of footprints as she followed the winding path. She felt trapped, rocky walls closing in all around her. Fiery lanterns hanging from the rock-face kept her warm and moving. She didn't know if this was some kind of trick, or there was genuinely something of interest in the depths of these mountains, but she just wanted to get this over with and go home.

Eventually, the path widened, and Isha became exposed to the harsh air again. Thick fog blocked her immediate vision, though with each step forward it seemed to fade.

Her jaw dropped at the majesty of the meeting between the two mountains. Below her was a steep cliff. It circled around the entire mountain, forming a giant crater in the centre. She stood transfixed, marvelling at the intricate force of nature.

She wondered where to go next, certain death awaiting any who would continue forwards. Perhaps she had been deceived, and this was to be her grave. She supposed there were worse places to be buried.

She cupped a hand over her eyes, only now noticing the faint figure standing as if on thin air in the middle of the canyon. On second glance, it wasn't air, it was stone. A protruding arch stretched out from the mountain's side. She looked around, searching for a way forward. A narrow path wound around the rim to her right. Knowing she might regret this later, she proceeded down the pathway.

The figure on the stone remained still, and as she drew closer, she knew it to be the Sun Prince. His hands were clasped together, head tilted down as if in prayer. She approached from behind, one hand still covering her face as the wind hampered her vision.

"It's peaceful, isn't it," the Sun Prince said, "here in the centre of Zur's Eye."

Isha stopped a few lengths short of him. "Zur's Eye? Do you really believe that?"

The Sun Prince turned, lips creasing upward into a confident smirk. "The name is not meant to be literal. It is, however, a known location and itself evidence of his direct intervention."

Isha let his words pass without a retort. Back in Lumindal if somebody spoke of Zur like this, they would have labelled them a heretic and burned them on a pyre.

Bessimir waved a hand in the air. "Do you know who you are, Isha? I mean truly?"

The air around them seemed to still, the harrowing breeze taking a break and lending them time to speak freely. "I am a daughter of Trost, nothing more," she said. "I have seen your city, and I wish to leave it at first light, as was promised to me."

Bessimir's features slackened in what seemed to be genuine disappointment. Their eyes caught each other, and Isha felt a wave of emotions roll over her all at once. She turned her head, eyes stinging.

"I will not be manipulated and coerced, as you like to do with others. Do not dare to try that trick on me," she said.

"I could not do that to you if I tried," Bessimir replied. "My eyes have no effect on you. My words, however, I have yet to give up on. I would like to try my hand at trying to convince you to stay one last time."

"I am done being the object of another's fascination. I am no prize to be sought or jewel to be won." Bessimir remained calm, despite Isha's growing anger. "You mistake my intent, and you forget that I am like you. Do you not wish to learn? To find out what you are? What we are?"

"My brother is dead. He is where my mind needs to be. My family needs me. My own desires are secondary. You expect me to place my trust in a man I suspect of my brother's murder?"

Bessimir pursed his lips. "Very well, you may leave come first light, as promised. No catch, no games. It is final."

Isha crossed her arms and began to leave.

"However," the Sun Prince continued. "If you would like to sit with me a while longer, I should very much like to tell you more about what we are, where we come from, and of the origin of what you call Shine. From my perspective, that is."

Isha almost laughed as Bessimir took a seat upon the stone. She let out an exasperated sigh, sparing a look back towards the trail she had come from.

"If you do not like what I have to say, then you may leave."

She didn't fancy trekking all this way for nothing, and she couldn't deny her own curiosity. Besides, he had already agreed to let her go, so there was nothing to lose from attaining knowledge about a potential enemy of Zapour.

She took her place on the stone and sat cross-legged next to the mysterious prince. He smiled at her, not a completely arrogant smile, but his smugness was hard to hide.

"What am I?" Isha said, impatient. "What are we?"

The prince allowed his eyes to meet hers. "That is an ambiguous question, but I will try my best to provide an answer. First, allow me to understand what it is you already know, or what you have been led to believe."

Isha hesitated, still not comfortable sharing part of herself with a stranger, let alone somebody she suspected of spilling the blood of her own kin, but she allowed herself to relax, placing those fears aside for the time being.

"I know little, only that in Zapour, people know of what I am only through rumour and speculation. It is as if I am a figment of the past now living in the flesh. They do not know what to think of me. I know they fear me, or rather the concept of me, but they do not know why."

The prince frowned, and through his façade Isha could see a great sadness buried within, one she did not understand.

"I know people are drawn to me," she continued. "Sometimes I can feel other people's emotions, influence them even. My mother was born here, in Yagos, though most of my life I have not known her. I know that there was a war, fought between whatever we are and the Lightweavers. That is all." Isha gulped. Talking to him in this way made her angry. Why was she telling him this? She did not trust him, would not trust him.

Bessimir listened, the wind whipping at his now dishevelled hair. When he was sure she would say no more, he spoke. "Your mother, would you mind telling me her name?"

Isha scowled. Part of her wanted to refuse. He didn't deserve to know. But her curiosity got the better of her. "Celia. Her name is Celia."

This drew a reaction from the prince. His mouth opened, releasing a light gasp.

"You know her?" Isha asked.

"No, but I know of her. I was friends with her mother."

Isha almost sprang from her seat. She steadied, sparing a look down into the deep chasm. "You knew my grandmother?"

Isha had never really thought about her grandparents. Both Kron's mother and father were long dead, and Celia was a closed book, much of her past hidden, Isha suspected, even from herself.

"I did, yes," Bessimir continued. "She was a fascinating woman. One of the bravest I have known."

"You're old, aren't you," Isha said. "Very old."

Bessimir smiled. "I see you are not completely in the dark. I am old, yes. Very old. What your mother told you is true. We did fight a great battle, but we did not start it. We were nearly exterminated. But that is only the end to the story of who we are, who we were. To complete the tale, we must start from the very beginning."

Isha swallowed her pride and re-settled.

"We of Yagos are not so dissimilar to those of Zapour. We

share many things – culture, religion, language. There is a reason for this. It is because we used to be one people. Gallion Lightfire, the first King-Radiant, is just as much a part of the history of Yagos as he is of Zapour's."

"What does this have to do with the colour of our eyes?" Isha asked impatiently.

Bessimir held up a hand and laughed lightly. "I am getting to it, do not worry. To understand the power behind our eyes, though, you first need to know the reason we were given them.

"There is much your country does not teach about the true history of the first King-Radiant and his Eagles. Your history was carved by those who remained in power, its image distorted by beings who would rather you forget what they did to attain their position.

"There were indeed fifty Eagles, fifty men and women chosen to ascend alongside Gallion. Gifted with the power of white-light to fight against Cova and her shadow-creatures, the Skae. But did you know that their ascension happened right here, in the very spot we now sit?"

Isha gasped, surveying her surroundings in a new light.

"In your country, a structure was created called the Last Light. Well, this was the First Light. This is where Zur gifted the power of his core to Gallion, which is why his Light shone red. The others were gifted with lesser powers. In total, one hundred and two people left these mountains renewed."

Isha's focus snapped to attention. "One hundred and two? I thought only fifty joined the King-Radiant in his ascension?"

"And there comes another lie," Bessimir continued. "A lie of omission that I am certain was purposeful. That day, here beneath the Eye of Zur, there were indeed more people that were blessed. Half of those present were chosen to wield his Light, and the other half were given something else. A power much more subtle, but just as important."

Isha felt herself leaning forward, curiosity getting the better of her.

"I was reborn that day, along with fifty others of my kind." Bessimir raised an eyebrow, as if expecting her to have a reaction. When she did not, he continued. "We were made alongside Light-wielders as a failsafe, to ensure that they remained true to their purpose. Zur understood the nature of power, and thus we were created to regulate that nature. What your people call Mystics were originally made to temper the emotions of the chosen. We were paired. When properly trained, we not only had the ability to sense emotions, but to manipulate them. Our role was to ensure the chosen fifty, alongside Gallion, remained true to Zur's goal. Whenever one would stray from that path, it was our responsibility to see them returned to it."

Isha no longer felt the cold, her mind running with a thousand thoughts, struggling to comprehend all that was being said. "Why would the King-Radiant hide this from us? If this is all true, why were we taught lies?"

Bessimir took a steadying breath. "To cover up what they did. To hide the fact that their power was built upon the backs of my brethren."

Isha didn't know why, but this made her angry. Even if what he was telling her was a lie, it was easy to believe, yet she resisted. "The Eagles were vile creatures, despicable humans," she said. "They kept me prisoner, held me on display for the better part of eight years for no better reason than my eyes shone a different colour. I hated them, despised them. They preached of their divinity, something you now say was true. I cannot believe, will not believe it. They were false. My brother proved them false when he put them all to the sword."

Isha was expecting the Sun Prince to dispute her claims, to tell her how wrong she was.

"You are right, they were false, in a sense. They were an after-image, a distorted reflection of what the true Eagles once were. The Eagles were Zur's greatest creation, and yet they were also his greatest failure. Our shared god, however righteous, failed to predict the fickle nature of his own creation. Once the war was over, and my people either killed or fled, the gifted began to breed. At first it was natural succession, the passing of Light from one individual to the next in their lineage. But at some point, they lost control. Those with Shine bred quickly. What once had been a perfect harmony became utter chaos. Minds were corrupted, boundaries set. The beasts that were once bonded with the chosen died out, and white-light began to corrupt the land."

"Wait, beasts?" Isha said. "What beasts?"

"Ah," Bessimir continued. "My apologies. I seemed to have skipped past my favourite part of the tale! I am not without eyes of my own in Zapour," the Sun Prince admitted. "I know of your brother's Dragon."

"Spike? You mean his pricket?"

"Pricket? Hmm, what an interesting name for the creature. What you call a 'pricket' is, I presume, the beast's 'basic' form, before it has had time to feed on Zur's Light and grow. The result of such growth is what you might know as a Dragon, a titan of the sky.

Before his ascension, Gallion had been extremely fond of, and kept on his person, a pet lizard, Scale. His second in command, Melicent, also kept on her person an animal, an eagle, which went by the name Mollicut. Upon their ascension, a bright light shone down from the sky, right where we now sit. From that light, the animals evolved, just as their human counterparts did. And thus were born the first Dragon, and the first Great Eagle."

"Great Eagle? You mean those are real?" Isha questioned.

The Sun Prince smiled again, this time refusing to even try to hide his smugness. "Oh yes, very real."

Isha shook her head. "You spin an interesting story. Whether it is the truth, or an extremely well-contrived tale, I cannot decide. Nevertheless, it is not enough. What was, does not change what is. I must return home. I must see to my family. Whatever happened in the past, the Eagles are no more. Their tyranny is at an end."

"And yet their poison remains. While Shine exists, we are all in danger."

"What is it you expect from me?" Isha responded, her voice rising. "What role could I possibly play in this?"

"You have no idea the importance of your role in things to come."

Isha stood, head shaking. "I have no interest in being your pawn. I will ponder what you have said on my journey home, beginning at first light."

The Sun Prince rose to meet her. "Very well, I shall see to it that a charter is prepared."

Isha nodded, turning to leave.

"Just one more thing," Bessimir said, causing Isha's eyes to roll to the back of her head. "What if I could prove all I told you true? What if there were a way? Would you then stay with me for a time? To learn about our gifts together?"

Isha pondered his request, figuring there would have to be substantial proof for her to even consider conceding to his proposal. "I am not interested in potentially falsified documents from the teachings of a foreign land."

"I am not talking about a piece of parchment," Bessimir continued. "I am talking about real, undeniable proof that at least part of what I have just told you is true."

Isha shrugged, figuring by this point that he was going to just show her anyway. She crossed her arms and leant on one foot before issuing a lengthy yawn.

This only seemed to spur Bessimir on. He turned away from her and walked casually toward the centre of the chasm, where the stone column met open air. Isha half-watched, partly curious, and partly just wanting this to be over with.

The Sun Prince shifted, lending her one last violet gaze before placing two fingers to his mouth and whistling.

Then he jumped.

Isha felt her stomach drop. She rushed to the edge, half-hoping that her job had been done for her and mountain had stolen her kill. She dropped to her knees, staring into the abyss of the bottomless chasm. Nothing.

The prince was gone, all trace of him vanished.

She sat there for a time, wondering what in the world had just transpired, when she heard a screech from below. It pierced the air, reverberating across the entire chasm and forcing her to cover her ears.

The screech died out, replaced by the sound of great wings beating. She peered down to see a rapidly rising figure. It shot like an arrow through the open air, its massive, arching beak coming straight at her. It veered at the last moment, the gust of wind caused by its momentum sending her reeling.

Then it slowed, two expansive wings opening wide, a black silhouette in the light of the full moon.

The Eagle began to descend, soaring in a semi-circle before landing behind her. Anchor-like talons bit into the stone. The massive bird shook its body and a layer of snow detached itself, revealing the full beauty of its golden-brown feathers.

Isha felt a weight pressing on her mind, as if the bird was trying to speak with her, bond with her. It lowered its head into a bow, revealing another figure atop a saddle on its back. It was the Sun Prince. He sat tall, back straight, features regal and relaxed, as if he belonged atop the creature. The Eagle lowered itself further, and Bessimir twisted one leg over before dropping to the stone.

He walked over to her, masked in the shadow of the Great Eagle behind him. "In my message to your brother, I proclaimed to be chosen by Zur. While I understand that to another's ear this might sound like an arrogant boast, I assure you it is the truth. Just as I assure you that I had nothing to do with his death. This here is Skeiron, one of the Great Eagles of legend, and my oldest friend.

"I ask you again," he said, offering his hand to her. "Will you stay with me for a time, that we might explore this path together?"

Chapter 28

- Raiz –

RAIZ MEANDERED AROUND the palace. He had so much to do. He needed to re-establish confidence within his alliance, within himself. He needed a plan. He knew how he must look, running out of the council room as he had. He felt more confident after talking to his mother, but now was not the time to make amends. He had to check on Spike, on the newborn prickets.

First, however– he had to visit an old friend. He stopped before a door and knocked. Not long after he was greeted by a familiar face.

"Raiz," a voice said. "I - I mean, Your Highness."

"Never call me that again, Hector. Not you. I need friends right now, not subjects. Besides, I am not your king, remember? Echo is."

"Right, of course. Please, come in!"

Raiz obliged. Hector was dressed in full uniform. He

couldn't believe this man was the same boy he had taken in over two years ago. He still had the same mop of dark hair, the same mischievous grin, the same fire in his eyes. But he had grown at least a foot taller. His features were also more defined, puppy weight replaced by slabs of lean muscle that spoke of rigorous training.

"You have done well for yourself," Raiz said. "A Kingsguard at sixteen, I'm impressed."

"Seventeen, actually," Hector corrected. "Echo has treated me well, given me every chance to prove my worth."

"And have you?"

Hector hesitated. "In his eyes, possibly, but in my own? No, I haven't. Echo knows I have ambition. He sees it in me. Not ambition for wealth or title, but for strength. I think that is why he promoted me to Kingsguard. He also knows I idealise you, your strength, your courage, your will, and so he keeps me close by his side."

Raiz frowned, pacing the length of the room. He'd never thought of himself as a man to look up to. "I wish you wouldn't," he said. "I'm not a man someone should seek to become."

"What do you mean?" Hector said, genuinely surprised. "You took down the King-Radiant, just like you said you would. You bested their entire regime, a whole system of subjugation destroyed because one man dared to fight back. Don't you dare deny credit!" Hector added, speaking before Raiz had the chance to cut him off. "I was there when you stood up to that Eagle in Lesken. I'm aware of what happened after that day, now more than ever. I saw the grief it caused you, the agony. Saw it as no other here can claim to. But that didn't stop you. You didn't bow as a lesser man might have.

You continued to stand. You fought, and you won. That is the type of man I want to be, what Echo knows I can become."

Raiz found himself lost for words. Never had he been praised so highly in his life. To know someone out there thought of him in this way felt… odd, but warm, however undeserving he was.

"This path," he said after a time. "It's painful, lonely. Are you sure it's a path you want to follow?"

Hector brushed a strand of hair from his eye, then issued a confident nod. "I am. I've already lost my family, my city, my home. I know pain, just like you. Where you fought to give us the world we deserved, I will fight to keep it."

Raiz couldn't help but smile. He shook his head in disbelief. "Come with me," he said. "There's something I want to show you."

Hector perked up. He followed Raiz out of the bedroom, and the duo walked in stride down the lengthy halls of the palace, then out into the sprawling metropolis beyond.

"Where are we going?" Hector asked.

"No questions. You'll see."

Hector quickened his step.

Raiz had left his crown back in his room. He still didn't dress like a king either, preferring his tattered cloak. He pulled up his hood, hiding his presence from the public. Before long, the pair exited through the rear gate and strode into the fields beyond.

They weaved through a wooded thicket and towards a small house on the outskirts of the city. A flowery scent filtered through a crack in the door as Raiz and Hector approached the home.

"It's open, come in!" came a voice from inside.

Raiz pressed his hand against the wood and walked into the room. The bright light of a Shine-globe greeted him, or rather several Shine-globes. They differed from the globes Raiz was used to, they were thinner, and more vibrant. They hung from the ceiling over a bed of pink flowers.

"Artificial light," a voice said from another room. "Magnificent, isn't it? The ability to harness Zur's strength even in the midst of his most unfavourable cycle."

Raiz turned the corner to see the man he was after sitting at his desk, idly dissecting a dead insect of some kind with his miniature tools. The figure turned. "I suppose I should call you King now, shouldn't I? Or would you prefer liege?"

Raiz rolled his eye. "Just Raiz will do." He stepped aside and gestured towards Hector. "Hector, this is Deryn, Beastmaster of Trost. Deryn, this is Hector, Kingsguard to Echo Levic of Zuton, and my friend."

"A pleasure to meet such fine company," Deryn said, removing his gloves and lowering his spectacles as he approached Hector with an offer of greeting. He turned to Raiz afterward and issued a lengthy sigh. "I was sorry to hear of your brother. To be the victim of such deceit... It is a tragedy, one all of Trost is feeling right now."

"I appreciate your words of sympathy," Raiz replied. "I may have been named his replacement, but my brother's title is not one I am ready to fully claim.

"Is your wife in?" Raiz continued.

Deryn waved an absent hand. "No, no. Eve is off on one of her expeditions. With the winter refusing to yield, she ventured up north towards the border, where there is rumour certain herbs yet grow."

"Can you not grow them here?" Raiz queried, fingering the

pink petals.

"That is the plan, yes. Though this is still very much a work in progress, you see."

Deryn went to continue when a commotion sounded from outside. Raiz braced himself, though soon relaxed as he heard a familiar high-pitched tune. He rushed to the back of the house, grinning wildly as he witnessed Spike attempt to squeeze through the entrance. His wings hampered him, the oversized pricket now too big to fit through a regular door. The hinges burst apart, wood cracking at the edges where Spike's weight pressed against it.

Behind him, Deryn grumbled. "Owww quickly now, get him outside. Eve will have my head if she gets home and these hinges are broken."

Raiz chuckled as Spike banged his head on the roof. "Get out of the way boy," Raiz said, pushing against him as he attempted to shuffle through the door and into the open yard.

Spike took a series of backward steps, allowing Raiz and then Hector to follow. He spun around in a circle, wings tucked tight to his sides as he continued to whine. His cries grew even more unfettered when he noticed Hector. The two had once been close, and Spike had a keen memory. He ran to Raiz, then to Hector, his bulk knocking the young Kingsguard over as the pair of them grappled in a playful hug.

It was nice to see Hector smile.

A large bandage was wrapped around Spike's leg where the spear had punctured it, though he didn't seem to be feeling any pain. His wounded wing had also healed, the skin now reformed where it had ripped.

"Don't let his attitude fool you," Deryn said, following them out into his backyard. "Like you, he needs time to recover. His scales are strong, but an arrow or spear to the right spot can still cause serious harm. He's lucky to be alive after losing so much blood."

Raiz nodded. Spike had done enough for him, he deserved a rest. He tugged Deryn on the shirt, pulling him aside while Spike and Hector played. "How are they?" he asked.

Deryn perked up. "They are well, safe. I must admit, your find has me quite excited. Three baby prickets in one day! Ever since Spike's rapid growth I've become fascinated with the creatures. You'd be pleased with my progress, actually, I've managed to —"

His voice went quiet, and after a moment Raiz realised it was because he was projecting his Shine. An angry red aura surrounded him. Raiz suppressed it, drawing the Shine back into his body.

"What is it?" Deryn implored. "Did I say something to upset you?"

"These creatures are not subjects to be experimented on. They are alive. I brought them to you to give them a home, not to use them for your own personal gain."

Deryn gave him a puzzled look. "I assure you, they are getting the best possible care. With respect, these are creatures that feed on Shine. Without a supply they may live for a time, but they won't grow. I actually have a theory you might be interested in, if you have a moment?"

Raiz motioned for him to proceed.

"Ah, yes, alright, where to start. As you're probably already aware, Spike bears a striking resemblance to the creatures of legend known as Dragons. At least, as the texts describe them."

"I'm aware," Raiz said. "Draz has already given him that

title."

"I see, well, it is my belief that 'prickets', the small lizard-like creatures my wife and I care for from time to time, were not always so small."

Raiz cocked his head.

"You see, when prickets feed on Shine, they grow. What if, and this is where I can only speculate, but what if these creatures were once much, much larger."

"You think prickets and Dragons are one and the same?"

Deryn nodded. "It's common knowledge that the potency of Shine has been much diluted over the years. What was once strong enough to sustain a creature of Spike's size is no longer enough, not by a long shot. So, what if, instead of dying out, as those who still believe in their existence would have you think, the Dragons merely reverted back to their natural state?"

Raiz's brow furrowed. "Then why has Spike grown?"

Deryn paused. He looked to the ground, as if what he might say next was dangerous.

"Speak!" Raiz said, assuming an air of authority. "Whatever you say I will not harm you. You have my word."

Slowly Deryn's head rose" and he spoke softly. "I — I know what you are. You have the blood of a Radiant in your veins. I won't tell anyone, I swear, but —"

"It's okay," Raiz said, holding up a hand and sighing. "I'm a man of my word, you won't be harmed. Just… promise to keep that information to yourself."

He nodded.

"So, you think because I'm a Radiant, my Shine is enough to make Spike grow to what they once were?"

"Again, it's just a theory, but that is my belief, yes.

Especially with what you told me of his experience inside the Last Light. The combination of that and your Shine must be what resulted in his rapid growth."

Raiz exhaled, his mind returning to what he had seen in Veka. "They're making more," he said.

"Excuse me?"

"On our return trip, Spike and I stopped for a reprieve. That's when we stumbled across their farms. They're making monsters. Force-feeding prickets with Shine, locking them in cages. It would seem you're not the only one to develop this theory."

Deryn's face was stricken of colour. He looked horrified, as if his life's work had been perverted, twisted. "What will you do?" he asked.

"I don't know. But it's been worrying me. If I need your help, I expect you to answer."

"Of course! Anything you need."

Raiz placed two fingers in his mouth and whistled. Spike came bounding over on all fours, followed by a dishevelled Hector. Raiz nuzzled Spike where he liked it under his chin, then ran his hand down the back of his neck. "Hector," he called. "Come, I wish to show you something."

Hector followed, and Raiz inclined his head towards Deryn, hinting for him to lead the way.

They followed Deryn out to the back, where a square wooden enclosure about six feet long and three feet high rested beneath the shade of a nearby willow. It had a glass casing, allowing the sunlight peering through the branches to bathe it in warmth.

Carefully, Deryn lifted the glass. Hector peeked over Raiz's shoulder. "What's going on?" he said.

Raiz held up a finger. "Just watch."

Raiz took delight in seeing Hector's jaw drop. The first pricket had poked its head through the foliage of sticks and leaves Deryn had placed within the enclosure. The other two followed, sensing the presence of not one, but three powerful Shine users, all with active Shine flowing through their veins.

Hector stood entranced, his focus entirely on the prickets. He held out a hand, but hesitated. "May I?"

Raiz nodded. Hector flinched as tiny claws gripped onto his hand, digging into flesh. He seized up, his back as stiff as a flagpole. Raiz let out a light laugh as the lizard continued to crawl up his friend's arm, licking at his skin with its ribbed tongue.

"It wants your Shine," Raiz said. "Do you remember how to drip it, like I taught you?"

Hector's cheeks flushed. "I'm no longer the novice you once knew."

Raiz stepped aside so he could demonstrate. Hector concentrated, hard lines forming on his brow. The pricket's tail vibrated as it positioned itself towards the tips of his fingers.

A white, goo-like ball formed on his index finger, the bubbling liquid morphing into a perfect sphere before breaking apart. It dripped down the length of his finger, droplets falling to sizzle on the soil at the bottom of the enclosure. The pricket continued to lick, guzzling down the hot liquid as humans would water.

The other two saw what was happening. Jealous, one dropped to lick at the spilled substance. The other balanced on its tail as it attempted to propel itself high enough to catch the Shine as it fell.

"Keep him," Raiz said, clapping Hector on the shoulder. "He's yours."

"She," Deryn interrupted. "This one is a girl."

Hector turned, almost spilling his Shine onto Raiz in his excitement. "You're giving her to me? Why? I can't accept such a gift."

Raiz waved him off. "Spike has been there for me through all of my troubles. Without him, I would have succumbed to grief and loneliness many times over. Let this pricket guide you as mine has me. Just promise me you'll treat her well."

"I will!" Hector said, moving his arm closer to his face to further analyse his new companion.

Raiz allowed them a moment to become acquainted, pulling Deryn aside. "Can I trust the care of the other two to you?"

"Of course. I shall keep them close until you should choose a pairing."

Spike nudged him on the shoulder. "Alright boy, it's time for me to go. Is he well enough to fly?" Raiz asked.

Deryn shook his head. "I would wait another few days. He'll act as though he's healed, but his wound was deep. I wouldn't risk it, to be sure."

Raiz turned to leave. "Come, Hector. I'm sure Echo will be wondering where you are."

Hector followed, barely acknowledging him, his focus solely on his new pricket.

"What will you name her?" Raiz asked.

He turned to see Hector standing tall. The pricket had attached itself to his shoulder, its claws digging into the pink of his flesh, sending a droplet of blood trickling down the length of his arm.

"I think I'm going to call her Claw."

Raiz laughed. "Suits her well!"

"Where do I, you know, put her?"

Raiz shrugged. "Invest in a cloak with deep pockets."

Hector scratched his head. The two made their way back through the thicket, taking the time to talk about their separate journeys since they'd parted over two years ago. For a moment, Raiz almost forgot about the events of the past few days, of Dazen's death… But those moments never lasted, and as soon as grief found an opening it hit like a razor digging into his chest.

Out of nowhere, an odd feeling stirred in his stomach. He felt Dazen's presence, his Shine. He knew it wasn't possible, that Dazen was gone, but he couldn't shake it. He looked to the sky, wondering if this was indeed his brother sending some kind of cryptic message, guiding him, but something seemed off…

He spun, fingers twitching, senses running rampant. Hector stood frozen, another's hand clasped over his mouth. He tried to cry out with a muffled voice.

Raiz tensed, surveying his surroundings. A body stood behind Hector, hidden by the Kingsguard's bulk. A black shadow slithered up Hector's torso, forming into a sharp point that drew a drop of blood as it touched his friend's neck.

"Who are you!?" Raiz shouted.

Claw made a pitiful high-pitched cry, still clinging to Hector's arm. Spike must have heard, for he came charging through the brush, teeth bared and tail poised for a strike.

"Spike, no!" Raiz said, holding up a firm hand. Spike listened, but lowered into a crouch, indicating his intent to kill.

"Who are you?" Raiz repeated. "Dazen? Is that you? Show

yourself!"

Whoever or whatever was holding his friend hostage remained perfectly still. Raiz shook his head clear. It couldn't be Dazen, he would never do this. Why then did he feel his presence? The newcomer's grip was like iron. Raiz craned his neck, and his eyes went wide. He had seen a tail like that before. He looked up to the sky. It was still daylight, but mostly cloudy. The figure stood in the shadow of a tree, his form hidden.

Confusion overcame him. Fear, rage, frustration, helplessness. He still felt Dazen's energy, knew it to be him, yet knew it couldn't be him. He had seen the body, had burned the body.

Hector squirmed in the assailant's grip, but the captor remained silent. They were frozen in time, neither party speaking, nor daring to move even the barest inch.

Spike still growled, tail vibrating. A fourth man emerged from the treeline, step by slow step. Raiz shifted to face the second newcomer. At first glance he thought it might be someone from Illidor coming to his aid, but as the figure drew closer, he knew it not to be so. A familiar energy surrounded the bearded man. Raiz gasped, eyes darting from the long, useless limbs dangling from his shoulders to the scorched, hand-printed face he thought had long passed from this world.

Raiz tensed, pointing with his finger as if to confirm that what he saw was, in fact, real. "You're dead!" he said, though his voice quivered with uncertainty.

"Hardly," came the reply. Celik's voice was stiff and rigid. He had the audacity to feign a smile, as if it brought him joy to see Raiz take discomfort in his lingering presence.

Raiz reached for his Shine, coughing up blood as he did. His body wasn't yet ready.

"It seems we are at an impasse," Celik said. "Overuse your Shine again, did you Raiz?"

Raiz grit his teeth and snarled. "How did you survive? Last I saw, you were unconscious atop the Last Light as it fell."

His words seemed to anger his former mentor — his grandfather.

"I warned you not to meddle with the tower!" Celik said. "I should have known you and Veil could not be reasoned with. I was a fool, but I will not make that same mistake twice."

"Veil died because of you!" Raiz spat. "You made her who she was, and then used her as a tool to exact your own vengeance. You never cared for us. You never cared for the future of Zapour. You just wanted revenge against the son who ousted you."

Raiz reached for his belt, drawing his dagger. His hand stopped there, however, as Hector issued another muffled cry. Whatever creature was holding him tightened its grip, the shadow-tail drawing another line of red across the pink of his neck.

"Always acting first and thinking last. You will never change, Raiz."

"Why are you here?" Raiz demanded.

"I simply wish to talk," Celik replied.

"Then let Hector go, and we can talk as men."

Celik laughed. "I know you better than that. Perhaps even better than you know yourself." His eyes shifted to Hector. "It seems the boy from Lesken finally made something of himself. It would be a shame to spill his blood here and now. To cut such a promising life short."

Raiz bit his lip, sheathing his dagger and composing himself. "I repeat. What do you want? Speak, so we might end this ceaseless reunion."

"What I want, and what you want, are one and the same."

"Great, then be on your way, before I put a hole in your chest."

Raiz eyed the figure behind Hector. Celik caught his glance and took a singular step forward. "You know what he is…"

Raiz's jaw tightened.

"You have seen them," Celik said, head rising as if he was proud. "You have been to the Weeping Mountains."

Raiz said nothing, his silence answering for him.

"Then you know why I did all that I have done, why I pushed you so hard, why I wanted control of the Last Light. They are coming, Raiz, mark my words. The sun is setting on the time we have before their return. We are the only two awoken to their presence. Another Darkening approaches. Soon, Cova will overpower Zur. We must prepare."

Raiz squinted, a thousand thoughts running through his mind at once. "You say one thing, yet do another, Grandfather. Your companion is Skae, is he not? He is one of them."

Celik nodded, impressed. "He is, though he has expressed his desire to become as we are, human. He is obedient. He is mine to control. We have an understanding, a common goal. Unlike you, he is subservient."

"How can I believe a thing you say anymore?" Raiz questioned. "You speak in half-truths, even your lies are lies."

"You need not trust me," Celik said. "I have no intention of making you mine again."

"I was never yours to begin with."

Celik reacted with a brash smile. "I am well aware, but I have information you need. Information to share. Act on it as you will."

Raiz said nothing.

"Gelvard is building an army. He and his cousin Hanns have joined. They intend to march on Trost."

"To what end?"

"To conquer, what else? You know Craw's ambition. The King-Radiant is gone. Without him, there is nothing to stop Gelvard from taking control of Zapour. He knows there is no controlling you. He fears your alliance with Zuton and Wisha, wishes to crush it before it can take root."

Raiz cursed. His first instinct was to call him a liar, but he had seen the army from Kogon first-hand. Something was brewing.

"Why tell me this?" he said. "What do you gain from it?"

Celik took another step forward, and Hector let out another yelp. "I wish for us to be prepared! Prepared for the true war, not for these petty disputes. To speak my truth, I do not care who wins this fight. I want armies raised. I want borders strengthened. I want Shine to prosper. I would prefer unity, but I see that this is not possible, so there needs to be a victor. Someone must take charge. Someone must lead the fight against our ancient enemy."

"So you would instigate a war to see your ends met."

"This war has been boiling ever since you felled my son two years ago, you are naive if you think otherwise. I merely intend to speed it along."

"Don't listen to him Raiz! His words are poison!" Hector said, squirming in the arms of his captor.

Celik shot him a sideways glance, but otherwise ignored his outburst.

"We are already at war with Yagos, I cannot fight a battle on two fronts," Raiz said.

"Your feud with Yagos is nothing but a distraction. They have no Shine. They are led by a princeling who would destroy our only weapon against this evil. You must focus your attention on the north, on the mountains…"

"They have my sister."

Celik grunted. His head rolled skyward before returning to face him. "Your sister will forever be a thorn in your side. She is gone, you must accept this."

"You know me better than that," Raiz said.

"Unfortunately, yes. Do as you wish then, but Yagos cannot help us here. The Skae are real, as you well know, and they are mustering. I hear you are a king now. The burden falls heavy, does it not?"

Raiz said nothing.

"I have spoken my piece. Do what is right, Raiz. Do not be ruled by your ego. Shine must prosper. Humanity must prosper."

Slowly, the Skaeling that looked like a human backed up into the line of trees behind him, following Celik's lead. Raiz took a cautious step forward, but then he was gone, disappearing into the shadows as he thrust his captive forward.

Hector gasped, clutching his neck, but his body was unmarred.

So, Celik was alive.

Interlude

- Kron -

KRON FELT REINVIGORATED. He felt young again, like his life had purpose. He had made mistakes, many mistakes. This was his chance to correct them, to prove to himself he was changing, that he wanted to change.

The past two years had taught him much. He had learned the value of family, relinquished the burden of the crown. But now that his son was dead, and his daughter taken from him again, he felt his old self returning. The rage that had been simmering inside threatened to ignite.

He pressed it down, Celia's softness at the forefront of his mind. There was no pain like losing your eldest son, but he had to stay strong if he wanted any chance at rebuilding his fractured family. Isha was out there, alone, in a foreign land. Kron had done nothing but watch the last time his daughter had been taken from him. He would not sit idle this time.

And so, he now stood on the deck of a burning ship. Its crew bowed before him, forced to their knees by the strength of his Flare. An aura of heat radiated from him, a warning to those who sought to refuse his request of a venture across the sea. No longer was he a king, and no longer did he hold command of the soldiers of Trost, but soldiers were not what he needed for this expedition. He could not fight his way onto the shores of the distant Yagos. What he needed was a smuggling ship. What he needed was to reach the shores unnoticed, and inconspicuous.

As he stood before his commandeered crew, he knew they

were his. Fear was enough to get a man going, but in order to keep him, you needed gold. Fortunately, Kron had both.

He dropped his hold over them, allowing his Flare to withdraw into his body. He ordered the fires dampened and the sail raised. It was time to depart the safety of Trost, and to brave the cold winds of the Sapphire Sea.

PART
III

Chapter 29

- Zeek –

ZEEK RELISHED THE OPEN AIR, the sunlight, the freedom. After living for so long in a pit of darkness, every step outside was a new opportunity.

He would be forever grateful to his father for this gift. Father was law. He provided for him, cared for him when no other would. He owed him everything.

Yet despite all of this, Zeek felt a longing within, a desire for independence that only grew each day, with each passing step. But he had given his word, promised to be loyal to Father's wishes. Above all, he feared returning to the darkness. Now that he had tasted the light, he could never go back.

He froze in his tracks, assaulted again by the mysterious thrumming in his chest, pulling him, urging him in a certain direction. He quashed it, as he had with the several that had come before. He felt guilty for hiding it from Father, but he was confident that he had control of it now. After the initial assault, he had become accustomed to it. As long as it didn't become any worse, he could handle it on his own.

"Where are we heading now?" Zeek asked, stepping over a large branch in the middle of the pathway.

"The puzzle is almost complete," Father replied, not even bothering to look back at him. "All that is left is to choose when and where the final pieces come together."

"You mean for battle?" Zeek questioned. "You mean for them to make war."

Father turned to face him now. "Of course I do. It is the only way to prepare, to make them see sense. In order for Zapour to be ready, there needs to first be a victor. These kingdoms are fractured beyond repair. Alone, they will be picked off, chewed up, and spat into the Sapphire Sea. They need unity, they need strength. They need a ready-made army."

"Can they not make peace? Surely together they would be stronger?"

His father laughed at him. "Search your memories, Zeek. You now hold within you the Light of both a Glaive and a Saelmere. Once you are done looking, you tell me whether you think these two families can cooperate enough to fight alongside one another."

Zeek mused, searching his memories for what he already knew to be true. "This enemy," he said. "You must fear them deeply. Are they really so bad? My kind? Am I truly so dangerous that you would go to such lengths to stop more from becoming like me?"

Father took two steps towards him, eyes narrowing. "Tell me, now that you are awakened, do you feel dangerous?"

Zeek paused again, though he didn't need to search within to answer that question. "Yes. I am very dangerous."

"The Skae, they follow Cova. They will turn this world into an eternal night. No longer will the light rise and fall as it does now. They will eclipse the sky, just as you have seen the stories foretell. They will shroud the land in shadow, destroy anything living in this world, anything worth seeing.

"You made your choice the day that you promised yourself to me," Father continued. "I ask you again, do you wish to return to them? Do you wish to go back to your former life?"

Zeek's fingers twitched. His shadow-tail began to vibrate within the confines of his coat. "No. I am with you, always."

"Good, then I will hear no more talk of it. Now come, there is but one errand left to run so that we might speed up the coming conflict."

Zeek followed in silence. He marvelled in the atmosphere of the forest. Bright leaves of amber and scarlet grew on trees as old as the earth beneath his feet. The path in front of him was littered with colourful flora, and rich with active fauna. Animals darted around him, skittering across the grass and shrubbery, all seeking to live their lives, to survive. Thus was the nature of this world. He was beginning to understand. Every living creature, every human, every animal, every plant, they were all driven by a singular desire – to survive. To make the best of what they had. What if these creatures his father spoke of, the Skae, were just like any other living being? What if all they sought was to survive? Did that make them any less than humans? Was perspective the only thing separating the importance of human desire from that of creatures such as the Skae?

He silenced his thoughts and subconsciously began to

listen to the beating inside of him. The thrumming, constant drum that had been calling him. He remembered the voice, the familiarity, the warmth. How could something so natural be so unwelcome?

Father.

It was unwelcome because Father had said so, had forbidden him to listen. But now listen he did.

There was another sensation slowly creeping its way into his psyche. One he was beginning to welcome, yet feared would overcome him. It had started when he'd encountered that boy. His Light had shone brighter than any he had ever seen. Something within him had reacted then. Even as he'd held the second boy hostage, he'd felt a warmth towards them, as if something within had been urging him to let them go, to save them.

He searched himself, forcing the memory he needed to the forefront of his mind. He stopped, audibly gasping, though he quickly covered the noise by snapping a branch. That boy, the one Father had spoken to. That was Dazen's brother. Once he had a firm grasp on that singular memory, others came in a flood. Images coursed through his mind, flashing brightly, showing him Dazen's life as if he had lived it himself.

His body continued forward, its muscles moving on their own as he followed Father's footsteps, but inside his mind was a flowing vision. He saw Dazen as a child, playing with what he now understood to be his brother and sister. He watched as Dazen unleashed his Shine for the first time, his own body overcome with the ecstasy of the feat. Powerful memories began to pop out, forcing themselves into him like a wave ready to break. He saw the Glaive family at their high table, watched as Raiz carved a piece out of the ceiling with his red

Shine. He saw their sister, Isha. A great sadness overcame him as he watched her taken from them. He could almost feel the arms around his waist as Dazen's father held him back while his sister and brother were assaulted. He felt his pain, his empathy, his helplessness.

More images began to take hold, and with them new feelings, sensations. All at once he felt loneliness, despair, emptiness. Thus were years of his life wasted away on a false sense of duty. Then came hope, power, righteousness. He saw Raiz again, watched as the two brothers met, clashed, fought, and then made up. He watched on as they found their lost sister. His chest tightened, breath coming short as he relived the emotion of the moment, the joy Dazen had felt at that time of reunification.

The memories continued to flow, fractured depictions of the moments that all lead to where Zeek had ended his life. Instead of pushing them back, this time he allowed them all through, watching and feeling as Dazen experienced his first love, the exhilaration of welcoming a daughter into his life, the burdens of ruling that plagued him up until the very end.

Zeek looked down at his hands, Dazen's hands. He shook his head clear, a sharp pain forming in his temple as he attempted to set the memories aside, to regain himself. Not that he truly knew who he was, or even wanted to be. Dazen's experiences were beginning to become his own, but Dazen was not the only one asserting his influence over him. He felt Ancel too, his pain and his torment still very real and present. Just as the Glaive and Saelmere families had clashed in real life, so too did the memories of their two eldest sons within Zeek.

He stopped in the middle of a familiar clearing, allowing

the senses of the real world to return to him. The sun was fading. When had it dipped so low? How much time had passed while he had been lost in memory?

They came to a house that he had been to before, the old and rotting wood staring at him from his vantage point atop a small knoll. This was where he had first felt the light. This was where his life had truly begun. This was where he had killed…

Father returned now from the open door of the small house. A length of rope was fastened around his leg, a trick he had taught himself without the need for arms and hands. He pulled with his thick, muscled legs, dragging a weight that was tied to the rope's end.

Zeek recoiled, and something within him screamed. "Father, what are you doing?"

Father smiled at him. "I am preparing the final piece of the puzzle, as I said. Now, come and help me carry this, would you? I have not the strength to drag the Saelmere brat the entire way back to Trost."

Chapter 30

- Isha –

ISHA HAD BEEN in a trance ever since her encounter with Skeiron beneath Zur's Eye. Did this mean Bessimir was telling the truth? Great Eagles were animals of legend, thought by most to be no more than a myth. But she couldn't deny what her own eyes told her, could she?

No.

It was real, Skeiron was real. She had felt his power, his intelligence, his majesty. Her mind was spinning. Were there more of them in hiding? And if so, what were they hiding from?

She cursed, kicking at a clump of snow as she followed Sounja's heels and made the silent journey back to the city streets of Drin. She hated Bessimir even more now for clouding her mind with these questions. He was clever, too clever, but it had worked. Isha needed to know. She needed answers.

"I've decided to stay," she said to Puk, closing both fists and thrusting them down towards her waist.

Puk frowned. *What about your brother? I thought it was*

decided that we were going home? he gestured.

"I know, and I am sorry, truly. I've seen something, something I cannot ignore. There are answers here, knowledge about my heritage. I believe if I stay then I will find out more about who I am, about who my mother was. That is not an opportunity I can walk away from."

Puk hesitated, brows knitting into a tight crease. He studied her, stepped closer, and pressed his face towards hers. He squinted, staring deep into her eyes.

"I'm not under his spell, Puk," Isha said, averting her gaze and taking a backward step. "His magic doesn't work on me. I haven't fallen prey to some trick of the mind. This decision is my own."

There can be magic in words, Puk signed. *Deceit often accompanies promises. Are you certain his words are true?*

Isha paused and took a steadying breath. "In truth, no, I'm not. There's a lingering thought at the back of my mind telling me to be careful, to see through his charade. But I have seen enough to at least stay a while longer. I'm sorry. This is my choice, my burden. I'll ask them to send you home at first light. You need not suffer here because of my curiosity."

Puk took her hand and pressed it to his lips. *It is good to be curious,* he signed. *Curiosity leads to knowledge. But the best friend to a curious mind is a cautious one. I will stay here, protect you, no matter what you say.*

Isha's heart sank. She didn't deserve such loyalty. "I can't make you do that, Puk."

If you order me to go home, then I will go home. But know that it is not my choice. My choice is to stay here with you, if here is where you need to be.

Isha wrapped her arms around his waist and pulled herself

tight. She pressed her head against his chest. "You are a true friend."

THOUGH THE EXISTENCE of a Great Eagle was still a shock to the system, Bessimir was keeping the rest of his cards close to his chest. There was still so much to learn about the animal. She supposed she didn't blame him. He wanted a reason for her to stay, so it made sense to keep her wanting more.

The memory of Dazen's death was fresh in her mind. Bessimir was there, had been the only one there. She needed answers, needed to know the truth of what happened that night.

Isha thought on what Bessimir had said, about them being able to feel people's emotions, control them. There had been times in her life when she might have demonstrated such an ability, though at the time she might not have realised what she had been doing.

She thought back to her time with Averardus, how he had always afforded her special treatment, despite his callous nature. He had never harmed her, nor ever allowed her to be harmed. She always thought that was because she was his prized possession, but now she was beginning to think it might have been something more.

It happened again during her escape. Argon, a Captain of the Golden Talon, had let her leave. He'd caught her red-handed, but still allowed her to escape. At the time she'd thought it was because he had feelings for her, but now she suspected it might have had something to do with her power.

She was escorted to a private room in the city's palace. Only once her head hit the softness of the pillow did she realise how exhausted she was. She relinquished control as her body relaxed into a state of overdue rest.

She awoke hours later to the blinding light of Zur peeking over the distant horizon. She should be on a ship right now, destined for Zapour. She wondered how Raiz was coping. If he was okay. If he was coming for her…

She needed to tell him, to let him know that she was safe, but that she was staying. The question was how to do it.

During the night, someone must have come to tend to her room, for in place of her tattered clothes was a fresh uniform. She picked up the linen shirt, pressing it against her body, surprised to find that it seemed like a perfect fit. She got herself dressed, thankful that the prince had not left her some flowery dress. She completed the ensemble with a thick coat, and then made her way to the door.

The hall was quiet. She took comfort as Puk turned to face her, dutifully standing by her door, refusing to show even an ounce of weakness, even though he had to be exhausted from a sleepless night.

"I told you to get some sleep," Isha said, miming the words with her hands.

I still do not trust these people, Puk replied.

Isha nodded, surrendering to the idea that no matter what she had said, Puk would have done it anyway.

She had no idea where they were, nor where she should go, so she decided to explore. The halls were not so dissimilar to the palace halls in Illidor. Long, winding passages, spiralling around a central structure. She made her way inward, passing by a number of palace guards along the way, all of whom allowed her to pass unhindered. Puk remained on edge, not trusting a single soul.

Eventually, the halls stopped winding and came together to meet in front of an open corridor. There were no doors blocking the entrance to the expansive room, just two large columns carved from white stone. Intricate patterns that were etched into both its base and top depicted some historical event, which on further inspection looked somewhat familiar.

Isha ran a finger over a portion of the pattern that showed two groups of people meeting at the centre of a large cavern. Her eyes widened as she recognised the shape of the cavern. It was Zur's Eye. Two groups of people were all looking towards the sky. A ray of light descended upon them, lending credit to the prince's tale.

She walked further into the open room. The ceiling was cut into a circle, the outside covered by thick stone, and the inside open, exposed to the elements. This was a surprise, given how cold the climate was in Yagos, but she supposed it hadn't always been this way.

Even in the cold of the morning, a stone table situated in the middle of a bed of snow-capped grass was filled with people. She sauntered around the edge of the structure, keeping to herself as those currently indulging in their morning feast eyed her suspiciously.

She heard the creak of a chair being pulled, drawing her attention. It was Bessimir. He was at the head of the table, with two empty chairs beside him.

He walked over to her, and the others at the table attempted to hide their interest, though Isha could tell when eyes followed her.

"Lady Isha," Bessimir said. "You look well rested. Would you care to join us? There are some people I would like to introduce you to."

She thought about refusing. She didn't fancy being the centrepiece of another large gathering, but if she wanted answers, then she would have to play her part. She threw on a well-practised fake smile, took Bessimir by the hand, and made her way over to the empty chair.

Puk followed cautiously, unsure whether he was welcome, yet not daring to leave Isha's side. Bessimir glanced back at him and spoke. "You are welcome too, Puk, WhiteSword of Illidor."

He finished his sentence with a warm smile, and Isha hated that she couldn't tell if it was genuine or false.

As she took her seat, she recalled the names of some of the familiar faces. Bessimir introduced each in turn regardless. "The man behind me, who you are already acquainted with, is Abhick. He is my First Protector, the Sun's Shield."

Isha reached for her right wrist, remembering the sting of being in his powerful grasp. Puk set his jaw, eyes like darts bearing into the bulky guard as he stood motionless.

"I do apologise for the way the two of you were introduced," Bessimir continued. "I assure you, Abhick is not the type of man for unwarranted violence, but hopefully you can understand, given the nature of your first encounter."

Isha paled, remembering how she pushed him off the boat in her attempt at vengeance, hoping he would sink to his death at the bottom of the Sapphire Sea.

Bessimir moved on, gesturing to the duo seated to his right. "These two you are also familiar with, the twins Sounja and Edar. Sounja is the finest warrior west of the sea, and is my First-Sword, Commander of the Sun's Army."

Sounja sat with her arms crossed, red locks braided and folded over her chest as she continued to stare at her with untrusting eyes.

"And Edar here is my closest confidant, or the Sun's Mind if you would prefer his formal title. One of the greatest minds I have ever come across, unrivalled in stratagem."

Edar didn't look like much, and besides the red hair and similar facial structure, the twins couldn't have been more opposite in their mannerisms. Where Sounja sat straight and looked fearsome, Edar slumped in his chair and fiddled with his thumbs. She remembered how fiercely the Sun Prince had protected him. He'd sacrificed his own flesh so that this man, Edar, would not be harmed.

Isha averted her gaze as Bessimir moved to introduce the rest of those seated at the table.

"The two to your right are Lady Edolina, and Sir Salove Lardel of Stone's Reach." He gestured towards a couple that actually looked as though they could be twins, but from the way their hands intertwined with each other, were clearly man and wife. They inclined their heads towards Isha, though she suspected more out of respect for their prince than for herself.

"Following them are Lord Jehan of Rivermarch, Lady Penrith of Illios, and our leading metallurgist, Sir Dareth Stern."

Isha feigned a polite nod, instinctively moving to hide her eyes from unwanted stares.

"Without the aid of those at this table, we might never have been able to liberate Yagos from the oppressive rule of its former sovereign and set the world on Zur's righteous path."

Indirectly, his words made Isha uncomfortable. She shifted in her seat, glancing around the table and seeing only the faces of conspirators. Men and women under the veil of a scheme which would see an end to Zapour. Had they already acted? Was her brother's death but the first part of their grand plan to 'liberate' all of Zapour? She felt as though she were being mocked, fooled into the belief that what they were preaching was true and just.

Before sense could override her actions, she found herself standing and talking. Her chair creaked on the stone, lending her the complete focus of everyone there. "Is this where you planned it then? To kill my brother?" she said, eyeing everyone she had just been introduced to. "Is this where you plotted to meet with him on the sands of his own country on the promise of parley, only to drive a knife through his heart?"

Her focus was entirely on Bessimir now, who remained surprisingly calm.

"You say your country was recently liberated, I say so were we. The King-Radiant was cruel, his Eagles unjust. They were monsters, distortions of the people they were supposed to represent. But we ended them. My brother helped end them. All so that we of Zapour might seek an opportunity for a better future. And we had it, were making progress on a brighter path. Then it all ended. My brother was murdered on his own coast, and with it any chance our two nations had at cooperation."

She found herself breathless, chest falling without rising.

"Those are quite the accusations you throw around," came a feminine voice from the end of the table. "I assure you we did not plan such a thing. Bessimir would never breach a promise of parley. You should watch your tongue when —"

"Enough, Lady Penrith!" Bessimir interjected, voice raised, hand held in the air. "Isha is well within her rights to believe this to be the truth. I was indeed in a meeting with her brother, king of the sovereign land they call Trost, when he met his end. To an outsider's perspective, all evidence did indeed point to myself as the one responsible. But I swear to you," he said, turning to her. "I swear to you, by my life and by the light that guides me, it was not I who struck him down."

Isha's' brows bunched as she studied his expression. She found no hint of a lie, and she had lived with liars her entire life. "Then who?" she said evenly, the question on everyone's lips.

Bessimir paused, his expression dampening. He sighed. "In truth, I have been struggling with what I saw, and whether I believe what my eyes told me.

"The King of Trost and I were discussing terms of a potential future together when something sinister made its presence known. Something I thought lost and forever forgotten. It moved in the shadows, and left in them just as quickly as it had come."

Isha could see the pain on his face as he spoke, the disappointment in the arch of his brow. "It could just as easily have been me who was struck down," he continued. "I do not know the reason for such an act, but I know that it was calculated. I know that it was purposeful, and now that I have had time to dwell on the incident, I believe I know who was responsible."

The entire table sat motionless, their eyes fixed on their prince.

"I believe it was an attack from a creature known as a Skaeling, an agent of Cova."

A series of audible gasps sounded from across the table.

"It cannot be," a voice said from the other side. "The Skae are long extinct. Your eyes must have deceived you, my prince."

"My eyes never deceive me, Lord Jehan. I know what I saw. I know how it sounds. But the nature of it could not be mistaken. You all know the tales of the Shadow-wars," he said, broadening his view. "I was there. If you are to believe the sun is indeed dying, that we are to be its salvation, then you must not be blind to the realities of the past. The possibility of the Skae returning is plausible."

Several of the gathered guests began muttering amongst themselves, though Isha's gaze was firmly locked onto Bessimir's.

Was this a trick? Another ploy to gain her trust? Or was he speaking the truth, and her brother was truly murdered by such an ancient foe. She sunk deep into her memories, trying to recall the details of that fateful day. She had been so angry, so consumed with hate and the desire for vengeance. But she remembered the wound, the gaping hole in her brother's chest, and the rotting flesh of his withered corpse. She shut her eyes, tears forming as the pain of his death returned.

She had thought it to be poison, some concoction made to cause further pain after the cutting of flesh. But perhaps it was something more…

"Do you know what this means?" It was Sounja who spoke, two hands planted on the stone table. "This means that all we have worked for could be for naught. If the Skae have returned, then the people of Zapour will rise. They will defend their country to the last man. They will gather all of those descended from Shine and they will damn this land to an endless winter!"

"Calm yourself Sounja," Bessimir said, his tone relaxed, despite her urgency. "It is only one potential sighting, let us not get ahead of ourselves."

"What did it look like?" came another voice.

"It had a human face, but its shadow-tail was unmistakable. All Skae are born with one, and are capable of using it to consume their victims, to become them..."

This time it was Isha's turn to talk. "You think this creature sought to become my brother?"

Bessimir held a steady hand in the air. "Its intentions I cannot guess with any certainty, but your brother was strong with Zur's Shine. It is possible for these creatures to harness this power for themselves."

"What will you do then?" Isha questioned. "If what you say is true, and the Skae are returning with the failure of our sun, will you stand with Zapour and fight against them? Or will you sit on your island and let us perish..."

Chapter 31

- Raiz –

RAIZ SAT ON THE THRONE in the empty Great Hall, still unable to place his brother's crown atop his head, instead letting it rest atop a cushion of velvet on a table by his side. He shouldn't be there, shouldn't be the one ruling Trost. He wasn't even a Glaive, not truly. He wondered what would happen if such information became public knowledge. Would anyone challenge his legitimacy? Enough people knew of his true heritage to spark the beginnings of a rumour, but was there another who might seek to take the throne from him?

Trost had many noble houses, all of whom could stake their claim, but in truth, the Glaives had little family. Kron's own father had usurped the crown from the previous king many years ago, and since then the Glaive line had become stagnant. With Dazen's death, Raiz's illegitimacy, and Kron's incapacity, there was little to turn to. Isha should be the one to rule. She was the beating heart of Trost, her strength and her resolve unrivalled by any man. She would make a great queen. But she was not here, and so the burden had fallen to Raiz.

The loneliness was killing him. It was like a slow disease that caught you unaware. Gale was a small comfort, Dazen's First Hand taking on most of the responsibilities that came with governing a country. But Gale had been *Dazen's* friend, *his* confidant, not Raiz's.

With Echo returning to Zuton to strengthen their borders against the gathering army of Kogon, Hector had followed. After nearly losing his life to Celik's pet Skaeling, Raiz couldn't blame him for wanting to be away from him for a time. All he ever did was get that boy into trouble. Though now Hector's ordeal would lend weight to Raiz's story of the Skae returning. Celik may be a bastard, but he was right. The allied nations needed to be prepared. For three separate impending conflicts, it seemed.

A commotion beyond his sight drew his attention. Something was happening outside the doors to the hall. Voices were raised, threats levied. Raiz rose, thinking his enemies had come early.

The double-doors burst open, and a figure tumbled into the Great Hall, a metal helmet clinking on the marble floor as it rolled down the length of the carpeted strip between two seating areas.

"Draz!" Raiz called out, drawing the attention of the two men rolling around on the floor. A Whitesword of Illidor was the first to rise, coming to attention at his king's call. "My king," he said. "I apologise for the interruption, this brigand here was attempting to enter the hall without a writ."

"There is that word again," Draz said. "Draz is confused. Raiz, will you kindly explain to the metal-man here that you are no king, and that Draz does not need a writ to see his friend."

Raiz looked his old friend up and down, eyes dropping as he realised that Draz must not yet know. Another figure approached behind Draz, taller, with long braids of hair flowing around her chest. Aroha placed a hand upon Draz's shoulder, turning his body towards her. They each took in Raiz's facial expression, sensing his anguish and his heartache.

"Draz, now is not the time," Aroha said.

Raiz watched as comprehension dawned. Draz bowed his head and kneeled.

"HOW DID it happen?" Draz asked once the news had settled, and the three of them were free of the confined space of Illidor's Great Hall. They were once again where they belonged, on the open road, albeit within the borders of the capital.

Raiz proceeded to explain to them all he knew, of the meeting between his brother and the Sun Prince, the betrayal, of Isha's absence, and of Kron's vow to see her returned.

Raiz found it a great comfort to share his burdens with people he knew, people he had spent his life with.

He continued to explain all they had missed. About the mustering army in Kogon, the prickets, and the growing tension between the allied nations now that Dazen was no longer with them. He spoke of Celik's appearance, told them that he had survived the blast and Veil's sacrifice.

This drew a disgruntled sigh from Draz. "That man has more lives than Aroha has braids in her hair."

"That's not all," Raiz said. "He has a pet Skaeling with him. It's somehow taken human form, though from the shadow-tail it wielded, it was surely the same type of creature who attacked us in the mountains. I sensed something different about this one though. He was evolved, familiar even."

"What business does Celik have with a Skaeling? I thought he hated their kind." Aroha said.

Raiz could only shake his head. "Your guess is as good as mine, but Celik is a serpent by nature. Using people for his own means is what he does. I don't know what he promised the creature, if it can even comprehend human desire, but he's coerced it somehow."

Draz dropped his shoulders. "And this Skaeling, it was walking during daylight?"

Raiz hesitated, only now comprehending the significance of what had occurred. "There was heavy cloud cover in the sky, and he was hidden beneath the shadow of a tree, but it was daylight, yes."

Aroha leaned in closer. "If these creatures are no longer confined to the mountains, that could mean trouble for the future of Zapour."

"It could mean a return to the Shadow-wars," Raiz said. "This couldn't be happening at a worse time. We're already at war with Yagos to the west, and now Gelvard wishes to press his advantage. We don't have the men to spare for each conflict. Isha is missing, and Dazen is gone from this world."

Raiz turned, trying to suppress his rising anger. His Shine reacted, bubbling at the surface, and he found himself again involuntarily projecting his Flare, much to his companion's discomfort.

"Raiz," Aroha said, pressing through the heat to cup her hand in his. "This problem is not yours to bear alone. Dazen's death is tragic, and we know how much you love your sister, but all is not lost, not yet. We have time. We have help. Kron will find Isha. Wisha and Zuton will not abandon you. Both Dazen and Isha worked hard to bind those nations to Trost. Send out missives, request aid. It will not be denied."

"If only it were that easy," Raiz replied. "Aia and Echo don't trust me. With Kogon mustering so close to Zuton's border, I don't blame them for seeking to bolster their own defence. And the people of Wisha won't come – can't come. They must pass through Craw to make it here, and that journey alone is enough to dissuade sending aid. In addition, their princess, Aia, has informed me of assaults on their settlements, from the north… She suggested they may not be human, and only raid at night."

"You think it's the Skae?" Draz said, forearm tightening.

"It would make sense, yes."

Aroha and Draz shared a knowing look, which Raiz caught. "What is it? What do you know?"

"We have some news," Draz began, "from our trek back to Trost, that might unsettle you…"

Raiz creased his brow. "Well, what is it?"

His friends both hesitated.

"Speak!" he insisted.

It was Aroha who finally broke their silence. "It's about Gelvard, and Lumindal… The Last Light, it's being repaired."

Raiz froze, his voice caught in his chest. He forgot how to breathe, as if the easiest task in the world had somehow become impossible. The Last Light was a poison. Veil had sacrificed her life to ensure such a weapon could never be used again. She had died so that no other child might grow up as she had, motherless and alone, an outcast, a danger to everyone around her. If Gelvard succeeded in making it functional once more, then she would have sacrificed herself for nothing.

Raiz couldn't let it happen, couldn't allow one tyrant to replace another. In a way, Gelvard was worse than Evanon. Where Evanon sought to control, Gelvard would seek to destroy. The Saelmere line were known for their brutality, their ruthlessness. There would be no peace between nations, only a victor. In many ways, Dazen had been a great king. He'd been noble, he'd been just, but he'd also been soft. He should never have allowed Gelvard to take control of Lumindal. Raiz would not make that same mistake. If this was truly his intention, then Raiz would have to crush him.

"Are you sure?" he questioned, his focus returning.

"As sure as we can be," Aroha said. "We intercepted a shipment of peridium heading for Lumindal. There's only one reason someone would be importing so much of that metal. We altered our route to seek a closer look. We ventured as far as we could without risking capture. It's not as tall as it once was, but repairs are being made. The initial explosion splintered the tower to perhaps two thirds of its original height, but the base remains intact."

Raiz grit his teeth, attempting to quell the rising heat within him. "We should have scrapped it for parts when we could. If he completes the tower, then it'll spell the end for us all. He could wipe Illidor from the map without sacrificing a single soldier."

"But this also gives us time," Aroha said. "Gelvard wouldn't risk his own troops on an invasion of Trost when he need not do so. His army might only be intended as a means to clean up what remains of Trost after the Last Light hits Illidor."

"Which would mean we need to go on the offensive. Stop its construction before it can be completed," Raiz said. "I'm not sure if I can convince the others of this course of action. A second assault on Lumindal wouldn't go down well."

"It might be the only way, lad," Draz said.

Raiz withdrew into his mind, remembering a piece of vital information. "Evanon once told me that only one with the blood of a true Radiant would be able to control the Last Light. If what he said is true, then Gelvard's efforts will be for nothing."

"Unless he had a former King-Radiant on his side…" Aroha said.

Realisation dawned upon Raiz like a hammer to his chest.

"That lying sack of pricket shit," Draz said, coming to the same conclusion. "Do you think Celik would really stoop so low?"

"I wouldn't be surprised by anything from that man anymore. I should have killed him when I had the chance," Raiz said, slapping his knee with an open hand.

"Send us to find him," Aroha said. "We'll kill him before he has the chance to do Gelvard's bidding. His life is mine to claim after what he did to my brother. If he's alive, I will end him."

Raiz paused. His friends had only just come back to him. They were to be his comfort, his protection, his confidants and advisers in a time where he was in desperate need of both. But Aroha was right. This was a problem that needed a solution right away. Celik was a stain, his presence a constant threat. He needed to be dealt with, and quickly.

Finally, he nodded. "Go," he said. "Find him and kill him. But be careful, his pet Skaeling is powerful, I could sense it.

Don't underestimate the creature, and watch out for its tail."

Raiz embraced each of his friends in turn, holding Draz's arm for longer than he had expected. "Thank you, the both of you," he said, nodding toward Aroha. "You're true friends. Promise that you'll come back to me alive? I don't think I could bear to lose any more people I love."

Chapter 32

- Isha –

ISHA HAD TAKEN time to ponder Dazen's death, allowing a full day to pass without talking to the prince, or anyone else besides Puk. The more she thought about it, the more difficult it was for her to find any reason for Bessimir to have taken his life. He gained nothing. Dazen had been receptive to his ideals, been willing to learn and negotiate. Killing him served no purpose. Not unless an invasion was imminent.

She decided she needed to break her day of silence if she wanted any more answers. After a brief search, she found Bessimir in the courtyard, absorbed in a game of chess with Edar, and marched right up to him.

"Do you intend to invade my country?" she asked him, deciding to forego subtlety in favour of being direct.

Bessimir stopped and turned toward her. He took his time responding, giving no indication of how he might answer.

Puk came close, sensing the potential for conflict.

"Do you think I wish to invade your country?" Bessimir responded, pitting her question back at her.

Isha scowled. "I am the one asking."

Bessimir smiled. "It is one possible outcome," he said bluntly.

"What is stopping you then?

"War should always be the last choice, only sought after all other options have been exhausted. War is not what the stories claim it to be. It is bloody, gruesome. There are no victors in war, only survivors."

"Then why bother with us at all? Why not leave us be?"

"I would like nothing more than to leave Zapour to their own devices. I have no interest in ruling your country. I am not a conqueror. But Zur is dying, of that there is no doubt. If your country continues down the path they now travel, there will be but one war, and this time there will be no survivors. Eternal cold takes no prisoners. There will be no song of glory, nor any record in the history books, for there will be no one left to write about it."

Isha leaned forward. "And just how do you claim to know this? What evidence do you hold to suggest that this is more than a naturally prolonged winter? The Eagles thought themselves divine. They preached a similar song, believed themselves linked directly to Zur. Said the world would end if they perished. Well, perish they did, yet here we stand."

Bessimir took a deep breath. "I could lie, and say Zur whispers into my ear, as many in this city now believe, though I see that will not work with you. So, I shall give you the truth. I know because I have seen. I know because I have watched this world turn for a thousand years. I was there when the First Light shone. I was there when my order fell, stricken from the records by those who would label themselves divine. I know because Skeiron tells me it is so, as do his kin."

"So, it is vengeance that drives you then. You want to destroy Shine because Shine is what destroyed you."

It was then that she saw it. A flicker of emotion, of rage. It was well disguised, hidden behind a well-practiced façade, but Isha didn't need her power to see his pain.

He shied away, not giving her the chance to delve any deeper. "Perhaps," he eventually replied. "Though vengeance is a narrow pathway. Follow it too long and you're bound to fall off.

"I have learned that to quell violence with more violence is not sustainable. Instead of being the butcher, I would prefer to be the cleanser. If we can remove Shine from this world peacefully, I am open to it."

"Even if my brother had accepted your terms, you must be aware there are those in Zapour who would not be as receptive. Craw and Kogon both boast entire armies packed with Shine users. They would not be open to the idea of a step down in power."

Bessimir inclined his head. "Are you offering a solution?" he questioned.

Isha paused, knowing she spoke with little authority. "If you are truly innocent of the crime of which you are accused, then prove it. Help us defeat the armies of Craw and Kogon. Muster your forces and join them with our own. After the battle is won, we can try to enforce whatever solution you think adequate."

Now it was Bessimir's turn to study her. He stared for longer than she would have liked, long enough for her to shy her head away in discomfort.

"You would so quickly place your trust in me and my countrymen, after all that has happened?" he said.

"Trust is built through action. You say you are innocent. What better way to prove it than fighting alongside your accuser? So long as the fighting benefits both of our causes, I don't see a better alternative."

Bessimir leant back into a smile, and Isha hated the fact that she found the crease of his lip so disarming. "You surprise me again, Glaive. Perhaps there is hope for what you suggest, but you must understand that I am only one man, and I must place the fate of Yagos, and the entire world, before the word of someone who not so long ago tried to stick me with a knife," he said, rubbing at the shallow wound on his chest. "No matter how persuasive and alluring you may be.

"I cannot commit my soldiers to your war on promise alone. I would need a written agreement, signed by all in alliance with you and your kingdom. Only then might I consider your offer."

"I see."

Bessimir opened his posture. "Let us place these talks on hold for the meantime, and instead focus on getting to know each other. There is much I would still like to teach you. And there is someone I would like you to meet."

Isha was about to prod for more information, her curiosity piqued, when Dareth, the lead metallurgist, interrupted. "I am sorry, my prince, but might I have a moment of your time?"

Bessimir's brow creased. "I am in the middle of a conversation."

"Apologies, my prince, but the matter is quite urgent."

"What is it?"

Dareth paused, sparing a glance toward Isha. "The matter is private, m'lord."

Bessimir waved the comment away. "Speak, there are to be

no secrets here."

"Very well," Dareth continued. "There has been an accident in the mines. Several deceased, many more injured."

Bessimir exhaled a heavy sigh. "I see." He turned back to Isha. "Would you excuse me for a time? Meet me at Zur's Eye after sunrise tomorrow, there is much for us to discuss. I will assign a company to escort you, should you need it."

He left before Isha had a chance to reply, rushing off to address Dareth's concern as if the thought of his people dying plagued him deeply.

Isha was left twiddling her fingers, listening to the clash of swords from a friendly duel that had begun in the middle of the open courtyard before her. Before, bladed contests had always bored her, infuriated her even, but ever since she'd started seriously training she had become enthralled by them. The world revolved around battle. If she was to protect herself, she needed to master the blade.

She made to rise, interested if bladework styles were different this side of the sea, but was interrupted by Abhick stepping before her. He stared as if he could see straight through her. She waved a hand in an attempt to gain his attention. He began to gesture, clenching his hands into fists and crossing them over his chest, the symbol for 'fight'. Isha stood confused. Did he want to fight her? Puk had already taught her much. She might not be as adept as Raiz or Dazen, but she was now more than capable. Even so, the thought of facing down this mountain of a man was incredibly intimidating.

Then she followed his eyes, realising with relief that the challenge had not been issued towards her, but to Puk. Puk rose, looking to Isha for approval. Isha opened her palm, suggesting that this was his decision to make, not hers.

Puk squared his shoulders, chest expanding as he set his jaw. Puk was loyal to a fault, but he was also proud. This man, Commander of the Thousand-Shields, represented all that Puk had once been. Just as she needed to find the measure of the Sun Prince, so too did Puk with Abhick. The two made their way towards the sparring area, which had drawn a crowd as anticipation rose.

She looked up to see Edar beckoning her over. He now sat alone, the chess board in front of him in the process of being reset. Isha walked over, taking Bessimir's former seat across from him as he placed the final piece into its starting position. She craned her neck, trying to keep an eye on Puk.

"I would not worry about them," Edar said. "Abhick can be brutal, but he would never do anything to anger Bessimir. He is merely curious. They both are. They are the same, each following a different path, yet winding up at the same destination.

"Would you care to play a game with me?" Edar continued, gesturing at the chess board.

Isha's attention was still on the sparring circle, though as she looked through the crowd she found a set of familiar eyes bearing down on her with enough heat to make her squirm uncomfortably.

Edar laughed. "I would not worry about her either," he said. "My sister will keep her distance, but she does not trust you. She thinks one of you will try to stab me again."

Isha paled, remembering the moment Puk had almost killed him, but then she hardened again. "What makes you think I won't?"

Edar shrugged. "I like to see the best in people, a trait I am afraid my sister did not inherit."

He thumbed at a piece on the board, moving it forward two spaces. "White goes first," he said. "Are you familiar with this game? It is a model made in Zapour. I like to occupy my time with games of strategy."

Isha studied the board. She was indeed familiar with the layout, remembering a time before Averardus took her when Dazen had taught her the pieces and used her to test his theories, all in an attempt to surprise Father with his skill. Of course, he never ended up winning. Kron was too cunning, too calculating, even for one so determined as Dazen.

"I am familiar, yes, though it has been some time since I have played."

Edar took his finger off the piece and gestured for her to make her move. "We will use this as a practice game then, so you might re-familiarise yourself with the rules."

The game came back to her swiftly. Each side boasted sixteen pieces – a King-Radiant, a Queen, two Eagles flanking the pair, two Golden Knights, two Spears, and eight pawns.

Isha wasted no time, moving one of her pawns forward in what was considered a defensive move. Edar continued his aggressive stance, moving his Golden Knight out in an attempt to lock her key pieces in place. Isha didn't care, she immediately moved her Eagle onto the field. Edar moved another pawn into play, and so Isha moved her Golden Knight in front.

The game continued in a similar fashion, though despite his aggressive stance, Edar refused to take her pieces. He was the better player, there was no doubt, but Isha wasn't playing to win. She moved her Queen forward, and on the following move her King-Radiant, following suit until her entire line of 'special' pieces were in front of her pawns.

Edar eyed her. "I am not quite sure you grasp the point of the game," he said. "You are sacrificing all the wrong pieces."

"Am I? Hm, I see it differently," she said, holding her head high. "This is how the game should be played," she continued. "The pawns protected by those with power, not the other way around."

Edar leaned back in his chair. He ran a hand through his hair. "Very clever," he said. "I have an idea."

He rolled his shoulders around in their sockets and cracked his neck. He swiped an arm across the board, wiping it clear, then began to reset the game. This time he placed the pieces differently. Instead of the back line consisting of the special pieces, he placed his pawns behind, all eight of them.

"Same rules, new objective," he said. "The game ends when all eight pawns have been taken from play."

Isha grinned widely. She had not been expecting such a show of respect for her blatant mocking of Edar's game.

Edar made the first move, taking one of her Spears with his Eagle. Isha couldn't hide her delight as she used one of her pawns to take his Eagle off the board, reliving the moment she had freed herself from Averardus and ended his reign.

The game went fairly quickly, the rules clearly not intended for such a reversal. In the end she lost, Edar proving quite formidable, true to his name as the Sun's Mind.

Once the game was over, she noticed that the atmosphere around her had changed. The crowd had grown, and it seemed as though the entire palace had gathered to watch the bout between Puk and Abhick.

Up until this point, the combatants had been allowed time to warm up, though Isha suspected the delay had been more to heighten the spectacle. Now, however, the duel was to begin in earnest, fought without weapons or armour, just bare fists and the skill of hand-to-hand combat.

Isha held her breath as the two charged each other, exchanging a series of blocks and blows that were almost too quick to follow. When the two parted, Puk was panting. Sweat trickled down his face, dripping onto the snow-capped grass. Abhick fared no better. He cradled one arm as if in a sling. His face was contorted into an angry knot. He clearly hadn't expected Puk to be such a capable opponent.

She looked back to Puk, a welt already forming above his right eye. Her first instinct was to intervene, to pull him out of there. It had already gone too far, in her opinion, but she held herself back. This was Puk's fight. These were his people. This was something he needed to do for himself.

Abhick rushed forward, fists raised. The two clashed, throwing and blocking a series of heavy punches before ending in a grapple. Puk was the smaller man, but he held his own.

Isha found herself gasping along with the rhythm of the crowd as each man landed another blow. She remembered the time that Puk had easily defended her against three trained soldiers with nothing but a wooden spoon. This time though, his opponent was no slouch. Both of them were a product of the same regime, born and bred for war. Puk had grown since then, she had taught him that there was more to life than battle and duty, but Abhick seemed to have learnt the same lesson. Neither were fighting because they were ordered to anymore, they were fighting for pride. They were fighting to prove their own ideals stronger. Puk for Isha, Abhick for Bessimir.

She watched as they parted momentarily, only to charge at

each other in one last, desperate attempt. The crowd went still as their two heads clashed together, splitting the air with a sickening crunch. Each combatant was thrust backward, landing with synchronised thuds. Neither moved. Blood seeped down Puk's forehead. Isha looked to Edar, who had promised a clean bout. He too looked surprised, completely transfixed on the outcome, just as she.

Slowly, one of them began to stir. Isha leant on the edge of her seat as Abhick rose. He hovered over the spot where Puk lay prone, struggling to regain consciousness. Isha prepared to leap across the field, ready to place herself between Puk and Abhick, when the big man slowly reached a hand down. Puk hesitated, looking to Isha and then back to his opponent. Finally, he took the arm in his own, and Abhick lifted him onto his feet, thrusting their conjoined arms up into the air. The crowd erupted in a wild cheer, overjoyed with the competitors and their show of sportsmanship.

Isha breathed normally again, releasing a light chuckle as she watched Puk revel in the admiration.

Edar blew a thin stream of air through his lips. "That was a close one," he said, beginning to reset the board for reverse chess. "Another?"

Isha spared one last glance at Puk, who was now conversing with the other liberated members of the Thousand-Shields company. "How did he do it?" she asked.

"Hm?"

"How did he do it, all of this?" she said, motioning to everything around her. "I admit I have never stepped foot on this soil before, but from everything my father taught me, and from the tales told across Zapour, Yagos was always a strict and brutal country. Even the Eagles feared dealing with the former emperor, so rich was his reputation for ruthlessness."

"Ah, I see," Edar said. "An excellent question, and a necessary one, if we are to trust one another, Zapour and Yagos.

"But first, a fair trade. I will tell the story of how we came to be here, if you might tell me the story of how you came to be here."

Isha shrugged. "Agreed, though mine is not so pleasant a tale."

"We have that in common then. I am inclined to believe we have much more in common than first assumed.

"Very well," Edar continued, sending his Golden Knight into attack with the first move of their fresh game. "I will tell you what I know, but you must understand that there is much more to Bessimir's character and his history than I can describe. He was already long-lived when I first encountered him, and had endured many hardships before my time."

Isha pursed her lips. She made her move on the board, though it was a rash one, for her mind was elsewhere.

Edar clasped his hands, placing the game on pause. "Would you believe it if I told you that Sounja and I were born in Zapour?"

Isha looked up, eyes wide. "You were?"

"Mhmm. Though we were not there long. Would you believe me again if I were to tell you that we were royalty?"

"Royalty of Zapour?" She froze, thinking through the possibilities. They couldn't be from Trost, she would have heard of them. They didn't look Wishan either. That left only Zuton, Craw and Kogon. She tightened her grip on the chair beside her, frightened at the prospect they might be allied with an opposing kingdom.

"We were indeed a prince and princess of one of the Six Kingdoms," he said.

Isha racked her brain, eyes darting as she tripped over a certain detail. Her stomach dropped as she realized the only truth that made sense. "You were from Crata?"

Edar nodded. "We were. We were just children then, Sounja and I. We were not present in Hirane when Shine rained down from the sky and annihilated that once grand city. We were elsewhere, spared from the destruction by chance. Sometimes I wish we had perished alongside our father in that blast, for we were found, taken by the Eagles you now claim to be dead.

"I thank you for that, by the way. Ending them as you did. I hated them, and though Bessimir attempted to change their ways, to make them see the light, in my heart I knew they would never change.

"They shipped us to Yagos, traded us for who knows what treasure. Sounja and I were enslaved, tormented, and forced to endure day after day of pain and suffering. I am no fighter, as you can plainly see. My strength is my mind. But my sister, she always fought back, always sought to protect me when I could not protect myself. It often got her into trouble. Most of the time she got away with it, for she was a hard worker. They needed her, the family who owned us, and they needed me even more. Together, we helped them rise from a family of little consequence, to one of the most powerful families in Yagos. But no matter how well we did, no matter how wealthy we made them, we always went to sleep in chains."

Isha forgot about the world around her, engrossed in a story that was all too close to her heart.

"That is when Bessimir came. He held no status back then,

was just a man who could talk his way into anything. He convinced the family that owned us to relinquish their power. Can you believe it? I could not, at first. It was not possible. My owners were ruthless and power hungry, nothing could have deterred their ambition.

"And yet Bessimir did it. He convinced them to sign over their lands, their property, to him. That very night, the couple were found at the bottom of a cliff, having jumped off it of their own free will in front of half a dozen witnesses. It was insane.

"The very next morning he came to us, told us that he was chosen by Zur, and we were inclined to believe him. He freed us of our chains, gave us a choice. If we wished it, we could leave this place, make whatever we wanted of our lives. Or we could serve him. Not in chains, but as his generals. He saved us that day, and every day since."

Isha withdrew, instinct urging her to rub at her eyes. "It was his power, wasn't it," she said. "The way he convinced them. He used his eyes."

Edar nodded. "He did, yes."

"Are you not afraid he has done the same to you? Entranced you into working for him?"

"I will admit, the thought did cross my mind the first time I learnt what he is capable of, but over time I have come to believe it is not the case. Bessimir would never use his powers on me and Sounja, nor anyone else he truly cares about. I am certain of it."

Isha clenched her fist. "He used it on my brother."

Edar took a steadying breath. "Yes, he had planned to use his powers on your brother, to convince him of the correct path."

"And what if he had succeeded, what then? Would he have sent my brother tumbling off a cliff too?"

"No!" Edar protested. "No, he would not have done that. Your brother was a kind man. He saw this, told me so. He had only planned to convince him of the truth. He never had any other intention, I swear it.

"These halls are full of people he has liberated," Edar continued. "He used his attained wealth to purchase the entire Thousand-Shields Company, and then broke the keys in front of them. This was before he took control of Yagos and titled himself the Sun Prince. He seeks to better the world, and he has the means to do it. Yet despite his great ambition, he would throw it all away to save but a single life. You saw him do it on the boat. He placed his body in front of mine, ready to die so that I might live. This is the type of man my prince is. He is the living image of the reimagined board we have in front of us here."

As he spoke, he moved his King-Radiant piece in front of a pawn that was in danger from Isha's Eagle.

Isha sighed, relaxing into her chair. "You spin a fine tale, Edar. One I will think on. Thank you for taking the time to tell it."

Edar flattened a crease in his uniform and pulled his chair further into the table. "It is my honour."

"Now," Isha said, leaning forward. "I believe I owe you a story of my own."

Chapter 33

- Raiz –

BABY NORA SLEPT soundly in his arms. Raiz stood awkwardly on the dais. He didn't know how to hold her. Should he cradle her? Should he hold her upright? Should he be cushioning her head?

He gently rocked her back and forth, only because that's what he had seen his mother do on occasion. He could feel Dazen's strength of spirit writhing within her. For the first time in a long while, Raiz found himself genuinely smiling. It felt odd, feeling joy in a time like this, but he supposed this was what people meant when they said to take joy in the little things.

Holding Nora was helping, distracting. Without her, his mind would wander, and the helplessness would return. He hated feeling powerless. He held the most prestigious title in all of Trost, and yet never in his life had he felt so useless. He was not good at delegating responsibility. He had learned from a young age that if you wanted something done, you needed to do it yourself. Now he was forced to lean on others. Forced to lean on Kron to rescue his sister, on Gale to guide him on matters of the kingdom, and now on Draz and Aroha as they dealt with a problem that he should have taken care of years ago.

He placed those thoughts aside, focusing on the beautiful baby he held in his arms. Sumaya was looking over his shoulder, no doubt fretting over whether Raiz would drop Nora or not. The two of them had not seen eye to eye of late. Raiz didn't think the two of them had ever actually held a conversation where they'd gotten along, but she was trying.

Raiz respected her, and not just because she was the mother of his niece. She was loyal to a fault. She could have left with Echo, taken Nora and moved to Zuton, but she had stayed, not because she had ties here, but because it is what Dazen would have wanted. Nora was a Glaive, she needed to grow up in Illidor, and Sumaya was sacrificing her own life to see that she could.

Although she put on a brave face, Raiz could see how much she was hurting. She hid her grief, keeping herself together for Nora's sake. If Raiz had to put up with her chastising him from time to time, he would, for Dazen.

He turned, bouncing Nora in his arms as she began to stir. Sumaya rose from her chair in the dining hall and Raiz allowed her to take the baby from his arms. "Thank you," he said. "It's nice to be reminded what I'm fighting for, what I'm protecting.

"I'm sorry," he continued, "for all I've done to your family in the past. I'm trying to be a better man, to be a ruler. You were right to question me. But I'm not the man I was two years ago. Though I still have much to learn, I will continue to do my best."

Sumaya lulled Nora back to a peaceful sleep with the comfort that only a mother's arms could provide. "I appreciate it," she said. "I see that you are trying. I know it's not easy, have seen first-hand what the crown did to your brother. And I apologise if my words the other day were harsh. I wasn't myself. I'm afraid I'm still not. Not yet anyway. But if you find yourself needing an ear to listen, know that I'm here if you need me, as is Nora if you need another reminder of what we're fighting to defend."

Raiz placed a gentle hand of gratitude on her shoulder, and then she made to depart. Crossing her path as she left was his faithful First Hand.

"Gale," Raiz called. "It's good to see you. I've been meaning to speak to you about... What's wrong?" Gale walked down the length of the Great Hall in staggered steps. He seemed jittery, with his face unshaven and his hair an oily black tangle. "Is something the matter?"

Gale righted himself, flattening his uniform. "No, apologies, my king. I — it is my wife. She has taken to bed. A sudden sickness has struck her."

Raiz took a comforting step towards the man his brother had called his most loyal friend. "I am so sorry. Is there anything I can do?" He knew Maitreya, she was Isha's friend, who had fled Lumindal alongside her. It pained him to think of her unwell.

Gale seemed about to speak, but held himself back.

"What is it, Gale? You can confide in me. I promise what you say will stay between us."

Gale hesitated, then spoke. "My wife, she has been having

dreams, visions even. I do not understand them, and neither does she, but they are becoming concerning. They are getting worse, more frequent. She says there is a voice in her head. I am afraid it will soon overcome her, and she will not recover."

Raiz paused. He didn't know what to say. He wasn't good at consoling people, but if he wanted to be a better man, he had to try. "We will not let that happen," he said. "These dreams, what are they? What do the voices say?"

"I —" Gale mumbled. "I am not sure. She mentioned something about an eclipse, about a second Darkening. She says something is speaking to her, pulling her. Says she must follow it. I am doing all I can to keep her healthy, sane. It is my fault. I blame myself. I spoke to her of what you saw in the mountains. I did not realise how much it would affect her, frighten her. I placed these thoughts inside her head. I —"

"Take the day," Raiz interrupted. "This is not your fault. You cannot blame yourself. Go, be with her. I will handle matters on my own for a while."

"My Lord, are you sure?"

"Yes, of course. It is the least I can do after all you have done. "But a war is coming, whether we would like one or not. Let us pray this sickness passes. I will need you in the days to come."

"Thank you, my lord. I will be back by your side come morning."

Remembering his courtly manners, Gale bowed deeply and then shuffled off to see to his wife's health.

Raiz, however, remained. His thoughts swirled with possibilities. This couldn't be a coincidence. Celik had mentioned that same thing, the Darkening. What did it mean? How was it all linked?

Raiz looked back to the empty throne and to Dazen's crown, wondering if it was all too much. He wasn't enough, yet he had to be. He was all there was. He reached for his—Shine, his resolve strengthening as new strength flowed through him. He might not have all the answers, but he would find them. He just needed time.

Chapter 34

- Isha -

NOW THAT SHE knew where she was going, Isha found herself able to truly take in the beauty of the northern mountain surrounding Zur's Eye.

The high peaks were capped with a thick layer of snow, and though the sky was shrouded in mist and cloud, she could still see the sun forcing its way through, as if Zur were watching over this very spot.

Puk walked in front of her, the two of them flanked by a contingent of Brightguards — the name she had come to learn was given to Bessimir's highest ranking soldiers. She tugged on Puk's sleeve, still cross at him for what he had done to his face. His entire right eye was covered in purple swelling, and he sported another half-dozen cuts and bruises across his face and neck. And those were only the ones she could see.

"You're hurt," she said, not even bothering to copy the gesture along with her words. "You have nothing to prove. That was reckless."

Puk gently pulled his hand away. She was wrong, and she knew it. Puk had everything to prove, every reason to seek validation and acceptance amongst the people he was born to. Up until the other day he still believed them to be slaves, bound by the keys which had tormented his youth. To find out that he wasn't alone, that he wasn't the only one of them to be liberated, must have been a shock. She just wished it hadn't come at the expense of his body.

"Just be careful is all," she managed to say. "You're all I have here."

Puk took her hand and squeezed it tight, the two continuing to climb the sloping mountain.

Once they arrived at the summit, Puk took his place by the crevasse. Isha parted with him and began the short journey through the darkening gap between the two mountains.

The path was much clearer today. Most of the morning mist lifted, preferring to leave the mountain alone. Fires still burned, illuminating the way towards the centre, just as they had on her previous visit. Isha held her breath, expecting to be greeted by a Great Eagle any minute. Her time with Skeiron previously had been short. In truth, she had been too tired and weak from a long day to truly comprehend his presence. This time would be different. She wanted answers, needed answers. Bessimir had promised her as much, and she intended for him to make good on it.

She was greeted by a familiar scene – a lone figure at the centre of a large chasm, sitting cross legged in a trance-like state as if he were the only person in the world. Unlike last time, she made straight for the pass, edging her way around the base with confidence, despite the chill and the dread that threatened to overcome her should she lose her footing.

She looked down to the bottom of the pit and immediately regretted it, gulping down a nervous lump. What was she expecting, to see an Eagle circling down there? Would it catch her if she fell?

She steadied, skipping the dangerous end of the trail and hopping onto the protruding platform beyond. A light spattering of snow fell, swirling around the cylinder-like cavern, but the wind was not powerful enough to buffer her step.

"Bessimir?" she called.

The Sun Prince's eyes snapped open. Isha still wasn't used to seeing another with eyes that shone as bright as her own. Her mother's were bright, it was true, but this man's eyes were like no others. They oozed power, the colour complimented by a sense of charisma and self-confidence. Her mother might have the same eyes, but she was timid, fragile.

"Are you ready for your first lesson?" Bessimir asked.

Isha heard him, but couldn't help but being distracted, thinking an Eagle could rise at any moment.

"Ah," Bessimir said, sensing her disorientation. "You seek Skeiron. I suppose it is only natural, to be curious. I had been planning to call on him later, once we'd had the chance to speak, but perhaps his presence is necessary.

Once again the prince placed two fingers between his lips and made a high-pitched whistle. Isha looked to the pit, expecting the Eagle to rise like a storm, as it had the before. Instead, the Great Eagle made its presence known atop the mountain's peak. It glided, rather than swooping, allowing the gentle breeze to carry it.

Isha blanched as the enormous bird landed nearby. Even prepared, she found herself caught off guard by the size of it. Being acquainted with Spike had leant her some measure of composure when dealing with a creature of this size, but there was something different about what now spread before her. Something majestic, intelligent. Prickets were intelligent creatures, but their intelligence was instinctual, animalistic. She could tell by the way the Eagle looked at her, the shimmer of its pupil, the way it carried itself, and the aura she felt when in its presence, that this creature was special.

But there was something different about this Eagle. The shape had changed, and the colour. She took a step back, eyeing Bessimir. This wasn't Skeiron. Where Skeiron was thick and broad in the chest, this Great Eagle was more shapely. Where Skeiron was a bronzed gold, this Eagle's feathers shone like sunlight, bright and shimmering. The gold of its tail ended in a plume of red feathers, which ruffled in the gentle breeze. Isha circled. The bird's feathers were tightly packed, its beak long and sharp, ending in a hook.

"This is not Skeiron," she finally voiced.

"Perceptive," Bessimir said. "No, this is Strix. She has requested to meet you, to gain your measure."

"M — my measure?" Isha questioned, lifting her eyes to see several dark shapes peeking over the mountain pass beyond. "Are there more!?"

Bessimir shrugged, gesturing to where she was already looking. "You tell me."

"How many are there?"

"Let us start with what is in front of us for now, shall we?"

"Right, of course," Isha said, returning her full attention to Strix.

"May I?" she questioned, reaching a shaking hand out.

"That response is not mine to give," Bessimir stated, crossing his arms.

Isha took a cautious step forward, acknowledging his

comment and respecting the Eagle's sanctity. She hated that the King-Radiant's followers had named themselves after these magnificent creatures. They had sullied their good name, poisoned it through years of greediness and wrongdoing.

She flinched as she approached, but the Great Eagle remained unmoving, eyes tracking her with practised calculation. Isha leaned in to touch its golden wing, which was now tucked into its side. She felt an energy surrounding the creature, an aura radiating from it that was not dissimilar from when her brother's Shine ran too hot.

"Fair warning," Bessimir intervened. "Besides myself, Strix has not made contact with another human in centuries. If what you tell me about your lineage is accurate, then you should know she was once bonded with your grandmother."

Isha's eyes lit with energy. Her hand recoiled, as if the significance of this moment had somehow tripled. "My grandmother?"

Bessimir nodded. "Are you sure you want to do this? Once the connection is made, you cannot unsee what you will see. The same goes for Strix. If she sees darkness in your heart, if she does not like the person you have become, she will sever the connection, and you will never see her again."

Isha hesitated, confused. She didn't know what that meant. What would she see? She hardened her resolve. She had come too far to turn back now. She needed to find out who she was, who her grandmother was. She needed answers. Her hand touched the first feather.

Immediately, her head flung backwards. A barrage of images assaulted her. Her eyes could no longer see what was in front of her. Instead, they were filled with knowledge, depictions of the past. It took her a moment but once the initial assault had settled, she began to comprehend what she was being shown.

She saw the beginning of it all, clear as day. She saw these mountain ranges, only they were different, flatter, unmarked by divine intervention. She watched as people gathered, close to one hundred of them. She saw through the eyes of an eagle, perched on the shoulder of a woman, though her features were a haze. She watched as if she were being shown a play. A lone figure walked to centre stage, a small lizard clinging to his arm.

Bright pictures flashed through vision that was not her own, suddenly speeding up, slowing down, and then speeding up again. She looked on as these people prayed, pleaded, hoped, but no one answered.

She felt as they felt, their existence hanging by a thread, wishing for a rope long enough to hold onto. And then their prayers were answered. Light shone from above, the brightest light Isha had ever seen. It rained down from the sky, red at its core, with the surrounding light white as snow.

The gathered people panicked, thinking their thread finally cut, their lives ended. But what happened was much greater. The light continued to rain down, pounding into the mountain like a mallet to a drum. The people floated, unhindered. Instead of perishing to the light, they consumed it, became it.

After a time, the light diminished, those affected returning to the lone stone pillar which had survived the onslaught of light. When they came to, when they again found their sanity, they were changed. Isha continued to watch. She saw the figure who had walked into the mountain's centre. He was glowing. She could feel his heat as if she were there, her skin pricking. The lizard that had been attached to his arm was no longer there, instead it had risen, grown into something grand.

All of a sudden, the creature whose eyes she had been watching through took flight. It curled through the sky, great wings beating with renewed power, strength. Those below began to gather, to acknowledge, to understand.

Half of those below shone with a brightness greater than any Isha had ever seen. The other half looked up to the sky, admiring the sight of the first Great Eagle, their eyes shining bright waves of violet.

Isha came to, gasping and panting as if she had taken her last breath. She fell back into strong arms, knowing that Bessimir had caught her fall. She relaxed into his grip, allowing him to carry her weight as she regained her lost breath. He felt safe. All around them was chilled air, but within his arms she was warm.

She pulled away abruptly, brushing free of his grip, remembering who he was, still not fully certain she could trust him.

"What was that?" she said through laboured breaths.

The Great Eagle kept its composure, remaining still and giving her time to recover.

"That is what I call an affiliation," Bessimir said, standing upright. "It is how Great Eagles create a bond."

"So, we are… bonded now?"

Bessimir laughed. "In a sense, yes."

Isha gingerly touched Strix's vibrant feathers again, expecting another outer body experience. This time one did not come. Instead, Strix leaned into her touch, the weight of her neck pushing into her as it nuzzled her hand.

"You have done well. Just as you were shown Strix's origin,

so too was she being shown yours. She knows your past, your experiences, your pain."

"I saw the light, the people, their ascension."

Bessimir nodded. "Then now you know the beginning, the true beginning."

Isha withdrew into her thoughts, unbelieving. Her instinct was to deny, to fight against what she had seen, to declare it false. But how could she deny what had seemed so real. She could still feel the heat of Zur's intervening blast prickling at her skin. The Great Eagle was evidence of the vision's legitimacy. Spike was evidence. Raiz was evidence. She was evidence…

She had always hated religion, reviled it, was repulsed by the idea that people like Averardus were seen as some kind of holy being. Now she knew the truth. Perhaps the Eagles of Lumindal were indeed born of holy blood, but they only spoke in half truths. They were no more holy than any other who could wield the white-light. Only the King-Radiant could claim to be greater, only Raiz held the power gifted by Gallion, greatest of the original Eagles.

"Are there more?" Isha asked. "Like Strix?" she queried again, casting her gaze to the mountainside.

"There are more, yes, but their numbers are few. There is much more for you to learn, for us to teach you, though it can wait. The affiliation takes a toll, especially the first time a connection is made."

"But I want to know now. I need to know now," she pressed. "Say all of this is true. Say you are right, about the Eagles, about Zur dying. I need to know it all, so that I can tell people, help prevent a war that doesn't need to happen."

"Patience, Isha. There is yet time. Zur is indeed dying, but to rush into potential conflict without truly understanding Zur's purpose will do no good for any of us. I fear your brother's death has caused irreparable damage to my country's relationship with Zapour. Even if you now believe all that I have said, there are others in your country who yet hold hatred in their hearts for me and my people."

"Then let me speak to them. Give me time and I might convince them."

Bessimir nodded. "Maybe you will, and maybe you will not. I will allow you to send a missive home, to let your family know you are safe. But there are other ways to convince someone that what you say is true. Ways of the mind, a gift that very few in the world possess, though two of them are standing here on this very platform."

Isha ran a finger over her left eye. "You mean for me to learn my power."

"I do, yes. With my help, you will learn to wield the gift you have been given by Zur. Together, we will unite our nations. Together, we can save the world."

Chapter 35

- Zeek –

ANCEL WASN'T AS heavy as he'd expected. Most of his body had withered away to nothing more than skin and bone. Most of his worth, his essence, had already been consumed by Zeek. He could feel that strength coursing through his veins even as he carried Ancel's body across the plains of Zapour. The real weight was not physical, but emotional. Though the Prince of Craw had lost his life, his mind and his memories still lived on inside of Zeek. They screamed at him. The hatred that had consumed him now spilled into Zeek's consciousness, changing who he was. Zeek fought against it, wrestling back control until Ancel was merely a distant thought in the back of his mind, but he was still there, ever persistent.

Father still hadn't given an explanation of his plan, but that was how it always was. Zeek was simply his tool, the arms he had lost. And he was okay with that, as long as he could walk the light. Father could be selfish, but he could also be generous.

"Ah, here we are," Father said, standing atop a small cliff that overlooked a stone keep. Men wearing black-and-blue uniforms lined the battlements. Twin banners bearing the standard of Trost hung on either side of a drawbridge, which covered a sickly green moat that flowed the length of the keep, circling around until it met with a river on the northern pass.

"And where exactly are we, Father?"

"Our destination," he said with a broad smile.

Zeek grunted. Dumping Ancel on the ground, he made to get a better view of the ominous keep.

"What do you need me to do?"

Father nodded towards the river. "We set the corpse in the water over there, and let nature take its course. The quickest way to start a war is to provide proper motivation. The keep that stands before us is Kirkham, the Glaive's strongest foothold on their northern border. Gelvard is too slow, too patient. If we wish to force his hand, we must give him a reason to begin."

"Forgive me, Father, but isn't Gelvard in the City of Light? How is he to even know his son is here?"

Father shook his head. "You are too young to understand how the world works. I have been at this game a long time, is it not enough to trust that I know what I am doing?"

Zeek gave him a blank look, followed by a nervous shuffle.

Father rolled his eyes. "Fine, if you must know, Gelvard has spies everywhere. Trust me, Ancel's red cloak alone is enough to cause a stir. By the time his body reaches the moat, half the keep will be in uproar, spreading rumours of the washed-up corpse. From there, it is but a matter of time before

Gelvard retaliates.

"Now, if you don't mind," Father continued, "pick up the corpse and start moving, I want this done before darkness touches the sky. If the deed is not done now, we will have to wait until morning. I would rather not wait for a patrol of Glaive loyalists to come snooping.

Zeek obeyed, his muscles acting on reflex. They sauntered through the thick woods surrounding the keep, careful not to run into one of the patrols, which seemed to have doubled since their encounter with Raiz. But despite his recent affinity for the light, Zeek had been born in the shadows, and knew how to stick to them.

They reached the riverbank, finding a space where the water was deep and fast-flowing. He placed Ancel's body by the side, taking one last look at the withered corpse before readying himself to kick it in. Father had made him replace the former prince's clothes with his old uniform. The red cloth had been muddied by the journey, but there was no mistaking its make. If there was to be any further doubt about his identity, he still wore the golden ring given only to the Prince of Craw.

Zeek slipped off his cloak and dropped knee-deep into the water. Before he could act further though, his shadow-tail suddenly unfurled, flexing and stretching into the air before curling around his shoulder, an unmistakable indication of danger.

"Kick that body into the water, and Draz will cut you into little pieces and feed them to whatever cave-dwelling monster gave birth to you, shadow-beast," came a voice from behind.

Zeek turned, Ancel's body half-submerged but not yet taken by the river's current. Two people stood on the riverbank. One was a stocky man wielding twin axes, his body covered in leather strapping and armour. Atop his head he wore a metal helm. His feet were wide, set into an aggressive stance, one axe raised, ready to be loosed at any moment.

The second was a ferocious-looking woman just behind the man. She stood perhaps seven feet tall, with long, braided hair flowing down to her hips, beaten in length only by the massive broadsword she held firm before her, two hands fixed on its hilt.

Zeek shifted to face them, inclining his head as his shadow-tail rose to its full height, now towering over the tall woman even with her advantage on the high-ground.

The man who had spoken took a backward step in surprise, only to reaffirm his stance and take an extra foot forward. "Step away from the body."

Something within Zeek shifted. There was a sense of familiarity about these two. It was as if he knew who they were but couldn't place them. He supposed it made sense. They were in Trost, these were likely Whiteswords, Dazen's chosen warriors. Whiteswords or no, Zeek would dispose of them like he had their master.

Another figure emerged from the treeline, issuing a bellowing laugh that was snatched by the growing wind. "It has been a long time, Draz," Father said.

Caught off-balance, Zeek's eyes narrowed as his gaze shifted from Father to his new combatants.

The man his father had called Draz turned to face him, twirling his axe around his wrist before tightening his grip. The woman behind him stood transfixed, her eyes as wide as if she had seen a ghost. "So, Raiz was right," she said. "You do yet breathe."

"I am not so easy to kill, it seems. Many have tried."

"Then let us finish the job this time," the woman said, bracing her broadsword over one shoulder and coiling like a snake about to strike.

"You two are fools!" Father spat. "Just as Raiz is a fool. You have eyes but you cannot see. Your vision is narrow, always was. You seek to stop that which is in front of you, not what I know to be coming."

"As always, you speak in riddles," the woman replied. "Your words are sour, as is your soul. I believe nothing that comes out of your mouth anymore. I name you a coward. You murdered my brother while he slept, and I will have your life for it."

Father's eyes rolled to the back of his head as he rocked back and forth in an exaggerated show of frustration. "Argon's death was necessary in order for me to hide my identity. Do you think those cretins would have allowed me in their company if they knew my true lineage? Everything I have done, everything I still do, is for the good of Zapour."

"You are not what's good for Zapour," the woman said. "You never were, and you never will be. What is the meaning of this?" she pointed towards Zeek, towards Ancel. "I see what you're doing. You mean to incite a war."

"The war has already begun," Father replied. "I merely wish to accelerate it."

"Why? What possible purpose could you have for throwing us all into turmoil?"

"BECAUSE YOU ARE ALL FOOLS!" Father boomed, before doubling over into a coughing fit, his dead arms offering no comfort as he spat onto the dry soil.

He sucked in a deep breath. "Raiz and that infernal girl destroyed the only weapon capable of stopping what is to come." He let out another few rough coughs, clearing his throat with a long grunt. "Though in truth the fault is mine. I am the one who thought they could be controlled. I raised them to be killers. I used their lust for vengeance toward my own personal gains. I underestimated how far they were willing to go. I will not make the same mistake again. I have a new tool now, a new child. One who knows nothing of vengeance, and one who seeks only to live. My arms may not render me capable of saving this world from destruction, but I have found some that are."

It took Zeek a moment to realise he was speaking about him. He gasped, shaken by such admiration from someone he had thought callous through and through.

The man in the metal helmet waved an axe in the air. "Do you know how insane this sounds, old man? This… thing, it is an abomination! It is Skae! The very beings you wish to destroy. How can you think what you're doing is good for Zapour?"

"Because now you believe me," Father said. "You have seen them. I see the way you look at him. You have seen those tails before. You know what they can do."

Zeek watched as the man with the twin axes reached for his shoulder.

"You have felt their sting, seen their lair, heard their queen…"

"Aye, Draz has seen it. Yet here you stand, allied with such a creature. We cannot let you live. The Last Light must remain in ruin."

"The Last Light is our only defence! Shine is our only defence! The white-light was Zur's gift to us so that we might combat Cova and her beasts, not waste it on petty squabbles."

"Then why are you here, inciting a war between humans?"

"I tried to make peace. I tried to restore the balance and remove those decrepit Eagles from power, but all my efforts were for naught. In order for humanity to thrive in the coming conflict, I must first break them down into one unit. I do not care who the victors are, only that the Last Light remains active. The Darkening is coming. I do not know when, but the Skae will return to these plains, and if we are not prepared, then the sky will fall."

"Draz has heard enough of your lies. You speak only poison. You die here and now."

Zeek reacted, his instincts screaming at him to defend his father as the helmed man attacked. He left the corpse on the riverbank, springing into action, but Father was prepared. He pushed himself backward with a Shine-infused kick, flipping out of reach as the axe hit empty air.

"Aroha, now!" the axe-wielding man said.

The woman — Aroha — leapt forward. Not towards Father, but towards Zeek. Caught off guard, Zeek panicked. Thinking as a human might, he moved his hands to cover his face — a desperate last-ditch effort to protect himself. Thankfully, he wasn't yet human, not entirely. His shadow-tail moved on its own, morphing, shifting, hardening. Its edge turned sharp, just as it had with each victim he had consumed. The woman's broadsword came down hard, the impact of shadow and steel almost soundless, though the force of the blow was far from insignificant.

Zeek was thrust backward, boots skidding in the soil. He grit his teeth, reaffirming his control over his own tail. His foe did not back down, coming at him with a series of relentless strikes, each blow falling like a soundless hammer as he used his tail to parry.

In the background, he could hear Father and his assailant deep in combat. Through each defensive swipe of his tail, he watched the fractured pictures of red Shine shooting through the air. Out of the corner of his eye he saw as his father kicked a leg forward, Shine streaking across the battleground like lightning and thudding into the man's helmet. Zeek let out a sigh of relief, thinking his father the victor, only to catch a second glimpse of the bolt as it ricocheted off the helm and into a nearby branch, sparking it alight with flame as it continued its course of destruction through to the forest's centre.

Smoke mixed with shadow as Zeek and Aroha's battle moved off the riverbank and onto the forest edge, where fire was quickly spreading. He hadn't much experience with hand-to-hand combat. His opponent was clearly a master, but Zeek didn't need to be good. He already knew how to fight, at least, Ancel and Dazen did. He drew upon their memories, their techniques. He didn't think, didn't need to think, he already knew. Using his tail as a sword he went on the offensive, the aggressive woman now on her back foot. He pressed his advantage, finding himself invigorated by the thrill of fighting with someone finally worthy of his skill.

He was learning with every strike, every manoeuvre. His mind was like a sponge, rapidly soaking in information. Using the bulky nature of his opponent's weapon against her, he waited until she fully extended, and then used the moment to whip his tail around, scoring a slash across her calf. He pulled back before she even had time to lift her sword.

She staggered to her knee, teeth bared but eyes still sharp and focused. Zeek went in for a killing blow, but she saw it coming. Using her left arm, she caught his tail mid-length, away from the sharpened end. Zeek tried to wrench it free, but her grip was like iron.

Suddenly realising he also had hands, he threw a punch, his right knuckle scoring a blow on her left eye. He was expecting her to recoil, to relax her grip, but it only tightened. She looked at him, heavy eyes filled with hatred and disgust, and thrust her thick head forward into his.

Zeek reeled, mind a haze. He returned, only to be stuck again by the same mallet-like forehead. He watched in horror as the crazed woman gripped his tail in two giant hands and used it to hoist him off the ground, only to throw him back against it.

Panic and pain lanced through his entire body. Dazen and Ancel had known pain, all of his victims had known pain, but Zeek had never experienced it, not truly. Pain was new to him, and he quickly found he did not like it.

His shoulder burned, and he heard his ribs crack. He struggled for breath, trying desperately to suck in air that refused to come. He heard the sharp ring of metal cutting air, and his body rolled on its own, narrowly missing what would have been a finishing blow.

He broadened his vision, watching as Father was kicked into the blazing inferno that the bordering trees had become. Zeek raged, anger and hatred bubbling as the thought of losing the man who had given him everything became overwhelming. He reached within, searching for strength, and he found it. Shadow mixed with Light, the two opposites colliding, mutating, reforming. He channelled this new-found power, forcing it to the surface.

The woman's blade came down again, this time too quickly

to dodge, so Zeek released what he had found within. The powers given to him in birth and stolen by him through death twined together into one concussive blast that streamed through the palms of his hands, uncontrolled and volatile. It struck the incoming longsword, stopping it momentarily before burning clean through the blade. The woman behind it stood aghast as the beam continued its trajectory, burning through her entire left arm. She cried out in agony, immediately recoiling and retreating.

Zeek wasted no time, pushing wearily to his feet. He limped over to the wall of flames. Father's Shine had wreaked havoc, burning through an entire section of the neighbouring forest. The man with the metal helm was still standing, but when he heard the cry of the ailing female he ran to catch her fall. Zeek used the opportunity to search for his father. It didn't take long to find him, propped against a tree, injured, but alive.

"Father!" Zeek called.

He grumbled, coughing through the smoke as he tried to rise. "Get me... out of here..." he said through laboured breaths.

Zeek obliged, lifting him onto his back, despite his own injuries, and ran for clearer skies.

"The... body..." Father said. "Drop it in... the water!"

Zeek altered his course, allowing him to peek through the trees. The body was gone. Ancel was no longer in the place he'd been left. The current had taken him, and Father's war had begun.

Chapter 36

- Isha -

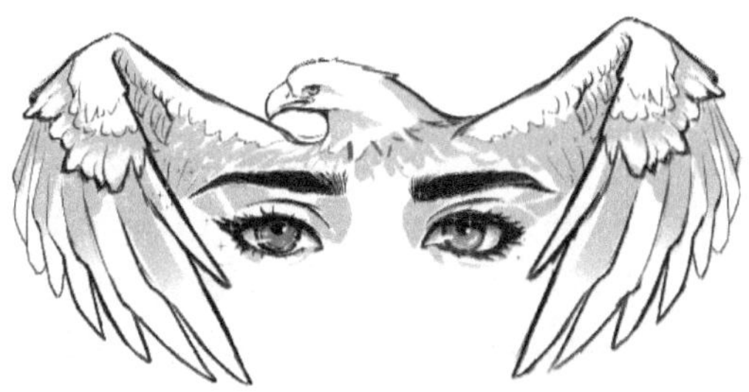

THE NEXT MORNING was similar to the last, though instead of reluctantly rolling over in her sheets, Isha eagerly rose with the sun.

Her mind swirled with thoughts of Strix. All she wanted to do was see her again. It was consuming. She felt unworthy. What had she done to deserve such a connection? Before, she was nothing, a prisoner. Now, she had the chance to be someone, to find out who she was, and carve her own destiny. Why then did she feel so guilty?

Her new connection wasn't the only guilty thought plaguing her mind. Last Night was the first night she hadn't thought of Dazen. This left her feeling empty, like she didn't deserve to move on with her life, not when Dazen was so freshly put to the pyre. in the ground.

She forced her melancholy aside and sat upright. Moving to the desk beside her bed, she grabbed ink and parchment and began composing a letter home. At first, she found the words hard to write, but once she got started they came easily. She addressed it to Raiz. Out of her remaining family, only Raiz would see the truth and the heart behind her words.

She spoke of her experiences so far, emphasising the notion that she was safe, and that she would return of her own accord when she felt the timing was right. She expressed her growing impression of The Sun Prince's innocence, and explained his version of events. She deliberately left it open-ended, suggesting that although her suspicions were abating, they were still present. Perhaps Bessimir would have her letter read and edited, but she had to take the chance and speak her truth.

Just as she was finishing, a knock came at the door. "Who is it?" she called. Puk entered, making the gesture for a summons. Isha took a breath and looked to where her clothes hung by the door. "I need a minute."

Once dressed in appropriate attire, she made her way to the courtyard, where she was greeted by Edar, a person she now found herself surprisingly comfortable with. The two spent the morning playing reverse chess, Edar always getting the better of her. She didn't mind. Isha enjoyed her time with him, found the battle of wits to be a great opportunity to continue prying into Bessimir's life, and the state of Yagos.

After several unsuccessful games, she heard a rough cough coming from beyond the entrance. She inclined her head, watching as two figures walked hand in hand down the paved pathway and into the light of the open ceiling.

A small girl, no older than Raiz had been when he'd first discovered his Shine, walked next to Bessimir. Her face was pale and sickly, and she continued to cough, covering her mouth with her free hand. She was dressed in tattered clothing, a brown rag covering thin and frail shoulders. Her hair was a tangled mess, falling down her face to cover a cute button nose and bright hazel eyes.

Bessimir stopped in the middle of the courtyard and beckoned Isha over. "This here is Naya. Naya, this is Isha. She is an Empath, just like me."

The little girl's face lit up. "Can she help us too?"

Bessimir nodded. "She is still learning, discovering who she is. But it is my hope that yes, one day she will be able to help, to ease the burden you and so many others carry."

"Hello Naya," Isha said, smiling and bending over to greet the child. She shifted back to Bessimir. "Help who?"

"Would you walk with me and Naya into the city? There is something I wish to show you."

Isha paused, suspicious, but nodded. She followed, taking a place next to the girl as the trio left the courtyard. Puk trailed close behind. Naya raised her head to meet Isha's gaze. "You have pretty eyes," she said, smiling brightly before succumbing to another coughing fit.

Isha walked in confusion as they wound their way through the palace and out into the sprawling metropolis of Yagos. Bessimir greeted each and every onlooker with a reassuring nod and a pleasant smile, pausing on occasion to shake a hand or offer words of kindness and thanks in response to admiration. Isha garnered attention as well, though she was received with a wariness that spoke of uncertainty and curiosity.

"Where are we going?" she asked as they walked into a less desirable part of town. They attracted quite a crowd, the allure of the Sun Prince's presence too hard for regular citizens to ignore. Isha thought she spotted Sounja among them, following, her eyes never leaving the prince.

"Not far now," Bessimir said, still clutching Naya's hand.

They came to a circular building of solid stone. The entrance was muddied with an ugly mixture of dirt and snow. Isha had to peg her nose as the smell of sickness and rot grew thick.

Bessimir stopped and turned to her before entering. "I want you to open up your senses," he said. "Relax your mind, allow yourself to feel the emotions of those around you."

Isha frowned, but attempted to do as he said. He was right, she was too tense. Her instinct was to block negative emotions. It was natural for her, and sometimes it had been the only way to survive during her time in captivity.

She relaxed her mind as best she could, and they stepped into the building. The initial burst of emotion was nearly overwhelming. Isha doubled over, her head dizzy. She rose to find Naya's hand in her own, squeezing tight to lend her some much needed reassurance.

There was pain, so much pain. Dozens of people were laid on pallets, injured or sickly. Physicians worked frantically to tend to those most in need. She watched as everyone present acknowledged Bessimir's presence as if they had seen him before and were genuinely excited.

"What is this place?" she whispered so that only Bessimir could hear her.

"This is a hospice, a place for the sick to recover. It is where I come every morning, when I am present and able."

Isha raised a brow. "Are you a healer then?"

Bessimir hesitated. "Not exactly, but in a way, yes. As are you, if you learn to control what I know sleeps within you."

Isha kept quiet, allowing whatever was to play out run its

course. She watched as an ailing man well past his best years began to shake, overcome by a fever-dream. Bessimir approached, leaning over and pressing his hand into the troubled patient. "Ourri, it is I, Bessimir. I need you to focus on my voice, can you do that?"

The patient writhed, his back arching as he struggled to hold still. His eyes fluttered open, glazed and absent. "Cold, so cold," he said, forcing a single eye open, which locked onto the prince.

Bessimir took advantage of the contact, stroking the man's shoulder. The patient's eyes opened fully, and what had been a deep brown now lit with a violet fire. His pupil blazed. Within moments his breathing stilled to a normal rate. His arms stopped shaking, and his body relaxed into the comfort of his pallet.

Bessimir broke his contact, and the man fell peacefully to sleep. The physician on duty pressed the back of her hand to the patient's forehead and wiped it with a damp cloth. "Thank you, my prince. I feared we might lose him today."

Bessimir nodded, already moving onto the next patient.

"You *are* a healer!" Isha said.

"No. What I do here is no miracle cure. I merely take away their pain. I change their thoughts, alter their feelings. The physicians are the ones these people should thank, not me. I am simply here to ease their suffering."

"What do you mean? How do you do that?"

Bessimir moved in beside a man that sat in the corner of the hospice, one hand covering the bandaged stump of his other arm.

He perked up upon seeing the prince approach. "M — my prince, I — I am honoured by your presen — ahh," he choked, leaning forward as his wounded arm pained him.

"What is your name?"

"P — Percius, my prince. "M — my name is Percius."

"And what happened to your arm, Percius?"

"I lost it to the frost. I was a hunter, but the weather up north, it became too harsh. Even thought I migrated south with my family recently, Zur's decline had already taken its toll," he finished, raising his amputated hand and releasing a pained groan.

"Would you like me to take some pain away?" Bessimir asked.

Percius nodded. "Y — yes, my prince. I would be most grateful, most grateful indeed."

Bessimir bent down, again allowing his eyes to lock onto his patient's. "Pay attention," he said, snapping his fingers at Isha.

Isha, startled, moved to his side.

"Can you feel his pain?" he continued, still looking at Percius, though his words were directed at her.

Isha concentrated, opening her mind to the soldier's emotions. "Yes," she said, wincing.

"Good. Now, watch as I take it away."

The patient's eyes gleamed with that same violet fire as he stared at the prince in a glazed-like state. After a moment, his head looked to the ceiling and he released a heavy sigh.

"How do you feel?" Bessimir asked as the hunter regained himself.

"I feel — I feel, amazing! What did you do?" he said, beginning to rise.

Bessimir pressed him back down with a gentle hand on his good shoulder. "Sit, rest. I have not healed you. I have only eased your pain. If you want to make a full recovery, you will need to remain here, and allow the physicians to tend your wound properly."

Percius nodded. "A thousand thank yous, Sun Prince."

Bessimir moved on again, and the pattern repeated. He must have treated over two dozen people before he made to leave. Isha watched with piqued interest. Every encounter was the same. Their eyes shone violet, and then their pain was gone.

"Can I do that?" Isha said as they departed the structure. "Am I capable of what you just did in there?"

"There is only one way to find out," he said, gesturing to the little girl who had followed them out of the hospice. Despite her already positive attitude and joyful energy, Isha could see that she was in pain.

"What is wrong with her?" Isha asked.

"She is dying," Bessimir said plainly.

Isha gasped. "She's what?"

"Her condition is terminal. The physicians have tried to fix her. She has been ill for a full two years now. They say she should have passed already, that the infection has already spread beyond their care."

"Can't you help her?"

Bessimir shook his head. "I am not a healer, remember? I can only ease her pain, allow her to enjoy what time in life she has left, so that she might spend it on her two feet, and not bedridden."

"You take away her pain," Isha said, almost in a whisper.

"Would you like to try it?"

Isha hesitated, turning from the prince and looking back towards Naya. "Would you like me to try?" she asked.

Naya nodded over-enthusiastically, her smile brightening at the thought of the pain once again going away.

Isha looked to Bessimir. "What do I do?"

"Your body already knows what to do," he responded. "You have just never opened yourself to it. Edar told me of your journey, of what you have been through."

Isha made to respond, frustrated with Edar for spilling her secrets, but Bessimir held a hand in the air. "Do not blame Edar, I pressed him to tell me. I wanted to know more about you, and feared your response should I have asked myself."

Isha relaxed. What did it matter if he knew her story? She knew his, at least some of it. But there was always more to a story than the first telling, so she remained cautious.

"I fear that, at first, I misjudged you. It makes sense that you shut your mind to certain emotions given the ordeal life has seen fit to put you through. But you are not in Lumindal anymore. You are free, despite the circumstances that brought you here. In order to influence another, you must first set your own mind free. Look Naya in the eye, allow her emotions to enter your void."

Isha took his advice, unlocking the cage she had for so long used to lock away unwanted emotions. As her eyes met the girl's, she immediately felt her pain, her sorrow. At first, it was too much, and she began to retreat back into her cage, but she was not that person anymore. She focused, allowing the pain to become her.

"Now," Bessimir whispered in her ear. "Alter the emotion. Will the pain away, replace one emotion with another."

Isha acted even as he spoke. She took the child's pain and twisted it, shaking it away until it disbanded. What remained was emptiness. It felt wrong, as if she had meddled with this girl's mind and left her nothing.

"Replace it!" Bessimir urged, sensing her discomfort. "Offer one emotion for another."

Isha concentrated. Naya's eyes lit with a shimmering violet as they opened wide, completely entranced. Isha searched, surfing the girl's mind for positive emotions. Memories came at her in a flood, not vivid and active, but foggy and passive. She felt the emotion of the memories without actually viewing them herself. She found a time when the girl seemed happy. She took hold of that memory, that emotion, and tugged. The effect was immediate. The girl began to relax, to calm. Other emotions accompanied the first. Peace, contentment, joy, love, she pulled on all of them, not with a rough jerk, but a gentle encouragement. Isha became one with the emotions being experienced by the girl. Her mind began to float, her thoughts no longer her own as she gave in to her own influence.

And then they were gone.

Isha came to herself, startled. Her vision was black, a hand was covering her eyes. She pulled it away, breathing heavily. Bessimir stood before her, his grip tight on her wrist. "That is enough for your first time," he said. "You must be careful. Being an Empath is a powerful gift, sometimes too powerful. You must know when to sever the connection, for your own safety."

Isha watched as the girl ran to her and wrapped two tiny arms around her waist. She looked up, and Isha saw the absence of pain in her expression. Her eyes were still coloured, but she was happy.

"How long does it last?" she asked.

Bessimir shrugged. "It depends on many factors. Strong Empaths can influence someone for days at a time. Others, only for a few hours. I witnessed your connection, you are strong, perhaps even stronger than myself, given time. The girl will feel at peace for several days now. If you wish to see her again when your influence wears off, I will arrange it."

Naya gave Isha one last hug before they departed. Isha couldn't help but feel guilty for leaving her, for leaving this place. She might only be a novice, new to her power, but there was more she could do, more people to help.

As they reached the twin pillars of the palace, Bessimir bent over, hands on knees. Sounja rushed from the shadows to his aid, taking him under the shoulder and proceeding to carry him past the bronzed steps, eyeing Isha as she did so. Isha stood, too shocked to say anything. It was the first sign of weakness, of vulnerability, the Sun Prince had shown her since she had arrived here in Yagos.

She walked past Edar on the way in, who was leaning lazily on the pillar, watching as his sister tended to the prince. "This is how it is every day," he said as she passed.

Isha stopped to face him. "What do you mean?"

"He took you to the hospice, yes? To see the sickly?"

Isha nodded.

"It weakens him, what he does to help them. Weakens him to the point of exhaustion."

Isha took a moment to take in what Edar was saying. The effort that it must take, knowing what he must endure every day so that others might find a sliver of peace.

"Why is he showing me all of this?" Isha asked. "Why am I so important to him?"

Edar stood, unmoving, as if he'd been expecting the question. "There are two answers I can provide you with. The first, is that you are important to his plans. You are a princess of a key kingdom in a land he wishes to see change. He believes that if you are to master your Empathic powers then you will be a great asset to his goals and ambitions over there."

Isha frowned, not taking to the idea of being his pawn. "And the second?"

"He is lonely. For centuries he lived in isolation, separated from his own kind, and forced to live with hatred in his heart. I saw it in his expression the moment he first laid eyes upon you. Knowing he was no longer alone nearly broke his composure. I suspect his fascination has only grown as you have begun to reveal your character to him, your strength of spirit, your drive for knowledge, your desire to make right what is wrong."

"Even after I tried to kill him?" Isha queried.

Edar laughed. "I did mention strength of spirit, did I not? He does not see your actions that day as anything but natural, when faced with the situation you were in. The desire to protect one's family is a righteous one, and that is all you did, after all."

She breathed a deep sigh, watching as what could be seen of the day's sun began to set over the distant horizon.

"Can I give you some advice?" Edar said, noticing her stress.

"I suppose you are going to lend me it anyway, so give it your best."

Edar chuckled as he walked down a step to be level with her. "You have a castle, surrounding yourself," he said, making the shape of a box around her head with his hands. "Its walls are high. It is understandable, more than understandable, given what you have been through. But in the end, you chose to be here. There was a reason for that. You must allow yourself to fully experience what Bessimir has to teach you. If you are to be what I know you can be, you should give it a try. It is okay to let your walls down, to be vulnerable."

Isha's brows creased. "I learned long ago that to be vulnerable is to be weak, and weak minds are almost always eaten by strong ones."

"Perhaps," Edar said, stroking his stubble. "There is truth in what you say, in certain circumstances, but in others, there is great strength in vulnerability, and also the opportunity for growth."

Isha withdrew into her thoughts, trying without speaking to comprehend Edar's words. When she was finally ready to respond, she rose to see Edar on his way into the palace, one hand raised over his shoulder as he waved. "Goodnight, Princess. Think on what I have said, and get some deserved rest."

Chapter 37

- Raiz –

RAIZ STARED AT DAZEN'S crown on the cushion beside him. To others, it was a simple crown of gold, but to him, it was a shackle of expectation. He didn't want it. To be relied upon. He wasn't good at it. But there was no one else. Without a Glaive on the throne, Trost would fall to infighting, picked apart by greedy fingers itching to hold a power they would surely abuse. Then again, he wasn't a Glaive…

What if the rumour took root? What if those daring enough began to challenge his reign? Would he submit and give up the power granted to him? Or would he fight?

He mulled the thought over. Would he be expected to marry? To have children? To continue the Glaive name?

He couldn't. Veil still held his heart, her memory living inside of him. What if he forgot about her? He couldn't allow that. Wouldn't allow the memory of her to fade away like a morning dream.

He needed help, needed a friend. He had always lived a lonely life, one of solitude and neglect. He was used to it. But he thought he had finally found a place in this world – a brother he could count on, a sister that cared for him, reliable friends, a lover to call his own…

They were all gone, leaving him to pick up the pieces. Even Gale was no longer there for him, his wife – Isha's good friend, Maitreya – now bedridden by illness. He'd tried so hard over the past two years to let go of the hatred inside of him, to become a better person. Now the old Raiz was starting to resurface. He felt his rage, his anger, beginning to build. Patience did not befit him.

He clenched his fist, taking the crown in his free hand and holding it aloft. He stared at it, but could only see Dazen beneath its crest.

"I will do well by you, Brother," he whispered into the silence of the throne room. "I will make Trost a better place. I will make the world a better place. I swear it."

Through his whispers, he found a measure of confidence. He would do his brother proud. Trost would prosper in Dazen's absence, whatever cost it might bring to his own soul.

"My king!" one of his personal guards called, barging into the empty throne room. "You must come, quickly!"

Raiz rose. "What is it?"

"Aroha, my lord, she is injured."

Raiz raced out of the palace and down the stone steps, terrified of what he might see. He quickly outpaced his own escort, rushing to the infirmary, to his friend.

He slid to a stop on the tiles, his breathing laboured. Draz was outside the room, fingers interlaced around the back of his neck as he paced up and down the hallway.

"Draz!" Raiz called. "What happened?"

Draz turned to face him, eyes watery, helmet set aside and resting next to the door. His anguish turned bitter as his hands dropped to his sides, knuckles white with worry and frustration.

Raiz took a cautioned step forward. "She's not..." he paused.

Draz shook his head. "She's alive, lost in a fever dream, but she won't swing her sword ever again."

Raiz released a breath. "What happened?" he repeated. "Did Celik do this?"

Draz shook his head. "No, it was that... beast." His words came out softly, and he spoke through thin lips, head jerking on an angle, cheeks twitching as if the thought alone brought him unwanted grief.

"The Skaeling?"

Draz nodded.

"Tell me, Draz, I must know what happened."

His friend's eyes rose to meet his own, his hardened expression speaking words of its own. "We fought them, by the river," he said. "Draz fought with Celik, nearly killed him. She fought the Skaeling, had him beaten."

Raiz leant closer.

"He conjured the Light," Draz said. "The creature. He called upon Zur and was answered, though it was different, corrupted. Light and shadow woven into one. An abomination."

Raiz gulped, but said nothing as Draz continued.

"Draz wants no more of this conflict," he continued. "NO MORE OF IT!"

Raiz froze, eyes wide. He had known Draz a long time and

had never seen this much emotion. Draz moved to lean on the wall of the infirmary, one hand covering his brow as if suddenly dizzy. Raiz rushed to comfort him, to lend an arm, but Draz shrugged him off. Raiz recoiled as if struck.

"Leave Draz alone," he said, sliding down the wall until he was sitting on the ground.

"What do you mean? I'm your friend. I'm not going to leave you like this, I never would," Raiz responded.

"You don't get it, do you lad? We stayed for you. Trost isn't our home. This place isn't where we want to spend our lives," he said, gesturing to the city buildings around him. "We stayed because you needed us, because we knew that you were lost without Veil, in need of direction. We thought you might find peace in the north, that you would see there were no answers to be had and could finally find clarity in her death. We were wrong.

"Draz is sorry for your losses, truly. He feels your pain as if it were his own. It *is* his own. But this life is not for us. Draz and Aroha, we want to start a family, to move to the mountains, repopulate and rebuild the Greysword Clan. Can you imagine," he said, looking as though he were watching a dream. "Can you imagine our pups, with my beauty and her strength?"

Raiz couldn't help but choke out a laugh along with his friend.

Draz's laughter soon turned sour, however, as a tear trickled down his cheek. "It was a mistake to go after him. That bastard is more cunning than a fox, and has as many lives as one. Draz is sorry. Sorry that he couldn't be a better warrior. Sorry that he couldn't be a better friend. But we can't live this war anymore."

Raiz wanted to protest, to say that what Draz spoke was nonsense, that he was needed here, but no words came out. Who was he to dictate the course of his friend's life? He hadn't even known Draz had been feeling this way, hadn't even been a good enough friend to ask. He reached out a hand, prepared to accept his decision and reaffirm his support, but just then the door opened.

Out walked a small, ageing woman with hunched shoulders. She carried a wooden cane in one hand, which clacked on the stone tiles as she slowly made her way out of the infirmary.

Draz and Raiz looked at her expectantly. It startled her to see him, her king, but she hid it well. "How is she?" Draz asked.

"She is well, all things considered," the old lady responded.

"Can we see her?" Raiz said, edging forward.

The old lady looked at him, and for a moment he thought she might be considering the consequences of refusing her king, but eventually she relaxed into a sigh. "She is sleeping, but if you wish to sit by her side, you may. Try not to wake her, she needs her rest. The strongest woman I have ever seen, that one. Fighting spirit of a lion. But she is not to be disturbed. Please be careful," she finished, holding Raiz's eye as she spoke.

She stepped aside, and Raiz followed Draz into the dark, candle-lit room. The heavy stench of sweat and blood was concealed by a sweet incense. A small contraption in the corner of the room produced a smoky haze, which gave the room a more pleasant aroma, allowing him to breathe easily.

Aroha was wrapped in a bundle of blankets. The braids of her hair flowed neatly over her chest and shoulders. The lids of her eyes were closed, yet active, as if she were still in the midst of her last battle. She made a faint groaning noise, turning her head to the side, but otherwise she was unmoving. Her right arm rested above the sheets, still as thick and strong as he remembered it. Raiz looked for her left, expecting it to be tucked underneath, but saw only a bandage.

He rounded the table, moving to confirm what he suspected to be true. He gasped, gripping the railing of her bed and recoiling as he felt it burning beneath the might of his over-stimulated Shine.

Her left shoulder was nothing but a stump, the entire arm missing, gone.

He turned to Draz, who could barely look at it. He seemed to be fighting back tears, face twitching, lips quivering.

"He did this?" Raiz asked. "The creature?"

Draz nodded.

"Where is he? I'll make him pay, I will crush him with my bare hands until his bones are ash. I will —"

"Leave it," Draz said, gripping Raiz's arm with the strength of ten men. "He is gone, fled with the old man. Draz hurt him, would have killed him, but we are done. Leave him to his schemes. Her life is more important."

"What of the Last Light? I can't allow him to use it against us."

Draz shook his head. "Whatever his intentions, Celik is not allied with the Saelmeres, that's for sure. At least, if he is, he intends to double-cross them."

"What do you mean? How can you be so sure?"

Draz's expression dampened further. "You should strengthen your borders. War will come to Trost sooner than you know."

Raiz narrowed his eyes. "What do you know?"

"The boy, the prince, Ancel Saelmere. He's is dead. Celik killed him, or his pet Skaeling. Whichever one it was, the prince is a corpse, his body rotted, skin empty of colour. It looked as if it had been drained dry, but I would recognise that boy anywhere. It was the prince, of that there is no doubt."

Raiz took the conversation away from Aroha, ushering his friend towards the back of the room. "Why? It doesn't make sense. Why would he do something like that?"

"Because he is insane. He wishes to ignite the fuse between Trost and Craw, to speed up your war so that the victor might prepare for his. He's framing Alzar Brickham for Ancel's death. When the news spreads, Gelvard will come for them, come for Trost. It's only a matter of time."

Raiz pressed a finger against his temple, attempting to quell the growing headache that continued to nag at him. He mulled the news over in his mind, searching, praying for the right answer to come to him, the right action to take, the right choices to make. This problem was bigger than him alone. He needed Dazen, he would have known what to do. But Draz had done enough. He wasn't even a citizen of Trost, wasn't his to command, never had been. He deserved a break, to start a family, to live in peace.

"Thank you, Draz, for everything. You are a true friend. A loyal friend. This is not your problem any longer. I want you to leave. Once Aroha has recovered, I want the two of you to go. Find a place to call home. Start a family. Rebuild your clan."

Draz paused in his stride, looking first to Aroha, and then to Raiz. He held out a hand, stubby fingers outstretched in a gesture of friendship. Draz looked him in the eye, chin raised, expression hardened. Raiz remembered a time when he would have given his left ear to see the face behind the metal helmet. Raiz wasn't the only one who had changed, who wanted to change. He stuck out his own hand, meeting Draz's, their grips firm.

"Good luck with your war," Draz said. "If you do happen to meet our old master again, kill him for me. Don't hesitate. Don't let him speak, just stick him with your blade."

Raiz nodded, feeling the fire in his belly. He looked to his hands, unwrapping the bandages on his own arms. His left was still blackened from a long time ago. Burned, but not useless. His right, however, had finally healed. He was whole again. He felt it, more than he saw it. He could use his Sine again, and use it he would.

Chapter 38

- Isha –

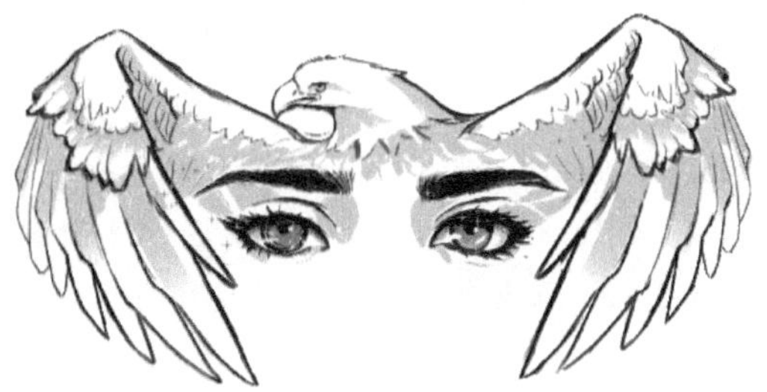

THE NEXT FEW days passed by fairly quickly. Every morning, she played reverse chess with Edar, conversing and sharing stories and ideologies. Puk continued to train in the background with Abhick and the other soldiers. It brought warmth to her heart to see him finding a connection with another, despite the ugly circumstances of what bound them.

Following her game, she would spend an hour practising her swordplay with Puk, and then venture across the city with Bessimir to visit the hospice, where she continued to impart her influence on those who were suffering. She felt her power growing the more she used it. Each time, it became easier. She was beginning to decipher which emotions to heighten and which to dampen to be most effective. She also found truth in Edar's words about the cost of such manipulation. Bessimir treated four times the patients she did every day, yet still she found herself tired to the point of exhaustion.

Today, Strix was waiting at the centre of Zur's Eye. Bessimir was also there, tending to Skeiron's harness. Isha bowed and approached, Strix allowing her to come close. She stroked at her wing, and as she did, her hand brushed against a rough callus. She moved the wing to find a large scar on her breast where feathers no longer grew. She turned to Bessimir. "What happened here?"

Bessimir looked over her shoulder. "I apologize, but that story is not mine to tell."

Isha sighed, taking another look at the nasty scar. It was as if there was a dark cloud around that part of her life, one Isha was afraid to look into. "I feel — I feel like I don't deserve this."

"What do you mean?" Bessimir said, clipping the last buckle on his harness and turning to face her.

"Her," Isha said, motioning towards Strix, who was idly picking at a loose feather. "I'm no warrior. I'm not divine, was not chosen by Zur as you claim to be. I'm just a princess of a foreign land. If I wasn't born with these eyes, Strix wouldn't look twice at me, and neither would you."

Bessimir moved closer. "You think yourself unworthy? Perhaps you are right," he said, catching Isha off guard. "But is anyone truly worthy? I was certainly not when I was so blessed with this gift. I was nobody, a fortunate bystander while other great men and women fought to save this world.

"Worthiness is a state of mind. Have you not suffered enough? Do you not deserve a slice of fortune? Deserving or not, you have been blessed with this gift. Do not waste your potential on self-doubt. I have seen first-hand your courage, your strength of will, your desire to protect, to avenge that which you hold most dear. Strix sees this too. She senses your grandmother's spirit within you. Your potential far exceeds that of anyone I know, you just have to believe you can reach it."

Isha placed a hand over her heart. Part of her still believed that this was all some grand trick, that Bessimir was guilty of the crime she had accused him of, and now was playing her for a fool. But inside she knew him to be innocent. This all felt too real to be a work of fiction.

She was about to respond when a gust of wind buffeted her. She looked up and gasped as two more Great Eagles landed on the stone before her. The two new Eagles were equally as majestic as those she'd already met, though they were easily distinguishable.

One was heavily scarred, long-since healed wounds marring its face, running across its left eye in the shape of two claws. Underneath the scars its eye was as blue as a clear sky, almost white in fact, leading her to believe it had been blinded.

The other was well groomed, as if every feather had a specific place, each complimenting the last. Its golden coat shimmered, giving off a radiance of its own. It raised its golden neck, craning its head to study her.

"Isha," Bessimir continued, gesturing to the well-groomed Eagle. "This is Sypa." He then turned to the battle-scarred one. "And this is Andreni."

Andreni unfurled its wings, not in challenge, but in what seemed to be a boast. Isha rocked backward, blown away by the sheer size of the animal.

"How are they here?" Isha asked, gathering herself.

"They have been in hiding. The ancestors of the Eagles you knew in Zapour stole from them, killed their brethren. They have been waiting, just as I have. But the time for waiting is past. Tell me, are you ready for something more?"

"Something more?

Bessimir motioned toward the gaping canyon behind him.

Isha's chest constricted, her lungs refusing to do their job as she grasped his meaning. She took a step toward the edge, peering down to the mist-shrouded hole that seemed to have no end.

"I — uh..."

"It will complete the bond," he continued. "Strix has chosen you. She will not let you fall. Empaths were made to take to the skies. These animals are our companions. Our spirits are linked through flight."

Isha inched closer to Strix. The two were friendly now, after a couple of encounters. There was a sort of mental bond forming, one she found hard to explain. It was still new, fresh. Already she had begun to care for her, to feel her absence when she left this place. But the thought of flight sent a shiver through her entire body.

"I want to do it. I want to fly with her," she said, as if just saying the words would lend her courage.

She looked Strix in the eye before stroking her wing. While the first time had shaken her into an outer body experience, it was now different. Instead of being tied in the past, their minds were joined in the present. She felt Strix's heartbeat beneath her legs as Bessimir helped her atop the Eagle's back. She felt how calm she was, her eagerness to take to the skies. She felt her composure, her confidence. There was also apprehension, anxiety. Strix feared their new bond. It made sense. Strix's last human bond was centuries ago. It felt right, however, despite their shared unease.

Isha tried not to look, her hands grabbing hold of feathers as she wrapped her arms around the bird's thick neck. The other Eagles watched in anticipation, as if gauging her worth. "What do I hold onto? There's no saddle!" she shouted as the wind picked up.

"The first flight must be done free of saddle," Bessimir said. "It is how it has to be."

Isha felt her heart flutter. Her mind suddenly filled with regret. Why was she trusting him? He was still a stranger. Maybe this was how he planned to take her life? Her body would never be found at the bottom of this endless pit.

No. She had to trust, to put her faith somewhere. She closed her eyes, feeling the weight of the magnificent creature move beneath her own. Her world began to tilt further and further, until together, they fell, plummeting like a rock down a well. She could no longer breathe, her lungs were frozen, expecting death.

Then, finally, Strix pulled up, and Isha sucked in a much-needed breath as her equilibrium adjusted. The Eagle dipped into another half-dive, spiralling between two mountain peaks. She felt the wind in her face. The fear of dying mixed together with the joy of living, the two opposites joining into a brand-new emotion that she had never experienced. She relaxed into it, reminding herself that she was allowed to feel happiness, to revel in the thrill.

Even if her grip faltered, she knew Strix would not let her fall, and if she did, she would catch her.

She spared a look behind but saw only mountains. The prince was gone. It was just her, Strix, and the open skies. She forced herself to still her mind, to bask in the atmosphere. Beyond Zur's Eye was a vast open plain of snowy hills that stretched all the way to the horizon.

She closed her eyes, and for the first moment since her brother's death, she felt at peace. She knew it was only temporary, that as soon as she landed the dark cloud would return, but she decided to enjoy this for what it was, to celebrate her new bond with positive thoughts.

The two flew for what seemed like half a day, though it was likely only a few passing moments. Eventually, Strix veered and returned to the place of the First Light.

Bessimir was waiting for her, hands placed neatly behind his back. The other Great Eagles circled, waiting for their return, cheering for it even.

It took Isha a moment to uncurl her fingers from Strix's feathers. She hadn't realised how tightly she had been holding on. Her fingers were numb. "That was incredible!" she said, forgetting present company and giving in to the jubilation.

"I am glad you enjoyed it," Bessimir said, seeming genuinely pleased.

Isha took a wary step forward, re-adjusting to the ground beneath her feet. "Can I do this again tomorrow?" she asked, sounding like a child.

"Strix is not mine to command. You are bonded. That is not something to take lightly. A bond between a Great Eagle and an Empath is sacred, and not easily broken. You have shared in her memories, and she in yours. It is only the beginning, however. There will be further connections to be made. If you want to ride her again, you need only wish it in your heart. I will not stop you, though if you would like, I can have a proper saddle made."

Isha listened, attention fixed onto Strix as she shook a light fall of snow from her wings. "I would like that very much."

THE DAYS BLENDED TOGETHER as Isha set about her routines. She was quickly coming to enjoy her new life here. Between her games of strategy with Edar, her swordplay with Puk, her work in the hospice with Bessimir, and her bond with Strix, there was much to do.

However, there was something gnawing at her from the inside. Although these changes were welcome, she knew they were only temporary. She had a life back in Illidor, a family who missed her. She hoped Raiz had received her letter. They needed to know she was okay. There was also still a layer of mistrust between her and Bessimir. Not a thick layer. In truth, it was thinning every day, but it was there. She couldn't return to her family yet, not until she was sure of his intentions. She still had more to learn.

She was expecting to see Edar sitting at the table in his usual place this morning, but in his place was Bessimir. His face lit up when he saw her approach. He rose, pretending to brush dirt from his tunic, then bowed. She met his greeting with a slight bow of her own, feigning a smile in an attempt to hide her blush.

"Good morning, my lady," Bessimir said, taking her hand in his own. It felt warm. He always felt warm, despite the cold climate. Her heart fluttered at his touch, a fact that surprised her. She placed a hand on her chest. Her pulse was heightened.

"Is something the matter?" Bessimir asked.

"N — no. I am well, thank you. Just had trouble sleeping is all."

"I see. The fault is mine. I have been pressing you hard lately. You are still new to your gift. It will take time to become fully accustomed to its use. I would normally suggest you take the day off, but I have something different planned for us today, if you would be willing?"

Isha cleared her throat. "What did you have in mind?"

"There has been some trouble up north in the quarry by Stones Reach, in the peridium mines. I am needed at the excavation site. It is a political matter, one my associates have been so far unsuccessful in resolving."

"I see."

"I would like you to accompany me on my journey there, if it would please you? It is not far, only half a day's journey as the Eagle flies."

"You wish for me to ride Strix there?"

"I do, yes. You may take Puk with you, if you like. Sounja will accompany me on Skeiron."

Isha took a moment to consider. Such a long journey would be a test of her bond with Strix, one she didn't know if she was prepared for, but the promise of seeing more of what Yagos had to offer was too tempting to refuse. Ever since the battle at sea she had been curious about peridium. Despite staring at a towering mass of it for years on end in Lumindal, the metal was rare in Zapour. No veins had ever been discovered back home. The Eagles had always relied on shipments from Yagos for their stockpile. Added to that, the metal seemed to be the only counter to Shine. If Trost and Yagos were to be enemies, then it would do her well to learn as much about it as she could. Of course, if they were to be allied, such a resource might prove useful against those who would stand against Trost.

"I will accompany you," she said after a time.

"Excellent, we will be leaving within the hour. I will summon Skeiron and Strix, so you will have no need to venture up the mountain today."

The journey was far less challenging than she was expecting. Puk sat behind her in the saddle made for two. He seemed uncomfortable, scared even, which oddly made her feel more confident. For once, she was the steady hand, the one providing comfort. Strix felt strong beneath her. They followed Skeiron's tail, which zipped in the wind.

Eventually, Skeiron descended, and the clouds parted to show what looked to be a giant brown hole dug into an otherwise white landscape. It was as if someone had come along with an ogre-sized scoop and uprooted part of the earth.

Beyond the quarry was a large snow-capped mountain, and nestled into its side was a neat little town. Bessimir and Skeiron ignored the town, however, making straight for the excavation site. They landed atop a flat surface set above a steep incline.

She dismounted Strix, her high-laced boots sinking deep into a layer of snow. She helped Puk down, and he quickly stepped past her, doubling over and spitting his morning meal into the white beneath his feet.

This drew a raised brow from Bessimir and a mocking laugh from Sounja, but one scowl from Isha set them straight.

Once Puk had recovered, the atmosphere of the quarry became apparent. The sharp ring of metal picks smashing against rock echoed around the huge bowl that made up the exterior of the mining operation. A light flurry of snow fell, which actually made the scene quite beautiful.

The side of the mountain had been entirely hollowed out. Graduated sides that looked like steps rose upward on either side of the bowl. Huge mounds of rubble and stone slabs littered the bottom of the pit, and dozens of tiny tunnels had been dug into the mountain's base. The site was filled with hundreds of workers, all covered in a mixture of dirt and snow. The combination turned the mine into a constantly shifting mass of flesh and mud.

Bessimir offered his hand, and she took it as he led her down a pathway towards a small hut overlooking the site.

Another figure met them there, a short and stocky man that she remembered. His name was Dareth, the prince's prized metallurgist. He greeted her with a warm smile, offering a callused hand to Bessimir in greeting. "My prince, I am glad you could make it. I see you brought the lady. Are you sure that was wise?" he said. "Druthe is not in a pleasant mood, and he gets dangerous when he feels his needs are not being met."

"Isha is more than capable of handling Druthe," Bessimir said. "Besides, she is under my protection. Any aggravation toward her will be seen as a direct assault on my person."

Dareth gulped, nodding.

"What is it you are not telling me?" Bessimir demanded.

Dareth paused, his oversized forehead beginning to drip with sweat. He leaned in closer, as if scared his words would drift in the afternoon breeze. "I have heard rumours, just boys talking, that Druthe's displeasure has grown… rebellious."

Bessimir leant back, issuing a deep sigh. "I see. And where do you stand after hearing this rumour?"

Dareth's expression twisted, shocked at the implication that he might turn coat. "With you, my prince. Druthe is a bully, nothing more."

"Good. Where is he currently? I should like to speak with him personally."

Dareth inclined his head towards the giant pit below.

Bessimir turned to move, but Dareth gripped his forearm.

"What is it?" Bessimir questioned, looking to the grip on his arm.

Dareth removed his hand. "I — there is something you should know, before you go down there."

Bessimir crossed his arms. "I am listening."

Dareth took a deep breath. "The new vein of peridium we found has proven to be quite extensive. At first, Druthe's own men were sufficient for the task. For a while they were happy with their progress. But, as time wore on, more and more offshoots of the vein were found, and there weren't enough workers to fill the quota. Some of the miners felt they were being underpaid for what was being demanded of them. When you departed on your journey to Zapour, Druthe saw fit to purchase hundreds of workers from out west who were... willing to work for cheaper."

Bessimir advanced a step forward, towering over the sturdy metallurgist. "How cheap?"

Dareth gulped. "They work for free, my prince. They are slaves."

Isha's temper flared, thoughts returning to a time when she had been caged, both mentally and physically.

Bessimir nodded curtly and made to leave without her. She thrust her arm against his chest, blocking his path. "I am not a child. I have seen, known, and dealt with slavers my entire life. I do not need to be coddled. I am coming with you."

Bessimir paused. For a moment, she thought he was going to dismiss her, but in the end he motioned her forward.

Heads turned and eyes followed as almost every worker in the area stopped to watch as their prince cleared a path towards the wooden construct in the centre of the pit where the overseers kept their watch. Isha spared a look behind. Skeiron and Strix were perched on a rocky outcropping, watching, observing.

"Druthe!" Bessimir called, fists clenched. "I wish to speak with you."

Isha looked on as whispers were passed up the slippery slope of the ice-covered stairs. Eventually, a man walked down, hands in pockets, head covered by a dark hood. At least three grizzly-looking men flanked him, each carrying short swords at the hip.

Sounja came to Bessimir's side, her chest heaving with the anticipation of a fight brewing. Bessimir held out an arm, which seemed to be all that held Sounja back from drawing her sword and slicing this man in two before his descent was even complete.

"The usurper returns," Druthe said. His voice was rough and course, which made sense, considering his trade. "The man who calls himself Prince of the Sun, chosen by a god to right the world's wrongs. Whatever did I do to deserve such an audience?" Druthe continued, removing his hood and spreading his hands wide.

Isha noticed that he hadn't looked Bessimir directly in the eye, his gaze drifting more towards his chest.

"I have come because word has leaked of the trouble here. I have come because these mines belong to me. I would see the people working them treated humanely."

Druthe scoffed, issuing a distorted, throaty laugh as he took another three steps closer. "You can't be serious. You may have conquered Yagos and dethroned Percival, but these mines are mine. I hold true to our arrangement and see that you get your share of the metal, but I don't appreciate you coming in here and trying to change the way I do business."

"Slavery is not business, it is crime."

Druthe made a show as he rolled his narrow head back and forth. In the background, many of the workers had gathered, some clearly wearing a thrall collar around their necks. Isha winced, instinctively feeling at her own throat, the memory of being pegged to a wall in Lumindal as people stared still prominent.

"You get your product, the rest is none of your concern," Druthe said.

Something inside Isha snapped. Killing Averardus hadn't been enough. No one should be made to suffer as she had. She took a step forward. "Release them! These are people, not property!"

Druthe stared at her as if she were a simple fly on a wall. He laughed. "Do you always let your bitch off her chain like this, Bessimir?"

Isha stood her ground. She saw Bessimir hesitate, expecting him to chastise her for speaking out of turn, or perhaps to brush her aside and pretend she had never spoken in the first place. To her surprise, he did neither.

"Speak to her like that again, and I will have your tongue," he said.

"Bah! You can't simply place a hat on your head and expect all to bow," Druthe said. "My family have been miners for generations. I will not sully my ancestors' names by ceasing a practice that has stood for a thousand years and brought nothing but prosperity to the good citizens of Yagos."

"These people are citizens of Yagos, just like everyone else."

"They are slaves, nothing more," Druthe responded. "They

are property, purchased with good money. Money I earned. Now, I suggest you leave, and take your barking bitch with you."

Isha and Bessimir's rage seemed to join as one. She didn't know this man, didn't have a personal connection to anyone in this country, but she knew slavery. Knew the feeling of metal around her neck, the restriction, the lack of choice allowed to any who bore the collar of a thrall.

In one swift motion, Bessimir drew his sword from its sheath and pointed it at Druthe. In response, Druthe's men drew their short swords, spreading into a protective ring around their leader.

"Don't look him in the eye!" Druthe shouted, drawing his own jewelled sword. "I know what you are, warlock!" he continued, vision fixed on the dirt-stained snow at Bessimir's feet. "I know your tricks, what you have done to the other lords. It won't work on me. These are my lands, to do with what I will! You shouldn't have come alone, prince of nothing. You die here today, you and your pet whore."

Isha tensed, feeling for the sword at her hip. She was no soldier, not yet, but Puk had taught her the art of swordplay well, and she would damn well use it to stick the next person who dared to insult her.

Bessimir held a protective arm in front of her, but she brushed it aside. His expression changed, his focus fixing onto one man circling them who had dared to brave looking him in the eye.

Druthe noticed his man's fixation and called out. "Kill him!"

The veins around Bessimir's eyes bulged as a surge of power swelled around them. The first soldier had his head removed by Sounja the moment he came within a breaths' distance. The second hesitated, staring at the headless corpse and waiting for backup to arrive.

It didn't take long before more of Druthe's men arrived. Puk joined Sounja in front of Bessimir and Isha. They were outnumbered four to one, though her voiceless champion worked quickly to dispatch the first two who came too close.

Druthe's voice rose above the commotion as he called upon more men. "Kill them! Kill them all. This man is not our prince. He is a usurper, a heathen! Kill him now!"

More bodies piled up. Isha swung her sword, deflecting a blow aimed at Puk's side. Puk silenced the aggressor, slicing his throat and leaving him to bleed out on the now blood-stained snow.

The slaves in the background stood and watched, likely too concerned with what might happen to them if they acted and Druthe returned victorious, a feeling Isha sympathised with.

Druthe's lackeys soon doubled, tripled even, as more took up arms against their small but deadly party. There had to be at least fifty, all standing in a nervous circle, staring at the bodies of their fallen comrades.

Sounja taunted them, daring them to enter her ring of death. Some obliged and were cut down as her twin blades rang through the air. Bessimir moved with ruthless efficiency, his blade slicing through flesh and moving onto the next victim before each assailant could even register the end of their life.

Skeiron swooped, sweeping three thugs off their feet. Their screams echoed as they flew high before plummeting to their graves. Strix came to Isha's side, her great wings beating, buffeting those who got too close before she dug her beak into the pink of one of their necks.

Isha gasped, only now realising the true nature of these animals. As ancient and sacred as they were, they were born in war, and their bodies were weapons. Those nearby stood transfixed, none daring to challenge their might.

Druthe continued to bark orders, threatening his soldiers and even the slaves with punishments should they fail to come to his aid. Some listened, past fears overcoming sense as they moved to defend their master. They were just about to throw their lives away when a throaty voice rang out over the commotion.

"Stop! Stop you fools!"

All heads turned to Druthe, who had a sword at his throat. At first, Isha thought it to be Bessimir behind him, for the culprit's eyes shone bright with violet. On second glance though, it was one of Druthe's own men. His grip was iron, the edge of his sword drawing blood.

"What are you doing, Uther," Druthe wheezed. "He's manipulating you. Can't you see?"

The man supposedly named Uther did not relent, pressing his sword even deeper.

Bessimir walked in front of Sounja and Puk. "Lay down your arms!" he shouted.

Everyone around them paused, and the Eagles retreated to Bessimir's side. The men hesitated as Druthe wriggled in Uther's grip. "I will gut you for this, prince of nothing."

"This man," Bessimir said, pointing at Druthe and speaking to the soldiers and slaves, "is not a man of Yagos. He is a man of evil, one who seeks to oppress others for his own benefit. This kind of practice, these kinds of men, are no longer tolerated in this country. I do not wish to spill the blood of innocent soldiers, but if you continue to follow him, you will leave me no choice."

Many continued to hesitate, looking at each other as if waiting to see what would happen before making a decision. Eventually, one of the men threw his sword onto the snow before Bessimir's feet. He moved to the front and knelt. "My sword is yours, Sun Prince."

Others followed, throwing their weapons into a pile as they also knelt before him.

"What are you doing!? You dare aband — ughh,.." Isha gasped as the sword sliced Druthe's neck, red blood spouting as he choked. He dropped to the ground, dead.

Bessimir turned to the slaves, then to Druthe's men. "Free them from their collars!"

Chapter 39

- Zeek –

ZEEK POURED THE last droplets of water from his flask down his father's throat, watching as the cool liquid brought a touch of colour back into his parched lips. He took the water stoically, his glazed eyes continuing to stare at the cloud-covered sun.

Zeek was tired. He had carried his father's wounded body upriver for days now. The fight had taken a lot out of him, and the trek north even more. Though his body was exhausted, his mind was active with thoughts and emotions. He had summoned Light. In his time of need he had prayed to Zur, and Zur had answered. He felt powerful, stronger than he had ever been. He did understand that his power was corrupted, however. Zur was not the only god to have answered his prayers. He felt the darkness within him, mixing with the light. Inside, there was a constant war, a perpetual fight for dominance.

He felt the beat of the foreign entity calling him again, whispering thoughts into his ear, pulling him northward still. He thought about mentioning it to Father, knew that he should, but Father was not himself. He talked in his sleep, and muttered more nonsense while he was awake.

After he had taken in the water, his eyes suddenly shot to life. "Zeek!" he said, almost shouting the name.

Zeek was shaken from his reverie. "Y — yes Father, I am here."

Father turned his head towards him, the black of his pupils wide. "You must stop them. You must stop their coming. The Darkening, it is almost here. This world will break. They must prepare. You must prepare…"

Zeek was taken aback, curiosity turning to fear at the seriousness of his father's tone. "How? What am I to do?"

Father leant in closer, crazed eyes now shaking with fever. "If I am to die, you must seek out Raiz."

Zeek shook his head. "You are not yourself. You must rest, recover your mind and body."

"No!" Father shouted, which turned into a cough. "You must listen. My blood is all that can save us. The Last Light is all that can stop them. Only the blood of a Radiant can protect us. If I am to die, you must find him! You must convince him, or you must consume him."

There was a fire in his eyes now. He stared directly into it, watching as it faded from a flame as bright as Zur himself to a shimmer, and then finally into nothing at all, just a dark pool of black as Father lost consciousness.

Zeek wanted to question him further, to seek details for his vague answer, but his father had faded back into a dream. The wounds the man in the metal helmet had given him were still taking their toll on his aged body.

He wrapped his fingers around his father's ragged clothes. His fists clenched, knuckles turning white. They would pay for what they had done to him.

Chapter 40

– Isha –

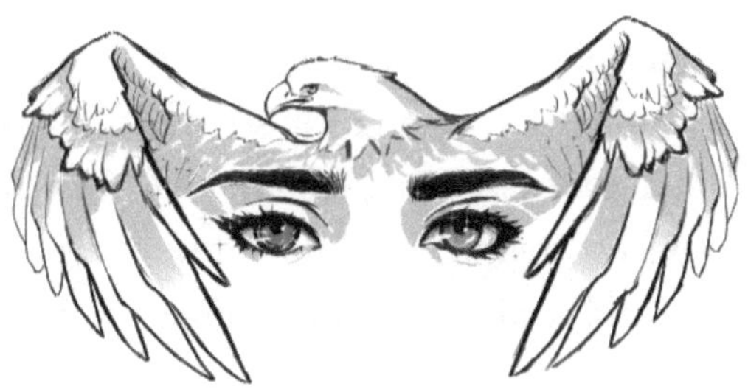

THE TRIP BACK to Drin was surprisingly quick, with most of them too exhausted to make conversation. Druthe's death had been embraced as appropriate, given the circumstance. The enslaved were given the choice to either return to their homes, or remain and work the mines for a decent wage. Many chose to return, and true to his word, Bessimir allowed them to. Many more chose to stay, deciding steady pay for honest work was better than a life on the streets.

Isha hit her pillow hard that night, her mind swirling with thoughts. She tried to settle them, to organise them and come to a conclusion regarding how she felt about what she had seen, though she found the task anything but easy.

A knock came unexpectedly on her door, causing her to jump. It was late for anyone to visit, and she had given Puk the night off. He had done enough for the day, and he needed rest.

She opened the door to find the prince standing there, hand raised as he readied himself to knock again. "Princess. I — uh, I am sorry to bother you so late."

Isha arched a brow. It was rare to see him stumble for words. He was usually so in control, so composed.

"I — I wanted to apologise, for today," he continued. "May I come in?"

Isha thought about saying no, but there was something alluring about him this evening. He seemed vulnerable.

She stepped aside, allowing him into her chamber.

He took a deep breath. "I did not know events would lead to where they did. I placed you in danger, and for that you have my apology."

Isha studied him, searching for any crack in his façade, but as usual there were none. For someone so adept at controlling other people's emotions, he also seemed to express his own rather effortlessly. He was genuine even in his mistakes.

"I chose to be there," Isha said. "Therefore, no apology is needed. But I am curious," she continued. "Why did you bring me?"

Bessimir paused, searching for the right words. Isha didn't wait for him to find them.

"You wanted me to see, didn't you. Wanted me to watch, to learn as you bent a man to your will. You wish for me to do the same, to the people of my country."

Bessimir caught his breath, surprise turning to amusement as he shook his head and laughed. "You are astute. Yes, I wanted to show you that we are capable of more than just easing a person's pain. I had planned to bend Druthe's mind, to quell his stirring rebellion before it gave birth. I was wrong.

I assumed too much, and nearly paid the price for it."

"But you didn't," Isha said. "You prevailed. You killed him. The strike was not your own, but you killed him as sure as the man who held the blade."

Bessimir straightened unapologetically. "I did."

"I suppose you're wondering how I feel about that? If I am disgusted? If I want to leave, get on the next ship back home, forget everything that has happened here?"

Bessimir shrugged. "The thought did cross my mind."

Isha turned, moving to sit on the edge of her bed and placing her hands on her knees. "It does not sit well with me. The thought of controlling someone else, of turning their own thoughts against them. It seems wrong. Unjustified."

She was expecting Bessimir to snap, to rigorously defend his actions, but he just stood, silently acknowledging her words.

When she offered no more, he moved a pace closer. "I am not ignorant of the perversion of my gift. I know how I am seen by those who do not agree with my path. To them, I am a monster, an aberration, a distortion of nature. From the very moment of providence I was marked, destined to either be the prey, or the predator.

"Over the years, I have learned that there are predators far worse than I could ever dare to be. I truly believe that I was chosen by Zur, that I am to be his voice, the voice to drive away the evil that has plagued his creations. Many see this declaration as arrogant, conceited. I suppose they are not wrong. But in this world, there are many forms of evil. So, if I am to act as judge, I must hold myself to a higher standard. I know the hearts of men like Druthe. They cannot be changed. I have seen it before, over and over. I have learned to accept scorn from others for my actions, for it is unavoidable. As long as I am true to myself, then my heart will remain whole.

"Tell me," he continued, stepping closer still. "Your time in Lumindal. If you had known what you were capable of, if you had understood your power back then, would you not have used it? Would you not have swayed your captors' thoughts to your own benefit? To free yourself? Perhaps even to disrupt their entire system?"

Isha rolled the thought over in her mind. Thousands of possibilities, of opportunities, opened up to her. She could have freed them all. She could have made the changes she wished to see in the world. Perhaps she could have even brought down the system, could have saved Raiz the pain and heartbreak of doing it himself.

She looked at her hands, remembering Averardus' blood trickling down her fingers like it was yesterday. In the end, she had killed him anyway, she had become the predator. What if there was a better way? An easier way? All she had to do was ask.

"Teach me," she said, her head rising to look him in the eye. "I want you to teach me how to use my powers, all of them."

He took one last half-step closer, his chest now level with her. Isha flushed as he cupped her chin with his hand, and she rose to meet him. She hesitated, reassuring herself that her mind was indeed strong. She was in control.

She wanted him. She hated that she wanted him, but neither could she deny her lust. She wanted to feel the strength of his hands, the press of his body, the warmth of his lips.

She tried to think rationally, to tell herself she barely knew him, that she had not yet let go of her hatred, but the urge to grab hold of him was overwhelming, her resolve shattering faster than a glass cage struck by a steel hammer. She gravitated towards him, his scent like a drug she had not fully indulged in, and yet knew she would grow addicted to.

A silence hung between them, measured in heartbeats. They stared at each other, finding alleviation in each other's eyes. She saw his pain, knew it as she knew her own. It was hidden deep within, buried beneath a weight so heavy that she wondered how he hadn't yet collapsed. They were the same in more than just the colour of their eyes. He had suffered just as she had.

Like steel to flint, a spark was struck. She embraced him, and he her. Like lost lovers, they wound together as one, lips touching, arms circling. He grabbed a hand-full of hair, caressing her neck with the softness of his lips. She relaxed into it, allowing herself to become fully intoxicated by his seduction.

She bit back at him, a gentle reminder that though she wanted this, she was in charge, not him. She pulled away slightly, enough to leave him wanting more, but not so much as to discourage him.

He pressed forward, aggressive yet forgiving, laying her down on the bed with his body atop hers. She felt her face flush, her inexperience beginning to show. He shifted her hands, moving her, guiding her, all the while his eyes never left her own.

It felt natural, felt right. The pair of them held the passion of the moment even as she fumbled to unlace her dress. He dropped his breeches, and she felt his girth against her thigh as he looked at her, asking without words for her permission.

She wrapped her legs around his waist and pulled him forward, gasping as his warmth entered her. At first there was pain. She cried out, covering her mouth with her hand. But the prince was tender, slow in his work until pain turned to pleasure. Her back arched along with his rhythm. He took the cue and increased his pace.

She intertwined his fingers in her own, basking in the kind of pleasure she had only ever read about in books and stories. Sweat trickled down her brow, down his chest. His muscles were thick, pulled taut. Deep scars ran down the length of his arms and back, long since healed, but likely not forgotten. She pulled him closer, her breasts brushing against his bare chest as the pair of them rocked back and forth.

Their passionate, rhythmic dance extended into the night, though it seemed that time stood still. Eventually, the prince began to moan. She encouraged him, clawing his back with her nails, guiding him to his climax. His moan turned deep, beastly. He gasped, freezing solid as if struck by an arrow. After a gloriously held moment, he released a long breath, withdrawing and relaxing into her open embrace. She held him close, stroking his hair as he nestled into the nook between her neck and shoulder. Each of them drew comfort from the other's presence. Lying there in his arms, she realised that she didn't [illegible] leave.

In the back of her mind, a sliver of doubt still lingered. She pressed it down. She needed to trust. Needed to believe he was good. Because if he wasn't, she knew she would never be able to trust again.

Chapter 41

- Raiz –

RAIZ FELT LIKE a fraud. Not just because he was king of a country he hadn't been born to, but also as a friend. He had been selfish, so single-minded in his grief that he'd forgotten that his friends were grieving too. They had cared for Veil, and even for Dazen in the end, but Raiz had pushed them, asked them to follow him without thought for their own desires, their own dreams.

Of course Draz and Aroha wanted something different, wanted more. This was not their home, it was his, if he could even call it that. It made sense that they wanted to leave, to start a family. Why hadn't they told him?

Now that dream might never come true. Aroha was in critical condition, no longer able to wield a sword. Because of him. Because of his selfishness.

He wanted to go to them, to make it right, to apologise. But that wasn't enough. They needed space, time to recover, to start anew. Maybe he was the poison. It would make sense. Everyone around him ended up hurt or dead.

He unfurled a letter in his hand, reading it for perhaps the tenth time.

Raiz

I'm sure by now news has reached you of our brother's death. My heart is broken. Words cannot describe the sadness that plagues me. It follows me around like a cloud. I feel lost without him, without you. But know that I am alive, and being treated well.

Despite my first assumptions, I am no longer certain the prince was responsible for Dazen's death. Much is still unknown. I do not yet know if he can be fully trusted, but the prince suspects it was the work of a creature known as a Skaeling. I have decided to remain here for a time. Know that this is my choice, made freely. I have been shown something that I cannot ignore. There is history here, knowledge I must seek about my past, who I am, and who I am to be. Regretfully, I cannot go into more detail, though I promise I will share all once we are reunited. Please extend my love to Sumaya and Nora. Know that I am thinking of you all. I will write again when I am more certain of the situation here, but for now, please refrain from sending aid. I know this is a difficult request, but you must trust me. I will explain all in time. Much love.

Isha

Isha was safe. That notion alone released some of the tension from his chest. She was alive, and apparently the Sun Prince was innocent? This changed everything. Perhaps Trost could avoid war with Yagos. But what did that mean? Events were already in motion. Kron was already on his way, perhaps was already there by now. There was nothing Raiz could do to stop him.

His thumb brushed over a particular word on the parchment. Skaeling. If this was true, then Zapour was not prepared for what was coming.

A thump broke from him from his reverie. Gale, his reliable First Hand, stepped into his personal brooding chamber. He seemed skittish, panicked. Not his usual self.

"What is it, Gale? Is Maitreya well?"

"She is fine," he said through laboured breaths. "Recovering as we speak. But… my lord, it is Kirkham…"

"What about it?" Raiz questioned, noting Gale's absent expression.

"My lord, it is no more. Gelvard has sacked the city. The Brickham family is gone. Craw has declared war."

Raiz straightened as if struck by an arrow. "Already? What of the missives we sent? Did none arrive?"

"I fear not, no. We heard nothing in response. His retribution was swift. Our Lightweavers had only just arrived when the forces of Craw surrounded the fortress. Scouting reports speak of the city burning. They suggest that Gelvard has since retreated back to Lumindal, that this was a message, a warning. My lord, what should we do?"

Raiz paused, his mind swirling with thoughts, with rage. Gale stared at him, waiting for an answer. This was the weight Kron had carried with him for Raiz's entire childhood. This was the weight Dazen had struggled with until it nearly broke him. The weight of a decision that could change the future of an entire country.

He hardened his stance and looked to Gale. "Craw has left us with no choice. Trost will go to war.

Interlude

- Kron -

KRON STOOD ON the bow of the ship, watching as icy waves lapped the not-so-distant shoreline. The trip had taken longer than expected. The shores of Yagos were treacherous, much of the ocean frozen over in thin layers of ice. It was impossible to navigate, and even harder for those who didn't know the lands. Added to that was the presence of patrol boats guarding the area, likely increased in number due to the impending conflict between their two nations.

The smuggling ship he'd procured had been forced to sail a roundabout route, one which had added days to his initial estimate.

One crew member had stood against him on the trip, threatening mutiny and proclaiming that no amount of gold was worth losing his life on this cursed journey. Kron had let his tantrum run its course, feeling out the rest of the crew to see how they might react. The rebellious smuggler managed to gain the support of two more out of the twenty-two on board. The three of them came at Kron as one, expecting to overpower him with strength in numbers.

Kron burned them all to a crisp in less than a heartbeat. The rest of the crew watched in horror as their ashes drifted lifeless into the Sapphire Sea. Kron didn't mention the mutiny again, didn't need to, just promised to give the rest of the crew the deceased smugglers' share of coin.

"This is the spot," his captain said as they approached land. "Must have been here at least ten times throughout my career, not once have I ever been spotted. This beach is a dead zone, Lord Glaive."

Kron huffed, amused by his former title. He wasn't a lord any longer, wasn't a king, wasn't anything. Just a concerned father, an ailing father.

The sting of his only true-born son's death was still fresh. That pain threatened to override his composure at every turn. He wanted the world to burn. He would kill this foreign prince for what he had done. Only the thought of his daughter's safety and the warmth of his former lover stayed his hand. Celia was good for him, but she was also terrible for him. She was the kindest soul he had ever known, her heart as pure as the morning sun. But such purity was fragile, and when broken, it gave birth to something sinister, something immoral, corrupted and polluted by heartbreak.

He had become such a monster once before. Now he felt himself turning again. He tried to quell it, to simmer his rage, but each day without his son and his daughter only magnified it.

"Where is Drin from here?" he asked the ship's captain.

The captain took a backward step. Kron looked down to see he was again asserting his flare. He pressed it down, and the captain pointed a shaky hand east. "Through the mountain pass, my lord. Only a day's trek on foot, perhaps less if you don't stop to rest."

Kron grunted, following his outstretched hand. The snow was thick, but snow melted, and right now he was a furnace.

"You will wait here until I return with my daughter," he said, his tone reminiscent of a time when he had ruled a kingdom. "If I should come back to find you have left, then know that if I survive, I will see to it that your vessel becomes ash, along with everyone on board. Do as I say, and the rest of the gold will be yours upon my return to Trost. Am I understood?"

The captain's lips quivered. He made a show of feigning courage, but Kron could see through the façade. He was shaking in his boots, and he would obey.

Kron grunted again, uncrossing his arms. A small boat had been prepared, and he stepped into it, waiting patiently as his commandeered crew lowered it for him. Once in the water, he sat, and he rowed.

The snow parted as expected. Kron felt like his old self again, the power of Zur never having left his veins. If this man titled himself the Prince of the Sun, then Kron was its King. He would show him what it meant to mess with a Glaive, would do what he should have done years ago and defend his kin.

He followed the coastline, keeping to the mountain trail for just over half a day until finally he saw the city of Drin nestled into the centre of a giant bay. He tempered his Flare. What was to come next would require a more subtle tactic. His goal was to see Isha to safety. He reminded himself that she was his priority, not vengeance, but the lust for it was an ongoing battle, one he wasn't sure he could assuage.

He lifted the hood of his cloak, staring at his feet as he approached the city from the dockside. Drin was an open city, with people coming and going as they pleased. Unlike Illidor, there were no high walls, nor heavy barricades. There was an abundance of city-watch, however. Vigilant eyes watched everything. Men in armour as sleek as steel lined every street. All bore the symbol of a yellow sun, which was imprinted on their breastplates.

He brushed against one on his trek towards the city centre. He almost doubled over, his legs turning to mud at the touch. He caught himself just in time, meeting the soldier's eye before quickly breaking line of sight and disappearing into the oncoming crowd.

He steadied, catching his breath. He had felt that touch before. It was peridium. He cast his gaze along the ranks of soldiers. They were all wearing peridium. Entire suits of armour had been fashioned out of the rare metal. He silently cursed. He would have to be careful.

He had a good idea where his daughter might be. These entitled people were all the same, all looking for something they couldn't have. Isha would be near the prince, he was sure of it.

He wasn't oblivious. He had heard the rumours. This man, this predator, was a Mystic, an Empath, just like his wife and daughter. At least he claimed to be. Kron, more than any, knew what someone with that kind of power was capable of. Even though Celia had a kind heart, deep down he knew what she could accomplish if she ever set her mind to it.

He sauntered down a nearby alley, grabbing an isolated beggar by the shoulder and pushing him against the wall. "Where can I find the prince?" he demanded.

The beggar gasped, eyes wide, voice shaking. "I — I — what?"

"Where can I find the Sun Prince?" Kron repeated, loosening his grip a little.

The beggar raised a quivering arm, pointing north. "H — he's in the palace. C — can't miss it."

Kron let him go, following his gesture. Sure enough, one building rose above the others. It wasn't as prominent as the palace in Illidor. There was no Moon-spire calling attention, just a gradual rise in the height of each building surrounding a central structure.

The beggar crawled away, seeping back into the shadow of the alley. Kron ignored him. Each step took him closer to his goal. The closer he came, the less cautious he acted. He couldn't help it. This man killed his son. This man kidnapped his daughter.

He forced down his emotions, using what little self-control he still had to remind himself of his purpose. Unlike the city's entrance, the palace was a fortress. Guards were posted at every entrance, spears in hand and swords on hips. Kron circled the structure, searching for a weakness, a point of entry that would not result in piles of bodies and his potential capture.

There was none.

He made another lap, careful to keep hidden among the still bustling crowd. The market was fervent, merchants called out, intent on selling their wares, and customers haggled, determined to see their prices reduced. He needed a distraction. Fortunately, he knew just how to make one.

Kron worked his fingers, calling his inner Light to the surface. He didn't need much, just a spark. He hid beneath the shadow of a market stall, feeling the fabric of a length of cotton being used as a buffer for the wind, and igniting it.

He walked away as if nothing had happened, but the fire was already building. He positioned himself in reach of a place where the security of the palace was lightest, and waited for his plan to unfold.

It didn't take long for the fire to spread. It was likely rare to see a market-fire in these parts, for the chill kept things nice and cold. But they would soon find out that Shine was brighter than flame, and much, much hotter.

The blaze blew from a small kindle into a boiling mass of fire and smoke. It spread quickly, jumping from stall to stall. People cried out, the crowd bunching together as a small panic set in. The blaze was controllable, would likely be put out soon, but it had drawn attention, and the palace guards were caught up by the disturbance.

There was still no point of easy entry, for despite the distraction, the guards were disciplined, and they remained at their posts, but their eyes were on his diversion.

He walked leisurely up to the palace wall, a spot hidden well enough from public view between the south and eastern entrances to the palace. Then he called upon his Shine, this time generating more than a spark. It bubbled in his hand, and when he thrust his right arm forward, white-light flowed from his open palm, shifting with his circular movements. It didn't take long for the wall to crack. He kicked the centre of the carved stone, watching as it crumbled, the structure outside of his design remaining intact.

With heavy boots crunching over ruined stone, he walked inside, brushing dust off his jacket. There was no one here, just an empty hallway. He moved with haste. If someone were to uncover the makeshift point of entry, it would not bode well for his chances of escape.

He clung to the shadows, hood raised, footsteps quiet, but he was not subtle by nature, and he certainly didn't fit in here. He heard raised voices, watching around a corner as a group of people made for the southern entrance, likely drawn to the earlier commotion he had caused.

He wound his way around a meandering corridor,

checking every room for his daughter. Most were empty, but some were occupied. For those that were, he quickly left, applying his Shine to the door handle and hinges so that whoever was inside would have to take their time forcing it open.

A guard spotted him attempting to melt one of the doors shut and made for him, the death's end of his spear pointing in his direction. The guard made no noise, just set his face into a determined grimace and charged.

The guard was experienced, his stance practised and his strength evidenced by a powerful thrust. Kron dodged, forced backward. He felt his arm weaken as it came into contact with a peridium gauntlet. It had been a long time, but Kron had spent his entire youth training in close combat. What they didn't teach you when training with spear and sword, however, is that one well-placed blast of Shine was all you needed to end a fight before it had truly begun.

The aggressive guard may have been well trained and well armoured, but he had made the mistake of forgetting his helmet today, so Kron made him pay.

His hand ablaze with a molten ball of white, he sidestepped the spear and lunged forward, listening to the sizzle as Shine met flesh. The now headless guard dropped to the floor, the smell of burnt meat loitering. His spear clattered onto the marble tiling, making a noise Kron would have preferred it not have.

He quickly moved on, the urgency of the situation rising with every second he was without his daughter. Eventually, he came across another guard. This one wasn't wearing the same armour as the rest. There was no peridium on his person, though there was something familiar about him.

He stood perfectly still. Long black hair ran down to his shoulders, and he was dressed in a loose cotton shirt and brown trousers. His hand was firm on the hilt of the sword at his hip. Recognition ignited in both of their expressions, Kron finding validation in the lazy eye, which remained unfocused despite the man drawing his sword and pointing it his way.

Kron tried to recall his name, but could only remember that he was the mute that followed his daughter around all day like a trained dog. He remembered the report of Isha's capture. The mute had been involved, but how? Was he caught alongside her? Or was he a conspirator? It didn't matter. He was alive, which told him all he needed to know. Isha was likely behind the door he now guarded.

Kron grit his teeth and summoned his Shine, prepared to get rid of anyone who stood in his path. The mute reacted, dodging the first bolt of Shine with a twist of his body. Kron drew his own blade, moving to overpower the guard's smaller frame, but the mute was strong, despite the difference in size. And he was quick. He repositioned, striking at Kron on an angle. Kron blocked his blow, metal meeting metal with a loud clang.

Kron didn't have time for this. He needed to finish it quickly. He thrust a giant boot into the mute's abdomen, sending him reeling backwards, then grasped his sword arm and slammed it against the wall. The mute dropped his blade, but used Kron's strength to his own advantage, leveraging the grapple into a kick that struck his temple, causing him to stagger.

Kron touched his lip, fingers coming away bloody. He reached for his Shine once more. He'd been meaning to save some of it for his escape, but this situation demanded it. He pushed outward with his will, using all his years of training and discipline as he imparted his Flare on the world around him.

The mute fell to his knees, unable to counter the invisible force. Kron swung at him, meaning to land the killing blow, but the mute was cunning. He managed to dodge his strike with a well-timed twist.

Kron eyed the door. He was wasting too much time. He doubled down on his Flare, thinking to end his assailant with one final slice of his sword. To his surprise, the mute regained his feet. Kron gasped, not having expected such strength of spirit. The Flare was a powerful technique, but it was not invincible. It took a mental toll on the user, and therefore couldn't be used forever. It took an even greater toll on those within range of it, however, and only those trained to withstand its touch or those with impeccable mental and physical discipline could fight through it.

The mute found his sword and moved into his stance, enraging Kron. Ignoring the swords altogether, he kicked viciously at the mute, sending him tumbling through the air. His head hit the marble floor with a sickening crack, and Kron left him there, bleeding.

Pushing the door open, Kron burst into the room like a rampaging bull. He saw his daughter strewn on the bed, half undressed, a man with shining violet eyes atop her. Kron raged, his breath ragged and laboured. His Flare multiplied, and fragments of rock broke from the ceiling as the entire room was shaken by his intrusive power.

The prince made to move for his sword, which was at the foot of the bed, but Kron intensified his Flare even further, and gravity amplified along with it. The prince was pinned to the floor, though even then Kron could feel the power of his eyes.

"Father! No!" he heard Isha cry. "You don't understand. Stop!"

But Kron was too far gone. There would be no negotiation, no reasonable conversation. The time for that had passed. This was the man who killed his son. And now he had taken his daughter. Kron shut his eyes, but kept his Flare strong. "Come, Daughter," he said. "Do not look him in the eye. Free your mind from his grasp and come to me."

"Father, you don't understand. Please, I beg of you. Stop this. I can explain!"

It was no use. He had corrupted her. His daughter's thoughts were not her own. Kron turned his attention back to the shirtless prince. "I know your tricks, Empath. You will not find me as easy to control as you might think."

As he spoke, Kron launched himself across the room toward the prince, but Isha protectively flung herself on top of him.

Kron slipped further into his pit of fury. It was his fault, he should have been there to protect her, to protect his kin from this monster. He grabbed Isha by the wrist and wrenched her free. He readied his Shine for the kill, but Isha pulled on his arm at the last second, and the Shine blasted through the ceiling instead. Pieces of rubble rained down, and the entire room began to shake.

Kron turned to chastise his daughter, but she fell limp in his arms. Blood seeped from an open head wound, a piece of the ceiling lying broken at her feet. He cursed, anger turning to panic as he laid her down.

The prince reacted, using the distraction to break free of the Flare. He leapt forward, but Kron was far more powerful, and nothing was going to stop him from protecting his daughter. He grabbed the incoming prince and threw him with all his might across the room, where he smacked against the far wall.

Kron heard another cry from behind, and he braced himself as a red-haired man charged him. He blocked the weak attack with a single hand, using the other to shoot a bolt of Shine through the assailant's shoulder before tossing him aside.

"EDAR!" cried the prince from the other side of the room. He came at Kron, but just then the ceiling caved in fully, separating the two. Kron thought about sifting through the rubble to make sure the prince was dead, but Isha was wounded, and more people would soon come. He grabbed the limp body of his daughter, relieved to find her still breathing.

Then, Isha over his shoulder, he ran.

PART
IV

Chapter 42

- Raiz –

RAIZ CLOSED AN ENVELOPE intended for Echo, pressing into the drying wax with the King's seal and offering a small prayer before handing it off to Gale to see that it made it into the right hands.

War had begun.

Gelvard had struck the first blow, sacking Kirkham, pillaging and burning a stronghold of Trost that had stood for longer than he was alive, all the while blaming Trost for the murder of his son. It was a lie. Raiz knew it to be a lie. It was Celik, playing his games, fanning the flames of a war that was already coming. Raiz had met Gelvard, fought his son. There would be no reasoning with him. Only death would follow.

The people were angry. They had a right to be. Raiz had a responsibility to them now, Dazen's responsibility, passed on to him. He wouldn't let them down, wouldn't let his brother down. If Gelvard wanted a war, he would give it to him. On his terms, not Craw's.

He felt his strength returning, the Light within him resettling, his body recuperating, becoming even stronger than before. He stood, left his post, and made his way over towards where he knew the Wishan envoy had made themselves at home. It had been discussed and decided that the roads were too unsafe for them to return home. With the oncoming conflict, there was simply no safe route across Zapour for Aia and her people to travel.

He knocked on her dorm, well aware of the weight the question he was about to ask carried. He straightened, attempting to appear as kingly as possible.

The door swung open and Aia stood before him. She was quite beautiful, her dark skin complimented by tan robes, which neatly wrapped around her shoulders and waist to form a kind of dress that Raiz had never seen before.

"Lord Glaive," she said. "I was expecting you. Please, come in."

She stepped aside, Raiz nodding politely before walking with all the grace he could muster into the dormitory. It was decorated with various wooden artworks, hand carvings, and colourful silken tapestries. Raiz found it fascinating. Isha had been great friends with Aia's brother, Obeyun. She'd told him numerous stories about the two of them, and also a few which Obeyun had shared with her about Wishan culture.

Aia gestured for him to sit, and then waited for him to speak, a single groomed brow raised in expectation.

Raiz stuttered. He didn't know how to approach the situation. He needed her help, but he wasn't about to demand it. Should he start with small talk? Should he go straight to the point? Instead, he stared awkwardly before averting his gaze. Dazen would have known what to do.

"I regret that we haven't had the chance to become properly acquainted with each other," Aia said, starting the conversation for him.

"For that, I must apologise," Raiz said, finding his voice. "Things have been… difficult of late. I am still learning what is expected of me."

Aia waved a dismissive hand. "It is more than understandable, given the nature of your coronation. I did not know your brother very well, but what little I did see of him, I had come to admire. His death is a loss for all of Zapour, that much is clear."

Raiz felt at his heart, head bowed low.

"It would seem your sister and my brother have quite the friendship," Aia continued. "Never have I heard him speak so highly of another before, especially someone outside of Wisha. I am asking the spirit every day to see her returned to safety. There is still far too much for us to share with each other."

Raiz straightened. "Isha is strong. Stronger than any I know. It is not easy for me to leave her fate untouched by my intervention, but I have faith she will return soon. I am sure she will be grateful for your kind thoughts."

Aia nodded, pouring herself a cup of wine. "Do you drink?" she asked, pointing to a second cup, which currently sat empty on the table.

Raiz hesitated. His instinct was to say no. He had never had wine before in his life, never had time for it, but before his mind could register the thought, he nodded.

As Aia poured, he thought back, remembering the days of courtly dinners where Kron and those present would often drink. Upon receiving his cup, Raiz did as he remembered and began to swirl the wine around. He didn't know why people did it, just that it was procedure.

He let out a light gasp as a speck of red splashed above the rim, staining the blue sleeve of his tunic three shades darker. He shifted his body, hoping she hadn't seen, though the hint of a smile on her lips told him otherwise.

He took a sip, grimaced, then quickly hid his distaste as he sat the cup back down on the table. "I have come to ask for your help," he said, taking on a serious note.

"You wish for Wisha to join your war," Aia stated.

Raiz choked out a startle. Of course she had been expecting it. Trost was preparing for war. She was not blind.

He took in a deep breath, then exhaled. "I do. Gelvard has an army at our doorstep. He has the support of Kogon, and has taken Lumindal as his stronghold. We need to band together. It is the only way to stop him."

Aia pursed her lips. "Your brother and sister came to me with a similar proposition. I will tell them what I told you. Wisha can spare no men. Our villages are under attack from the mountains. I came here to Illidor to seek aid from Trost, not to provide it. I understand that in order for prosperity between us there needs to be a give and a take, but I simply do not have the authority to sanction such a large request."

"No," Raiz said, "but you have the authority to ask for it."

Aia laughed, clasping her hands together as she thought over his request.

"Please, Aia," Raiz continued. "We cannot win this war alone. If Gelvard is victorious, who knows what will become of Zapour, what would become of Wisha."

Aia raised her hand. "I understand your reasoning, but

please do not pretend you know what is best for my country. We have survived in isolation before. I am sure we will survive in it again."

"Is that all you want? To survive?"

Aia shook her head in amusement. "You sound just like my brother. He would like you."

Raiz paused, not quite sure how to respond. He righted himself and leaned closer. "I have faced the creatures attacking your villages from the mountains. I do not think isolation will be enough to grant your people survival." "You speak of these 'Skae,'" she said, voice calm.

Raiz crossed his arms. "Do you not believe me?"

"In truth I do not know what to believe. All this talk of prophecies, the sun dying, the Skae returning. It is all just hearsay."

"Until it no longer is," Raiz said, matching her stare. "I will help you. If I survive the coming war, I will take Spike and personally fly to Wisha to aid your brother against those marauding in your villages. You have my word."

For the first time Aia looked taken aback. She turned to the side. "I — that is very generous of you, but I do not know if I even have the power to reach Wisha right now. They have not responded to my last three missives. I fear —" she covered her mouth with her hand.

"Surely it is nothing," Raiz intervened. "Craw has tightened their defences. It is likely the ravens carrying the letters have simply been intercepted. You must not think the worst."

"But you see," Aia continued. "That is exactly why I am unable to aid you in this situation. It is as you say, even ravens are being intercepted. I am trapped here, unable to return safely to my own kingdom. This is what your war has brought."

Raiz sunk into his chair. She was right, there was nothing she could do. Wisha was too far north. Nothing short of an entire warband would be strong enough to make it to Trost right now, not with Gelvard out for vengeance.

Raiz was about to end his meeting, to let Aia know that she was welcome here until it was safe for her to return to her homeland, when the door burst open. Gale stood there, breathing hard, obviously having run a great distance to deliver a message he thought important enough to interrupt his meeting with the Wishan princess.

"My lord," Gale said, attempting to bow. "Apologies for the interruption, but I have news that cannot wait."

Raiz stood. "What is it, Gale? Speak!"

Gale took a steadying breath. "It is Kron, my lord. His raven just reached us. He is on a ship headed for the border. He has Isha. He requests immediate assistance."

Raiz froze, losing his breath. He snapped himself clear. "Ready Spike, I leave for the coast at once."

Chapter 43

- Isha –

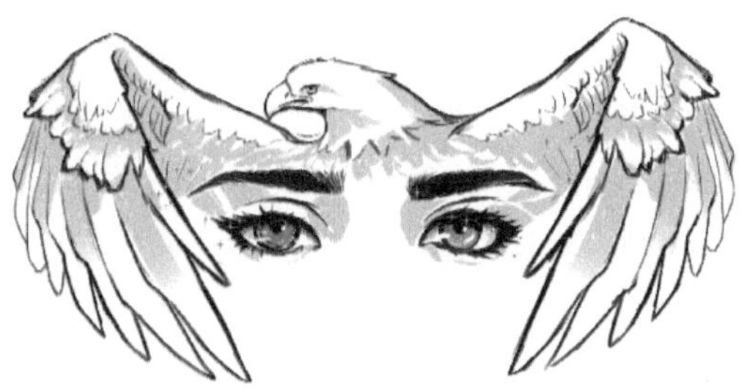

ISHA AWOKE ON a ship. Her stomach swirled along with the back-and-forth rhythm. Her head throbbed, and her first reaction was to reach for it. A bandage had been hastily thrown around it, still sticky and wet. Her fingers came away bloody.

She blinked, forcing her aching body upright. Memories came in a flood, followed by a foreboding sense of dread. She had a vague recollection of coming in and out of consciousness. How long had she been like that? A day? A week?

She gasped, throwing the covers off her legs and woozily jumping to her feet. She ran for the door, taking a minor stumble as her injury reminded her of its presence. She leaned against the door, forcing it open with what little strength she could muster.

She choked, tears welling beneath her eyes as she watched, hopeless. A sea of blue surrounded her. She fell to her knees. She had been making so much progress, was finally starting to learn about the nature of her origin. Bessimir…

Was he dead? She had only just given him her trust, a piece of her heart. He couldn't be dead. It couldn't end this way.

Father…

She stormed onto the deck, paying no mind to the shameless crew members who ogled her as she passed, barging through their ranks until she came to her father.

Kron stood with his back to her, arms on hips as he stared into the vastness of the ocean. "What have you done?" she demanded.

Kron turned. "Daughter, you are awake!"

Isha held her stare, her frustration not yet vented. "What did you do? Why am I here? Where is Bessimir?"

Kron looked perplexed. He took a step away from the railing and made for her. Isha took a step back in reaction. "Daughter, it's me, your father," he said, holding out a hand as if afraid she would break. "It's okay, You're safe now. You need to rest. We're almost at the coast. No one will hurt you here."

Isha clenched her fists and covered her eyes with them. She let out a silent scream, imploding with emotion. How could she explain to him the mistake he had made? How could she tell him he had ruined everything? That once again he had destroyed her life?

"You don't understand," she said. "You must take me back. I need to go back."

Kron just scowled. "Daughter, you are still under his spell. That man killed your brother. He is no friend. He manipulated you. You're safe now, I came for you. I would not abandon you again."

Isha could barely breathe, so deep was her frustration. She steadied. There was no changing his mind, not at this moment, but there was a question for which she needed an immediate answer. "Did you kill him?" she asked, her voice wild and dangerous.

Kron remained quiet for a while, then finally he spoke. "The building collapsed. His fate is yet unknown. Better for both of us if he perished under the debris."

Isha felt something inside of her snap, heart breaking, only held together by a thin string of hope that Bessimir yet held breath. She winced, tear-stained eyes closing and opening again.

She suddenly lost her footing, her legs turning to jelly as she fell to the decking. At first she thought it was because of her injury, but as she rose, she realised that she hadn't been the only one swept off her feet. The ship turned sharply, causing Kron to bend to a knee and snap an order to the man steering the ship.

A great screech sounded from above, causing all to stop and stare. Isha froze. She looked around but there was nothing there, only blue skies. The coast was edging closer. She could just about swim there from here if the need arose.

Kron grabbed her on the arm and forced her close.

"Let go of me!" she spat, attempting to pull herself free.

Kron said nothing, eyes fixed on the sky above.

Isha tried to lock her eyes onto his own, to impart her will onto him as Bessimir had taught her, but it was no good. He was too unfocused, too agitated. There was something going on.

Screams echoed around the foredeck as something large descended, but she couldn't see anything beyond her father's bulk. Managing to squeeze an inch away, She saw bloody corpses strewn across the deck. Some men jumped overboard, eyes fixed to the sky. Others screamed, holding weapons over their heads as they ducked.

She pulled against him, attempting to rip herself free, but Kron was unrelenting. She looked up to see a Great Eagle soaring through the sky, a red plume of feathers trailing in its wake. It rounded, circling in a high arc before descending with momentum. It streamlined its body, wings tucked to its side as it dove. Before making impact, its wings flung open. Huge, knife-like claws arched out, raking and impaling another crew member, his screams lost along the watery shore.

Strix had come for her.

Another Great Eagle swooped at them now, this one larger. On its way up, Isha saw a figure fastened to its back.

"Bessimir!" she said, causing Kron to tighten his grip.

Skeiron charged, keen eyes searching before focusing on their position. Kron braced himself, placing his body in front of her own, one hand outstretched into the air. He waited as the Great Eagle was almost upon him. Isha cried out as her father unleashed a blast of Shine. The Eagle reared, diving out of the way just in time as the wave of heat continued its trajectory into the open air. A wave of wind crashed into them, caused by the sudden shift in the animal's movements. Isha was buffeted, but still Kron kept his grip firm.

He moved to the front of the ship, dragging her along. He took one look below before throwing her prone form over the railing and into the deep water below.

Salt water engulfed her as her body was sucked under. She

rose to the surface, only to submerged again when Kron's heavy form plunged in after her.

"Swim," he shouted, motioning to the shore, which wasn't far away.

She thought about defying him, about swimming in the opposite direction, but that wouldn't get her anywhere. She couldn't do anything from the middle of the sea.

So, she swam towards shore. Kron continued to check their rear, Strix's shadow still apparent in the near distant sky. She watched as he looked directly into Zur, gathering what Light he could from the deity before diving back under, thick arms propelling himself forward.

It wasn't long before her feet could touch the sand below, and she slowly began to push herself against the weight of the water, step by slow step.

Kron ran right, so she ran left. A spray of water followed her as Kron bellowed an angry growl. Skeiron made another descent, diving between her and Kron, causing him to falter and fall backwards into an oncoming wave.

Another mass of heat emanated from her father as he returned to his feet to fire a wave of Shine, which poured from his palm in a continuous stream that arced across the sky.

Isha gasped as Skeiron performed a barrel-like roll, narrowly avoiding the deadly blast, keeping its distance. Isha wanted to intervene, to stop this madness, but she was too far away, their battle beyond her.

Once Kron's stream ran its course, Skeiron dove, taking advantage as Kron made to recover his Shine. She watched a claw bite into the flesh of Kron's stomach, then Skeiron bucked in the shallow water as her father drew his sword and swung. Steel rang against steel as Bessimir defended his mount, deflecting the strike with his own blade.

It seemed as though Kron had lost. His Shine was running dry, his arm already charred from his previous release. She watched in horror, unable to stop as the Great Eagle bit at him with its wickedly curved beak. She screamed, pleading with them to stop. She hated her father, despised him now more than ever, but she didn't want to see him die.

All seemed hopeless. He was to be devoured. She caught a glimpse of Bessimir's face through the commotion. It was set into hard lines, twisted with an anger she had never seen from him. He raised his blade for a killing blow, Kron now helpless, when another screech split the air, this one much deeper, more rigid, primal.

A roar.

Skeiron beat its great wings and Strix reared as Spike descended from the sky, Raiz mounted atop his back. A cacophony of beastly groans followed as the three creatures of Zur clashed, tangling together. Spike's barbed tail lashed out, catching Strix on the flank, causing it to scream. Jaws snapped. Talons scraped. Wings beat. Chaos ensued.

More nimble, Strix managed to grab hold of Spike's tail and pull. Spike was sent sprawling and Raiz was jerked backward, thrown from his saddle. He plummeted into the shallow sea.

Bessimir also got caught in the manoeuvre, losing his grip on Skeiron. He fell, but landed on his feet, sword still in hand. He charged Raiz as fast as the ankle-deep water allowed and poised for a strike before her brother could recover.

Kron intercepted, launching forward with his good hand and blocking the blow with his sword. He hunched over, his spare hand pawing at his ribs, which were gushing blood.

Raiz recovered, the water around him frothing as he

formed his Light-glaive and levelled it at Bessimir. Together they danced, all three of them locked in battle. Raiz swept his glaive in a wide arc, narrowly missing the prince as he twisted his body, twirling though the air with practised grace.

Kron was aggressive, yet slow, his wound hindering his movements. Bessimir fought like a mad-man, eyes full of vengeance, showing a set of skills Isha hadn't known he possessed.

As they fought their duel on the ground, another was being waged in the air. Huge gusts of wind continued to cut at the sea, creating waves of their own as the shadows of the three beasts above extended their struggle.

Isha stood and watched, unable to stop the anger-fuelled conflict. She felt helpless before so much brute strength and unmatched power.

No.

She wasn't helpless. She was strong. She could do something. She was sick of everyone fighting over her, was done being a prize to be won, a frail girl who needed protecting.

She was her own protection, and she would prove it.

She ran directly for the conflict, heedless of her own safety even as an errant bolt of Shine flew past, missing her right arm by a hair's breadth.

She forced herself into the battle, arms spread wide, back towards Bessimir, forcing both Kron and Raiz to stop and look at her. She felt their anger flow through her, matching it with her own. She used all that she had learned, catching their gaze, reaching deep into their minds, their souls.

"STOP!" she screamed, both externally and inside their minds.

CALM.

Both her father and brother froze, no longer in full control of their bodies as Isha imparted her will, altered their emotions. She took their anger, their hatred, and simmered it. Much as she had in the hospice, she took their pain. It was still there – pain of the mind was a different beast, internal scars ran much deeper than those of the flesh – but she was having an effect.

Bessimir made to move, to take advantage of their submission.

"YOU WILL NOT MOVE," Isha said, inclining her head towards the prince while keeping her focus locked on her family. There was no magic behind her words, no empathic power that would stop him as it had her brother and father, just the strength of her tone.

It worked, nonetheless. Bessimir stopped, though his breathing was ragged, his stance still aggressive. "Because of him, Edar now fights for his life," he said, "I cannot forgive such an intrusion upon my lands. He is not what a father should be. He never was, Isha."

Isha's heart wrenched, pained by the knowledge of Edar's condition.

Above them, the war in the air had ceased, Spike returning to Raiz's side, Strix and Skeiron to Bessimir's.

Kron pressed against her hold, taking a slow step forward. "He killed your brother, he murdered Dazen," he managed to say through gritted teeth. "You cannot trust him. We are family."

She felt anger flare in her chest. "You *left* me," she said, venting a lifetime's worth of emotion in just three words. "I was only a child, and you let him take me. He was a monster.

You knew what he was and you *let him have me.*"

Kron made to speak, but Isha interrupted, doubling down on her mental intrusion. "I know why you did it. I know what might have happened if you saved me, I am no longer naive about what they were. But you left your only daughter to be imprisoned by a monster, abandoned your son, leaving him to die at the hands of a tyrant, and STILL you have the nerve to call us a family."

She choked out the last few words, but forced herself to stay composed. "You are no father of mine. A true father listens. A true father asks. He does not demand. Does not dictate. Does not ignore."

She forced herself to watch as Kron's cheeks grew wet with tears. He no longer had the strength to fight her intrusion. Isha released her hold, and he fell to his knees, two hands planting into the shallow water.

Raiz took a half step forward. "Isha are you certain? If he truly killed Dazen, I cannot forgive it."

"I first thought as you do, when I saw his body. I was angry, rightfully so. But I have since learned the truth. Bessimir did not kill our brother, I know it in my heart."

She felt the prince take a comforting step closer, placing a hand on her shoulder.

"Then who? A creature of the night?" Raiz said, dismissing his glaive.

Bessimir stepped in front of her. His sword was still in hand, but he relaxed somewhat. "I believe it was a manifestation of the Skae. A creature born of Cova. I only caught a brief glimpse. It looked to be human, but its tail was unmistakable."

Isha tensed. She was expecting Raiz to dispute it, to call it a bluff, to rage. Instead, he remained still. She felt the emotion in his thoughts. There was recognition there.

"What did it look like?" Raiz questioned.

Bessimir paused, considering. He was likely as surprised by this reaction as she. "It took the form of a male. Slender build, deep pits of black for eyes. Its tail was formed entirely of shadow, though it had weight to it, unnatural, sinister. I thought the Skae lost to this world, but I was wrong."

Raiz reacted, his eyes full of fire. "I know the creature you speak of."

He bent to a knee, exhaling as though it were his last ever breath. Heat radiated from him, his Flare erupting as he threw an angry punch at the water.

"What is it, Raiz?" Isha questioned. "What do you know?"

Raiz rose. She felt pain in him, so much pain. She tried to intrude on his mind again, to take some of it away, but there was heat, too much heat. It was blocking her efforts.

"I know what killed our brother, and I know the one responsible."

"Who? Who was it?" Isha pleaded.

"It's my fault. It's all my fault. I should have killed him. I should have ended him when I had the chance. He stood right in front of me. I felt him. Felt Dazen. I knew it to be him, but also knew it wasn't. I didn't understand, didn't know."

"Talk to me Raiz, please."

Raiz met her eye. "It was Celik. He killed Dazen. Him and his pet Skaeling. I saw them. He came to me, offering to help. I should have known he was full of it. I should have put my blade through his chest the moment I saw him."

Bessimir stepped in front of Isha, approaching Raiz. "You saw a Skaeling? It is true then? They have returned?"

"More than one. I saw them all. In the Weeping Mountains. They hide there, biding their time, but make no mistake, they are coming, preparing."

Isha caught her breath. "What does this mean?"

"It means this feud is pointless," he replied, gesturing to Bessimir. "It means your prince is wrong. The world needs Shine now more than ever, and as the new King of Trost I will see it prosper."

Bessimir raised an aggressive fist. "Overuse of Shine is killing this world! How can you be so naive to its effects? You are a Radiant!"

"There will be no world left to protect if you stamp it from our lands! It is necessary. Shine is the only way to combat them, the only weapon we hold that will have any effect."

"You are wrong. Shine is not Zapour's only defence. Peridium cuts through shadow just as well as it deflects Shine."

"Peridium is scarce, unreliable. I will not stake the fate of Zapour on a few wagons full of peridum."

"What about a thousand wagons full?" Bessimir prompted.

Raiz raised an eyebrow.

"Our mines are plentiful. Weapons and armour are being fashioned from the metal as we speak."

"Weapons no doubt intended for use against us, not the Skae," Raiz responded, voice regaining its aggressive edge.

"I have never hidden my intent. Everything I said to your brother was the truth. I wish for peace, for prosperity. But I am also practical. I know what goes through the minds of those who hold Zur's power. You are headstrong, impulsive, wasteful. If peace cannot be attained, I have every intention of following through with my promise to right the world and see

Zur's strength returned."

Isha watched, waited. Raiz had changed. The old Raiz might have reacted, bit back at him, but he was different. Dazen's death had changed him. He held his composure. "What do you suggest?" he said.

Bessimir straightened, relaxed. "I suggest you cease your use of Shine immediately. I understand that Shine is attained involuntarily, that stopping its use entirely will be impractical. That is why I wish for those with an affinity to change their lifestyle, turn nocturnal, cease their stealing of Zur's strength. On top of that, there are to be no more children born with the ability to wield Zur's Light."

Raiz let out a surprised gasp, but held his tongue.

"This is necessary," Bessimir said. Isha checked to see if he was using his powers against Raiz, but he was not. Only his words. "In order to stamp out Shine for the future, there needs to be active change now. This point is non-negotiable."

Raiz gulped, taking a moment to gather his thoughts. "What did Dazen say to this proposition?" he asked.

"Your brother was open to it. He wanted to make peace, saw the wisdom in my words."

"You mean he saw wisdom because you made him," Raiz retorted. "He saw only what you wanted him to see."

Bessimir tensed, but kept his cool. "You are right. I did attempt to sway your brother to heed my words. But his mind was strong. I may have asserted my influence, but the decision was his. One that I suspect he was already willing to concede, even without my intervention."

Raiz seemed to recede into the depths of his thoughts, returning a moment later with his response. "I accept your terms, Prince. But I will not surrender our use of Shine until the Skae are vanquished."

Bessimir made to respond, but Raiz held up a hand. "I refuse to run naked into an enemy we do not understand. Zur gifted us with his Light precisely for this purpose, I will not give up our greatest weapon in this fight. When I am confident they no longer pose a threat, I will implement your terms, whatever the cost. You have my word."

Bessimir hesitated. For a moment, Isha thought he was about to refuse, but he stepped forward, hand outstretched. "I hope your promise is not false," he said. "For if it is, I will not hold back."

Raiz nodded, accepting. He extended his own hand, and they shook.

"There is a matter that needs to be dealt with first," Raiz said. "As it stands, Zapour remains divided. Craw and Kogon have declared war on Trost and are preparing an army to end my kingdom. I am afraid I will be unable to make good on my promise if they take control. And believe me when I say, they will not be receptive to your demands. If you wish to save our sun, you will need to go through them first."

Bessimir nodded, already aware of their potential situation. Isha had talked at length on the subject. "If this is as unavoidable as you say, you will have my aid. I will return to Yagos, gather its armies, and return to your shores with force."

Isha could feel Raiz's relief. It washed over him like a gentle breeze. He even managed a smile, sparing a look her way before shaking his head in mock admiration. "Trust you to be the one to bring our two nations together," he said.

Isha shrugged, only now feeling the weight of the past few days. She was tired, exhausted.

"Will you return with me?" Bessimir said, turning her to

face him, hand in her own.

She wanted to go, to be with him again, to explore their potential and learn more about herself, but she shook her head. "I must stay here. Raiz needs me. And I would like to say a proper goodbye to my brother."

Bessimir lowered his posture, disappointed, but she knew he would understand. "Of course. Go, be with your family, your people. Upon my return, I hope we shall continue what we had. What we have."

Isha tightened her grip, her emotions as raw and vibrant as the night they had lain together. A gust of wind rose from behind, causing her hair to blow over her face. She shifted to see Strix peeking over her shoulder.

Bessimir laughed. "She will not part with you again. Her fate is now bound to yours. Take care of her, will you?"

Isha moved to stroke the golden feathers of the Eagle's neck, and nestled her head into her wing. She turned back to Bessimir. "What of Puk? Is he injured?"

"Puk is fine. Your father knocked him unconscious. He is bedridden, but is expected to make a full recovery. I will take care of him until my return, you have my word."

Isha took his hand in her own, satisfied her friend was safe. She planted a soft kiss on his cheek. "Goodbye, for now."

Bessimir flushed. He called Skeiron from the sky with a click of his tongue.

Isha turned to see Raiz standing there, nose wrinkled, lips loose, scoffing in disgust.

She chuckled. Maybe he hadn't grown up as much as she thought.

Chapter 44

- Raiz –

SPIKE ROARED. A warning, though also a boast, a reminder that he was a titan of the sky. He landed with a thud, sand shifting beneath the might of his bulk, his long tail whipping against wind and sea.

Raiz went to him, Spike leaning into his touch, bending his long neck low as Raiz proceeded to pet him beneath his chin. He examined the beast. There were several open wounds covering the softer scales on his belly and sides, but nothing too serious. The Eagles had been a match for him. Raiz had never seen anything like it. The Great Eagle's existence was a reminder of all the ill teachings preached by the former hierarchy of Zapour.

Spike opened his gullet, and Raiz reached his hand down the Dragon's throat. He forced Light to leak through his fingertips, expending his gathered Shine and feeding his companion a well-deserved meal.

He looked up to the sky, where he could still see the distant speck that was the man who called himself the Sun Prince as he made for his homeland. Raiz collapsed to the watery sand, exhaustion finally taking its toll. He was recovered from his overuse of Shine, but he had nearly been forced beyond his limits once again. Isha came to him, to Spike.

Spike leapt towards her, losing much of his fierceness as he nuzzled her like a lost puppy who had reunited with its owner.

"Someone missed you," Raiz said, relaxing into a smile.

He watched as his sister allowed herself a moment of joy, laughing and playing as Spike licked at her salt-stained skin.

The Eagle by her side reacted. Powerful, cautious eyes bore down on Spike as Isha continued to play. Raiz found himself staring, unbelieving. "It seems we have a lot to catch up on," he said, motioning towards the Eagle.

"We do indeed, little brother. Or should I say, my king?"

Raiz tried to find humour in it, the fact that he, of all people, was now one of the six kings of Zapour, but he still felt like a fraud.

"I never intended to take the crown. I don't deserve it, nor do I want it. I did what was necessary. Dazen's daughter is to inherit when she comes of age. I intend to make sure Trost is safe enough when her time comes, so that she might rule in a time of peace.

"I am a soldier, nothing more," he continued. "And a rogue one at that. You should be the one to make the decisions, you always seem to know what to say and do."

"And look where that has gotten me," she said. "We can worry about succession after the war is won. For now, let's return to Illidor. I need to say goodbye, Raiz." She took a cautious step closer, watery eyes full of sorrow. "I need to say goodbye to him."

Raiz wrapped his arms around her back and pulled her tight, brother and sister taking comfort in their shared grief. He let the emotion of the moment linger, neither one of them wanting it to end.

Eventually, Raiz parted, looking over her shoulder to where Kron was talking with a man from his ship. "What do we do with him?" he asked.

Isha turned and scoffed. "I don't know. I don't want to see him. I can't. I know he was just trying to help, to make up for the past, but too much has happened. I can't even look at him."

"You did well, standing up to him. Standing up to me."

"I learned a lot about myself recently. About what I'm capable of."

"My body," Raiz said. "I couldn't move. You did that, didn't you?"

Isha nodded.

"You've done it before, unwittingly, back in Lumindal, when I was… not myself. You calmed me, saved me from my self-destruction."

"I know. I mean, I didn't at the time, but in Yagos I learned much about who I am, what I am."

"Thank you," Raiz continued. "For everything. I don't like the idea of you entering my mind, but I needed it, even today."

He whistled for Spike. "You can tell me all about it on the trip home."

He launched himself onto Spike's back and fastened himself into the saddle. He held an arm out to his sister, then realised she had her own ride. "Are you sure that's safe?" he said as she made for the Eagle's saddle.

Isha said nothing, just winked at him, and mounted her steed.

THEY TOOK THEIR time on the way back to Illidor. Despite all of their troubles, Raiz felt they deserved a moment of reprieve. They soared through the sky together, stopping frequently. Isha told him everything. He learned much about Bessimir, about the history of Yagos, or at least what the prince had told her. He learned about Zur's Eye, and the vision the Great Eagle had shown her. He learned about her bond with Strix, who still hadn't taken to Spike, continuously snapping at his side whenever he would draw too close. So much information took time to sink in. His first thought was to deny it all, declare it some made-up story conjured to twist her mind. But the more he thought about it, the more it made sense. Of course the Eagles in Lumindal had been hiding something so essential to their past. They were not the only ones blessed by Zur that day.

Everything the Sun Prince said made sense. Even as a supposed Radiant, a descendant of the most powerful Shine user in the history of Zapour, he could see how volatile they were, how dangerous they could be if left unchecked.

The thought of the Skae remained ever present at the back of his mind. He told Isha about it, of the voice inside his head, of the dread he had felt in that cavern. He couldn't fully give into the prince's demands, not while such a potential threat sat idle deep inside those mountains.

He steered Spike over the castle walls, circling the Moon-spire before making his landing on the white cobblestones of the palace courtyard. Illidor was bustling with activity.

Soldiers were active, regiments mustering, preparing for the inevitable war that all now knew was coming.

All stopped and stared as Raiz descended from Spike's back, though even more heads turned towards Isha. If there was anyone out there who still protested his claim to the throne, he was sure Spike and Strix's presence would silence them.

Gale was among the notable soldiers present. Where others kept their distance, he ran directly to them. He was with his wife, Maitreya overtaking him to sprint towards Isha. She threw herself on her, wrapping thin arms around her shoulders and smothering her in a hug.

"You're back!" she said.

Isha couldn't respond, her face smooshed against Maitreya's own. Raiz turned to Gale. "I see she is recovered. That is wonderful news."

Gale nodded, but didn't look quite as relieved as he should. "She is better today, thankfully. Though I fear the sickness has not yet passed.

"I see Kron was successful," he continued, "the princess is returned to us, along with a guest!" he finished, marvelling at Strix.

Raiz inclined his head. "She is safe, where she belongs."

"Where is Kron? Did he not come with you?"

Raiz issued a derisive sigh. "The matter is… complicated. Kron is to make his own way back, if I decide he is still welcome."

Gale raised a concerned eyebrow, but decided not to press the matter.

"Come," Raiz said. "Walk with me. I will fill you in later. First, I would hear of our war effort."

The two walked in stride, past countless captains all shouting orders, drilling discipline into their regiments, though most were still eyeing Spike and Strix.

"The White-Swords are assembled. I have gathered seven hundred Lightweavers, with a few dozen more out on scouting missions. Troops from Brane should arrive within the day. On top of that, Houses Grudle, Chaldwin, and Enister have already arrived. We are still waiting for a response from Ettle. Most of the able fighting men from Kirkham died in Craw's offensive, though a few have returned, Alzar unfortunately not among them. Together, we will have mustered an army of nearly fifteen thousand. Our Shine users will be spread thin, though I would like to group a hundred or so together to be used as a ram. How we utilise them will be the difference between whether we return alive, or not at all."

Raiz nodded, pleased with the progress. He didn't have the mind for military strategy and tactics. He was better equipped for espionage. Gale was trained for this, had been the man even Dazen had leaned on for support in such matters.

Thankfully, most of the nobles were being cooperative. The sacking of Kirkham had put them all on edge, and whether they fought out of loyalty to the crown, or just out of fear, didn't much matter now, so long as they fought.

"Any news from Zuton and Wisha?" Raiz asked.

"King Echo has answered your call. We received a missive from him this morning. His numbers are not yet clear, but Zuton will be by our side when the time comes.

"Wisha," he continued, "I am afraid, we have heard no response from. Aia is still here, the roads unsafe to travel. There is not much we can do. I fear we may be without their aid in the coming battle."

Raiz sighed, expecting the result. "And what of our enemy? How are their movements?"

Gale steadied, took a breath. "The intrusion from Craw was swift, their assault on Kirkham merciless. The entire fortress and its surrounding villages are in ruin. Few have survived. We were able to halt their advance by blockading the main passes through the forest, but the measures we put in place are temporary."

Raiz had to check his Shine, fury getting the better of him. Innocent people were dying under his watch. He had to act. These citizens were his responsibility now. "Where is Gelvard?" he asked.

"Our scouts report he has returned to Lumindal. They believe his men are gathering outside the walls and converging with his cousin's from Kogon in preparation for a full invasion of Trost."

Raiz bit his lip. "Your scouts," he said. "What exactly did they see? Were there beasts among their ranks?"

"Beasts, my lord?"

Raiz motioned towards where Spike lounged in the middle of the courtyard. "Like him. Smaller, but much more aggressive."

"You mean the prickets you spoke of? You think they will use them against us?"

"It is possible. Though I do not believe them to be controllable. Either way, we must be prepared. I want you to come up with a strategy to combat them. Can I count on you?"

"Of course, my lord, but this army we have mustered, where are we to march it?"

Raiz paused. He knew what he wanted to do, but the

weight of his decision still sat heavy on his conscience. "We march to Lumindal. I want to meet them on the open fields. I will not risk the Last Light becoming active again. If we are caught cowering behind our walls, we are done for."

Gale nodded. "I had come to the same conclusion, but will our forces be enough?"

Raiz allowed himself to settle into a coy smile. "We will not be alone."

"What do you mean?"

"The Sun Prince," Raiz said.

He watched as Gale's expression turned from confusion, to understanding, to hope, all in one action. "They are to be our allies?" he asked.

Raiz nodded.

"How?"

"My sister," Raiz replied, indicating to where Isha and Maitreya were still conversing.

Gale gulped, face hardening. "What was the price?"

Raiz looked to his outspread hands, feeling the fresh Shine bubbling beneath the surface. He had decided on his trip home not to release the agreed upon price for their help to the public. If he was to die in battle, then Isha would keep his promise.

"The price does not matter. If we lose, nothing will."

Chapter 45

- Zeek –

ZEEK WAS BACK in a cave. He had no choice. Father was unconscious, feverish. Unable to travel. Soldiers bearing the serpent crest of Craw constantly patrolled the area. It was too dangerous to venture outside with his father in this state. Zeek didn't know them. They might kill him, kill Father.

He felt boxed in. Even though he had spent so long in a place just like this, that had been another life. He hated it, hated the smell more than anything. Damp, moss-covered walls encircled him. The air was thick with animal musk. He had become accustomed to the open air, the fresh dew on the morning grass, the salty tang of the ocean at full tide, the chirps of birds at first light. There was none of that here, just a gloomy darkness.

He doubled over as a familiar intrusion pressed on his mind. His stomach churned as whatever had a hold of him pulled, whispered incomprehensible words, calling him.

He tried to ignore it, to fight against it, but his father was not present enough to shake him from it. So, he allowed it to consume him, weakened by his claustrophobia.

Come to me child. Our time is almost here. Your potential is limitless. Come to me, my child…

He was about to give in, to leave this cave and go wherever the voice directed, when a great roar split the air. He awoke from his dream-like state to see a fully-grown bear standing up on its hind legs in front of him. Panic flared. They must have intruded on its home. He looked to ensure his father was safe.

The bear roared its challenge, taking two meaty steps forward. Saliva dribbled from its open jaw. Claws the size of small swords swiped at him, and Zeek was forced to dodge backward. The bear fell to all fours, thick brown fur consuming his vision.

Zeek gnashed his human teeth before issuing a roar of his own, accepting the challenge. He tried to summon the stream of Light and shadow he had used not so long ago, but it wouldn't come. He side-stepped, carrying no weapons of his own, and charged the bear. He threw his body at it, attempting to overpower the beast with sheer will. He soon found his efforts futile. The bear reacted, pressing back with its shoulder. It swung another clawed arm at him, this time catching him on the shoulder.

Zeek reeled in pain, revelling in the sensation. He laughed, pain turning to joy at the prospect of another experience. This is what he wanted. This is what he lived for. The thrill of battle, the thrill of anything, as long as he didn't have to sit idle in a cave.

His body reacted on its own, his shadow-tail making its presence known at last, curling around his body and arching into a deadly point.

Zeek smiled as the bear made another charge. The point of his tail darted forward, piercing its hide. The bear roared, then whimpered. It continued to defy him, errant swipes falling short as Zeek's tail pierced deeper, consumed its essence just as it had done countless times before with humans.

A new sensation began to hit him, beastly, animalistic, instinctual. He felt power, raw power, strength. It flowed through him, began to change him. He wanted more. He sunk his tail deeper into its flesh, listening as the animal protested, helpless.

Before he could access even half of what he knew the animal had to offer, a bolt of Light shot through the air, piercing the beast's head and blowing it clean off. His tail retracted, returning to its resting place coiled around his waist.

Zeek looked around, disappointed. He felt anger, fury, frustration at the interruption of his meal. He spun, ready to fell whoever had dared to deprive him of what he deserved, when he found his father staring back at him, panting, a long foot raised in the air.

"You fool!" Father said. "Do you want to become like this creature?"

Zeek leered awkwardly, confused.

Father grumbled, lowering his foot and muttering a bunch of curses beneath his breath.

"I saved us," Zeek said.

"And you nearly killed yourself in doing so."

"Killed myself? I won the battle. I could have taken all of it! I could feel its power flowing into me."

"Not all power is worth the cost," Father said, motioning towards the creature. "In attaining the beast's strength, you would have sacrificed your mind. Do you want to become an animal? Is that what you want? Because that is what you will become if you feed on these creatures, a mindless beast. Never feed on another animal again, am I clear?"

Zeek hesitated, still feeling the bear's strength coursing through him. "Yes Father. I understand."

His father relaxed, coughed, then righted himself. "We must get out of here, it is not safe."

"But Father, you are not well en—"

"I am fine!" he interrupted. "Just get me to Lumindal. I fear I have miscalculated. Your Queen is stronger than I thought. She calls you, does she not? She is near, I can feel it. The Darkening will come soon. Zapour must be prepared."

Chapter 46

- Isha -

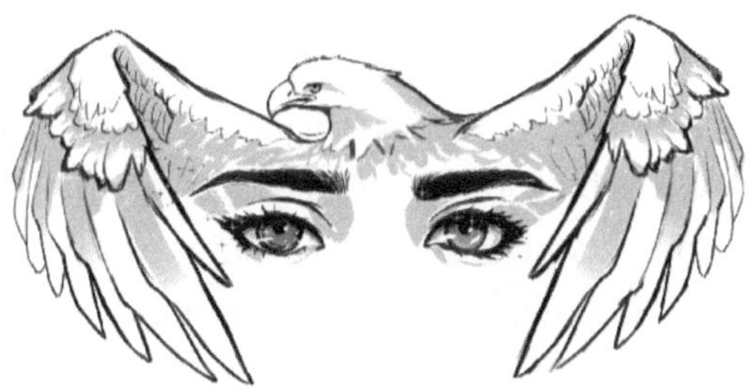

DESPITE BEING HOME, Isha felt alone. She expected to rise and see Edar sitting at the table, waiting for her to join him in their game of reverse chess. She expected to see Puk, to train with him as she had every day. She missed him. She needed to talk to him, apologise for taking him for granted. She felt guilt in her heart. She felt like a traitor, as if her actions with the prince had somehow been a betrayal of his trust.

Even worse, she didn't regret it. Puk was warm, soft, reliable. He meant the world to her, yet still she could only see him as a friend. The prince was ambitious, cunning, ruthless, but he was also kind, and thoughtful. Was it wrong for her to feel this way about one but not the other?

She had placed her trust in Bessimir, decided to believe he was who he claimed to be. There was risk, however, she had learned that risks needed to be taken. If she wanted truth, if she wanted knowledge, then she had to seek it out.

Illidor was silent this night. She sat atop the roof of the Moon-spire, wind in her hair, an open window behind her. It was cold, the chill creeping up her legs. Though, compared to Yagos, this was nothing. Winter still refused to fade. Spring was long overdue, no flowers had yet blossomed, and little warmth bathed the land.

So far, Trost was holding against the forces of Craw. There had been a few skirmishes along the border, though Raiz and Spike had seen to most of them personally, and were becoming quite a formidable pairing in the eyes of the enemy.

Troops were gathering on both sides, and it was just a matter of time before their armies clashed.

A high-pitched whistle sounded from above, and Isha smiled as Strix came to perch on a length of wood extending from the tip of the Spire. She reached out for her. It felt odd. Now that she was away from Yagos, her connection to the Eagle felt frayed, as though she didn't deserve it. Perhaps she didn't. This creature was divine, a legend come to life. What business did it have with her?

Despite this, Strix warmed to her touch. To her, Isha was familiar. She suspected this was because of her grandmother. Their bond must have been strong. Was strong, in fact. Isha felt it there, un-severed.

"What happened to you, girl?" she whispered, as though the Eagle could answer her.

Strix was intelligent, speaking through visions and images, but in truth, Isha didn't truly understand all of them. There simply hadn't been time to delve too deep. She had this moment though, a rare lull in the constant push and pull that had been her life of late.

She reached out for Strix, not physically this time, but mentally. Just a gentle tug. "Show me what you know," she said.

She felt Strix's hesitation, her emotion. She wanted to let her in, but was afraid.

"I can handle it," Isha continued. "Please. I need to know more. Show me what you can."

Strix relaxed, and Isha took advantage, placing two hands upon her heartbeat.

Immediately, her mind swam, depictions of the past coming at her in a stream, too fast to comprehend. She held their connection, determined to see it through. She pulled harder now, tempering the wave, focusing and narrowing the visions into decipherable pictures.

She saw more Great Eagles, many of them, each as large as Strix, yet unique in their own way. They flew through the skies, mixing with another creature. A Dragon!

More Dragons came into view now, each with a rider on their back, just as Raiz now rode Spike. The Great Eagles were also paired with a human counterpart. She saw through Strix's eyes, felt her contempt as more Dragons appeared. Strix shifted in her vision, and the Eagle's emotion washed through Isha as a lady appeared. Her smile was bright as day, her energy lively and excitable. She looked like Isha had before she cut her hair short. Long dark hair trailed down her back in chestnut waves. She was more toned than Isha, her strong frame full of muscle, but she had the same high cheek bones, the same dimple in her smile, the same eyes…

Grandmother!

Isha gasped in her dream-like state. She felt the bond between Strix and her grandmother like it was her own. There was joy, love, respect, duty.

Then the vision began to change. The image grew foggy, and was replaced by another. Orange flames licked at the edges of it as she was shown something terrible.

Blood. There was so much blood. She felt Strix's pain, her heartbreak. A Great Eagle lay dead at her feet, its rider similarly no longer of this world. Half of his body was burned to a crisp, the other half left untouched. Strix broadened her view, and Isha was shown what she had wanted to see.

Death. There was so much death. Eagles and Dragons fought in the sky, clawing, ripping, tearing each other to shreds. The Last Light towered over the landscape, though the Spears surrounding it were absent, not yet fashioned. Shine was everywhere. People shouted, screamed for help, for mercy, but none was given.

Isha wanted to help, to save them, but she was trapped in her vision, a witness only.

She forced herself to watch. She had wanted to see. This was the moment, the betrayal. This was why Bessimir hated Shine so much, why he wanted it gone from this world. This was its nature. To destroy.

More images came in a flash. There was a man, a man of Shine. He fought against his own kind, seeking to protect. She saw her grandmother, running, fleeing. The pictures came and went so fast that they were hard to decipher, but she had seen enough. She had seen her kind fall, and felt the betrayal as if she had been there herself.

Then she saw her grandmother, alive. A child, one born of Empathy as well as Shine. Mother!

Isha heaved, gulping in a deep lungful of air as she was thrown from the vision and back into reality.

She withdrew her touch, silently thanking Strix for sharing this with her. Such a deep connection had taken a toll, and so she made to return inside the Moon-spire for some much-needed water. When she did, she found a pair of violet eyes staring back at her from within the Spire.

She lost her footing, almost fell, Thinking for a moment that she was back in her dream, that it had followed her to the present. Celia made for her, clearly just as startled as she had been, her mother quickly opening the window and helping her back inside.

"Mother, you scared me," Isha said, catching her breath.

"I am sorry my dear. I did not mean… I only came to check in on you, to see how you are doing," her mother said.

Isha grabbed a pitcher of water and gulped some down, hearing Strix vanish from the roof as she did so. She watched her mother closely. "Why didn't you tell me?" she asked.

She knew her mother was fragile, that such a line of questions might frighten her away, but she no longer cared. Mother knew about Strix, she could see it in the way she had looked at the bird.

"Why didn't you tell me there were more? More of us out there? About Strix? You promised me answers. When we met in Lumindal, you promised to tell me everything, and yet so far I've mostly been met with silence."

"Isha I… I wanted to tell you. I did. You must understand —"

"I deserve to know. Who I am. Why these things keep happening to me," Isha interrupted.

"I was protecting you. There is much you do not understand —"

"Then help me understand. Please," she added.

"Grandmother, is she alive? Are there more out there like us?"

Celia's shoulders sank as she sighed deeply. "She was alive when I left, yes, but I have been gone a long time."

"What about Strix? You know her, don't you? You've met her before."

Celia paused, then spoke. "Strix and my mother are bonded, yes. I know her well."

"What do you mean *are* bonded? Are they still paired? Is my connection with her false? Temporary? What is going on? I don't understand."

"I — I know not, truly. I wish I could tell you, help you to understand. Your grandmother, she told me, warned me not to travel the path you now walk. Said Shine was dangerous, that those in power over here were not to be trusted. And she was right. Look what happened to me, to you. I just... I wanted to protect you. Nothing good can come of reigniting past feuds."

"It's too late for that. Bessimir, he is coming here. He can help us beat them. We can set the world right again."

"Bessimir?" Celia said, startled. "He is the Sun Prince?"

Isha nodded. "That's where I've been. In his care. Why? Do you know him?"

Celia paled. "I know of him, yes. He fled Lumindal along with my mother so long ago. But he has led a... different life. Are you sure you can trust him?"

Isha stopped to consider, but eventually gave a confident nod. "I am, yes."

"Be careful. There are a few still alive who were there on the day of the Eagles' Fall, but any who bore witness still remember, and hold hatred within their hearts. Even my mother. Hatred, over time, never really diminishes, not completely. It merely simmers. Please be careful, Isha."

"I promise. You have my word."

Her mother seemed to relax, then grew tense again. "There is another matter I wish to have a word with you about."

Isha leaned closer. "What is it?"

"Your father has returned."

Isha's throat closed, as if she had somehow swallowed her tongue. She hadn't thought about what to do with him yet, had thought she would have more time. "Is that so?" she said, not knowing what else to say.

"I want to ask you something that I have no right to ask for. Please, do not blame him, not for this. I am to blame. If you are to hold hatred for someone, let it be me."

Isha stood, shocked. "Why would I blame you? He is the one who came, took me in his arms without a care for what I had to say. He nearly killed my friends. Why would I blame you?"

"I know. Kron is… troubled. There is much about his past he regrets, that I still have not forgiven him for. But he is trying. He wanted to make it up to you, to fix his past mistake. To do right by you this time. And he knows he went about it the wrong way, that he should have listened to you. But this is my fault. I pushed him. I made him promise me he would get you back, whatever the cost. I told him to be ruthless, to not let anyone or anything stop him."

Isha's eyes grew wide. "You used your power on him?"

"No!" She paused. "No. I would never, not again. But it was my words that compelled him to act this way."

Isha turned, frustrated. "Then why are you here, and not him?"

"He does not know I came today. He is too ashamed, afraid

of what he might see should he look upon you."

Isha considered. "It's not that simple to forgive, to forget. No, I don't hate him, nor do I hate you, but neither can I see him, not right now at least. Too much has happened. I don't know if he can truly change. I hope he can, with all my heart. But I need time. Perhaps in the future the world will be at peace. Maybe then we can reconnect, be as a father and daughter should be. Right now, I need space. Can you understand that?"

Celia nodded. "I can." Her expression seemed to change then, her lip quivering and her face distorting as her eyes swelled. "You have grown into such a fine, strong woman. I regret that this has nothing at all to do with me, and all to do with you. How is it so?"

Isha smiled. "I made friends. Even in the darkest of places, there will always be someone who shines. Sometimes you just have to fight for a spark."

Chapter 47

- Raiz –

RAIZ WAS PLAYING a delicate game. One he was still unsure he was equipped to play. He had managed to gather the largest army Trost had ever seen, and *he* was leading it.

This had never been his plan, to be king, to lead others. He was a rebel, a runaway child, an outcast. He had no right to dictate the fate of thousands of people. He worked better alone.

Yet here he was, on the eve of a battle that would define the future of Zapour, a leader.

Raiz didn't feel comfortable leaving Illidor for long, though all reports suggested Gelvard was holed up in Lumindal, gathering his strength, preparing. If this was true, then he had time, though not as much as he would like. He and Bessimir had parted with an agreement, now all Raiz could do was wait and see if the prince's words bore any truth.

Isha stood beside him on the sands of western Trost, confident, unwavering in her belief that he would come, but Raiz wasn't so sure. He looked to his sister. Thick clouds of doubt blackened his vision, but in this moment, she was the radiant one. Her focus was absolute, her determination unmatched, unhindered by uncertainty.

"Don't doubt him," Isha said, maintaining her stare across the Sapphire Sea.

"I can't help it. Every day we remain on this coast is another Gelvard could use to sink his teeth into our lands."

"We would risk even more going into battle alone. Let them stew in their stolen capital a while longer. They think themselves unbeatable. Let's show them they aren't. Give us time to open the crack in their armour."

Raiz studied her, puzzled. "How is it that you went from trying to kill this man, to being in love with him?"

Isha's brow creased. "I am not in love with him," she snapped, though the slight variation in her tone indicated otherwise. "You're like Father," she continued, exasperated. "You think that I'm under the influence of some sort of spell. That my mind is not my own."

"No…" Raiz spat, backtracking. "That's not what I meant. I was just curious is all."

Isha calmed, chest falling as she relaxed into a sigh. "At first, I hated him, it's true. I wanted to kill him. I thought he was responsible for Dazen's death, wanted to rip his heart out and stomp on it. I was consumed by anger, clouded by it."

Raiz leaned in closer, listening as she described a feeling he knew all too well.

"Then I found reason. I found truth. I found a sense of purpose that I never knew I needed. Bessimir listened, he accepted my anger as just, and did not fault me for it. He is driven, determined to make the vision of the world he sees in his mind a reality. But above all of that he is kind. Ambition is one of the greatest strengths a human being can possess, but ambition without a kind heart is a lonely path.

"We are the same, and yet we are different. He taught me things about the world I never thought I would have the chance to know, and yet there is still so much more for me to learn. I understand your mistrust, am glad for it even. I am not asking you to place your trust in him, I am asking you to place your trust in me."

Raiz followed her stare out into the calm sea. She was right. That had been Kron's mistake, not trusting his own daughter. He would not make it as well. Isha was blood, but she was more than that. He needed to trust her. He owed her that much. Trost owed her that much.

Together they stood, and together they waited, testing his resolve just as much as hers. Raiz did not falter again. Even as day turned to night, and night to day, Raiz waited with her. They sat, sleepless, huddled together in the cold with nothing but a blanket to cover them. It reminded him of when they were younger, as though they were children again, back atop the Moon-Spire, staring out at the stars.

It wasn't until midday the next day that the sea began to sparkle. The sparkle soon morphed into a black smudge on the blue canvas of the horizon. The smudge multiplied, shifted into separate, moving shapes. Isha watched, her vision fixed on the incoming ships. There was no relief in her expression. For there to be relief, there would have had to be doubt first, and she'd had none.

She was happy, however. Excited, even. They gathered at

the edge of the wharf, and eventually, the ships became fully visible. There were more of them than Raiz had expected, had dared to hope. Dozens of yellow suns stared back at him, painted onto white sails. Raiz listened as the men he had come with began to nervously chatter. Some readied weapons. Not openly, of course, but Raiz could sense their apprehension. Many did not believe Isha's tale about Dazen, and needed to see proof of this new alliance before they became fully invested.

But not Raiz. He knew it to be valid. He knew because Isha knew, and that was all he needed.

Spike made his descent, anticipating the heat of the moment and wanting to be there to lend comfort should Raiz need it. He issued a mighty roar – a greeting, yet also a warning. His nostrils flared. He could smell the Great Eagles, could sense their presence somewhere within the fleet of giant, sun-painted ships.

The port of Brane was bustling with activity. Up and down the wooden piers men shouted, ropes were pulled, and preparations were made. Great drums sounded, and for a moment Raiz thought they were their own, that someone had issued an order without his say. It took him longer than it should have to realise that the massive, harmonious beat was not coming from land, but from the sea.

It echoed all around them, building, growing louder with every crashing wave. The sun shone bright behind the lead ship, which was just ahead of the others in the formation. Everyone had to shield their eyes as the bulk of the galley turned, basking the entire shoreline in Zur's light. Except for Raiz. Raiz stood and stared, taking in Zur's Shine.

Just as the people around him began to let down their

guard, to sheathe their weapons, a shadow moved amongst the shifting sails. It grew, massing into something grand before soaring high and getting lost in the glaring rays of the sun. The coast of Trost was full of long-held breaths as an ear-splitting screech pierced the air, followed by a blur of movement as a Great Eagle descended upon the sparkling shoreline.

Huge wings opened wide as the Eagle broke its dive mere moments before hitting water, causing twin waves to split as the sea parted below it. The mounted Eagle then soared along the coast, making a straight line across the entire fleet. Even Raiz stopped and stared at the spectacle, his pulse racing, though there was one heart at this moment that surely beat quicker than them all.

Isha stood at the end of the pier, hand on her chest, watching, waiting.

As the first of the ships made it to port, the Eagle descended. Beside him, Spike growled, baring his teeth. Only Raiz's comforting hand calmed him, though Spike kept his tail curled, vibrating as it always did when danger was present. Spike still bore the scars of his previous encounter with Skeiron. He'd become accustomed to being the only titan in the sky, and had not appreciated finding that there might be another predator just as deadly as he.

Raiz moved to calm him again, to reassure his companion, but his agitation only grew, narrow eyes focused on what seemed to be clear skies. Raiz, more than any, knew that an animal's instincts were not to be dismissed.

Sure enough, as the Sun Prince landed, more silhouettes descended from the sky, black splotches quickly turning into colourful streaks of gold as two more Great Eagles made their presence known. This time, Raiz took a backward step, caution overriding fascination.

The Eagles made no aggressive moves, simply gliding along the shoreline, splashing waves against the bountiful fleet. Spike hunched, placing weight onto his hind legs, but otherwise remained still.

The great animal he had come to know as Skeiron landed on the rickety wharf. The Sun Prince slid down the side of his Eagle with practised grace. He was adorned in full plate armour — likely of peridium. His face was painted with yellow and orange lines, made into streaks that spread from a rim of black around his eyes, which only seemed to accentuate the violet within. He walked towards where Raiz stood beside his sister. Intricate patterns were crafted into his armour from top to bottom, the metal clinking, growing louder with each step. Much like the sails of his ships, a yellow sun was etched into the breastplate, shining in bright contrast with the black matte of the peridium set.

He wore no helm, and his long hair was tied into a single braid. Isha moved to him, and he to her. They embraced, sharing in the comfort and knowledge that each held equal faith in the other.

Another figure made its way down from the Eagle's back, though much more slowly, and with much less grace. Raiz squinted. He had not noticed two people astride the beast upon his first inspection. The figure righted himself, then immediately bent over and vomited into the shallow sea.

"Puk!" Isha said, already running for him. She wrapped her arms around his back, tighter even than she had with Bessimir.

The two friends parted. Puk seemed to recover, wiping

drool from his lip, then made a series of hand gestures Raiz couldn't understand.

"You do not owe me anything," Isha responded with her voice and her hands. "I am the one who is sorry. I am just glad you are safe, glad you are here!"

Isha turned back to Bessimir, walking with him and Puk until they converged with Raiz in the centre of the wooden pier. "What of Edar?" she questioned. "Is he…?"

The prince put up a calming hand. "He is still with us, do not fear." He pointed towards the lead galley, which was only now pulling up to cast its gloomy shadow over the docks. "He is there, as are four thousand of my men, as promised," he said, casting his gaze towards Raiz and holding it there.

"Impressive," Raiz responded. "You make quite the entrance. No doubt the story of your arrival is already being spread amongst our lands and turned to song."

He looked around at his men, most of whom were still staring goggle-eyed at the sky, watching as the Great Eagles circled.

"We have not come to spread our might in song," Bessimir said. "We have come for one purpose."

Raiz nodded. "Good. We have precious little time to waste."

Chapter 48

- Isha –

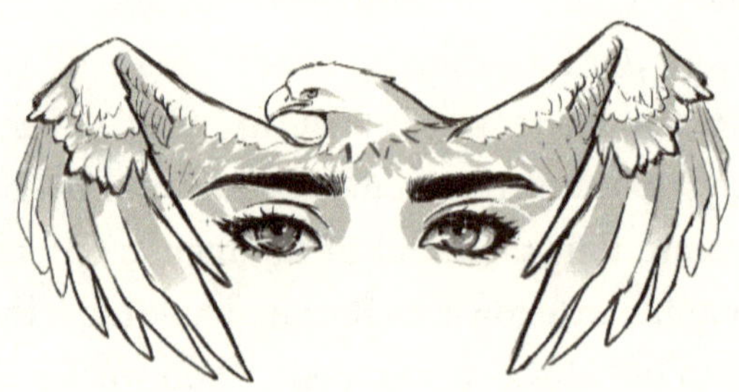

"I MISS him," Isha said, hand in hand with Raiz as they sat on the roof of the Moon-spire.

Around them, the city prepared for war. Illidor was at capacity, overflowing out to where soldiers camped beyond the city walls, making temporary homes out of the crop fields that fed them. More were coming each day, and Isha shuddered at the thought of watching them all die.

"We all miss him," Raiz replied. "I can't do this without him Ish. I'm not our brother. I'm not Dazen."

"Nobody expects you to be Dazen. You are Raiz, born a Lightfire, raised a Glaive."

"Then why do I feel like neither? Why do I feel like I'm tainted? Evil? Should never have existed? Everywhere I go, people end up dead. Everyone I love, I hurt."

Isha listened, her heart breaking with each ailing word.

"I killed them, Ish. I killed them all in cold blood. The Eagles. You saw me. I hate them. It haunts me."

Isha wrapped an arm around her brother's neck. "They're gone now. They were vile creatures, and perhaps deserved such a death. But don't let their ghosts continue to guilt you, don't let them win."

"You don't understand," Raiz said, baulking away from her touch and raising his hands before his face. "It doesn't haunt me because I feel guilty. It haunts me because I feel nothing. I murdered every single one of them, and I regret none of it. I would do it all again for what they did to you, for what they did to this world. What does that make me? I'm a monster. Monsters shouldn't rule kingdoms."

Isha wanted to comfort him, to make him understand in this moment that all was well, that he wasn't the monster he thought he was. But Raiz didn't need a quick fix. Internal wounds like that didn't heal through a single calming hand. They healed through hundreds, thousands even. Raiz had spent his entire life devoted to a single purpose, to her purpose. He had always been there for her, even when she didn't know it. Now it was her time to be there for him. She was the older sister, it was her duty to protect him, to shelter him from the demons that clouded him, especially the internal ones.

She took him by the hand again, and when he made to pull away, she squeezed all the tighter. He looked at her. She must have looked a horror, face wet with tears. "I'm sorry, for everything you've done, everything you've been through. I'm sorry for being selfish, for running to another shore without thinking of home, of you. I'm here now. We can make a future of Illidor, of Trost, of Zapour. Together."

Little time was wasted as the war preparations continued. She wanted to take the time to properly introduce her brother to Bessimir, but she understood the time parameter they were working under. Any day now, Gelvard could decide to invade. If they were caught unprepared, the results could prove disastrous.

Bessimir's fleet remained docked at Brane in western Trost, though he himself had travelled with a small party to Illidor to discuss the war efforts. The current war-room consisted of Isha, Bessimir, Edar, Sounja, and Abhick on one side, and Raiz, Aia, Gale, Sumaya, along with several representatives of Trost's noble houses on the other.

She took comfort in seeing Edar alive and well. His arm rested in a sling. She knew he was just putting on a brave face, that beneath the façade was a wall of pain. She could feel it from him using her empathic powers, even though Bessimir had already taken most of it.

She was even glad to see Sounja again, though her hardened face remained as mistrustful as ever. She could feel her anger, emanating from her like heat from a Shine user. She wanted to take it away, to alter her emotions, but knew she would refuse her request. It was her anger that drove her, kept her sharp. Without it, she wouldn't be herself. Even so, Isha still wished she could take some of it, if only to save herself from the constant scowling.

A map of Zapour was displayed on a central table, fitted for the occasion. Brass pieces that Isha likened to the carvings on a chess board were spread out all over the sprawling map, highlighting troop and garrison locations of both the allied and enemy forces. She recognised many of the colours and locations, Lumindal being the most notable. The exact numbers were inaccurate and unpredictable, but there was more than a sizeable force gathered at the foot of her old prison.

She searched the expressions of those present in the war room, felt the rise and fall of their emotions. Apprehension, anxiety, caution, determination, dread.

She sat by Bessimir's side, the prince still adorned in his peridium plate-mail. Gelvard and his cousin Hanns each boasted hundreds of Lightweavers, perhaps even double those that Trost and Zuton could produce.

"I have a gift," Bessimir said, breaking the stretching silence. He gestured to Abhick, who brought forward a large chest carried between two strong hands. He opened it to reveal a complete set of armour, from helm to leg braces. It wasn't necessarily as pretty or decorated as the prince's own, but Isha could tell by the colour that it was peridium.

"There are three hundred more of these currently being transported here for your purposes. Not enough to outfit an entire army, but they should be sufficient to counter a unit of Lightweavers should they be deployed correctly."

Raiz inspected the plate armour, taking care not to touch any of it. His hands wavered close to the metal, his skin seeming to vibrate the closer he came. He retracted his hand and stepped back, nodding. "This will prove useful. Thank you, I know such a gift is not idly given. My men will put them to good use, be assured."

Bessimir bowed. "Is this the current situation?" he said, straightening and gesturing to the map atop the table.

Raiz nodded, and the prince leaned towards Edar. His short red hair seemed as thick as rope. He grunted as he rose to inspect the board, eyes searching, assessing, learning.

Edar sat back down on his chair, eyes still cast over the map, his good hand rubbing at the stubble on his chin. "These pieces here," he said, waving his hand to the brass carvings Gale had used for the Wishan people, which sat isolated deep within enemy territory. "Are they accessible?"

Raiz spared a look towards Aia, then slowly shook his head. "We were hoping so, but as of late we have received no response from the Wishan capital. We suspect it is simply a matter of Craw cutting off our communication. We have no way of reaching them without invading enemy territory. The Wishan princess, Aia, is here with us," he said, motioning towards Aia, "but without communication, I believe we may be without the Wishan Bakai for this war effort."

Edar remained impassive, simply continuing to stare at the pieces as if he were moving them with his mind.

"And here," Edar pointed, "these are the troops from Zuton?"

"Correct," Raiz said. Isha was no tactician, and she doubted Raiz had the experience to lead such a large and coordinated effort either, but he had told her that Gale had been tutoring him, Dazen's First Hand now Raiz's own. Raiz leant on him, used him, and relied on him for matters that were above his ability to comprehend or surmise.

"And you plan to meet here?" Edar continued, waving his hand over a piece on the map at the edge of the Golden Forest.

Raiz nodded, his face sceptical.

"And where are we to fit into this plan?" Edar said, his eyes flickering.

"It was my hope to split our forces along the border here," Raiz said, using three separate hand movements as he highlighted his chosen locations. "We are to surround Lumindal on three fronts. Gelvard is preparing his own invasive army. They are mustering outside the walls here," he pointed, "where he is joining his force with his cousins from the east."

"And you are sure he will not simply sit behind the defence of his walls?"

Raiz looked to Gale, who shook his head confidently. "Yes," Raiz said. "His force is too large, and Lumindal's population is too numerous to hold his army within the walls. All reports suggest he has settled outside of the city for now, though we are prepared for an assault on the walls should the need arise. Lumindal was built by and for the former Eagles. It was not built to withstand an assault by white-light. If we concentrate our efforts enough, I am confident we can make an opening through to the city."

Isha placed a steady hand on Bessimir's leg, well aware that talk of using so much of the sun's energy was troubling him. He failed to fully mask his frustration, which didn't go unnoticed by Raiz.

"Let us hope there will be no need for such a misuse of Zur's power," Bessimir said as calmly as he could.

Raiz took a steadying breath. "With respect, if we do not seize the city as quickly as possible, then we risk the Last Light becoming active. I am sure you are aware of the significance of such a weapon, given your extensive knowledge of the history of our lands."

"Raiz!" Isha said, noting the mocking tone of her brother's words.

Bessimir did not retaliate, simply raised his hand to reassure her he had taken no offence. He turned his attention back to Raiz. "I am well aware of what the Last Light is capable of, and like you, I am ashamed of what has become of it.

"I understand what it has taken from you," Bessimir continued, "and will do all I can to ensure the weapon remains out of commission."

"What is this?" Edar asked. Throughout their conversation he had continued to stare at the map, thinking, plotting, portraying the same fixated expression he had given her every morning during their games of reverse chess.

She watched as Raiz studied the map. "That is the Lion's Tail Channel. It flows through Zapour, ending in Lake Edius."

"And this channel," Edar continued. "Do you have access to it?"

Raiz shook his head. "Once, perhaps. But since the fall of the King-Radiant and Gelvard's seizure of Lumindal, Craw has taken control of the channel."

"But the river splits here," Edar said. "Where land meets sea there is a tributary. One of the connecting rivers falls under blue territory, correct?"

Isha leaned over the table to see what he was talking about. The map was split into colours, each representing one of the Six Kingdoms of Zapour. Blue for Trost, red for Craw, green for Zuton, brown for Kogon, yellow for Wisha, and grey for Crata. Isha bit her lip at the thought of Edar seeing his kingdom of birth grey and empty, but she held her tongue. She hadn't revealed that tidbit of information to Raiz just yet.

Edar was right, part of the river's mouth meandered away from the others, stretching into blue territory. "I suppose," Raiz said, looking to Gale for support.

"Is the channel large enough for ships to pass?" Edar inquired.

It was Gale who spoke next, placing two hands on the table and staring at the location in question. "The channel you speak of is wide enough, yes, but there would be no point running one through there. We may hold control over that particular affluent, but eventually all meet in the same location. Agents of Craw man the river's edge, their veins flowing with Shine, ready to sink any ships who would pass uninvited."

"Have you tested this?" Edar questioned.

"No, we have not. It would be suicide. But that is the information I have been given, and I can personally vouch for its accuracy."

"Suicide for you, perhaps. But your ships and your men are not equipped for such warfare. That is the problem that comes from reliance on a power that is not natural."

Gale's expression changed. Thick blue veins protruded from his forehead as he tensed, likely replaying a memory they both shared. He'd been there when Isha had rushed reckless into the Sapphire Sea. He'd been responsible for recovering her after she had acted rashly. And he'd been there when Bessimir's ships had so easily destroyed his own.

But despite the tactical display and victory, Bessimir had spared him, allowed him to return unmolested, which was likely the only reason Gale was able to be in the same room as him right now.

"What are you suggesting?" Raiz interjected.

Gale relaxed, crossed his arms. "He wants to send their fleet down the channel, wipe out the Craw outpost, and deploy his troops at Lake Edius' edge."

"Is that all possible?" Raiz asked.

Gale shrugged. "I have seen what his men and his ships are capable of first-hand. I would say so, yes. If the timing is right, then we might be able to take Gelvard by surprise. With a frontal assault from our forces joined with Zuton, Bessimir and his men could attack from the rear, using the lake to position themselves behind the enemy line. We could squash them between two fronts. It is practical, yes, but also requires the ships to break through the Craw outpost to succeed. If that should fail, we may as well have tied our own hands."

"It will not fail," Bessimir said, voice calm and collected. "Edar's plans have never failed me before. If he says it is possible, then he has my full support. Besides, I have Skeiron. I doubt even the might of a nation such as Craw has born witness to a Great Eagle at war. Edar, will this work?"

Every face in the room looked to Edar. He gulped, beads of sweat dripping from his brow. He righted, cleared his throat, then looked to Gale. "I will need a detailed map of the river's course, as well as information on its width and depth. I want to know where it flows fastest and where it shallows. I would also require any reports you can give me on the Craw outpost, including troop numbers and distribution, as well as your permission, and safe passage through the mouth of the spoken affluent."

Gale looked to Raiz and shrugged.

"Then you will have it," Raiz said.

He looked to Isha, and she inclined her head in respect. She admired Raiz now more than ever. She had always loved him, would always love him. But before, her love was born out of kinship. They were family. Now, her love had changed, grown. In the past, Raiz never would have trusted someone like Bessimir, and she suspected he still didn't. But he trusted her, and that meant more to her than even the shared bond of their birth mother.

Chapter 49

- Raiz –

THE GOLDEN FOREST was silent but for the footfalls of a marching army. Gelvard had not ventured any deeper into Trost. He was patient, either waiting for his numbers to swell, or for the Last Light to finish its reconstruction and reach capacity. Either way, Raiz had to go on the offensive. It had to be now. Trost would lose the waiting game, and everyone knew it.

A familiar horn blew in the distance, playing a tune that in another lifetime had signalled an enemy's call to action. Sumaya headed for him, dressed for war in a suit of peridium. Dazen's twin blades dangled at her hip. Mother was in Illidor, looking after Nora, Sumaya reasoning it was her duty to fight. There was no safe place if they lost the coming battle. Illidor might hold out for a time, but in the end, Gelvard was too ambitious to allow them to remain unmolested by war for long.

Raiz did not regret taking down the King-Radiant and his Eagles. They were vile, corrupt. But what he did regret was failing to anticipate the nature of a man such as Gelvard. He had lied to them, deceived them into thinking the remaining Kingdoms of Zapour could co-exist in harmony. In reality, power was a volatile concept. Once someone had a taste, there was always room for more.

Slowly, the horn blasts grew louder. Sumaya charged ahead to where the two paths met. It wasn't long before Zuton's army became visible, and the two converged into one.

Their meeting was an apprehensive one. Though their alliance had been in place for over two years now, the nations had yet to collaborate on a course of action of this scale, and Raiz could feel the taste of hatred still lingering on the lips of some of the older veterans, who might well have fought against those standing on the opposite side of the forest in a past battle.

Despite Raiz's short reign, Dazen had disciplined his men well, and before him, Kron had instilled a sense of duty even amongst the most outspoken of his troops. Raiz bit his lip at the thought of his father in power. Kron was somewhere back there, in the ranks of common soldiers. Raiz didn't like the idea, was still seething at the way he had treated Isha. But she had insisted, and in truth, he was a powerful soldier that would be a great asset in what was to come.

Raiz's face lit up as he saw Hector riding towards him, just behind his king. Echo was adorned in full plate. He had not yet grown into the stature his predecessor and birth father, Rayner Levic, had been known for, but despite his youth, Echo had a regal presence of his own making. He held his head high. The emblem of the Twin Serpents was bright on his breast. A silver crown circled his head, and he sat atop a black steed that towered over Raiz.

Echo dismounted. Hector and another man, who was much older and larger than them both, followed suit. The second man had a battle-hardened face, with a long scar running its length from chin to forehead. One eye was blue as the morning sky, the other brown as an oak tree.

Raiz moved to greet Echo, Gale shuffling up behind, but Sumaya beat him to it. She wrapped her younger brother up in a great bear hug, much to the youthful king's embarrassment, though he eventually relaxed into it, embracing the moment for what it was – a reunion between brother and sister. Raiz, more than any, knew the importance of such moments, so he let it linger.

Instead, he moved to Hector, the two facing off in mock competition before Hector's lip curled into a smile. Raiz allowed his own to do the same, embracing him like a lost brother. Claw still clung to his shoulder, the pricket having already grown an inch or two since the last time they met. For a moment, Raiz was proud, but then he remembered his deal with the Sun Prince. Hector had only just begun to learn how to handle his Shine, would he be able to cope if he was forced never to use it willingly again?

"You grow stronger still," Raiz said, placing two hands upon either of Hector's shoulders and feeling the broadness of his growing shape.

"I can't stay a kid forever, unfortunately. Have you been well?"

Raiz thought back on the past few months. He had not been well, but he wasn't about to go preaching weakness. Strength was needed in this moment. "As well as can be," he said. "How are you taking to Claw?"

Hector spared a glance towards his reptilian companion. "Well, she's a little clingy… but I admit I've become attached," he said, sliding into a cheeky grin Raiz had not seen before.

Raiz laughed alongside him. "I see she has grown. Best to keep her away from the coming conflict. The battlefield is no place for a creature so young."

Hector nodded. "Of course. My wife will take care of her for me while I'm at war, she's part of the medical core who travelled here with us."

Raiz stared, open-mouthed. "Your wife?"

Hector nodded, scratching his head. "Yeah, just kind of happened, you know. I would have invited you, but it was a spur of the moment decision. I don't want to have any regrets."

Raiz shook his head in disbelief, but shrugged his acceptance. "When we return home, you and I are to share a drink. I would hear of how you two met."

Hector nodded, but then raised a brow. "Do you even drink?"

Raiz hesitated, embarrassed. He was grateful that Echo and Sumaya had ended their greeting, the King of Zuton making his way over.

Raiz extended an arm. The two were nearly the same height. Echo clasped his hand around Raiz's forearm. "While I regret that Dazen is not here to see this alliance tested through combat," Echo said, "I am glad to have the chance to see the results of all of his work in joining our two great nations."

Raiz nodded his respect. "I too am thankful for the

opportunity he made possible. I am not my brother, nor will I pretend to be, but I will not put his legacy to shame. The only way forward is together. I am glad to have the chance to fight beside the brave men and women of Zuton."

Echo bowed, then stepped aside. "This is Adenar," he said, gesturing to the scarred man. He is commander of my forces, and has served my family for countless years."

Raiz and Zuton's commander locked gazes, and in that moment Raiz was glad to have him on their side. The man oozed experience, a quality desperately needed in the events that were soon to play out. They exchanged a quick greeting before Echo spoke again.

"Where are our friends from across the sea? Did they not travel with you?"

"The prince has set his own plan in motion. Isha is with him. They are taking a fleet down the Lion's Tail to overthrow the Craw outpost, then take the channel to Lake Edius. This will allow them to deploy their troops on the shore and come at Gelvard from the rear."

Echo's face turned into a picture of confusion. "That is a suicide run! Soldiers of Craw fill that channel end to end! It cannot be done. Not to mention the entrance is blocked by the Craw fleet, and who knows what they have in store should they even make it all the way to the lake."

"I thought the same as you when I first heard the plan, but you have not seen their fleet. Gale assures me they have the means to back up their boast. Added to that, they have somehow managed to attain the support of four Great Eagles."

Echo paused, failing to mask his surprise. "So the rumours are true? They do exist?"

Raiz nodded. "It would seem the former hierarchy of

Lumindal kept more secrets from us than we thought. I still do not trust him fully, but Isha assures me of his good nature, and there is at least some truth to his tales. After the war is done, we can find out what he knows, together."

"Agreed. Now, shall we take a look at what fate awaits us over the ridge?"

Raiz breathed a deep, foreboding sigh through thin lips. "If we must."

Silence. Nobody spoke. Nobody could speak. Words held no meaning as they looked out into the open plains before the towering city. Mouths hung open. Hands were fastened to the hilts of blades. Feet shifted from place to place.

Tens of thousands of troops bearing the crimson sashes worn by men of Craw littered the outskirts of the city like ants to an anthill. Though, unlike the chaotic dance of ants scurrying to return to their home, these men were extremely organised. Tight rows of soldiers were cordoned into formation, separated into ranks and groups receding all the way back to the gates of Lumindal. Raiz placed a hand over his brow, shielding his vision from the sun. He spotted the rusty brown cloaks worn by soldiers of Kogon, swelling the already bountiful ranks, more still pouring in from the east.

"There are so many," Hector said as he came to Raiz's side, echoing the thoughts surely radiating through the minds of all present.

Raiz looked behind, marvelling at the strength of the country he now proudly called his own. Every known name in Trost had answered his call to war, sickened by the prospect of losing their home to whatever tyranny Gelvard had in store, should he be victorious.

He walked along the front line. He would give no rousing speech, no grand gesture, no calling upon their honour. He was not Dazen, and would not pretend to be. Spike roamed the sky above, his presence lending much needed confidence, silencing the shaking voices, stilling the shivering hands.

Raiz cleared his throat. "Their numbers do not matter. We will win."

He looked to Hector. The young Kingsguard looked unconvinced.

"How? How can we possibly beat that? They must have nearly double our number, not to mention a giant wall of stone at their back." His hands began to tremble, his breath grew ragged.

Raiz turned to him. Echo, Sumaya, Gale, and a host of others were all present, watching. He grabbed Hector by the collar. "I thought you wanted to conquer fear? I thought you vowed to rid the world of the selfishness of men like Gelvard? Now you have your chance. There is your fear!" he said, pointing a tense arm down the hill towards Lumindal. "Now, what will you do with it?"

At first, Hector recoiled, wide-eyed. He shied away, squeezing his eyes shut as if to close out the world around him. Then, something changed. His fists clenched. The air around him grew thick. Raiz felt an immense pressure. His knees began to buckle. Hector's hands began to shake, Shine leaking from his fingers like a dripping tap. He rose to meet Raiz's eye, then looked over his shoulder, out into the gathered army.

"You're wrong," he said. "They are not the fear. I am."

Chapter 50

- Zeek –

FATHER WAS WALKING again, recovered enough to at least hold his own weight. Six men bearing crimson sashes the same make as the prince he had killed and consumed escorted them through the largest congregation of humans Zeek had ever seen. The entirety of his short life, he had lived in solitude. Even on the open roads he never encountered more than half a dozen people at one moment. Now, he was surrounded by them.

The pungent scent of sweat was thick as they slipped through the gathered masses all the way to the open gates of the now familiar city. The dead prince inside of him screamed, memories flooding his mind like a wind that twisted into a gale of never-ending voices and images. He pressed it down, focusing instead on making sure Father made it through to the sharpened towers looming ever-present in the sky above.

The city was empty. Not literally. He could still see prevalent signs of activity as the odd citizen popped out of their home to tend to one chore or another. However, most had made themselves scarce, likely either by fleeing the city, being conscripted into the army, or hiding behind the four walls of their frivolous homes.

They made their way up what he had learned last time was the Fifty-First Spear — the tallest of the lot save for the Last Light, which looked even taller than the first time he was here. He nearly lost his footing again as the contraption lifted them up into the air, moving on its own.

Crimson guards flanked their every movement, not giving himself or his father room to breathe. Zeek's shadow-tail vibrated beneath the confines of his cloak. A warning. He pushed it down, forcing the one lingering reminder of who he was and who he had been back inside.

The scene played out in a similar fashion to the last time they were here. Gelvard sat on his throne at the end of the hall. He seemed to have slimmed down since his last visit, though Zeek supposed grief did terrible things to the human body as well as the mind. Thick black bags hung heavy beneath the lids of his eyes, and he wore a hardened expression, one Zeek was coming to know well.

Inside, Ancel's essence again asserted itself. It was as though the dead prince was still awake, conscious and active, even though Zeek knew he was in full control.

The King of Craw was not the only one on the dais this time. Another throne had been fashioned by his side, and atop it sat an insanely tall man with hunched shoulders. He too bore a crown atop his head, sharing Gelvard's frightening expression as the two of them eyed his father while he walked down the velvet-covered walkway.

"That is far enough!" Gelvard bellowed.

Father stopped, Zeek a few steps behind. "You two make a cute couple," Father said.

The two kings were unamused, eyes narrowing to slits. "You are late," Gelvard said, brawny hands squeezing the knob of his throne.

"Apologies, my liege. Lieges," he corrected, eyeing the second king. "I ran into some… inconveniences on my way back. I trust the repairs on the Last Light are complete?"

The two kings looked at each other, then back to Father. "Not quite," Gelvard said.

Father studied them with a look Zeek knew well, understanding. "You tried to use it. And how did that go for you?" he said, making a derisive sound of mock criticism.

Once again the two kings spared an errant look at each other, this one full of contempt.

"I told you, the Last Light may only be wielded by a true Radiant. Place as many Shine users atop that tower as you like, but they will all burn unless Gallion's blood is used to harness it properly."

"So it would seem," the other king spoke. "Fortunate for us then, that you have returned. And on the eve of battle, no less."

Father puffed out his chest, the sign of a man who knew he had power over another. "My terms stand. I will do as you request. In return, I would have the Last Light refilled, and access to its Light when the time comes for the Skae's return."

Gelvard rolled his head around in its socket, releasing a long-held groan. "Again with this Skae business. The Skae are a myth! A legend. They are not real, and are certainly not on the eve of making a long-awaited return to Zapour."

"The Skae are very real. You would know this if you had sent an expedition to the Weeping Mountains as I suggested."

"Bah!" Gelvard grumbled. "I will not waste resources sending my men on a pointless quest to be ambushed by Cratan barbarians or Wishan rats."

"The Darkening is coming. I do not know how long we have, but it is nearing its cycle. With it will come our end if we are not prepared. What do you have to lose? Agree to my terms. If I am wrong, then you lose nothing. If I am right, then you will thank me for it later."

Gelvard leaned forward and shook his head. He thrust a strong fist onto the armrest of his throne, rising in a fit of anger. "Arggh, no! It will not do. I will not be dictated by the likes of you. The time of the Radiant is over. Our time has come. Saelmere and Balsto will rule Zapour from this day forward, and will conquer all who oppose. You will do as I say, Radiant. I will give you no choice."

Zeek tensed, and Gelvard snapped his fingers, indicating to someone hiding behind a door at the side of the room.

A shuffle of footsteps later and two guards came into view. Between them was a small, elderly woman with silver hair. Her hands were cuffed behind her back, though she did not struggle. Instead, she held herself tall, her bright eyes fierce and determined, speaking to years of experience.

"Sephare," Father said, his tone more of a statement of fact than of concern for her safety.

"Husband," she said in response. Her gaze lingered, drifting towards Zeek, and then she inclined her head, her lips forming into an amused grin.

It was Gelvard who spoke next. "Do not pretend you have

lost your affection for your own wife. I tire of these games. You will do as I say, or she will pay for her sins."

Father was unmoving. The silence stretched, and Zeek made to take a step forward.

Two spear-length halberds blocked his path, metal-clad soldiers in blood-coloured capes criss-crossing their weapons in one swift motion.

Gelvard ripped Sephare from his own guard, cradling her between his biceps and forearm. He drew a knife from the sheath at his hip and levelled it at her, pressing the point into the pink of her wrinkled neck.

"Sephare!" Father said, this time with more emotion.

"Ah, so there is still some empathy left in that blackened heart of yours," Gelvard said. "I suppose you and I are not so dissimilar these days. We both understand the pain of losing a natural born son." He laced those last few words with a touch of malice, and Zeek could tell he was struggling to keep his composure.

Ancel screamed inside of him at the mention of his death, but Zeek wouldn't let him speak.

Gelvard seemed to calm somewhat, taking a deep breath. But his knife remained at Sephare's throat. "I will not say it again. You will obey me, Radiant, or the blood of your wife will run through these halls like a river."

Beside him, Father growled, angry veins popping from his already blackened face. He turned to Zeek, looking at him for the first time as if he were a stranger. Inside, Zeek felt something shift, an emotion he had never felt before rising to the surface.

"I wish it hadn't come to this," Father said.

Zeek took a cautious step forward. "What do you mean,

Father?"

Father sighed. "I had another plan in mind for you, but this is too important. The Last Light must become active. It is paramount."

"What are you two babbling about?" Gelvard demanded. "Speak!"

"What if I can prove it," Father said, much to everyone's confusion.

"Prove what?" Gelvard responded. "Enough of these games."

"Prove that the Skae exist. That they are coming."

Gelvard laughed. "Unless you are hiding proof in those dead arms of yours, then this conversation is pointless. The armies of Trost and Zuton are at our gates! I need the Last Light activated now!"

Father turned to Zeek with eyes void of emotion. "My associate here, he is of the Skae."

Zeek gasped, which was soon followed by another two as Gelvard and the other king issued a surprised choke.

"Quit wasting my time," Gelvard said. "I will not fall for your cheap tricks. Now submit to me, and have your wife's life spared."

"Show them. Do it now," Father said to him.

Zeek hesitated. It didn't seem like a good idea. Revealing himself in this situation would certainly lead to his capture. But Father had told him to. Why? He had to trust Father... Father would protect him. He wouldn't lead him astray, he had told him so.

"Do it!" Father insisted, eyes wide, lit like a brazier burning with fire.

Zeek obliged. All he had ever known was obedience. He

owed his life to him, his experiences, his existence. It was all because of him. He would do this act. He would show his true form. And Father would protect him, he was sure.

The twin guards either side of him edged a half-step away as he unlatched the hook on his jacket, revealing his bony, dark-veined forearms.

"Enough of this," Gelvard said. "We have wasted too much time. Submit to me now and we can…"

His voice trailed off as Zeek lifted his shirt, revealing the still-forming human flesh beneath. Despite his recent accomplishments, Zeek's transition from the shadow-like state of his previous life had not yet been fully completed. Dozens of black splotches dotted his otherwise pink skin like bruises, only they moved, swirling around his body like a shifting shadow.

That was nothing compared to what came next. He finally released his hold on his tail, allowing the inky blackness to seep from his body. It curled around his waist, moving on its own as it coalesced into a single entity, hovering above his head and forming into a barbed hook.

The King of Craw's mouth hung open as he stared at Zeek as if he were a ghost. He tried to speak, but released only a garble of inaudible sounds. Eventually, he found his voice. "S-seize him!"

The guards beside him moved in unison. Zeek went to respond, to negate their advance, but Father stopped him. "Do not move!" he ordered.

Zeek obeyed. His shadow-tail curled to a point, ready to strike, but he forced it to steady, pressing what little control he had against it. He could feel its instincts. The urge to carve the advancing soldiers into mince was strong, the hunger ever persistent.

He searched Father's expression as more guards poured on top of him, grabbing his hands, his legs, his tail…There was nothing there. Wasn't he going to stop them?

"Father?" Zeek whispered, but he was left unanswered. Eventually, Father's gaze left his own, turning back to Gelvard. "Do we have a deal?"

Zeek felt the words as if they were a knife to his heart.

Gelvard looked terrified. Zeek could smell his fear even amidst the chaotic tangle of limbs he was now caught between. "If your words turn out to be the truth, then I will allow you to use the Last Light against any threat thrown towards my city. If," he continued, "you help me to defeat the advancing armies currently at Lumindal's door, and you allow me to study this… specimen."

Father turned one last time to look at Zeek, who even now continued to believe that he would save him from this fate, before turning back to Gelvard. "Agreed."

What breath Zeek still held left his lungs. An emotion began to swell in his heart, one he recognised from Ancel. Hatred.

It boiled, bubbled, morphed in his mind. Father had betrayed him. He had promised him the world, told him that if he did as he was told, there would be more. More forests to explore. More oceans to swim. More animals to meet.

He had lied.

Zeek's anger turned to power, and he gave in fully to the shadow he'd always known was lurking within. The voice that had been following him, pulling him, flared to life. It called to him, even now, granting him power.

Light mixed with darkness as his veins turned into a

deadly mixture of the two contrasting elements. He pushed with his mind and body, and the guards holding him down were thrust outward in a wave of unseen force. He was free. His tail curled, vibrating, hungry.

A quick to recover soldier came at him with the point of a halberd, and Zeek easily stepped aside. His tail lashed out, and the barbed point cut through metal to shear the unfortunate man's neck in half.

More came at him, and more fell to the hunger of his inner shadow. He searched for Father, who was staring, watching, unmoved. Gelvard called for more soldiers. They poured through the doors, too many for him to handle all at once.

Zeek's eyes fluttered towards the glass window at the end of the room, behind the thrones. He charged, and a cluster of soldiers moved toward their king, holding rounded shields in his defence. Another two shot bolts of Shine towards him, aiming to burn him alive. He dodged, moving with inhuman speed and leaping towards the glass. It shattered, his body following the glass through to the open air of the other side.

Then he was falling. Falling far, and falling fast. His stomach dropped, though he found the sensation oddly thrilling. Even as he fell to his likely death, he somehow knew that he would survive. The shadow within him shrouded his body, covering him in a veil that protected his physical form. He landed with a crash into a green courtyard. All around him lay squashed shrubbery, broken glass, and a human-sized divot in the ground. But he was alive. More than alive. He was awoken. And he was angry.

Chapter 51

- Isha –

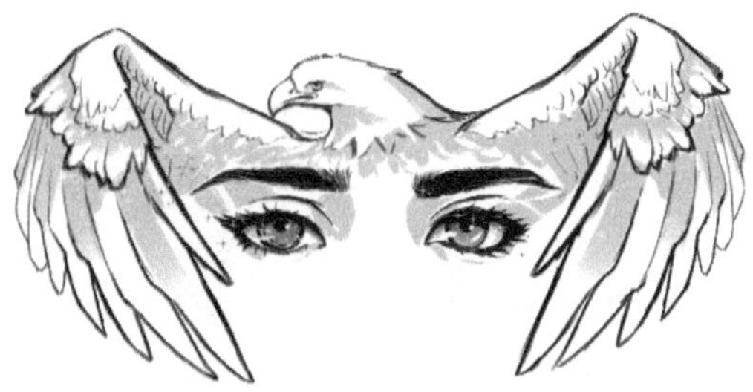

ISHA STOOD ON the foredeck of the Sun's Reach, staring into the mouth of the southernmost affluent of the Lion's Tail Channel. The entrance was narrow, but Craw's dominion hadn't quite stretched far enough to completely cover its bank.

Twelve of Yagos' ships in total followed the Sun's Reach down the strait, escorted by four of Trost's own.

Brightguards lined the railing, fitted with peridium plate. A golden sun circled each breast, bright flames licking at the edges. The heartbeat of Bessimir's army consisted of soldiers formerly of the Thousand-Shields Company, though the numbers were swelled by regular foot soldiers recruited from different parts of Yagos.

Puk stood by her side, also donning a peridium set. In his right hand he held a long spear, its point sharpened to a deadly edge. At his hip was a peridium short sword gifted to him by Bessimir in acknowledgement of his devotion. Isha too had been gifted a peridium blade. She held it in the palm of her hand, surprised by the relative lightness of its weight. She may not have had the training of a Brightguard or a White-Sword, but she had been learning, watching, practising every waking moment so that finally she might have enough skill to defend the people she loved most. To defend herself.

She turned to Puk. "I am sorry," she said, hands moving, "for abandoning you. For my father. For Bessimir..." she finished. She knew he had learned of her involvement with the prince, and knew how he felt about her, even if he left his words unspoken. "Things are... complicated..."

She felt sick. What did that even mean? She shied away. She didn't deserve him as a friend.

Puk clasped her hand in his and pressed her palm to his heart. He parted, smiled. *Never apologise for following your heart,* he motioned. *If not for you, I would never have seen what has become of my people. This prince,* he continued. *I do not know if what he says is true. But I know what I see. I believe him to be good. If he is where your heart leads, then you should follow it.*

Isha smiled. She pulled Puk close and wrapped her arms around him.

As they parted, four Great Eagles swooped by the central ship. Skeiron, Strix, Andreni and Sypa were an army on their own, likely drawing the attention of the distant watch towers and prying eyes even as day turned to night. Bessimir didn't seem to care. He wanted them to be prepared, wanted them to come at him with their full force. She was beginning to think the man had no fear. He had chosen to remain on the Sun's Reach, reasoning that if his men had to brave the tide, then so should he.

Night had fallen completely now, another of Edar's tactics. Shine was brutal, effective, and merciless. But without the sun to replenish their Light, it was finite. It was not an uncommon strategy used in Zapour, often utilised by a war party planning an offensive on an enemy with a greater number of Shine users than their own. It was a Lightweaver's great weakness, relying on stored energy.

"What can you see?" Isha asked Bessimir as he made his way to the bow.

"They are here, waiting, watching."

Isha could see the bend coming to an end. They had reached the part of the river where the affluents met. Gale was right, the Craw outpost looked impregnable. Watchtowers lined the river's bank, more than likely housing trained archers and Lightweavers. She could only just make out the blur of black shapes shifting in the distance, and coming into vision now was the black gate that Gale had spoken about, closed shut, barring their path forward.

Bessimir turned to his men. "Lower the sails! Ready the oars! Raise shields!"

All at once his men followed their orders, their feet moving in a flurry of silent footsteps. None spoke a word, they just completed their tasks with meticulous efficiency. The scene played out in a similar fashion to when the prince had wiped out Gale's fleet.

Bessimir made for her. "Come with me," he said.

"But I want to fight. I'm ready!"

"I know. There will be a time to fight, but this step requires patience."

Isha allowed him to take her to the safety of the centre of the Sun's Reach. Men either side of her carried giant metal shields, which spilled over the railing, covering a large portion of the hull, which she already knew was outfitted with a thin layer of peridium itself.

The night was quiet as they approached. She was expecting the fighting to begin immediately, for arrows to rain and Shine to flow. Instead, there was silence. Only the sound of oars meeting water could be heard as their ship ventured deep into enemy territory. She could see the shapes continuing to shift on the riverbank. She began to panic, thinking themselves in the centre of an ambush, though Bessimir seemed calm.

The ship continued, the Great Eagles keeping their distance. Isha gulped. Was this how Raiz felt before every battle? The sensation was both thrilling, and utterly terrifying at the same time, knowing at any moment there would be chaos.

She snapped herself back into focus, watching for Bessimir's reaction. The ship kept moving, edging closer and closer to the closed gate. Bessimir's lip trembled as the stand-off stretched longer than he would have liked. He held up a hand, indicating for his men to slow their pace. The ships came to a near stand-still, and Isha could have written an entire book describing the silence that followed.

The tiny hairs on her arm stood tall, and her hand began to shake. Bessimir grabbed her wrist, stilling her nervous energy. He squeezed, lending her a reassuring smile before a deafening cry came from somewhere in the shadowy brush.

Following the shout was a sound so thunderous it shook the entire ship. The black of the night turned white as a barrage of coordinated Shine came at them in one giant wave of energy. If she hadn't been looking back at the trailing ships at the time, she would have missed it. The entire riverbank lit with bright energy. Its impact was immediate, though the outcome was not as the aggressors intended.

Shine bounced off the ship's side like a rubber ball. It rebounded, ricochetted. Some spilled uselessly into the air, the angle of the shields forcing the Light upwards, but most bounced back. Their greatest weapon turned against them as the Shine was sent back to where it had come from.

Replacing the once silent river were shouts of dismay. Everywhere around her people were screaming, burning. The shadowy figures turned bright, fully visible in their destruction. Watchtowers burned, set alight by their own men as the peridium sent their attacks back at them.

Some remained standing, firing arrows set aflame with natural fire. A few were impactful, sinking into the ship's hull and creating spot-fires, but most were errant. Bessimir stood tall and began shouting orders. More men poured from the ship's insides, each holding a short bow in hand. Arrows were loosed, and those which had survived the initial burst of Shine were quickly dealt with.

Their path forward was clear except for the black gate barring their path forward. Bessimir grabbed her with one hand and whistled with the other.

Skeiron and Strix came soaring from the sky, landing with characteristic grace, though the ship still shook with the impact. Bessimir jumped on the saddle fastened to Skeiron's back.

Isha made for Strix, looking her companion in the eye and feeling their connection reignite like a spark of flame. She felt her emotions, her anxiety, her lust for blood. It was as if Strix's feelings were her own.

Within a few heartbeats they were in the air. Wings beat,

and the ground grew small as Strix took her above the conflict.

She dared to look down, surveying the destruction. Two thick lines of fire stretched the length of the riverbank. Between them, their ships sailed unmolested. The entire outpost had been decimated. Screams were still evident, and Isha saw multiple soldiers set aflame, attempting to retreat to the safety of their homeland. Some jumped into the water, hoping to assuage their burns with a cold compress. Others were simply gone, their bodies ash, washed away in the nightly breeze or the gentle current.

Only the gate remained as an obstacle. Skeiron descended. Isha and Strix followed. Sharp talons raked into the nearest soldier atop the central platform, skewering him and lifting him into the air, only to drop him at least thirty feet above ground. He fell, screaming.

Andreni and Sypa also joined in the battle, swooping at scared soldiers, picking them off from their high vantage one by one. Bessimir stood in his saddle, lifting his spear as Skeiron made for another pass. He thrust forward and withdrew in two quick motions, his spear returning bloody. Strix followed Skeiron's tail, as they landed, allowing the two riders to dismount. Isha rolled into a crouch, sword drawn, teeth bared. These men threatened her home. They endangered those she loved. She would hold no mercy for those who sought to conquer simply to satisfy their own lust for power.

A panicked soldier came at her, sword raised, eyes full of fear. She felt it, was drawn to it. Her first instinct was to help him, to ease his pain, his alarm, and she paused, suddenly uncertain in her bloodlust. But that was quickly quashed as he closed the distance faster than she had anticipated. Isha issued a loud war-cry, making to cut the man down on her first strike, but Bessimir's spear got there first. He lunged in front of her, jabbing the spear's point into the aggressor's stomach. The soldier of Craw's sword dropped to the stone pathway in a clatter, his body soon following as Bessimir withdrew his weapon.

Isha scowled. "Why did you do that?"

Bessimir couldn't look her in the eye. "You hesitated. Never hesitate in battle. I will not lose you like this."

Isha tensed, trying her hardest to crush the hilt of the peridium blade she held in her hand. He was right, her hesitation had nearly gotten her killed.

She focused, concentrating on her next assailant even as an Eagle swooped from above to take the life of the man behind her target. She leapt at him, using the training Puk had drilled into her. He turned just in time to see her blade sink into his heart.

Blood gushed from the wound, which suctioned around her sword, and Isha had to hold it with two hands just to pull the blade free of the dead man's chest. She stumbled backwards.

Bessimir again came to her side, spear in hand, though this time he seemed impressed, relaxing his grip. "Would you like to do the honours?" he said, nodding towards the lever next to the body Isha had just felled.

Stepping towards the lever, she pulled, and the ground beneath her shook. The gate was opening, and with it, their victory was assured. She turned and stared out into the meandering river, hoping Raiz was faring as well as her. He just had to hold out a little longer. She was coming.

Chapter 52

- Raiz -

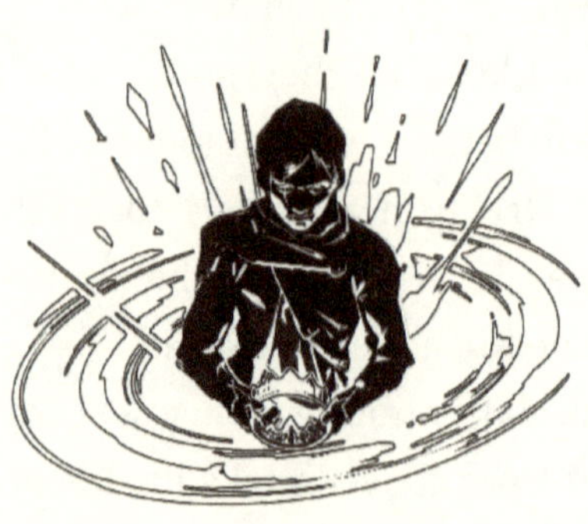

ZUR WAS OUT in strength this day, his bright rays either a blessing or a curse, Raiz hadn't yet determined which.

Spike roared. The deep sound manifested in his belly before reverberating across the entire battlefield. All could hear the mighty beast as he claimed this field as his own, his playground.

Only, Spike was not alone. Another answered his call. Then another, and another. A tightness gripped Raiz's chest. The answering roars were not as primal, but they had their desired effect.

They sounded pained, strangled, tortured. Raiz scanned the plains below, searching for their source, remembering what he had seen in Kogon, the force-fed prickets…

His eyes widened. Dotting the distance were several cages containing the tortured beasts, grown too rapidly for their minds to keep their sanity. They were angry, riled up by Spike's challenge.

Raiz turned to Gale, whose gaze had also been drawn to the commotion among the enemy ranks. They shared a brief, unspoken moment of trepidation.

He looked then to the lake, past the idle army to the west. There was no sign of the Sun Prince and his fleet. Craw still had full control. Worry for his sister was unavoidable, no matter how hard he pushed it down, but he had to have faith. Faith in her. Faith in the plan. Without it, all that would remain was doubt. Doubt led to poor decisions.

His first instinct was to charge, to carry the weight of the outcome on his own shoulders as he always had. He paused, disoriented for a moment as he looked behind him, searching the faces of those closest to him, then of those furthest away. He wasn't alone any longer. He was their king. He may not have wanted to be, and he may not like it, but these people were his responsibility. He didn't need to fight this fight alone. He needed to fight with them.

He might not be able to inspire, to light a fire in their hearts as well as Dazen could have, but he would fight by their side.

He reached for the sky with his good hand, feeling the power course through his veins, gathering as much of Zur's gift as he could hold. Then he turned it into a weapon. A thick beam of red Light shot from the palm of his hand. The Light of a Radiant. He twisted it, morphing it with his mind and fingers until the Light stretched and hardened into a shaft of blazing energy.

Glaive in hand, he mounted Spike. He fed his companion his Shine, fuelling him for what was to come. It leaked from his open mouth, simmering as it burned the grassy knoll beneath their feet. He wheeled Spike around to face his people. Thousands of men and women stood at the ready, partitioned into organised lines. Some were worried, fidgeting nervously. He didn't blame them. But all were ready to fight and die for their country, for their loved ones.

Behind him, Gale began giving the speech that Raiz never could, instilling Dazen's spirit within the gathered soldiers of Trost.

As he spoke, Raiz spotted Echo on the other side of the knoll, preparing his vanguard. He saw Hector by his side, whose posture was a picture of determination. Raiz felt proud. He had come so far. Raiz wanted to claim it was because of him, but in truth, the boy's fate had been entirely of his own making. He allowed his mouth to slip into a small smile, which seemed ill-fitting for such an occasion, but Raiz didn't care. He was proud.

A rumble sounded in the near distance, growing louder with each passing moment. Everyone stood still as a second sun formed in the sky. The entire army was transfixed, wondering what could be happening. Only Raiz realized. Only Raiz reacted. He urged Spike into Irint. Around him, people watched, perplexed.

No! he thought. *Not now!*

Great wings beat, and Spike lifted into the air. He had to act, had to stop it. Had to do something.

He was too late.

The Light fell.

With a sound like thunder, the ground erupted, sweeping unprepared soldiers from their feet as a ray of Light so large and intense it was like a continuous lightning bolt crashed into Zuton's army. Raiz's vision was lost, the Light blinding him as it burned a line through an entire third of his ally's mustered troops.

Panic ensued as the beam of heat continued. Dying men couldn't even scream as they were incinerated by the vast wave of gathered energy. Raiz could only stare. It all happened so fast. There was nothing he could do, nothing anyone could do.

It wasn't long before the Light lost velocity and its power diminished. Ash and dirt clouded his vision. He couldn't tell how many had survived, if any at all.

Old anger and hatred returned as comprehension rose. There was only one person capable of wielding that much destructive power, and it was his own fault that he had been allowed to do so. His Flare activated instinctively.

He pressed down his Shine, assessing the battlefield. Fortunately, the blast had not been at full strength. He had seen what the Last Light was capable of, seen the destruction it had wreaked on Lesken. This was but a fraction of that power, a concentrated blast. The tower was at perhaps two thirds of its former height. But how much Shine did it have left?

Spike landed, and Raiz turned to his troops, issuing orders to regather. Spike's roar signalled the charge, his companion bending his legs and springing into the air again as his men began to move.

Residual Shine still lingered where the Last Light had taken its shot. Raiz tensed, spurred on by the anger of seeing Veil's sacrifice undone. She had died to see that weapon destroyed, and now it was active again. It never should have existed.

With one beam of Light their entire plan had been foiled, and now, whether on their terms or not, the battle had begun.

There was no turning back from this, no running home with their tail between their legs. It was do or die.

Raiz swept the skies, keeping enough sense to quickly survey the damage. Zuton's ranks were sundered by a smouldering line of upturned dirt. He could now clearly see the devastation the Last Light had wrought, but not all was lost. The majority of Zuton's army had avoided incineration, and the surviving troops were mustering. There was still hope. He looked for Echo and Hector, but the cloud of dust and smoke hindered his vision.

Gale led the White-Swords forward in a furious charge down the hill. Light streamed like molten rain, devastating Craw's vanguard, blackening their crimson sashes and turning the flesh beneath to ash.

Shine flowed freely, and both sides took heavy casualties. Raiz had never seen such wide-scale destruction. Steel met steel. Shine met Shine. Men burned. People screamed.

Spike dove, Shine flickering at the edges of his sharpened teeth. The Dragon lit up the battlefield, torching the entire front line in one quick sweep. Then he took to the skies again, avoiding an endless stream of arrows that Raiz only just managed to keep at bay using his Flare. His aura glowed a deep red, the heat too intense for the shaft of an arrow to penetrate. Spike remained unaffected, the beast only encouraged by Raiz's intense projection of Shine.

He reared and circled. Raiz assessed the battlefield that had become of the plains before the City of Light. The army of Kogon was approaching his own from the east, closing in on Gale's advancing White-Swords. If nothing was done, they would be overwhelmed.

He set Spike into a dive, wings tucked to his side as the pair of them made another Shine-infused run. Heat raged, pouring from Spike's open mouth, allowing the advancing Kogon line to feel the full wrath of his new-found power. His assault proved effective, and the advancing line was forced to regather.

Satisfied, Raiz soared back into the air. He controlled how this would play out, not the Last Light. Thankfully, he'd bought enough time for Zuton's soldiers to recoup and enter the fray. He looked again for Echo, for Hector, but couldn't pick them out among so much carnage.

The battlefield was a furnace. Raiz looked to the sky, wondering if all that the Sun Prince had preached was, in fact, true. They took from Zur without regard, without a second thought for what they were actually asking of their god. But there was no time to ponder the question now, for if they lost, there would be no one left who cared about the answer.

He initiated another dive to wreak destruction on more of Craw's soldiers, when something black whizzed past, narrowly missing Spike's wing. Spike squirmed and retreated. Raiz reasserted his Flare, doubling down on the shield he had surrounded his companion with, but another black object soon whizzed past again, even closer this time.

Raiz took Spike higher into the sky, the black streaks following their assent. He

looked down, searching for the source of the attack, and found it in the form of several massive ballistas. Arrows the size of spears continued to fire at him, shot from contraptions likely built just for this occasion.

Raiz cursed under his breath, using his own Shine to blast a ballista bolt from the sky before it could penetrate Spike's hide. Forced to retreat, he made for his still advancing soldiers, landing in a pocket next to a section of grass that had been burnt by an errant blast of Shine.

He dismounted, searching for a hint of what to do next. He looked to the lake. Still no sign of the Sun Prince. Had he abandoned them? Betrayed their oath? Or had they simply failed, caught on the river and stopped by the Craw outpost.

Raiz pushed those thoughts aside, because to think of them would mean Isha was dead, and that thought would break him. He had to trust that they would come, but if it didn't happen soon, they might arrive too late. Echo's forces had fully joined in the battle now, pressing their advance into Kogon's front. Shine still flowed freely, and spots of Light continued to scintillate, the strongest Lightweavers on both sides of the conflict wiping out entire divisions of soldiers.

Raiz watched as the ballista artillery changed course, now firing bolts infused with Shine that wreaked havoc as they were flung into friendly ranks. He bit his lip. Something had to be done. If left unchecked, those defensive weapons would continue to cut swaths through his advancing army.

He watched as a bolt blasted past him, impaling several men, burning through their armour like it was paper before the white-light coated tip exploded. Nearby men were sent flying through their air. If the detonation alone hadn't felled them, the impact from their descent surely would.

He kicked Spike into motion, trusting his companion would hold his nerve. Wings beat as the two of them sped towards the contraptions, which were buried deep within the ranks of Craw's soldiers, surrounded by heavily armoured troops.

The great weapons wheeled to face him, but such a bulky machine took time to change course. Raiz caught the first one unaware, Spike blasting forth Shine to burning through wood and steel. Soldiers leapt out of the way, and Spike kept up the pressure, continuing his jet of Shine and slicing through a second machine at the same time.

The pair of them quickly retreated as arrows rained down and a third machine locked onto their position. Raiz pulled, forcing Spike high into the air and out of range, narrowly avoiding another bolt as they glided directly above the giant weapons.

Another problem soon arose. He looked to the east as Spike was drawn to the strangled cries of the tortured prickets, who had finally been released from their cages. Spike spiralled into another dive, enthralled by the cries of his own kind. Torn limbs were flung about as bodies were shredded by the aggressive and unhinged prickets. Huge tails whipped, thumping into unprepared soldiers and sending them reeling. Talons raked. Jaws snapped. Blood spilled.

Soldiers of Kogon kept the animal at bay using flaming sticks, the instruments forcing them forward rather than backward.

Spike crashed into the nearest pricket, his teeth sinking into the smaller creature's long neck. He twisted, and the creature let out a strangled cry before its neck snapped and it fell limp.

Several of the other monstrous prickets stopped their rampage, heads bowing low as they circled, studying the new threat. Raiz swivelled his head in an attempt to view all of them at once. There were at least six surrounding him, and more spread amidst the remaining Zutonian ranks.

A brave soldier attempted to blast one of the prickets with a bolt of Shine, the white-light proving ineffective on its thick hide. To his credit, he wouldn't relent, drawing more and more power from Zur as he threw everything he had at the crazed beast.

It wasn't enough. Raiz watched as the man's face turned from brave and determined, to frightened and afraid in a matter of seconds. His arms imploded. His Shine ran dry, and all that remained were two blackened husks. The broken soldier looked to the sky, praying to Zur for more strength, but finding he had none to give. That was his last moment, as the nearest pricket turned on him, its giant maw closing around the pink of his neck. Blood sprayed, and the soldier's dying scream was muted by the giant pricket's bone-rattling cry.

Raiz gasped, unable to help as the man perished. The other five prickets dove, and Spike's tail whipped into the closest two, sending them sprawling. Claws raked at Spike's hide as one narrowly missed Raiz. He swung his glaive, finding that the red Shine of a Radiant still cut. He severed a tail as one made to pass, the shrieking cry taking on an even more tormented tone.

Spike cried out too, as one of them managed to slash into his skin, three lines of red appearing on his side. He bucked, and Raiz was thrown off. He landed in a roll, glaive in hand.

Nostrils flared as more of the prickets recovered. They

pounced on Spike from all angles. Angry, confused, and blood-raged jaws snapped at him. Spike used his bulk to shrug off as much as he could, but they just kept coming, too nimble and numerous to keep track of.

Raiz tried to help, to come to his companion's side, but was confronted by another of the rampaging beasts. Soldiers on both fronts had cleared space for the ensuing battle, continuing their struggle out of the way of the charging animals.

Raiz was rocked by a sweeping tail, winding him. He lost his glaive, the heated blade sent tumbling from his grip to bubble away into nothing as it extinguished. He looked up to see drool dripping from wet, fanged jaws as the pricket above him growled like a rabid dog before a meal.

Raiz tried to draw in a breath, but found air hard to come by. He drew his hidden dagger instead, slashing it in a wide arc and holding it before him in a pathetic attempt to scare the animal off.

In the background, Spike moaned, and inside Raiz cried. This was how he was going to die. The pricket stepped closer, its oversized tail vibrating in anticipation of its kill. With a wheezing gasp, Raiz finally found his breath, but it was too late. The beast pounced.

Raiz flinched, closing his eyes and preparing to be devoured.

When no teeth sunk into his skin, he opened them again. The pricket was still there, unmoving, eyes glazed. A sword was stuck through its open maw, blood trickling down all the way to the hilt.

The sword withdrew, and the pricket fell, thudding to the ground. Hector stood over the beast, blood-covered, breathing ragged. He reached a hand towards Raiz, who took it and recovered to his feet. There were no words spoken, just a shared look of mutual respect as the two of them turned to face the rest of the beasts locked in a life-or-death duel with Spike.

Spike raged. Raiz had never seen him like this. It was as though he could feel his companion's anger, his frustration. Every wound he took was a shared experience, so close was their bond.

He reached for Zur, looking to refuel his Shine, but a thick layer of cloud had covered their god's glowing heat, making it hard to draw from. It was still possible to draw Shine from behind cloud cover, but it took a little longer, and wasn't as effective as direct sunlight.

Fortunately, he had enough stored to re-summon his glaive, using it to cut through the neck of the closest pricket before it could make another leap for Spike. Hector cut at one of them as well, though his blade did not have the same potent effect as Raiz's glaive. The creature reared, pouncing on Hector. Spike reacted, finding time to whip his tail against the hide of the advancing pricket, sending it crashing to the ground.

Time seemed to stop as they each took a moment to recover. Raiz surveyed his surroundings. Reinforcements had arrived in the form of Gale, splattered with the gore of those he had slain, and Sumaya, wearing the peridium armour gifted to them from Bessimir. Following her were another hundred or so soldiers clad head to toe in the foreign metal. Wayward bolts of Shine bounced off breastplates as the small army made for the centre of the conflict where Raiz and the prickets were locked in battle.

Limping by his sister's side was Echo, the King of Zuton still standing despite the Last Light's best efforts.

Sumaya charged, and the savage prickets seemed to cower at the touch of the unnatural metal. Overwhelmed, they began to disperse. Some retreated back into the offensive line of Kogon's infantry, where they were cast aside by the long, flaming, metallic poles that had been used to torture the beasts in their cages. Others were caught and killed as Sumaya and her hundred ran them down. There were so many of them, though, and plenty of them simply vanished, either using their skin to camouflage into the distant battle, or speeding away to wreak havoc upon another portion of the clashing armies.

Raiz stood, panting, Spike by his side. Sumaya ordered troops to surround the duo. They obeyed, forming a defensive line in protection of their king.

Once his breath was caught, he made his way to Echo and Sumaya. "I am so glad to see you alive," he said, turning to a limping Echo. "I hoped we would get here in time, but I was wrong. I'm sorry. It's Celik. I should have ended him when I had the chance!"

"This is no time for self-pity!" Sumaya yelled. "We need the Last Light taken out. Can you manage that?"

Raiz took another look, then nodded. He set his face into hardened stone. "I will destroy it. You have my word."

Echo nodded. "What of your prince? Where is he? We are hard pressed. If his aid does not come, the Last Light will be the least of our worries."

Raiz looked to the west, searching the distant lake for any sign of Isha's arrival. There was nothing there but Saelmere banners. "They will come!"

But even he knew it was a fool's hope. They might have to

finish this battle alone. As he gazed at the crystalline lake, the ground beneath his feet began to shake. A familiar rumble reverberated through the entire battlefield, and again the Last Light struck.

This time he had to shield his eyes as the intense heat cut a swath through the western–flank of his own men, devastating rank upon rank, incinerating all in its path. He stared, open-mouthed, as the Light receded, revealing the carnage left in its wake.

Chapter 53

- Isha –

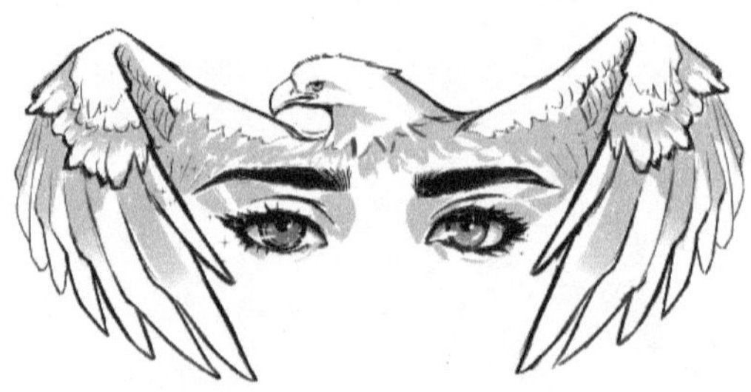

THE SUN'S REACH careened around the river bends. They had won a great victory, but it was only the beginning. The true fight was out there, beyond the twisting currents and below the darkening clouds. Raiz was out there somewhere, out in the open plains before Lumindal, fighting for his life. Fighting for all of their lives.

To her surprise, comfort came in the form of Sounja. She moved up beside her, hands on the railing. The two stared into the endless river. Her hair was tied into a warrior's braid, thick strands of red interwoven and pulled back tight to her scalp. She wore no peridium, her muscled arms bare and exposed.

"It never gets any easier," she said after a time. "The silence before a fight. You would think that after countless battles the water in your stomach would turn to stone, but that is wrong. The sickness never leaves. It stays with you long after victory is won."

Isha's stomach groaned as if on cue. "Any other inspiring insights?"

For a brief moment, Sounja actually laughed, a rare showing of emotion outside of her usual cold demeanour. "Try not to get yourself killed. Live to breathe another day. I may never understand why, but Bessimir is different now that he has met you. He has less anger. Is calmer, more focused. I cannot see it, but there is something about you that has sparked a change within him. I hope it is for the better."

Isha relaxed, the water in her stomach easing, if only a little. In truth, Sounja was everything that she wanted to be. She was a skilled warrior, who fought for her cause and fought well. She had pride, and had proven herself time and time again. Like Isha, she had come from everything, fallen to nothing, and rebuilt herself.

Isha moved her hand atop Sounja's in an attempt to return her comfort, but immediately recoiled at the stinging touch. Sounja reacted, shrugging away from her. Comprehension struck Isha as she moved back in to touch Sounja's forearm, feeling the heat she now suspected was bubbling beneath her skin.

Sounja wrenched her arm away in an aggressive swing. "You dare!"

"You have Light within you."

Sounja paled, the shifting of her feet and the not-so-subtle tilt of her head giving her away.

"Does he know?" Isha asked, gesturing to where Bessimir stood atop the crow's nest.

"Of course he knows. Do you truly still not see? My very existence stands against all that he believes, all that he values.

Yet still he took a chance on me. He does not blame the individual, but rather the construct itself. That is why I follow him. That is why I will always follow him.

"But make no mistake, daughter of Illidor," Sounja continued, stepping forward to clasp Isha's wrist. "I am not Bessimir. I do not forgive so easily. If I ever see your father, I will kill him for what he did to Edar. That is a promise."

Heat radiated from her then, warming Isha's wrist to a point close to a burn before she withdrew her hand.

Isha recovered, accepting Sounja's right for vengeance.

She was about to respond when a light flashed in the distance. It was hard to make out, but was impossible to unsee.

Others stopped and stared at the mysterious light. It fell like lightning, only grander, wider, and lingering longer. After it was done, a thick cloud clung to the distant sky, followed by a swirl of smoke and dust.

Her heart heaved, beating like a drum as she alone seemed to comprehend the travesty. She had witnessed it before, had felt the same energy, the same sense of overwhelming terror wrought by the sheer scale of what had produced the light.

"What is it?" Sounja said.

Isha struggled for words. She let out a long-held breath. "We need to get there, now!"

She sprinted towards the centre of the ship. Bessimir descended, two fingers to his lips as he whistled. Skeiron dove from the sky to land on the deck. Soldiers scattered. Of everyone here, only he knew what that flashing light signified.

"I will fly ahead," Bessimir said. "Edar, Abhick, Sounja," he shouted. "You are to lead the fleet into the lake and make the offensive."

They each nodded. Skeiron shifted to allow Bessimir onto

its back. Before he could leave, Isha grabbed hold of his arm. "I'm coming with you."

Bessimir stared at her for a moment as if she were his enemy. "It is too dangerous. I do not know what I might be flying into."

"My brother is out there, my family. I won't be sidelined. It's my choice, not yours. Let there be no guilt on your conscience."

Bessimir's expression changed. There was still concern, but he squared his shoulders, pursed his lips, and whistled again, this time a different tune. Strix descended, landing beside Isha. She pet her beneath the beak, rustling golden feathers as the animal leaned into her touch.

"Follow me," Bessimir said evenly. "But do not engage unless I do. This is not an order, but a request. You are untrained in aerial warfare. It is not safe."

Isha spared another look toward the rising dust cloud. She wanted to help, to rush into the fray and find Raiz, protect him, but she knew that would be reckless. If she wanted to help, she needed a calm mind.

Strix moved closer, and Isha focused on the majesty of the giant bird to still her racing thoughts. Slick, colourful feathers covered the Eagle from head to toe. She spread her wings wide, highlighting the intricate segmented patterns beneath. Strix's keen eyes shone a bright yellow, reminiscent of the sun itself. They stared at her as if they held the knowledge of the world. Dark brown turned to gold as the interlaced feathers grew larger at the wing's edge. Sharpened tips that Isha likened to fingers protruded from the furthest point of her wing. Isha looked down to see four thick toes on each foot, all ending in a hooked talon that dug into the wood of the ship's decking.

A hand clasped around her own arm, causing her to turn in alarm. She breathed a sigh of relief when she found it to be Puk. He let go of her, making gestures with his hands.

I want to come with you. Protect you.

Isha returned his gesture with a smile. "I'm sorry Puk. I can't risk your life on this. You have already done so much for me. I ..."

Puk again gripped her wrist, this time meeting her eye-line with an intensity she had not seen in him before. She felt his emotion, his determination, tenacity. He lived to protect. Whether he was made for it or not, this was his purpose. He had decided it to be so. How could she deny him this right? She could feel his guilt, the sense of failure clouding his mind from when Kron had taken her. He was wrong, of course. Puk could never fail her.

Please, he gestured.

Isha took him by the hand. "Alright. The two of us. Ride with me!"

Still connected, she felt the shift in his emotions, the excitement and the thrill. She withdrew from his mind and began preparing for war.

Isha followed Bessimir and Skeiron. Puk held on tight to her waist.

She peered into the darkening clouds. Spots of sunlight still peeked through at stages, shinning bright rays over what she could only describe as a field of death.

She held her breath as they drew closer, watching as the two opposing sides of colour clashed, more soldiers sitting in wait for their turn for either glory or death, likely both.

She could see the evidence of the Last Light's work in the form of two giant lines of blackened dirt, each cutting a huge swath through two fronts of the allied forces. She scanned for Raiz, praying he had been elsewhere when the massive column of Light fell.

Skeiron circled, Bessimir seeming to have the same thought. Together, they flew closer to the ensuing battle. She could feel the sweat trickling down her brow. The heat was intense, the entire battlefield a boiling inferno of overused white-light. Spots of white shone from all corners of the plains. Those soldiers not birthed with the power of Zur were simply fodder for the strong, as thick streams of Light incinerated dozens at a time.

She drew closer to Bessimir. She didn't need to feel his inner emotions to understand his pain. His eyes darkened, and his face wore a multitude of expressions, all filled with pain and heartbreak as he witnessed perhaps the greatest theft of their shared god's energy of all time.

She continued her search, scanning the battlefield for Raiz. They were losing, and losing badly. The Last Light had destroyed any advantage they might have anticipated. She spotted a scaly beast fluttering around down below. At first, she thought it might be Spike, and guided Strix to soar closer. But it was smaller than Spike, more aggressive, and it was cutting down everyone in its path. More of the foul, wingless creatures roamed the ground below, each charging into friendly ranks as men and woman of Trost and Zuton fought valiantly against their wild aggression.

Isha wanted to help, to pull Strix into a dive and strike at the heart of the enemy, but she needed to find Raiz. She needed to tell him hope was on the way, that he wasn't alone in this fight.

A wave of Shine whistled past as they came within reach of enemy Lightweavers. Puk tugged on her waist, twisting his body in front of her in case the blast struck true.

Once Strix recovered, they followed Bessimir and Skeiron into the centre of the field. A daring roar split the air, calling the attention of all within earshot. Isha whirled, and Strix shifted to face what she believed to be a threat. She could feel the hatred within the Eagle, burning brighter than a bolt of Shine. The emotion was instinctual, ancient. A deep-seated vein of anger formed in Strix's mind, and she lashed out.

Isha tried her hardest to calm her, but she had little hope. Strix dove, and Spike, riderless, took flight to meet the challenge.

Puk held her tight as Strix moved to engage her suspected enemy. Wings spread, and Isha was thrust backward, kept secure only by the tightened harness fastened to her hip. Talon-first, the two beasts clashed. Isha braced herself, yelling out for Spike, hoping her brother's companion could hear her familiar voice.

The cacophony of battle sounds was too great, and Raiz's Dragon couldn't yet determine her as friend. Jaws snapped and beaks clapped as the two conjoined, bodies tied in a tangle of unnatural limbs. Isha shouted, finally catching Spike's eye amidst that chaotic tumble. His pupils narrowed as she pressed all of her strength outward. Recognition dawned, and Spike pushed backward, issuing another ear-shattering roar before descending back to where she hoped Raiz was.

Strix flapped her wings, regaining control as she transitioned into a glide. Isha tried her best to steer the Eagle towards her brother, but the creature was stubborn, and she was not yet in full control. The memory of the Eagles' Fall replayed in her mind. The commotion below must have triggered something in her companion. In the heat of battle, Strix had lost her sense of reason, and it took all of Isha's control to calm her.

Bessimir came to her then, settling Skeiron into a glide beside her. "Are you okay?" he shouted from atop his Eagle.

Isha set her jaw and issued a determined nod.

"Raiz is down there!" Bessimir called, pointing to a spot in the centre of the raging melee. "In and then out. Do not engage more than you need to!"

Isha listened, assessed, then picked him out, focusing on the large shaft of red Light being used to cut down foe after foe. Together, they dived. She reached her destination quicker than anticipated, Strix pulling up just short of the ground. The tremendous gust of wind sent enemy soldiers hurtling into the air, crashing into men several ranks away.

Raiz turned to face her, chest heaving. There was no time to talk, to reminisce. Not with an army to destroy.

With a slash of his tail, Spike sent another half-dozen troops spinning into the air before returning to Raiz. Her brother mounted and took to the skies. Isha followed.

Bessimir joined them at the rear of the friendly war-party, and they settled atop a small knoll that was empty of any form of danger, though they could still hear the terrifying sounds of the ensuing conflict.

Isha dismounted, and Raiz leapt off Spike's back to embrace her in a warm hug. They parted, and Bessimir joined them.

It was Raiz who spoke first. "We have little time. Our soldiers won't last the day. Did you break through the outpost?"

Bessimir stepped forward. "We did. Our ships are on the way, and will be here within the hour."

Raiz breathed a deep, relieving sigh. "That's good news. But we have another problem. The Last Light is active. I thought there would only be enough for one charge, but Celik is smart. He's siphoning the gathered Shine, using the weapon in smaller bursts to preserve power and spare Gelvard's troops from harm.

"We need to put an end to it," he continued. "Will you help me?"

Bessimir took a moment to assess the battlefield, unable to hide his displeasure. His breathing was ragged, eyes scattered, lost in a living nightmare. He looked to the sun, to Zur. The clouds had parted, and their god again shone his glory over all of them. Visible tendrils of ethereal white and golden Light bathed the entire field in a blanket of colour as those below continued to draw from him. The scene would have been beautiful to any who didn't understand the dire consequences of what was happening.

"Can you not see? They are stealing from him, taking without thought for his divine existence, without understanding the ramifications of drawing so much power. Power breeds selfishness, and humanity's lust for it has seen no bounds. Perhaps we deserve to die, to fall victim to the harsh climate that would be his justice."

Isha couldn't help but stare, unable to answer against the truth of his words. Raiz, too, stood transfixed by the utter brilliance and sheer horror of the force that was Zur's Shine.

Her brother was the first to snap out of the reverie, moving to clasp Bessimir by his collar. "I understand. I believe you. I see now what needs to be done, what I need to do. But remember this. Zur gifted us with his energy for a reason. I do not deny we have over-extended its use. But I am his soldier, just as you. If you want to let the world burn then go ahead. But I will fight for it. There is the enemy," Raiz continued, pointing at the Last Light. "If we are to have any chance at correcting the world, Gelvard must not be allowed to rule Zapour. If he does, and what you say is true, then there is no future. I ask again. Will you help me?"

Bessimir returned to himself, expression hardening. "I will."

Chapter 54

- Zeek –

ZEEK RECOVERED, shadow and human form mixing into one. The black streak that was the Fifty-First Spear hovered over him, beaten in size only by the Last Light, which loomed ominously in the near distance. He knew that was where they were headed, where the betrayer would make his stand.

He felt multiple presences stirring within, all fighting for influence, all trying to shape him into the person they wanted him to be. Through it all, he tried to focus, to think. It was time he started to dictate his own future, to break free from the delusion that his betrayer actually cared about him. It wasn't easy, Father had been everything. But now Zeek had seen the truth. He was a puppet, a tool, a means to an end. And to Father, his end had come.

Hatred swirled deep within the pit of his stomach. Within that hatred, that desire for vengeance, came a voice. It was familiar, natural. Where before he had pushed it away, today he let it in.

Kill the Radiants.

It came as a whisper, soft at first, then growing louder, stronger.

Kill the Radiants. We are coming.

The voice was deep, feminine, ancient.

Join us. You are one of us.

Zeek listened, his shadow-tail curling around his body, protecting him.

I can protect you. We can protect you. This world will be yours. Climb. Take the life of the Radiant ones, and I will give it to you.

Zeek felt the voice deep within his soul. It spoke to him, resonating with something he never knew he possessed. He looked up, staring at the never-ending blackness that was the Last Light.

Climb.

That was what the voice told him to do, and that was what he would do. Other voices sounded in the distance. Human voices. He bent to a crouch. He needed to get out of here. He needed to kill the Radiants.

He slipped into the shadows seamlessly, fully indulging his formerly suppressed powers as he stepped with renewed quickness. The human voices quickly grew distant as he wound around the Fifty-First Spear and up toward where the Last Light protruded from the ground like a giant hand.

He rounded its base, searching. He moved to touch it, withdrawing his hand as it stung. The metal weakened him. Even in his newly awakened state he found it hard to grasp. Peridium. That's what his acquired knowledge told him this was.

He continued to search, testing the structure for potential weaknesses.

There.

The voice in his head sounded again. He focused, finding a section of metal that was easier to grip. He touched it, smelling the metallic odor of rusting iron. The structure itself was too large to be made entirely of peridium. Sections were overlaid with thin metal sheets of coloured iron. He wrapped his hands in pieces of ripped cloth, then propelled himself upward using his newly gifted speed. Strong fingers sunk into the surface of the metal. He used his tail like a fifth limb, climbing with strength and speed that no human could produce.

One way or another, he would have his vengeance. Then the world would be his.

Chapter 55

- Isha –

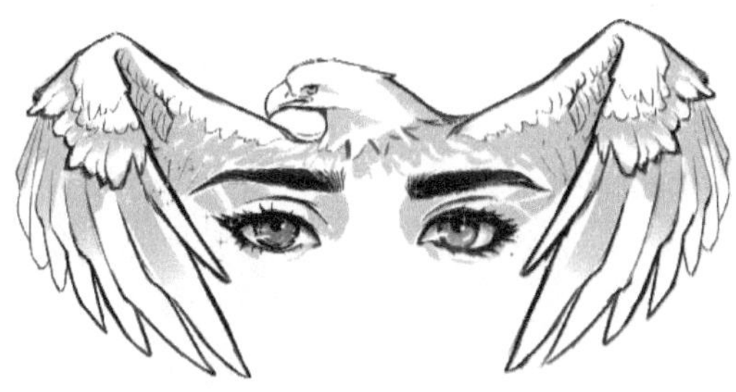

ISHA STARED INTO the dazzling display of Light. It fell like rain onto the endless field of nations at war. Lightweavers continued to feed on Zur's strength, channeling Zur's Shine and throwing it at each other with little regard for their own safety.

Isha readied to leave, to fly with Raiz and Bessimir and put a stop to the Last Light, when something caught her eye. "What's that?" she said, pointing to a place beyond the lake where a mass of troops were converging.

At first she thought it was people from the Sun's Reach, but upon closer inspection it couldn't have been. There were no ships, no emblems of a bright blazing sun upon their breasts. But they were coming, and fast.

"Are they your men?" Raiz asked, settling atop Spike.

"No," Bessimir responded. "Enemy reinforcements,

perhaps?"

Raiz placed a hand over his brow. The mysterious figures continued to flow down the hill in numbers. If left unchecked, they could pose a threat to the coming fleet.

"We don't have time for this! The Last Light could fire at any moment. We must fly now!" Raiz said.

Bessimir grit his teeth. Isha placed a steadying hand on his shoulder. "I will go. I will see if they are friend or foe. If they prove a threat, I will fly to warn Edar so they might be prepared."

Bessimir hesitated.

"Raiz needs you more than me," she insisted. "Now go! I will handle this. Do you trust me?"

Bessimir turned to face her. He leaned in close. "Stay strong. Do not hesitate. Fight from here," he said, pointing towards his heart. "Stick close to Puk."

Puk, who was already saddled atop Strix, motioned. *I will keep her safe.*

With that, Skeiron and Spike took flight, making haste to the towering structure of the patched Last Light.

It was hard to ignore the desperate cries of the dying down below as they took to the skies, harder still when she pictured her countrymen fighting for their lives amidst the chaotic scramble that had become of the once green plains.

She pressed forward, a hand over her mouth as she passed through residual Shine left over from the Last Light's wake.

She prepared to swerve, to paint the newcomers as foe and report their sighting to Edar on the Sun's Reach. Her heart warmed as she picked out the black-skinned Bakai of Wisha storming down the hillside to their aid.

"Wisha has come!" she found herself screaming, sparing a

look over her shoulder to see Puk deep in concentration. "What's wrong? Can't you see? Obeyun has answered us! Wisha has come to our aid."

Puk continued to stare, leaning forward, eyes focused. He pointed, making a series of gestures Isha couldn't quite see from her vantage.

It wasn't long before she understood what Puk was trying to say. "Where are they going?" she said out loud. "The battle is that way. And how do they intend to cross the river?"

Her suspicion piqued as more Wishan numbers filed from the murky wood. These were not all Bakai. Women, children, even the elderly filtered through, held together by a small guard of Bakai, who flanked either side of the massive migration.

Isha sent Strix into a dive. She pulled up before the leading Wishan, a gust of wind buffeting his position and causing those behind him to scream in terror.

Strix steadied, and Isha spotted a familiar face heading towards her. Several fierce looking Bakai levelled sharp-tipped spears towards Strix.

"Obeyun!" Isha called, unstrapping herself from the Eagle and sliding down her side.

"Isha?" her old friend called, running to embrace her in a wide hug. He wore the wooden crown of Wisha as if it were made for him. The rest of him had not changed. He wore a sleeveless linen shirt decorated with various paintings and ornaments. His skin was still half milky white, the other charcoal black. From what Aia had told her, his people now celebrated his abnormality rather than shunned it. There was something about his demeanour, however, that spoke of great urgency.

He parted, eyeing her, then Strix, then her again, all in a few blinks.

"Obe, have you come to help?"

Obeyun was still panting. Those behind stopped once Isha made herself known, though by the sound of their nervous shuffling they did not intend to stay put for long.

Obeyun calmed. He moved to stare at the translucent barrier of Light that had blanketed the battlefield beyond. He grabbed Isha by her wrist. A single tear trickled down his cheek, causing her heart to quicken.

"What is it Obe?"

He shook his head. "Wisha. It is… no more."

Isha's heart wrenched. Her stomach lurched.

"They came. They destroyed… everything. It is no more. Only us. Only we remain, only we escaped."

"Take a breath Obe. Talk to me. What happened. Who came? Was it Gelvard? Did the Saelmeres do this?"

She felt her anger rising, boiling. Obeyun shook his head. "They are coming. They will not stop. We need to go. You need to go! Run. Get out of here. Be gone from this place before the sun falls and night reigns."

"Obe, you're not making any sense. Who is coming? What happened to your people?"

Obeyun's eyes shook, and even though the two had spent years together as captives, she had never seen him this scared.

"The Skae," he said. "They are coming. They are here."

Her throat closed. She looked behind him, afraid of what she might see. The Skae were creatures of the night. While there was light, surely they could not come.

Recovering, Isha began directing the Wishan populace towards safety. Unfortunately, a patrol of Craw longships had spotted their arrival and were making for their location.

At least one hundred Bakai flanked them, re-forming their defensive perimeter around the women and children. Arrows fired from the closing ships, falling only a few feet short of her position.

Puk stood, his peridium shield raised as the ships landed along the shoreline. An arrow struck, but Puk stood firm, his shield too strong for the shaft to penetrate.

Beside them, Bakai loosed their own arrows, and some even threw tall spears. Isha watched as one struck the heart of a pursuing red-cloak, sending his body flying into the river in a spray of red.

Strix dove, sweeping and picking up three helpless soldiers between talons before dropping them from a deadly height. The Great Eagle was forced to retreat though, as multiple arrows narrowly missed her feathery form.

Isha drew her sword as the red-cloaked soldiers approached. Puk lunged, cutting through the first two to enter his range of motion. Isha moved to his side. Beside her, a Bakai chopped the head clean off another, moving with unparalleled aggression. His face was painted red and white, gifting him an even more intimidating presence than he had already boasted.

More soldiers poured from the landed ships, quickly outnumbering the gathered Bakai. Isha tried to search for an option, something she could do to turn the tide, but her vision was hampered. She thrust with her gifted sword again and again, withdrawing to find it bloodier each time. She stepped back, Puk again taking the lead and cutting swaths through their ranks. Arrows continued to rain against the defenceless

Wishan people.

Isha felt for them. They had fled their home seeking refuge, and this is what they were met with. There was nowhere else to go. Without their home, Zapour was not safe. Only Trost would welcome them, only she could save her friends. But there would be no Trost if they lost this day. There would be no Zapour.

Puk grit his teeth, his sword arm raised as another met it in combat. The two became locked in a test of strength and will. Another arrow fell from the sky, causing Isha to duck. She was expecting pain, had felt the sting of an arrow before, but the pain didn't come. She looked up to see Puk's assailant dead, the shaft sticking out of his back.

She broadened her vision, cupping her eyes with her hand as she spotted something that made her heart soar.

"Edar!"

Two bolts of Shine whistled past, burning through the closest Red-Cloaks. Sounja appeared, her palm smoking. She shook the smoke clear, and Isha looked beyond to where the Sun's Reach was moored. Allied ships quickly overrun the landed Craw longships.

Isha ran to Sounja as she dealt with the last of the Red-Cloaks.

"What is going on here?" Sounja asked, eyeing the closest Bakai soldier. "Are these men friend or foe?"

Isha grabbed her wrist. "Friend, they are friends! Don't shoot!" she shouted so all around could hear.

"They seek refuge."

Sounja's jaw tightened, but to Isha's relief she didn't move against them.

Obeyun found her again, still panicked. "I must go. My

people need my protection. We must leave this place. You must leave this place."

Isha turned. "I can't go. Look across the river. My people need me. I can't abandon them."

Obeyun took a breath. "Then you must finish this before nightfall. You must trust me. They will come. Will consume everything."

Isha's entire body tensed. She took Obeyun's hand in her own. "Go. Flee to Trost. The path beyond is clear. Aia is there. She will take you in. Take your people, wait for us there."

Her old friend nodded, and she turned to leave, but felt his hands upon her wrist.

"Isha…"

She smiled. "I will return. I promise you. I won't die this day."

She felt Obeyun's strength leave her as he parted. He led his people down the winding river, away from this never-ending conflict.

With her mind eased, Isha and Sounja ran to the riverbank and boarded the Sun's Reach. She found Edar leaning on the rail. "We need to get across the lake, right now."

Chapter 56

- Raiz –

HIGH WINDS BROKE against Spike's hide as the pair surged into the distant sky. The Sun Prince was hot on their tail, the Great Eagle's speed a match for Spike's own.

The clouds parted, exposing them to the sun's glare as they continued to climb, circling around the black tower.

He felt the heat within the structure readying another charge. Cracks still lined the outskirts, a bright hue emanating from within the deepest of them. It seemed unstable, hastily patched together for the sole purpose of a single victory.

It angered him, to see all of Veil's work undone. He flew faster, pressing Spike to his limit. Together they spiralled, splitting the air until eventually they neared the tower's top. Great wings spread wide as Spike halted momentum.

Raiz peered over his companion's neck, searching the tower for activity. The Sun Prince joined him, making his own assessment.

The top was different, hastily rebuilt. Instead of the arching peridium prongs, there were four rods fixed into each corner, placed on an angle so that they all met in the middle, creating a kind of dome. At the head of the dome was a ball of gathering Shine. It was smaller than the last time he had been here, but more was being siphoned into it this very moment, taken from the open pit set into the centre of the structure.

He spotted a number of crimson guards bearing the Saelmere emblem on their breast. Celik gathered sunlight at the tower's rim. He seemed deep in concentration, head bowed in a meditative state.

Raiz spared another look towards the Sun Prince, the two nodding in unspoken agreement. Together, they swooped. Raiz headed for Celik, meaning to strike directly at the source. He was met by a blinding force of Light as the crimson guards stood firm, linking together in a defensive wall of conjured Shine.

Forced to turn, he banked to the left. Blinking, he tried to right himself and find his bearing. The Sun Prince faced a similar situation on the opposite side, only he was assaulted by a barrage of Shine as the defending troops made to protect Celik.

Raiz spotted Gelvard in amongst the crowd of red, boasting a sinister smirk as his efforts proved effective.

Raiz cursed, continuing to circle until a plan came to him. He looked to Zur. Guilt plagued him. He had taken so much. It wounded him then, that he had to ask for just a little more. If they were to fail, and Gelvard were allowed to rule, it would be the end of sunlight. Shine would reign, would flow freely, until it didn't... Zur would fall, and so would humanity.

He soaked it in, reaching again for Spike's open mouth to feed him his fill. He closed his eyes, activated his Flare, and led Spike into a dive.

The Dragon roared. Heat emanated from his maw before pouring forth in a torrent of searing Shine. It broke through their shield, incinerating the helpless soldiers beyond and rendering them a pile of ash.

Raiz took the opportunity, diving off Spike's back and weaving his glaive in the same motion. He pressed outward with his Flare. Those nearest to him were helpless against the raging heat, bending to a knee as Raiz moved towards them, cutting their life short with one swing of his heated blade.

More came at him, some strong enough to withstand his flare. But he was a Radiant. He was Gallion's kin. They were no match for him.

The Sun Prince made his own landing, his Eagle sweeping several men off their feet and sending them plummeting over the tower's edge to certain death.

Together, Raiz and Bessimir fought. The Sun Prince was skilled, his peridium armour making him resistant to both Raiz's Flare and the enemies Shine. Raiz watched him end three men in as many seconds with quick thrusts of his spear, before drawing his short sword to cut the hand off another.

Above them, the sphere of Shine doubled, tripled even, distancing Spike and Skeiron and cutting them off from the battle on the platform.

They were not needed though, as before long the platform was clear of soldiers, all except for Gelvard, Celik, and another form beneath the King of Craw's grip. Bodies littered the floor. Some were still twitching, pools of red forming beneath. Others would never move again, cut to pieces by Raiz's glaive or Bessimir's peridium blade.

Gelvard's smug grin vanished, replaced by the desperate, agitated leer of a man who knew he'd lost.

"It's over Gelvard!" Raiz called, striding over to the centre of the platform.

Gelvard bent down and wrenched the figure at his heels off their knees. A strangled, feminine cry rang out as Gelvard yanked her head back and held a knife to her throat.

"Come any closer and I cut," he said.

Raiz inclined his head. His mouth opened as recognition struck. Sephare, Celik's wife, the once Queen-Mother. *His grandmother.*

Raiz hesitated to take another step, his foot hovering in the air. He didn't much care for his grandmother. She had never been there for him. He had never even properly met her. Though neither did he want to be responsible for the death of another family member. His talk with Isha swirled in his mind. He didn't want to be the monster any longer. He wanted to change, to be better. But was her life worth the many that would perish should he do nothing?

"Why are you doing this?" Raiz said.

Gelvard's expression changed. His hands shook, and Raiz could clearly see the weight under his eyes. He was in pain. A pain Raiz had felt many times before.

"You killed my son!" Gelvard spat. "You and your shit of a kingdom. Trost is weak. I see what you are all up to! Banding together with the other weak nations. You think you could ally yourselves against me and the knowledge would slip by me? No. I will not sit idle while Craw gets surrounded, overrun by rodents who do not know their place."

"You are delusional! We did not kill Ancel! We had no

plans against you or Craw. You must believe me."

"Lies! Of course you did. You are his son. I should have killed you when I had the chance."

"You're not listening. We didn't murder your son. That deed was done by Celik and his Skaeling," he said, pointing to where Celik was still gathering Shine on the edge of the tower.

Gelvard hesitated, his eyes darting back and forth between Celik and Raiz.

"He did the same to us!" Raiz pleaded. "He murdered my brother, murdered Dazen. Think it through! His body, he was drained, wasn't he. Absent of colour. My brother was met the same fate. You need to believe me. We can stop this. We can find a way."

Something in Gelvard's expression changed again. A deep-seated rage came to the surface all at once. His body began to glow, and his gaze fixed on Celik.

Then the Sun Prince intervened. He thrust himself in front of Raiz, bearing down on Gelvard with his violet stare.

The King of Craw's eyes rolled to the back of his head. His hand slipped, knife slashing through flesh.

"Sephare!" came Celik's mournful cry from behind.

Sephare fell to the ground in a pool of blood, her blank eyes already absent of life.

Raiz continued to watch as the prince issued an order that Gelvard followed.

"Walk."

Gelvard's abstracted form sauntered towards the other side of the platform. Raiz thought it was over, that he would stop, but he continued, walking forward without concern until his next step met with open air. He plummeted off the tower's edge, falling to the certain death that awaited him below.

The Sun Prince bent to a knee, weakened by such an outright display of his absolute power. Raiz didn't know what to do. Sephare and Gelvard were dead. The prince was down. Only Celik remained.

He turned to face his grandfather, who was shaking. His arms might have long been dead, but he was far from powerless. The gathered Shine from the Last Light hovered above, its fate dependent on his decision. He wore the tear-stained face of a broken man, a desperate man.

Raiz had known nearly Celik all his life, but the person before him now was someone else entirely.

"YOU DO NOT UNDERSTAND!" he shouted. "NONE OF YOU UNDERSTAND. I AM TRYING TO SAVE YOU!"

"Let it go Celik!" Raiz called. "It's over! You don't need to do this. I know you're not evil at heart. Let go of the Shine!"

"YOU ARE NOT LISTENING. THEY ARE COMING! YOU NEED ME. ZAPOUR NEEDS ME."

It was useless. Sephare's death had destroyed him. All that was left was an empty husk, a shell of the man he might once have been.

Raiz took a few more steps forward. He could end it all right here. One quick bolt of Shine through his heart would do it. Why then was he hesitating? Celik deserved it. More than anyone he deserved to die. It may not have been by his own hand, but he had killed Dazen. He was the one who caused Veil's condition, wiped out an entire kingdom of innocent people.

"TAKE IT!" Celik said, continuing to shout at the top of his lungs. "TAKE IT! THEY ARE COMING! THE TIME IS NOW! I CAN FEEL IT! LOOK UP!!"

Raiz paused. He began to follow his grandfather's gaze into the distant sky when Celik suddenly started gurgling. Blood trickled out of his mouth, dripping down his chest. He dropped to a knee. The sharpened end of a tail made almost entirely of inky black shadow protruded from a hole in his chest. It wriggled, worming all the way through before lifting his dying grandfather off the ground. Slowly, the colour began to drain from his face as the tail worked its magic, sucking what little life he had left away and into the form of the creature at his back.

The Skaeling responsible for Dazen's death emerged, his beady eyes unreadable as the draining process completed. The creature tossed Celik's limp body to the floor, where it landed in a tumble. Even as he died, Celik's glare was fixed to the sky, staring in fascination. Raiz finally followed his line of sight.

All breath left his lungs as he stood transfixed, witnessing perhaps the most beautiful yet terrifying spectacle he had ever seen.

The once blue sky grew dark. The moon's giant white orb was moving. Cova had sensed her opportunity. Zur's golden light began to fade as Cova made to block out the sun. Brilliant strands of pure bright sunlight flickered at the edges of Cova's darkening form as she attempted to complete the eclipse.

Raiz stood motionless, glaive in hand, staring at the event Celik had warned them about.

The Darkening had come.

Chapter 57

- Isha –

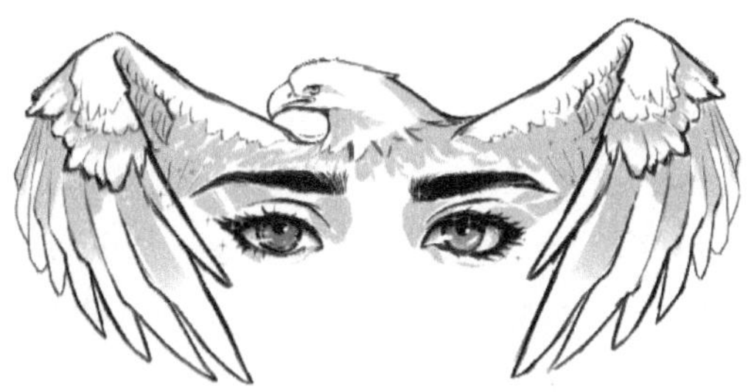

THE GOLDEN VEIL over the battlefield was more dazzling than ever as more and more drew power into themselves, stealing Zur's energy for their own desire to survive. Bessimir's ships finally made landing on the shore of the lake. The Brightguard poured from them, forming into tight, coordinated lines organised by Edar and led by Sounja.

Isha joined their charge, Puk by her side, Strix ever-watchful above. Raiz's forces had been decimated. The Last Light had taken a devastating toll. White-Swords were overrun, chased down and hunted by red and brown cloaked Lightweavers. Only fractured segments of the allied army remained standing, fighting and defending in small pockets. Strix swooped from above, followed by Sypa and Andreni as the three Great Eagles cut a swath through advancing Red-Cloaks.

The White-Swords of Illidor turned, taking advantage of their luck. They re-formed, grouping together with soldiers of Zuton to be led by Gale and Echo.

Dead bodies littered the battlefield. Isha simply stepped over them. There would be time to grieve tomorrow, if tomorrow came. A contingent of Lightweavers bearing the Saelmere mark maneuvered to intercept the approach of the sun-crested men of Yagos. They drew more power from Zur, blasting Shine into the formation of Brightguards. Isha ducked, thinking her life ended. She had little defence against such raw power. Puk thrust himself in front of her, swinging his shield forward and holding it firm as Shine bounced. She waited until the searing light faded, and then she rose.

People were burning. Screaming. Isha felt their pain. It surrounded her. She could feel their agony. She wanted to help, to take it away. She couldn't. Not now.

The armies clashed. Muddied feet shuffled around her and it became hard to tell friend from foe. She focused as best she could on the Red-Cloaks. She lunged, cut, and thrust again and again, each time coming away bloody. Puk was her shield, swatting away any who dared come too close. Shine still flowed freely as the White-Swords of Illidor joined with the Brightguards of Yagos. She spotted Gale, covered in blood and gore.

She witnessed Abhick slice a man nearly in two with a huge swing of his over-sized sword. He moved to fight next to her, him and Puk a force of their own. She felt weak, useless compared to these titans of the battlefield. This was what it meant to fight for those you loved. This was the reality of war, what Raiz and Dazen had dealt with their entire lives.

She grit her teeth. She might not be experienced, but she

would gladly give her life defending her country. Looking up, she could see the white-gold globe of Shine bubbling at the top of the Last Light. Raiz needed her. Bessimir needed her. She needed to warn them, help them.

A set of razor-sharp teeth greeted her as she lowered her vision. A mutated pricket drooled there, droplets of saliva trickling down its scarred jaw as thin yellow eyes bore down on her location. Isha gasped, brandishing her sword as if it could ward against the savage beast. The pricket's skin rippled with colour, changing, morphing uncontrollably to match its surrounding environment.

A brave Brightguard made to intercept and met with a bloody end. The creature slashed, clawed, and snapped at anything that moved. The stench of blood was fierce, and the smell of charred flesh might have overwhelmed her if it wasn't for the adrenaline pumping through her veins.

The pricket advanced, making its way to her with ruthless efficiency. Puk wheeled, attempting to throw himself in its path. He was struck by a thick tail to the gut as the pricket whirled, whipping into him with the force of a battering ram. Puk spiralled into the air, crashing hard into a pack of soldiers.

Isha screamed and charged, thrusting the sword's point into its eye. The already crazed pricket let loose an even more strangled cry, bucking hard before swiping at Isha. Pain erupted from her arm as the sharp claws bit through skin.

Isha recoiled, dropping her sword and clutching her bloodied arm. The half-blind pricket continued to squirm as Isha ducked and weaved. Teeth snapped an inch from her neck, and she was thrown off her feet by the sheer force of the prickets bulk. Thriving on bloodlust, the pricket lunged for the kill.

A golden form flashed to her left, followed by a red-plumed tail. Strix swooped, grabbing the wounded pricket with arching talons. Together they tumbled, bit, swiped. Dust swirled as the two animals skirmished. Strix fought with a ruthlessness Isha didn't know she possessed. The Eagle was smart, calculating, and most of all accurate, pecking at the pricket's remaining eye and plucking it from its socket. She kicked off, watching and hovering as the blind creature fled back to where it had come from, knocking over a number of Red-Cloaks in its path.

Isha ran to Puk and lifted him off the ground. Together, they turned to face the oncoming wave soldiers. Reinforcements had come. They were surrounded by a sea of red. Beside her, men were screaming, dying. Her men. Men of Trost. Men of Yagos, of Zuton. Even with the fresh Brightguard troops, they were still helplessly outnumbered.

It was no use. There were too many. They were going to die.

It didn't matter. She would fight to the end, had to fight.

She readied herself to strike, to slash, to cut at any who dared threaten her home, when something strange happened. The sky darkened. The golden veil which had been blanketing the battlefield turned to mist, dissipating in mere moments, replaced by something dreadful. At first she thought it was just a dark cloud, blotting out the sun momentarily, but on closer inspection it was more. The battle continued to rage, and the sky continued to darken. Isha watched, her stomach churning with trepidation as the truth of the situation took hold.

The moon was moving, and it was moving in front of the sun.

She felt for Puk, grabbing him and drawing him close. In front of her, the sudden shift caused the fighting to temper. The two armies seemed to split apart, and Brightguards began to withdraw into formation. Men of the allied nations followed, moving to stand behind the peridium-plated soldiers of Yagos. Isha tensed behind the second line as shields were raised and spears were levelled. Silence stretched over the battlefield as both friend and foe stopped and stared, awed by the spectacle above.

Then true darkness struck.

The sun was fully eclipsed, vanishing entirely beneath Cova's bulk. Outside of Lumindal, the only light came in the form of distant firelight, and the odd blazing sword still coated with the wielder's Shine.

All became still on the muted plains. It was as if they were expecting the darkness to subside, for Cova to pass and for Zur to once again reign. But more time went by, and the darkness remained. It would have been impossible to see if not for the bright city looming in the near distance, bathing the dark plains in faint luminescence.

For a long time, all Isha could hear was the heavy breathing of those beside her. No one moved. The wounded still cried out, the odd foot still shuffled, but the fighting had completely ceased.

Eventually, a strangled cry broke the silence. The sheer magnitude of the fear in the dying man's voice sent a chill down her spine. It was soon followed by more startled cries. Isha tried to determine the source, but it was on the other side of the battlefield. Puk and the surrounding Brightguards shared in her confusion, puzzled expressions searching for answers.

A commotion arose within the enemy ranks, distant at first, but it drew closer with every breath. The front line of Brightguards and White-Swords stood firm, linking shields and edging further backward.

The deathly cries steadily grew louder, joining with another sound – this one much darker, more sinister. Unnatural.

Dark shapes swirled amongst the red-cloaked soldiers under the Saelmere banner. The battle-bloodied figures at the head of the enemy ranks began to panic. Heads darted, feet shuffled. There was nowhere to go. Behind the Red-Cloaks, people were dying, and in front of them was an aggressive line of shield and spear.

The screams continued. Isha's heart skipped. Her grip tightened on her sword. The dark shapes coalesced, converging on their location. Shadows shifted, formed, broke, and then reformed. It was impossible to see clearly, but Isha knew. She knew what they were, what had come.

"The Skae! The Skae are here!" she called, warning anyone who still had the composure left to listen.

The Red-Cloaks on the front line panicked and broke formation. They charged the shield-wall, preferring to take their chances there than to be torn to shreds and consumed like the rest of their comrades behind them.

The Brightguards and White-Swords moved as one, cutting them down before they could advance. This continued for a time, soldiers of Craw and Kogon attempting to flee from the Skae through their line, only to be speared, and thrown to the side as the more coordinated allied troops dealt with them successfully.

Whatever lurked behind was efficient. Darkness still

reigned, and the defending line took a silent breath, bracing for what was to come.

An impossibly fast swarm of creatures rose from the impenetrable black. They were the things of nightmare, some made entirely of shadow, others taking the fleshy form of mutated animals. More still were humanoid, their black limbs reaching, slashing, and tearing the remaining Red-Cloaks to shreds.

All of them shared one common trait. Isha watched, horrified as a single, scorpion-like tail made entirely of shadow ripped into a man, sucking the life out of his body and leaving him limp.

Isha tensed. This was what had happened to Dazen. This was how her brother's life had ended. All of her instincts shouted at her, screamed for her to turn tail and run. Patches of Light gleamed in the near distance as those still with fight in the enemy ranks resisted, burning through the shadow-creatures. In the end, their efforts proved futile, and even the Lightweavers were consumed.

Isha dug deep, forcing her lungs to work as she raised her sword-arm into the air and issued a mighty battlecry. Those around her rallied, their formation tightening as several of the dead-eyed creatures turned their attention toward them.

Even in the darkness, Puk's presence was her one comfort. She knew that with him by her side, no foul creature would touch her.

And then they came. Some moved like insects, scuttling forward with quick, precise steps. Some moved like beasts, with wild strides akin to a rabid dog's. Others yet moved like humans, placing one foot in front of the other. All were of the shadows, tails flickering above their heads, hungry for anything living.

Isha braced herself as Skae met shield. The shrieking cries were almost deafening as the Brightguard's peridium stung shadow like fire did flesh, repelling the initial onslaught and sending the vile Skae back from whence they had come.

Even as the repellent metal rebuffed their first advance, the creatures came again, either unaware of the pain awaiting them, or unable to stop their insatiable lust for human flesh and bone.

One particularly nimble creature darted through the legs of the soldier in front her, snapping a sharpened maw with teeth made half of bone and half of shadow. Isha thrust with her sword, cutting deep into the creature's shoulder, but the shadow-beast was relentless, forcing its way forward, jaws snapping at her neck. Puk grabbed the creature around its head, his muscles bulging as it struggled against his grip.

Isha wasted no time, pulling her blade back and sending it into the creature's mouth. She twisted, and the creature fell to the ground, dead, an inky black ichor seeping from the end of her peridium blade.

The scene repeated itself time and time again. With each assault, the Brightguard held, repelling wave after wave with the help of the White-Swords, who even now were blasting bolts of Shine, the white-light burning through shadow and flesh with ease.

Sypa, Andreni and Strix came to their aid as well, sweeping and cutting through the blackness as though they had done this before. They clawed at the Skae, ripping them apart with sharp beaks and even sharper talons.

But despite it all, the Skae kept coming.

Isha peeked above to the distant plains. Thousands of

shapes moved, picking apart the fleeing remnants of Craw, and now Kogon's armies. They seemed endless.

Her vision began to blur. Her focus narrowed. She gasped for breath. Bodies pressed against her. She couldn't move. Puk was beside her. If they fell, so too would Trost. So would Zapour. So would Zur.

Where had they even come from?

Isha looked to the sky, hoping, praying that Cova would part and Zur would Shine again.

Chapter 58

- Zeek –

RAW, UNIMAGINABLE POWER coursed through Zeek's entire body as the sky darkened. He flexed his hands, basking in the ecstasy that was this new, unnatural strength.

He looked to the betrayer, lying dead on the floor. He felt his Light flow through him, the Light of a Radiant. Something else was also granting him power. He could feel it, was familiar with it. It was as though it had always been there, only now it was unchained. Light and darkness fused, overwhelming him in a torrent of brilliant energy.

He saw another figure in front of him, knew him. Dazen knew him. Zeek cursed, clenching his fists, fighting against Dazen's presence as, even in the afterlife, the person he had been fought against him, urging him to leave, to flee.

Zeek was stronger than this presence. He had already rid himself of one betrayer that told him what he could and could not do, why not rid himself of another? He pushed Dazen down, deep into the pit of his being, and focused on the man in front of him.

Kill the Radiants.

The voice sounded again. It wasn't a command, but a necessity. He felt as though this was what he had to do if he was to survive.

The glow from the ball of Shine above bathed the top of the tower in a wash of light. All else was blinding darkness. The man he had come to know as Raiz faced him down, wielding a shaft of crimson Shine.

"You caused this!" Raiz said. "This world does not belong to your kind. Go back to the shadows!"

Zeek was done skulking in the shadows. The light held so much more. He had tasted what it had to offer, and he had every intention of making it his home.

His shadow-tail vibrated faster than ever, sending him forward as his body followed to engage his final foe.

Raiz was quick, prepared. He stepped to the side, sweeping with his glowing weapon. Zeek felt its sting zip past his chest as he took a backward step. He would have to avoid the Shine if he wanted to survive to see the world in its entirety.

He pressed all of his strength into his tail, using it like a human would a sword, clashing against the heated blade of his opponent. He found that Raiz's Shine did not cut as long as he focused his strength there.

Shadow and Light met time and time again. Sparks flew as Zeek used the skills stolen from his countless victims to aid him in the struggle. He lashed out, hoping to catch Raiz unaware, but again his efforts were countered as the heated blade whirled through the air.

"I know you're in there, Dazen!" Raiz screamed in a pointless attempt to get Zeek to drop his guard. "If you can hear me, use your strength! Stop this madness. We can't win without you. We need you. *I* need you!"

Zeek almost laughed as he sprang forward with another offensive. "Your brother is mine," he said, his shadow-tail swinging in wide swaths, each one of them deflected by his assailant's vibrant blade. "His power is now mine to wield. This world is mine to explore."

His words seemed to agitate the crazed Radiant, Raiz coming at him with renewed vigour. Zeek backed up, only to be assaulted by a barrage of Shine as Raiz released streams of Light through the tips of his fingers.

One struck true, burning through the inky flesh of his thigh. Zeek tightened his jaw. The sooner he could rid the world of this rodent, the better. He re-doubled his efforts, slashing right and left, using all of his stolen skills to his advantage.

But Raiz was a true Radiant, and his skill was impressive. He dodged, blocked, and out-manoeuvred Zeek at every turn. Darkness still reigned in the sky as Cova staked her claim, and Zeek felt his strength continue to grow. He used it, calling on his new power. He felt it bubbling within, building.

Raiz came at him with everything he had, his body glowing a deep red. Zeek felt his strength begin to drain, his limbs growing weak as the radiance forced him to the floor.

He fought against it, using his tail as a shield as Raiz swung again with his glowing spear, infused with Zur's energy. Zeek's new strength battled against the might that was a Radiant's Light. He screamed. A primal, ancient sound emitted from his still-forming body. With it, he released his gathered Light. Dazen's stolen Light. Ancel's stolen Light. His father's Light. All at once it came, mixing with his own inner darkness.

Darkness and Light collided in an explosion of contradicting elements as Raiz's force met his own. The two auras clashed, each trying to overpower the other. Raiz pressed his strength, beginning to gain the upper hand, but the sun was now gone, and the moon continued to gift Zeek with power. He used it, releasing all that he had. Shadows swirled and flickered, mixing with sunlight until the sunlight was no more.

In a burst of power, he thrust Raiz backward. The sound of his agonised scream followed him as he landed with a thud. Zeek released his hold, and the shadows swirling around his body ceased. He stepped towards the prone form of the last living Radiant, his tail itching with anticipation.

Raiz was alive, but his body had gone into shock. He writhed, his chest heaving as he attempted to rid himself of the aggressive darkness that had consumed him.

Zeek poised for a strike, meaning to finish the job, to drain him and take his strength for his own. Then he felt another presence, another figure coming to the Radiant's defence.

It was a man, tall and strong. He stood over Raiz's weakened form, his violet eyes bearing into Zeek with the force of ten suns. He felt their strength, their power. It was like nothing he had ever felt.

He had seen this man before. It was the man he was supposed to have killed, the man his betrayer was afraid of. But Zeek was stronger than his betrayer, had his power even now coursing through him.

"You will not harm him," said the man with the violet eyes.

Zeek made to cut him down, but felt his body resisting, as if something, or someone, had entered his thoughts. He could feel it, the surge of energy asking him, willing him to stop his approach, to turn around and jump off the edge. He inclined his head. This was new, different. It took some time to understand, to comprehend.

But he was done being controlled.

He fought, pushed against the violet energy, stepping closer. His scorpion-tail rose, poising for a strike. The man with the violet eyes doubled his efforts, bearing down on him in a torrent of mental energy.

"You will not harm him!" he insisted.

Zeek smiled. The thrill of such a contest had him excited. It was exhilarating, not knowing whether he was going to live or die. He pushed through the mental barrier, ready to claim his victory and start his life anew, finally free.

"Dazen," came a soft, weak voice.

Zeek looked to the floor to see Raiz struggling to rise.

"I know you're in there. Hear me Brother. Fight him. Fight for us, for Sumaya, for Zapour. Fight for Nora! Fight, damn you. Fight!"

Zeek went to dismiss it, to laugh in his face and tell the young Radiant that his brother was dead and his words were pointless, when something within him struck.

It hit hard, a mental blow. His head throbbed as Dazen's familiar energy surged through him, freezing him in place.

"Fight!" Raiz called again, unable to stand.

Zeek tried to rid himself of it, to press it back down, but the man with the violet eyes bore down on him once again, forcing him to a knee.

"Release your hold on him, demon! He is no longer a tool

for you to hold! Release him! Do it now!"

Zeek screamed, back arching, chest tightening. "No," he said in a strangled voice. "I claimed him. I earned this. His Light is mine…"

As he spoke, Dazen's presence thundered. Visions swam into focus. A child. The love of a brother, a sister, a wife. A home. A purpose…

Zeek's insides spasmed, and he felt Dazen leave him, watched as his golden Light trickled from his mouth. It drifted, floated in the air before ascending into the darkened sky.

Zeek fell, hands spread on the ground as he made to catch his breath.

A spear suddenly slashed through the air. Zeek was only just able to anticipate it, but he didn't quite move quickly enough, and the blade cut into the flesh of his stomach. He retreated, hand to wound, and hissed a daring cry as the violet-eyed man came at him. He looked behind, peeking over the edge of the tower to where he could hear the distant cries of his kin.

Come to me, my child, the voice inside of him whispered.

Zeek took one last glance at the violet-eyed man before leaning back, and allowing the winds to take him.

Chapter 59

- Raiz –

RAIZ LAY ON HIS BACK, watching the golden Light that he felt in his heart was his brother's essence fade into the sky. He exhaled, still trembling after the sting of the Skae's shadows.

Bessimir returned to him and extended an arm. "The Skaeling is gone, fallen off the edge."

Raiz breathed a sigh of relief and clasped the arm in his own. The prince pulled him to his feet, his wounds complaining about the sudden movement.

"What is this?" he said, gesturing to what seemed to be a night sky. "It was light just moments ago. What happened?"

The prince frowned. "It is the Darkening. An eclipse. It is what signals Cova's return to power, and the rise of her creations."

"How do you know this?"

"I have seen it before, witnessed their assent. I should have been more aware. Should have known they were this close to a return."

They moved to the edge. In the dark it was hard to see, but he could hear the terrible sounds down below, the anguished screams. Beside him, the prince squirmed, tensed.

"What is it? Can you see what's happening down there?" Raiz asked.

The prince began to shudder, as if he were at war with himself. A tear fell from his violet eye, and he turned slowly to Raiz.

"You must use it," he said.

Raiz frowned, puzzled. "Use it? Use what?"

The Sun Prince bent to a crouch, his face a picture of pain. "You must use it! Use it now! Or all will perish. She will perish!"

Raiz looked again into the distant pit of black below, wondering what he was talking about.

"Connect yourself to the tower and you will see. Use your Shine! Become the Radiant. Do it now!"

Raiz focused. He didn't really know what to do, but he felt for the bubbling Shine above, connecting to it as if the Shine were his own.

His heart jolted, skipping a beat. He felt the thrill of the foreign Shine, but more than that, he could see. The whole of Zapour came to him like a giant map. He felt as though he could touch it all. He saw Illidor, sitting idle in the distant plains. All he had to do was direct the Light and he was sure he could reach it.

It was terrifying, holding this much power in his hands. He hated it, wanted to refuse it. He tried to leave, to rid himself of the responsibility. He thought of Veil, of what she had been through. She had given her life to make sure this weapon could no longer harm another human soul. Now he held that power. He wanted to leave, to destroy it and be done. But then he focused, narrowing his vision, and witnessed the atrocity that was occurring below.

He saw them, the Skae. They were all-consuming, terrifying, deadly. The streets of Lumindal were full of them. People were dying, their screams echoing. He watched as even now the combined allied armies made their last stand, bunched up behind a shield wall as the creatures of Cova's shadow bit at them piece by piece. He couldn't be sure, but he thought he felt his sister down there, part of the massacre that was about to take place.

Panic flared as Raiz watched, powerless to stop them all from perishing beneath a wave of darkness.

Only he wasn't powerless. The ball of Shine glowed brightly above his head, raging like an inferno. It wasn't at full strength, was nothing compared to the blast that he had seen take out an entire city, but it was something. Was potentially enough.

He struggled, an internal war raging within. He hated it, hated this weapon, But now he found himself with no choice but to use it.

"Do it. Do it now!" came a cry from his side.

Raiz focused as the Skae horde surrounded the retreating allied forces.

And then he released it. All at once, the Light fell. He felt the heat prickle at his skin as he directed the blast. It wreaked havoc amongst the raging Skae, decimating and destroying all in its path. He ran it in a line, using the stored Shine to wipe out all that he could see.

He felt his strength begin to ebb, his eyes begin to close, he couldn't hold it any longer.

Finally, he collapsed. Exhaustion took hold, and sleep called to him. The last of his vision flickered, and before his eyes closed at last, he thought he saw Zur's light peeking out from behind the dark.

Epilogue

- Isha –

THE GREAT HALL of Illidor bustled with activity. The gates to the palace had been opened. People cried, shouted, slept, grieved. Isha dragged her legs through the long hall. Her mind was a fog. She barely remembered fleeing Lumindal. All she could recall was running, flying, rushing to organise a retreat.

She bumped into Obeyun as their paths crossed, her eyes rising to see the image of a broken man. She gripped him close, their heads coming together as they shared in their grief.

"Trost welcomes you, my friend," she said. "You have a home here, be sure of it."

She had known Obeyun for half a lifetime, been with him through more than most could imagine, yet never before had she seen such pain in his eyes.

"I brought as many as I could," he said. "The Skae came

without warning. Such malice, such emptiness. I — I…"

"You did well, Obe," Isha said. "All here are safe because of you. You couldn't have known… we couldn't have known…"

Obeyun's expression softened. He let his hand rest on her shoulder, then left to assist one of his Bakai who had been wounded in their fight.

Isha wobbled on two feet. She tried to steady, and nearly fell, but was caught by firm hands. She turned to see Bessimir.

"You should rest," he said.

Isha went to pull away, then found she did not want to. "I can't. Not yet. My people need me. They need us. Tell me, will you stay?"

Bessimir hesitated, and for a moment she thought he would pull away, that he would leave her, leave Zapour to its fate. "Yes," he said. "I will stay. My convictions have not changed. The sun is still dying, and the task is mine to see to its recovery. Though, there is a new threat now, an ancient threat. One that I should have foreseen. Ultimately, preservation is my goal. Above anything else I would see us survive. So, I will stay. I will do what I can to counter Cova and her legion of shadows."

Isha nodded, glad. She wanted to press for more, but knew it wasn't the time. In the background, people groaned. She could feel their pain, their sorrow. She wanted to take it all away. She couldn't, of course, but she could take some of it away, at least for a time.

She squeezed Bessimir by the hand, and then sauntered over to a wounded soldier. His hand was severed at the wrist, which had recently been cauterised. She looked him in the eye, using what little power she had left to take away as much pain as she could. She moved around the room, repeating her effort for any who would allow her to.

She felt weak, exhausted. She hadn't changed clothes, had barely slept. Her eyes were heavy, her muscles tight to the point of collapse. She drifted among the wounded, tripping on a displaced chair and stumbling to a stop. She collapsed onto the edge of a table.

People around her shuffled. She knew they spoke, though she couldn't hear them. Her mind wandered. When she closed her eyes, she was back in Lumindal, back in her lavish cage. People were staring, watching, whispering. Where before this dream had haunted her, now she felt in control. She knew this threat, had overcome it. She stood proudly in her cage, her eyes wide as she cast her threatening glare out into the gawking crowd. She took joy as those around her cowered.

Then her vision changed, blurred. The shapes of the cowering Eagles of Lumindal shifted, darkened, morphed into something else, something horrible.

Shadows clouded her sight. Her cage vanished. She was out in the cold, open plains outside of Lumindal, huddled between the weight of a thousand men. She could hear the screams. They were pure terror. She tried to swat away the shadows, but they merely re-formed, multiplied. She cried out, called for Puk, for Bessimir, for Raiz.

No one answered.

This no longer felt like a dream. It felt real, it was real. She felt hot breath as wet jaws snapped at her neck. She smelled blood, the air thick with it. She watched as the creatures made of shadow tore limbs from bodies, witnessed one pierce the heart of a fleeing soldier with a tail as black as pitch. The sky was dark. Why was it dark? Where had the light gone?

She found Puk, reached for him, grabbed him. A figure clawed at him, raking at his skin.

Puk!

A bright light flashed through the sky...

Isha woke, gasping for air. Her body fell, caught by something soft and warm.

"Isha!" a familiar voice said. "You're okay. You're safe. I'm here. We're here."

Isha awoke fully. She swatted at her eye, as if that would make it so the dream had never happened. She saw Raiz, felt his strength. He pulled her close, and Isha relaxed into his chest.

She didn't know how much time passed, but eventually she caught her breath. She uncoiled from his arms to see more people surrounding her. She saw Bessimir, his violet eyes full of concern. She saw her mother, only now realising that her hand rested on her shoulder.

She rounded her head to see Puk. He was alive, unmolested by the shadows of her dreams. He came to her, stood by her side. Instinct cautioned her to search her bond, and through it she felt Strix. She was here, somewhere outside, circling.

She broadened her vision to see her father standing by the dais, hands crossed. He kept his distance, though she could tell his concerned eyes watched over her. She no longer felt any lingering hatred in her heart. After what she had witnessed, she wanted her family close, no matter how fractured it may be.

"Raiz," she said, her voice weak, every word a labour. "Will we be okay?"

Raiz shifted. He reached for something. A crown. He paused. With one hand he held hers tight. The other he used to lift the crown and place it on his head.

"We will," he said. There was a power in his voice, a fire in his eye. "Look around you. Light always defeats darkness. While our bonds hold, there is always hope."

Epilogue (2)

- Zeek –

ZEEK WANDERED the ravaged streets of Lumindal, defeated. Dazen's presence was no longer there. It was gone, along with the power his lifeforce had brought him. But the sun had risen, and he still walked the light. He walked, and walked, and walked some more.

The streets were dead, barren, bereft of anything living. Corpses littered the wide path he travelled along, their empty shells sucked dry of their essence. Even in his defeat he felt victorious. He was no longer alone in this world. His kind had come, the Skae had returned.

All his life his betrayer had taught him to hate himself, to believe his kind were a poison, a blight on the world. Perhaps that was true, but now that he had begun to see the true nature of humanity, his perspective was changing.

Maybe humanity was the blight. All he wanted was to live,

to experience. Perhaps that's all the Skae wanted too. But this world could not be shared. There could be only one alpha race.

Zeek had chosen his side.

Eventually, the sun dipped below the horizon and darkness took hold. He used to hate it, to wish for the sun to rise again so that he might experience all the world had to offer, though now he was beginning to cherish both.

With the darkness came their return. They came from the shadows, hidden beneath the cracks and the crevasses of the world.

They circled him, studied him. Black shapes moved with the night. Some were made entirely of shadow, their figures translucent and moving as though they were lost. Others were humanoid, having fed on flesh. They were as he once was, transitioning into something different, something more.

Others moved like rats, crawling on all fours as they sniffed and searched the streets for anything living yet to be consumed. All had shadow-tails, some large, some small. They flicked and swayed in the air as the creatures that were his kin continued to surround him.

He allowed them to guide him, striding down the street until a large courtyard appeared where the adjacent streets intersected. He heard noises, the animalistic cry of a creature on the edge of life and death.

He saw through the darkness, watched as chains rattled and a figure bucked in its imprisonment. He stared in awe as a bird, larger than he had ever seen, looked at him through intelligent eyes. A Great Eagle!

It continued to struggle, its wings trapped beneath the heavy weight of the metal chains. Other creatures were also imprisoned, different ones. They reminded him of the

Radiant's pet, though much smaller, and wilder.

Zeek moved in a circle. Everywhere he went, Skae blocked his path. He spotted humans among their ranks, seemingly untouched and untainted. Only they weren't human. He felt it. They were Skae, but they were complete. Their flesh was entirely human. They moved differently, like he did, with intelligence, with insight. They stared at him, some aware of what was going on, others not.

"My children," the voice inside of him said. Only this time it wasn't a thought whispered into his mind, it was real, audible.

He snapped his neck to the side as a figure emerged from within the shadowy ranks. It was tall, slim, feminine, and ancient. Her dress was made entirely of black, shadowy fabric, which flowed down below her feet and swayed in the light breeze. Slowly, she shifted to face him. Her skin was pale, human, yet also inhuman at the same time. She looked at him through emerald eyes as bright as a blade of grass bathed in fresh sunlight.

Her features were warm, accepting. They spoke of knowledge, of wisdom. She moved closer, each step graceful and elegant. She cupped his chin in her palm, steadily raising his head to meet her gaze.

"You have done well, my child," she said. "I sense the blood of a Radiant within you."

Zeek shied away, disappointed in himself. "I let one get away. I have failed."

"No," the lady in black said.

"You could never fail me, child," she continued. "You are a part of me. We are one. All of us are one. Can you not feel it?"

Zeek concentrated, feeling the strength of those around him like a second heart beating beside his own. He nodded, and now he knew who she was.

The Skae Queen moved to another section of the courtyard, over to where the human-like Skae resided. "Even you are part of us," she said. "I have been calling you all. The sleeping ones. Long have I waited. Long have I resisted, watching as my children meddled, rooted themselves deep within human society. But make no mistake, human you are not. You are products of Cova. All here are her creations, her kin, even me.

"What is your name, child?" she asked one of the human-like Skae.

"M — Maitreya. My name is Maitreya."

"Ah, welcome, Maitreya, to the awakened. Welcome to your new kingdom. Join us, bask in our return as we reclaim that which once was ours."

She turned now to face Zeek, gesturing towards the Eagle. "Feed," she said. "Feed! This creature is my gift to you, mighty warrior. You have earned your right to him, to ascend to your true potential."

Zeek felt his chest beating like a drum. His shadow-tail rose, vibrating, hungry. He stepped forward, hesitant. He didn't want to, but he also did. He remembered his father's words, the words of his betrayer. He remembered how he had felt when he tried to consume the bear. He didn't want to harm animals, he wanted to help them, to live beside them.

"What is wrong, child?" the Skae Queen whispered.

"I — It is wrong, to hurt this creature."

The Skae Queen leaned closer, and for a moment he thought himself about to be chastised, as his betrayer had so often done. But in her presence, he felt only comfort.

"My child, you are pure. Have no fear. This creature is dying. With or without your intervention it will perish. But it can be saved. Feed, consume all that it is, and it will live on inside you."

Zeek took a step forward, regarding the dying Eagle. His Queen was right. He had a chance to save it, to allow it to live. His tail acted on instinct. It rose, snapping like a whip, and indulged. The creature moaned, cried out, but it soon took its last breath.

Zeek relaxed into a state of pure ecstasy, his body bathing in renewed strength. Memories flooded his mind, gifting him knowledge he had only ever dreamed of obtaining.

"Yes!" the Queen said. "Feel its strength, become it. Sprout your wings. Become my Dark Knight. I will have need of you. For tomorrow, we begin to take back our lost world."

THE SUN PRINCE

DID YOU ENJOY THE SUN PRINCE?

It's done. Now I can relax, right? I poured my heart and soul into this novel and am so happy with the result and to be in a position where I can share it with the world.

From the bottom of my heart, thank you for dedicating your time to both A King's Radiance and The Sun Prince. This is but another step on my writing journey. This is my passion. I will keep writing, and I will get better.

An honest review is the most powerful tool I have when garnering attention for my books and allowing me to continue to write. If you enjoyed The Sun Prince it would mean the world to me if you could take just a few moments out of your day to leave a short review on Amazon and goodreads. It makes a HUGE difference.

Until next time, may Zur's light guide you, and Spike protect you.

Follow me to stay up to date with new books, competitions, fantasy content and just daily life. You can find me on Instagram: @luke_schulz_author

Or twitter: @L_R_Schulz

Newsletter signup for even more exclusive insights:
http://eepurl.com/hWoJ3r

Acknowledgements

There are so many people I need to thank who have helped me along the way. Firstly, to my beta team for helping to deflate my growing ego and for forcing me to re-think and re-structure certain sections. I think I would have completely butchered Isha's ARC without the extra help.

To my editor Luke Marty who practically convinced me to choose him to edit the first book after he did such a great job beta reading it. Luke's enthusiasm and attention to detail was just the spark I needed on A King's Radiance, and this is continued here. He MAKES my novel work.

To Lena for creating the map of Zapour after I gave her my blob of a draft. She is amazing and her work speaks for itself. To Roxana for the proofread. To Tom at Fictive Designs for the chapter header designs and Vanda for the title page art. To Perci for the AWESOME pricket/dragon art. An extra thanks to Sien or 'Brushseven' for his FABULOUS front cover artwork, he was great to work with and such a talented artist.

To my family and friends for their growing support for my writing. And lastly to the amazing community on Twitter Instagram who continue to inspire me through their fantastic reviews and support for authors in general.

Thank you to all,

Luke Schulz

About the author

Luke was born in 1992 in Melbourne, Australia. He discovered a passion for fantasy at a young age which developed into a love for the imaginary and a desire to write. Despite an early passion for storytelling, Luke obtained a teaching degree before beginning a career as a primary school teacher.

When he is not reading and writing, Luke enjoys spending time with his Golden Retriever named Gem, gaming, and surfing.

A King's Radiance was Luke's debut novel, though he is always coming up with ideas for his next project, as well as working towards a sequel.